NL

CW00373425

Getting

Praise for A

'Warm, poignant and very funny' Marian Keyes

'Sidesplittingly comical and heartwrenchingly tragic . . . A brilliant debut' *Cosmopolitan*

'Maxted is a gifted comic writer and she manages to extract humour from even the most unpromising situations . . . had this reviewer laughing out loud' *The Times*

'Hugely funny. You often hear about books which combine humour and pathos, but very rarely do they live up to the billing; this one does . . . Maxted writes beautifully not only about death, but about regrets over what might have been, while at the same time writing a social comedy about current social movers with some seriously sharp dialogue' *Daily Express*

'Witty and clever . . . Like Bridget Jones, it refuses to gloss over life's ordinary squalor; unlike Bridget, however, its heroine's traumas are serious, giving it an edge which makes her predecessors' worries laughably small. It's compelling, humane and worryingly funny, and better written than many more "literary" novels' *Evening Standard*

'Readable, often poignant and always funny . . . Revealing a touch for comic timing and versatility, she paints scenes of hilarious pitfalls, biting sarcasm and heart-wrenching pathos. While comparison between this work and [Helen] Fielding's is unavoidable, Maxted's laugh-out-loud debut novel will come out ahead' *Publishers Weekly*

Anna Maxted lives in London with her husband Phil and their son Oscar. Anna read English at Cambridge and works as a freelance journalist. She is also the author of *Running in Heels*, *Behaving Like Adults* and, most recently *Being Committed*.

Getting Over It

Anna Maxted

arrow books

Reissued by Arrow Books in 2004

7 9 10 8

First published in the United Kingdom in 2000 by Arrow Books

Arrow Books
The Random House Group Limited
20 Vauxhall Bridge Road, London SW1V 2SA

Random House Australia (Pty) Limited
20 Alfred Street, Milsons Point, Sydney, New South Wales 2061, Australia

Random House New Zealand Limited
18 Poland Road, Glenfield, Auckland 10, New Zealand

Random House (Pty) Limited
Endulini, 5a Jubilee Road, Parktown 2193, South Africa

The Random House Group Limited Reg. No. 954009
www.randomhouse.co.uk

A CIP catalogue record for this book is available from the British Library

Penguin Random House is committed to a sustainable future for
our business, our readers and our planet. This book is made from
Forest Stewardship Council® certified paper.

MIX
Paper from
responsible sources
FSC® C018179

ISBN 0 09 941018 4

Typeset by SX Composing DTP, Rayleigh, Essex

Printed and bound in Great Britain by Clays Ltd, St Ives plc

To Leslie Maxted

Acknowledgements

So many people to thank: Phil Robinson for his love and jokes, Mary Maxted for courage and insight, Leonie Maxted for Russians and encouragement, Caren Gestetner for kindness, Jonny Geller for being the best agent ever, Lynne Drew for exquisite editing, Andy McKillop for excusing the missing chapters, Wendy Bristow for friendship, Emma Dally for pushing me into it, Jo Kessel for knowing everyone, e.g., Dr Michael Kessel, Dr Maurice Cohen for noticing the full catheter, Mark Curtis for explaining probate, Jeanette King for wisdom, Andy Robinson for the HK information, Evelyn Smith for expecting a novel from me since I was eight, Daniel Silver who doesn't wear Joop!, Jason P. Worsnip for being fabulous. Also enormous thanks to: everyone at Random House, Laura Dubiner, Mandi Norwood, Margaret Carruthers, Sarah Vassel, Heather Blackmore, Sybil Sipkin, Paul Bern, Paul 'TCB' Burke, Hudson and Gina Britton, Sasha Slater, Anna Moore, Lisa Sussman, Grub Smith, Alicia Drake-Reece, Martin Raymond, Dr Raj Persaud, Christabel Hilliard, Lynne Randell, Women In Need, Sam Leek, and James Buchanan.

Chapter 1

When it happened, I wasn't ready for it. I expected it about as much as I expect to win Miss World and be flown around the planet and forced to work with screaming children. Which is to say, it was a preposterous notion and I never even considered it. And, being so awesomely unprepared I reacted like Scooby Doo chancing upon a ghost. I followed my instinct, which turned out to be hopelessly lost and rubbish at map-reading.

Maybe I was too confused to do the right thing. After all, the right thing rarely involves fun and mostly means making the least exciting choice, like waiting for the ready-cook pizza you've torn from the oven to cool to under 200 degrees before biting into it. Or deciding not to buy those sexy tower-heeled boots because they'll savage your shins, squeeze your toes white, lend you the posture of Early Man, and a vast chunk of your salary will moulder away at the back of your wardrobe. If we always made the smartest choice we'd never get laid.

That said, the day it all began, I came close to making a very smart choice. Here it is, bravely scrawled in black ink, in my blue Letts diary:

I am dumping Jasper, tomorrow.

Words that whisk me back to another time. Barely one year ago but it seems like an age. Yet July 16th remains as sharp in my mind as if it was today. Maybe it *is* today. And this is how today begins:

I am dumping Jasper, tomorrow.

He deserves it for being called Jasper, for a start. And for a finish, he falls several thousand feet below acceptable boyfriend standard.

Funny thing is, at the age of five I knew what that was. I was dating the boy across the road and I routinely ate his tea before embarking on mine. I also tantrumed until he surrendered his Fisher Price wheely dog. And I refused to play in his bedroom because it smelt of wee. Then I grow up and start taking crap.

Unfortunately, Jasper is beautiful. Tall, which I like. The only time I've had dealings with a short man is when my overbearing friend Michelle set me up on a blind date. He rang the bell, I wrenched open the door, and looked down. And I'm five foot one. Two Weebles wibble wobbling their way down the road. Michelle's excuse was that when she met him he was sitting down. So Jasper, at six foot, is a delight. I wear five-inch heels so he doesn't notice the discrepancy. He has floppy brown hair, eyes so paradise blue it's incredible he actually uses them to see and, my favourite, good bone structure. And despite being the most selfish man I've ever met – quite a feat – he's a tiger in the sack.

I'm on my way there now. Sackbound. For one last bout. Except I'm stuck in traffic on Park Road. There appear to be roadworks with no one doing any work. I'm trapped in my elderly grey Toyota Corolla (a cast-off from my mother who was thrilled to be rid of it, please don't think I'd go out and buy one even if I had the money) and trying to stay calm. In the last twenty minutes I've rolled forward a total of five inches. I might ring Jasper to say I'll be late. The road converges on approximately fifty sets of lights and everyone is barging – as much as you can barge when you're stationary. It's 2.54. I'm due at Jasper's at 3.30. Great. My mobile is out of batteries. I pick the skin on my lip. Right. I'm phoning him.

I assess the gridlock – yes, it's gridlocked – leap out of the car, dash across the road to the phonebox, and dial Jasper's number. Brrrt brrt. Brrrt brrt. Where *is* he? He can't have forgotten. Shit, the traffic's moving. I ring his mobile – joy! he answers. 'Jasper Sanderson.' Never says hello like a normal person. He's so executive. I hate it but I love it. He sounds suspiciously out of breath.

'Why are you out of breath?' I say sharply.

'Who's this?' he says. Jesus!

'Your girlfriend. Helen, remember?' I say. 'Listen, I'm going to be late, I'm stuck in traffic. Why are you out of breath?'

'I'm playing tennis. Bugger, I forgot you were coming over. It'll take me a while to get home. Spare key's under the mat.'

He beeps off. 'You're such an original,' I say sourly, and look up to see the gridlock has cleared and swarms of furious drivers are hooting venomously at the Toyota as they swerve around it.

Forty minutes later I arrive at Jasper's Fulham flat. I ring the bell, in case he's already home, but silence. I kick the mat to scare off spiders, gingerly lift a corner with two fingers, and retrieve the key. Ingenious, Jasper! The place is a replica of his parents' house. There's even a silver framed picture of his mother as a young girl on the hall table – and a right prissy miss she looks too. Happily, he's never introduced me. His most heinous interior crime, however, is a set of ugly nautical paintings that dominate the pale walls. Thing is with Jasper, just when I think I can't take any more he does something irresistible, such as iron the collar and cuffs of his shirt and go to work hiding the crumpled rest of it under his jacket. I poke the scatter of post to check for correspondence from other women and see the green light of his answer machine flashing for attention. Jasper calling to announce a further delay. I press *play*.

As the machine whirrs, the key turns in the lock. Jasper flings open the door and I turn, smiling, to face him. Oof he's gorgeous. I'll dump him next week. This week, he's mine to have and to hold and to feel and to feel bad about.

He's like eating chocolate for breakfast – makes you feel sluttish, you know you shouldn't, you ought to stick to what's wholesome but Weetabix is depressing even with raisins in it. Jasper is un-nutritious and delicious. He opens his eminently kissable mouth to say 'Hiya babe!' but is beaten to it by a high silvery voice that echoes chirpily over the tiled floor and bounces gaily from one eggshell wall to the other.

'Hiya Babe!' trills the voice. 'It's me! Call me! Kiss! kiss!'

The smile freezes on my face. Jasper and I both stare at the answer machine which, having imparted its treachery, is now primly silent. Knowing the answer, I croak, à la Quentin Tarantino, 'Who the fucking fuck was that?'

Jasper is not amused. If this were Hollywood there would be a muscle twitching in his jaw and his chiselled face would turn pale under its caramel tan. As it is, he carefully places his sportsbag on the floor, and rests his tennis racquet neatly on top of it. I feel a rip of fury tear through my chest and I want to snatch up the Prince and wallop him. At least he *was* playing tennis, although he's so damn sneaky I wouldn't be surprised if it was an elaborate cover. He gazes at my red fear-ruffled face and says smoothly, 'My ex. She likes to keep in touch.'

I'll bet she does.

'When did you last see her?' I snarl.

'A week ago,' he replies. 'We just talked.' Ho really.

I'm like Fox Mulder. I want to believe. And Jasper wants me to believe too. He's tilted his face to a penitent angle. Cute, but from what I know of Jasper, plus the gut-crunching phrase 'it's *me*' induces scepticism. 'It's me' is as proprietorial as a Doberman guarding a chocolate biscuit. A woman does not ring an ex-boyfriend and say 'It's me' because for all she knows – and she obviously doesn't – there is now another me. *Me.*

'Did you have sex with her?' I roar.

Jasper looks hurt. 'Of course I didn't, Helen,' he purrs. 'Louisa calls everyone Babe.'

4

Names ending in *ah*. Argh! I narrow my eyes and give him my best shot at a cold stare. The big brave words 'You're sacked' are warm, ready to roll, but they stick, feeble and reluctant, in my throat. Now, I tell myself, is not the moment. Why, he'll think I'm in love with him! The only decent thing to do is to walk. 'I'm going home,' I say huffily. The rat steps gratefully aside. I intend to sweep out in a *Gone With The Wind* flourish and it's going to plan until I reach the doorstep and trip. I stumble, and I'm unsure if the snorty-gasp I hear is Jasper not quite trying to suppress mirth but I don't look back to find out. Face clenched, I stomp down his concrete garden path, plonk into the Toyota, lurch hurtle a three-point turn during which I dent the door of a parked MG, and rattle off into the fading afternoon.

You wanker. You wanker. I wrestle my mobile out of my bag in case he calls grovelling then remember it's dead. Piece of crap. I am driving as the crow flies. You wanker. I have no intention of gracefully erasing myself from the picture so Louis-*ah* can steal the scene. I can't decide if he rutted or refused her. Jasper likes to be in demand. But then he likes to lead a streamlined existence. When he first saw my bedroom he murmured, 'I think you've been burgled.' He also tells me with pride about the morning he sat next to a bearded guy on the tube and tried to read the *Telegraph* over his shoulder. The man rustled his property in pique and snapped, 'Papers! Forty-five pence from the newsagent!' Jasper replied narkily, 'Razors! Forty-five pence from the chemist!' Jasper – unironed shirts aside – likes his life and all that surrounds it to be just so. Shagging his moony old ex would be too messy, it would disrupt his timetable. Then again. You wanker.

She's reared her smugly head before. A month into our relationship, as I like to call it. Jasper called to say he couldn't meet as he was staying with his friend Daniel in Notting Hill. Beyond my surprise that Jasper *had* a friend in Notting Hill, I didn't question it. We were at that googly-eyed stage where you kiss in public and annoy everyone who is less in lust than you so I trusted him. The next afternoon, he suddenly said, 'I told you a pack of lies last night.' What. 'I . . . I stayed with my ex.' Turned out he'd missed the last tube home (he doesn't drive, his most unfanciable trait) and so he'd walked to Kensington and rung on the ex's doorbell. 'She was really good about it.' Good about it! I'm sure she was great about it! Further interrogation revealed that she'd fed him Cornflakes with brown sugar for breakfast. The sly witch – she was trying to nurture him! Happily, she was too needy to appeal and so a large bowl of cereal was wasted. But maybe she's sharpened up. And maybe *my* appeal is blunted. Oops, my personality is showing.

The first weeks were glossy enough. I met Jasper at a book launch – for a paperback sex manual. I'd gone from work with Lizzy and Tina. Partly because Laetitia our misnomered features editor didn't want to go and it is my job as features skivvy on *Girltime* magazine to pick up her slack. And also because Tina, the fashion assistant, and I are hardcore champagne tarts – anything for a free chug of Krug (or Asti, let's face it). And although Lizzy is health & beauty assistant in professional and personal life and her drink of choice is soya milk – she's so sweet, really walks the talk – she can be persuaded. We twisted her well-toned arm.

The launch was in a smelly Soho backstreet. I'd glammed up for the occasion – black trousers, black boots (five inches – that's the lowest I stoop and not just in the shoe department), black top. The celebrity funeral look. I'd also smeared a blop of metallic silver glitter on my cheekbones. It looked scarily Abba-ish but that evening I felt quite strongly I could not attend the launch without it. I'd have felt awkward and incomplete. The older I get and the more tediously responsible I'm forced to be the more I hanker for tokens of childhood. I now own: a tiny pink zippy purse

6

with coloured beads that you itch to pick off. A plastic heli-copter that you attach to the ceiling on a string, that whizzes round with flashing red lights. A kaleidoscope. A copy of *Elmer* by David McKee. A dartboard (well, it's not a sophis-ticated pursuit, is it?) And a spoilt kitten named Fatboy.

Usually I don't talk to people at parties. I survey the hordes of glamorous best friends all gabbling, laughing, bonding in inpenetrable cliques and I want to run away home. I feel my make-up turning shiny, my face creaks from one unsettled expression to another, and I'm the podgy teenager of twelve years ago, complete with dorky specs, a brown satchel and a blue scratchy duffel coat with shark tooth buttons and a huge hood. Now, of course, I'd be a fashion victim. But the Jasper party was different. I was one of a sparkly three-girl group, I glugged two glasses of sparkly wine in the first twenty minutes, and I was smeared in more sparkly glitter than a Christmas fairy. I sparkled! So it was only natural that Jasper appeared before me and offered me a fag.

'I don't smoke,' I said primly. In a flash of brilliance I added coyly, 'I'm a good girl.'

He didn't miss a beat. He replied, 'Well, you look filthy.'

It was the best compliment I've ever had. What could I do but shag him out of gratitude?

Jasper was 'in publishing' which turned out to mean he wrote press releases for a pipsqueak company based in Hounslow. I, therefore, terrier-torso assistant on *Girltime* magazine based in Covent Garden, was a great contact. Not that we review many books on Elizabethan sanitation or the indigenous insects of Guatemala but, roughly at the point I looked on his ravishing face and he gazed at my sparkly one, we decided to do business together. For a few weeks I upheld my airbrushed image. I exaggerated the importance of my job. Tina advised me on what to wear, i.e. grey, occasionally. I avoided taking him to the flat. And I edited all trace of squareness from my conversation and pumped up the wacky free-spirit factor. Like Bjork but better dressed. Shameful but it works. Of course, I realised after three days that we had bugger all in common – he called orange juice 'OJ' and was stockpiling to put his son through Eton (a tad premature as he didn't yet have one) – but I don't like sameness so it was fine by me.

He likes to be amused so it was fine by him. But sometimes, more recently, I've been sure the bubble is at bursting point. We spent an afternoon in the park last Saturday and I swear we had *nothing* to say to each other. He walked me to my car, and I was certain he was going to end it. Sure he was going to sock it to me sledgehammer straight in that efficient, emotionless, poshboy way – 'Helen, it's not working out.' But he didn't. He kissed me a breezy goodbye as if nothing was amiss.

I brooded all the way home. I dislike silence. I fear its potentiality. I prefer to fill it with my own voice which inevitably gabbers out something goonish. Last week, I blurted, to a shop assistant offering help: 'No thanks, I'm just mooching.' To the receptionist at Lizzy's health club who enquired how I was: 'Ready for a bout of exercise.' To Jasper, horny an hour after lunch at Pizza Express: 'I think I'm still digesting.' Sexy lady!

So, as the silences grow, I slowly blow my sassy cover. He doesn't seem to have twigged, but I feel increasingly uncomfortable. He doesn't get my jokes and I feel wrong and not right. I am so not right for Jasper and he is so not right for me but he still seems amused by me and he has a decent-sized penis. Breaking up is hard to do. Louis*ah* does not make it easi*ah*.

I swing into Swiss Cottage and begin the three-hour search for a parking space. You'd think no one ever went out around here. Sometime the next day I manage to squeeze the Toyota between a Saab and a Mini an hour's walk from the flat and start plodding down the road. I'm scrabbling for my keys when the door is wrenched open. My flatmate Luke looks, if possible, even scruffier and wild-eyed than normal.

8

'What!' I sing, to his loud silence. He is regarding me oddly. 'Jasper's rung!' I suggest. 'I've won the lottery! Not a pissy three hundred grand – an eight million rollover! You want a bike and a house! And a trip to Bali – we'll fly Concorde!'

God knows why Bali, I don't even *like* hot countries – I get heat rash if I stand too near the toaster – but Luke's expression makes me want to keep talking.

He shakes his head. Then he reaches and grasps my upper arm.

'No, Helen,' he says. 'Your mum rang. Your dad. Your dad's dead.'

Chapter 2

When I was fifteen and never been kissed (I meant what I said about the duffel coat) I fed the hunger on a gluttonous diet of pre-1970s Mills & Boons. The willowy innocence of these paperback heroines was as far removed from my fat chastity as a diamond from a lump of coal, but nonetheless gave me hope that one day *I'd* swoon at the sight of – ooh, let's say a gunfight, and a powerful, masterful, aquiline-nosed businessman would spring from his immaculate car, gather up my flaccid form, and spirit me away to a life of love, happiness, and endless passion.

Sadly, the closest I came to this swooning scenario was when I arose one Sunday feeling doddery, staggered downstairs in my pyjamas, and fainted in the hallway. The loud thud alerted my parents, and my mother grabbed my arms, my father grasped my ankles and together they huffingly hauled their too solid daughter on to the lounge sofa. The most unromantic part of it was that amid the heaving my pyjama bottoms wormed their way downwards and, semiconscious, I was wholly aware that the beginnings of my pubic hair were in full springy view of my dad.

At least, when Luke informs me of my father's demise I am, like a Mills & Boon heroine, well dressed. Furthermore, Luke keeps hold of my arm so when the words penetrate my skull and whirl crazily around my head and make me dizzy, I sway slightly but remain on my feet.

'Your dad is dead.' All that came before this moment hurtles into it. My dad is dead. My father is dead. Daddy is dead. But he isn't dead! He wasn't dead. He wasn't dead

10

yesterday, or the day before that. He's been alive ever since I've known him. A minute ago, he wasn't dead. And now he's dead? Both my parents are alive. That's how it is. How can my father be dead? Dead is old other people like Frank Sinatra. It doesn't happen to me. Or my parents. *Death*. Don't be mad.

'Wha-what? When?' My mouth is a gob of jelly, it's wobbling all over the place. Poor old Luke looks terrible. He isn't a drama queen like Michelle – she of the blind date dwarf incident – who probably has wet dreams of imparting news of such import. Breaking anything to anybody is purgatory for Luke. When he broke it to me that he'd just popped into our landlord's room to borrow a razor and that Fatboy appeared to have done a large pooh in the middle of Marcus' white duvet he was – until we both killed ourselves laughing – puce and stuttery with the stress of prior knowledge.

This is different. The words pour from him in a torrent. 'He just collapsed massive heart attack your mother rang she keeps ringing about an hour ago your mobile's off I didn't know where you were I thought maybe Jasper but I couldn't find the number looked in your room but it was a tip I didn't know where to start I thought of going through the phone bill but I don't know where Marcus keeps everything I don't know where he is to ask him she keeps ringing she's at the hospital she's really upset I mean really upset you've got to call her but they keep saying she's got to turn off her mobile so if—' Luke is very worked up and a large fleck of spit lands on my cheek. I surreptitiously try to wipe it off without him noticing. My hand is trembling. It's too late. Too late to decide not to come home just yet and to drive to Tina to moan about Jasper in blissful not-knowing. Too late to drive to Hampstead and buy a pair of shoes I don't need in Pied à Terre. Too late. Luke has said the words. They can't be unsaid. Saying it makes it real. Luke insists on driving me to the hospital.

*

11

Both my parents are alive. No, I mean it. My dad is nearly dead. Luke, the berk, got it wrong although – seeing as he spoke to my mother – I can guess how the misunderstanding occurred. Luke swerved into the car park and I ran dippety skippet into Casualty and started babbling at the first uniformed person I saw. She directs me to the relatives' room next to 'Resuss'. *Resuscitation*. Shit. I run down a corridor, past a man stripping sheets off stained mattresses. Then I hear the sound of my mother's voice and bolt towards it. Oh no, Nana Flo.

'Helen!' chokes my mother, and bursts into tears. Nana Flo, who thinks extreme emotion is vulgar and would adore Jasper, looks on disapprovingly. My mother clings to me as if snapping me in half will make it all go away.

Although I am gasping for breath, I manage to wheeze 'Wa, when did he die?'

At this, my mother flings me from her like a flamenco dancer. 'He's not dead yet!' she shrieks as I stagger to right myself. 'Oh Maurice! My poor Maurice!'

My mistake. My father is, as we speak, being fiddled with by experts after an almighty heart attack during lunch. As his lunch tends to involve four scrambled eggs – when I know, from Lizzy, that the recommended intake is two per week – this doesn't greatly surprise me. Also, he smokes like industrial Manchester. My mother, who was upstairs re-doing her make-up, found him slumped and groaning into his plate, egg on face. Being my mother, she wiped the egg off his face with Clarins and – I kid you not – *cleaned his teeth*, before calling the ambulance. I'm not sure if the teeth cleaning pre-empted her panicked attempt at mouth to mouth resuscitation. I say 'panicked' because he was still conscious. Thankfully, he'd shaved this morning and was wearing clean underwear and a nice shirt otherwise the ambulance wouldn't have been called till tomorrow morning.

There is nothing for us to do, according to some busybody calling herself the A & E sister, until the doctors have finished working on my father. She talks about drips, monitors, oxygen and blood tests, and drops the bombshell that he's 'very unwell'. So we sit in the drab peely-walled cafeteria. At least the coffee is filtered. My mother keeps bursting out crying and jumping up to ring everyone she knows. Then she decides she can't cope with anyone fussing so I have to ring back and dissuade everyone from descending on the hospital.

I gaze at Nana Flo. Shock has drawn her thin mouth even tighter, like a purse string. Her skin is as washed out as her beige nylon dress and her eyes are saggy like a salamander's. I feel a twist of pity but know better than to voice it. As ever, she converts all anguish into aggression and today, Luke is on the receiving end of it. Nana assumes he's my boyfriend and is grilling him. 'Your hair's too long, it makes you look like a young girl,' is one of her kinder observations. Her swollen hands are clasped on her lap but not tightly enough to disguise the tremor. And she doesn't look at me, not once, and I know it's because she won't let me see her pain. Indeed, if you weren't looking for the signs, you'd never think her only son was breathing his last.

I allow Luke to flounder and ignore his pleading glances for assistance. I stare unseeing at the peely walls, and my grandmother's gravelly voice, usually so penetrating, floats disembodied around me, a vague, scraping, far off sound. Everything feels unreal. Actually, everything feels nothing. I feel hollow. What am I doing here, sitting in a hard orange chair. I should be shagging Jasper. My father should be sitting in his study smoking a cigar and reading the *Sunday Times*. Parents are just there, a constant, in the background. Wallpaper. Peely walls.

Imminent death – the ultimate in suspense. An excuse to call Jasper and make him feel guilty. For both reasons, my heart is whapping along at 140 beats per minute. At least it *is* beating. First though, I ask Luke if he'd be sweet enough to go home and feed Fatboy.

He leaps up and cries happily, 'I'd love to!' before

glancing fearfully at Nana Flo and adding sombrely, 'Anything I can do to help.'

I give him detailed instructions. 'Whiskas kitten food, if he won't eat that, then try him on the Hill's Science Plan. If he's really stroppy then open a can of tuna and pour the juice into a bowl, *not* the oil one, he hates that, it has to be springwater. But don't let him eat the actual tuna or he'll be sick.' Fatboy, while greedy, has a delicate stomach. He pukes up ordinary, expensive cat food. Only the *really* expensive stuff which isn't sold in supermarkets and requires a long detour to Pet World stays the distance.

Nana Flo sniffs. 'Cats,' she says. 'Vermin.'

I feel sorry for Nana Flo. That is, I feel sorry for her in general. She finds very little in life to smile about. She's not at all what you want in a grandmother. No jolly fat legs and a bun, no five pound notes on birthdays, no cooking of mushy pea and poached fish dinners, no letting you plink-plank on her old piano, no talking you through yellow crackly photo albums and buying you sweets behind your parents' back. She's the Anti-Grandmother and I suspect she speaks highly of me too. My father – the few times he's ever spoken about her – rolls his eyes and says she's had a hard life. Well, excuse me but most old people I know have had a hard life, doesn't mean they're all miserable goats. Michelle's grandmother's a scream and *she* worked in a sausage factory for twenty-six years. Think Barbara Cartland but with more make-up. My grandmother just watches television. I leave her to her gloom and run to the payphone.

My conversation with Jasper is infuriating. He starts off with a wry 'Oh hi, it's you,' and I derive brief satisfaction from telling him the news and jerking him out of his indifference. I can't really believe it myself, can't believe I'm saying the alien words aloud. So, maybe not that amazingly, Jasper refuses to believe me! He keeps repeating, like a posh Dalek, 'I'm sure it will be okay.'

I say firmly, 'No Jasper, he *is* actually seriously ill,' but to no avail.

14

His last offer is 'Call me tomorrow and tell me how he is.' After Jasper's disappointing response I don't want to speak to anyone else.

Another hour of wall-staring and we return to the relatives' room next to Resuss. It's drab, poky, stinks of smoke and is a dead ringer for my sixth-form classroom. Finally, a red-eyed scruffy adolescent in black jeans and a nasty chequered shirt approaches and informs us that my father has been moved to the coronary care unit, and to follow him. The teenager has a stethoscope hanging round his neck, but even so Nana Flo looks like she wants to belt him. The lift ascends to the eleventh floor at the pace of a retarded snail, stopping at every floor. I start giggling. I can't stop myself. I'm shaking with laughter. I don't even stop when my mother screams 'stop it!' Then, I have the brilliant idea of biting my lip so hard I taste blood. It works. Minutes later, the house officer as he claims to be, stops in front of a wizened old man flat on a bed and it's a moment before I recognise him.

My father, senior partner, who makes Boss Hogg look like a wimp. My father, the quiet but respected king of every golf club soirée. My father who only ever wears tailored suits. My father who deems nudity on a par with Satanism. My father who only last week told me – via my mother of course – that he thought it was time I moved into a flat of my own and would I like him to advise me on location. This shrunken, helpless creature who lies motion-less, bare-chested, attached to a spaghetti of wires, smelling faintly sickly sweetly, pale and hollow-cheeked, rasping, unseeing, in an ugly metal bed. This is my father. He looks fucking dreadful.

While I am mute with shock – although I can't help thinking this is a week off work at *least* – my mother is loudly inconsolable. Nana Flo says nothing but she looks at her son, little more than skin stretched tight over a skull, and her hooded eyes glisten. I reluctantly place a hand on her bony shoulder. To my surprise, she pats it. Then I hug my mother, murmur useless words into her ear, and watch her hold my father's still hand and wail into his sheet. Nana Flo has blinked away the tears and sits silently beside her, like a grouchy angel of death. The adolescent quietly suggests that if we go to the relatives' room he'll explain what's going on, but as my boss Laetitia is always reminding me – demanding direct quotes from the Queen not a Buckingham Palace Press Office clone – you *must* speak to the organ grinder not the monkey. I run after his retreating back – 'Excuse me!' He turns around. 'I, ah, I don't mean to be rude,' I say. 'But, is it possible to speak to the specialist? To find out what's going to happen? I mean, how long . . .'

The adolescent sighs and says he'll fetch the medical registrar. Five minutes later, he returns with a bloke who I am sure is twenty-two, max. He introduces himself as Simon, and he tells us that 'Dad's very sick.' Surprise! Then he explains, in kindergarten language, what a heart attack is. He tells us they're doing all they can. Very powerful drugs. But so much heart muscle affected. No blood pressure. Kidneys failing. Fluid collecting on lungs. Hard to make a precise estimation. Doesn't have a crystal ball. Got to take it an hour at a time. To paraphrase, this heart attack was a vicious one. Judging by the woeful look on Simon's face, my father hasn't got long to live.

Nana, me, and my mother sit helplessly by my father's bed until the sky turns black and we're ushered into another dingy relatives' room. There are no curtains and when I press my face to the window I see all of London twinkling prettily under the dark sky. We spend the night sitting, pacing, staring, sighing. Hilary, a soft-voiced specialist cardiac nurse, keeps popping in to update us. Hilary happens to be a he which is a source of great displeasure to Nana Flo who keeps tutting, 'It isn't *right*.' Twice, thanks to my mother's wailing and gnashing, we're allowed into the unit for a brief vigil. Every time my father rasps I have to restrain her from pressing the red emergency

16

button. During vigil two, Hilary asks her to keep her voice down as other people in the unit are trying to sleep. My mother gives a shriek of rage at his audacity and runs into the corridor. I make an Englishy-apologetic cringe to Hilary and scamper after her. It's a long night. By 5a.m., I am indecently ravenous so I walk out of the hospital and into the corner shop and buy a pack of Pringles Cheez Ums. I *could* have bought my favourite, salt & vinegar, but feel it would be inappropriate. My mother 'can't eat a thing'. Nana Flo chows down at least half of my Pringles. She makes such a lunge for the tube I'm surprised her arm doesn't pop out of its socket.

Shortly after dawn, my mother goes to 'stretch her legs' and Nana Flo goes to the Ladies – which happily takes her twenty minutes. Hilary leans round the door and says, 'Would you like to see him?' I nod. My heart thuds. A second later I am alone with my father. A rash of dirt-grey stubble covers his chin and the shock hits me like a slap. I gently rest my hand on his. I ought to say something. But it's embarrassing. The most embarrassing thing, the thing my father would be most embarrassed by, is the large square transparent plastic wee bag which hangs from a tube that thankfully disappears under his bedcover. The other patients' bags are full of orange urine. My father's – I am relieved to see – is empty.

I hate to sound like someone who works for a women's magazine but you'd think they'd try for a more stylish, more opaque wee bag. I am idly wondering if Prada would agree to an NHS catheter commission or if Louis Vuitton might be a more judicious choice, when my father emits a loud rasp. Shit! Say it, say it, now, now, say it! But I am dumb. I clutch my father's hand and think, stiffly, I love you, in my head. Dad, I love you. Dad, did I tell you, Dad, I hope you know, Dad, I know we weren't, we didn't . . . Just say it. Can't. The words are glue. Think, 'you're sacked' but a million times stickier.

The hours pass and I still don't say it. Instead, I squeeze

my father's hand and bring my forehead to rest on it. This hand, this hand that's waved for taxis, summoned the bill, signed cheques with a flourish, caressed my mother's face, and walloped me on the backside, this warm, solid, big paw of a hand will soon be cold and dead, flesh rotting, peeling away deep under the cold hard ground. Jesus Christ. My mother bustles in with a copy of the *Daily Mail* and marches off to bother Hilary. So, instead of saying 'I love you, Daddy,' and crying daughterly tears all over my father's frail dying body, I read him extracts from the *Daily Mail* financial section.

Nana Flo returns and regards me suspiciously. 'He can't hear you!' she barks, before stalking off again. I get up, walk into the corridor, kick the wall and nearly break a toe. I lean against the wall and breathe deeply. Then I hobble back into the ward – ignoring the wide stares of the ill and wretched – and continue my private lecture. And from nowhere the quiet murmur of the ward becomes chaos, with screams of 'he's arresting!' and 'put out an arrest call!', and swarms of people in blue and white run towards me shouting, pulling, clanking the bed, pushing trolleys, yanking curtains, and in the blur as I am dragged away I see the orange reading on the black heart monitor screen is a wild scribble and my father has slumped on his pillow. So I am with my father when he dies, but each of us is alone.

Twenty minutes later, the medical registrar, flanked by the adolescent, is explaining to my sobbing, shaking mother and my silent, still grandmother. There is brief confusion when he says my father suffered a cardiac arrest and has now 'gone to another place' but the hurried addition of 'I mean, he's dead,' clears it. My father is dead. He dies at 7.48 p.m. He dies during the golden hour – when the setting sun cloaks the world in a warm yellow blanket of enchanted light. No more golden hours for Maurice. It is a beautiful day and my father is dead.

Chapter 3

Cinderella's glass slippers were made of fur. But when the French interpreted the original text, they translated fur-lined as *verre*. My mother's voice warms as she tells me this and I know she is reassessing Cinderella as a more homely, snuggly girl than the brash madam who click-clacked around the royal ballroom in hard shoes of glass. She loves stuff like this which is why, as an infant school teacher, my mother kicks butt.

That, and she shouts louder than any person I know. The children adore her, far more than she likes them. Her motto is, 'You can't get involved.' Not even when Ahmed's mummy rings to ask if Ahmed, five, can stay the night at school because the white people on their estate have been smashing their windows and beating up Ahmed's father and shoving dog shit through their letter box for three years and Ahmed needs to get some sleep. My mother does not take work home with her.

At home, my mother reverts to a fairytale of her own. She is a north-west London princess, with a handsome prince called Maurice to look after her. You'd never guess she was an intelligent, educated woman. She flaps if she has to program the video. She is famed for not returning phone calls from Nana Flo or anyone else who is emotionally taxing. She follows the thick ostrich school of thought – that if you ignore your demanding friends and relatives they'll go away instead of getting angry and offended. She wants everything to be *nice* and if it isn't she stamps her feet until it is.

19

This is partly why my father's death – my father's death! – is a problem. She doesn't want to get involved. She didn't want to 'view' his body (although to be fair, neither did I), she refused to see the hospital's Bereavement Services Officer – 'Don't say that word!' – and she wanted nothing to do with the funeral arrangements. So it's been left to me and Nana Flo who, amazingly, has become a whirr of efficiency.

Work have been great. I called Laetitia on Monday morning. She was sympathetic but pressured and suggested that I come into work 'to take your mind off things'. I said, 'Er, I think he's on the brink, actually.' She also offered to send me some magazines 'To keep you ticking over'. I accepted, it's rude not to. Anyhow I've got a week off, free, compassionate leave. If I'm still off next week, I get half-pay. Feeling mad and light-headed, I ring in to confirm what's happened to my Dad on Tuesday morning. I say the words but I'm not convinced. Immediately, the Editor's secretary sends a huge bunch of orange flowers to my parents' house. Luke's agreed to nanny Fatboy and my mother's a wreck, so I'm staying there. One thing I'll say about *Girltime*, they do a good bouquet.

Lizzy calls me, says how sorry she is, and asks in a hushed voice if I'm okay.

'I'm fine,' I say quickly, before I can think about it.

She says, 'Are you sure?'

Really, I tell her, in a brittle pantomime voice, I'm fine, I'm busy, my mother's freaking because she can't believe the Passport Office are 'cruel' enough to demand back my dad's passport.

Lizzy wants details and when I tell her about collecting my dad's clothes and his watch in a plastic bag and my mother not wanting to leave the hospital, she starts sobbing. Unfairly, I am annoyed by this. How dare she cry! She then tries to regale me with jolly tales from the office. Today, she says, the managing director showed the former hostage Terry Waite – she actually says that! 'the former hostage' – around the office and everyone ignored him because there was a beauty sale on. This is when the beauty department sell off all the cosmetics they've accumulated for 50p apiece and give the proceeds to charity. Everyone bites and punches in their determination to nab the designer stuff. I couldn't give a shit but I muster a small appreciative snort.

Then Lizzy says something no one else would dream of saying. 'Helen,' she says solemnly, 'I'm sure you were a wonderful daughter. I'm sure your father was very proud of you.' Jesus! That is *horrible*. What a horrible thing to say.

'Lizzy, please don't say things like that,' I whisper, and hurriedly put the phone down. I'm trembling. My head feels leaden and unstable, like a boulder about to topple off a cliff. I grit my teeth so hard my whole face is a rictus. I breathe in quick short sniffs until the comfort blanket of numbness resettles. Only then do I trust myself to speak. 'This house is pitch dark and freezing cold,' I say crossly to Nana Flo. I add spitefully, 'It's like a bloody morgue.' I stamp around turning on radiators and switching on lights. I remain chilly but feel calmer.

My mother is sitting on their, her bedroom floor sniffing my father's jumpers. I leave her a cup of decaffeinated tea as I fear the real thing would send her into a drug-crazed frenzy. I've also hidden the Nurofen. Meanwhile, Nana Flo and I have divided the death duties of which there are roughly a million. Lawyers, notices, certificates, application forms, wills, probates, pensions, policies, insurance, tax. Jesus. If I think about how much I have to do I will scream and go mad so I am trying not to think. All I'll say is I hate looking after people and I hate organising so today is not a great day. Ideally I'd like to slump on my bed and stare into space but my heart is still pounding so it's impossible to relax. It's doing wonders for my metabolism and I now know why bereaved people get so thin. Michelle will be *rabid*. Also, I never thought I'd say this but thank

21

heaven for Nana Flo. She managed to shake my mother out of her stupor for long enough to show us where Dad keeps his paperwork. She's phoned all our ghastly relatives and told them not to come round just yet *and* she insisted on registering Dad – which involves an exhausting trek to Camden Town Hall.

I make her take a cab. She starts to protest that the bus is fine so I say 'my treat'. I tell the driver to wait for her and drop her back and I'll pay. Hey, it's only money, my dad's dead, let's live a little. I don't know if it's the delirium but I'm beginning to talk in clichés. When I phone the local funeral home listed in the Yellow Pages – *home!* are they kidding? – I say, 'I'm ringing on behalf of my father.' Like I'm booking him into a hotel!

I haven't a fucking clue what I'm doing and am using a blue leaflet the bereavement woman gave me entitled 'What to do after a death in England and Wales' as a recipe book. It's a lot more use than my useless friends. Lizzy rings again to tell me she's been talking to the Health & Beauty Director who says there's an organisation called the Natural Death Centre which does eco-friendly funerals and biodegradable coffins. Then she says the words 'woven willow pod' and I say 'I'll stop you right there.' About six hours later, Nana Flo returns triumphantly with the death certificate – huffing because it cost her £6.50. I drop the cash into her purse while she's in the loo. She's also got the infamous green form everyone's wittering on about. It allows you to bury the body and dead people wouldn't be seen dead without it. Ah ha ha ha.

Despite the laughable horror of the situation the funeral guy is very sweet. He looks, as I expect, like Uriah Heep (or what I imagine Uriah Heep to look like having never got further than the first page of any Dickens novel apart from *Great Expectations* which we were forced through at school). He is tall, bony, with watery blue eyes, and grey hair in a critical stage of combover. His handshake is creepily limp. I brace myself for a grasping parasite but he

22

turns out to be kind. He ushers me into a room, the focal point of which is a very unsubtle painting of a stag in a dark forest, a bright ray of sunshine pointing directly at the stag's head. He offers me a coffee and talks me through the options. We flick through a coffin brochure. Any minute now Nicky Clarke will appear. Uriah says that if a client chooses a cremation, 'We recommend what I call a plain, dignified coffin.' He adds tactfully, 'It's not top quality wood, but you know what happens in a cremation.' I nod and smile as if I discuss cremating my father most days. Uriah continues, 'It looks beautiful and on the occasion, you would not be dissatisfied if you saw it.' Bless his heart.

He also shows me a wreath brochure full of big blowsy angel, pillow, trumpet and chair shapes. Weird – surely death is more of a lie down than a sit down. The cost of a grave is unbelievable and Uriah is suitably disparaging about London prices. 'A plot of land that would eventually cater for three people' – excuse me? – 'would cost a thousand pounds.' He sees my shocked face – although I'm less shocked by the rip-off cost than the prospect of a threesome – and adds, 'London land is very expensive. A plot in Highgate cemetery can cost fifty thousand! Whereas, not so long ago, I had cause to bury my mother, in Cornwall. The plot was five pounds!' At the punchline I raise my eyebrows and say that, despite the cost, I think my family want a burial.

My father's burial grave death body – a new vocabulary of ugly, alien, disgusting words. It's grotesque and I can't believe I'm here. I sit frozen in my seat, feet neatly together, and all the while my head is spinning like I'm riding on the big dipper and my brain is screaming *this is ridiculous it can't be real* and I want to run and run until it's not. Uriah, meanwhile, is keen to stress that he'd liaise with the hospital, the minister, provide the hearse, the cars, remove all the hassle from my girlish head, and until the funeral, 'Dad would stay here with us.' I smile and nod although I can't imagine anything Dad would like less. 'You can,' adds Uriah, 'pop in and see him whenever you want.' He suggests that I go home, discuss the finer details with my mother, and ring him tomorrow. He sees me off with another weak handshake and 'It's a horrible day, isn't it?' He's right. It's raining hard and the sky is as funeral grey as Uriah's grey suit.

'Thank you,' I say, and run to the Toyota.

I walk in the door and, do I believe my eyes! (I love that phrase – the Wizard of Oz says it – I even prefer it to my other favourite, '*Would* you credit it!') Who do I see sitting at the kitchen table charming the bloomers off Nana Flo – who is old enough to know better – *and* my mother – who has magically applied full dramatic widow's make-up plus long black dress – but Jasper.

'Jasper?' I say in a shrill squeak.

'Heeelen!' bleats my mother, sweeping out of her chair and crushing me in a long, sorrowful hug. 'You've been gone so long! I was terrified! I thought you'd had an accident!' Oh please! Like she ever hugs me!

'Mum, don't be silly,' I say. 'I was sorting out Da—, the funeral. I'll tell you about it later.' I wriggle out of her steely arms and kiss Jasper chastely on the cheek. Foolishly, stupidly, I am delighted he's here. Nana Flo and my mother show no sign of wanting to give us any privacy, so I suggest to Jasper that we go upstairs. We plod up to Dad's study, which is in fact my old bedroom. My parents turned it into a study the day I moved out.

Jasper has got something to say. His face is very serious. 'Helen,' he begins. 'I am so sorry for your loss. Poor you. At least he didn't suffer. And he had a good innings. And, I promise, time does heal.' He stops. I am furious. Mealy mouthed twit! What else? Try to keep busy? It's good to talk? Have a bubble bath?

'That's very comforting,' I say, not bothering to hide the sarcasm, 'although Jasper, I'd actually prefer it if he was still alive.' This throws him. In Jasper's world of Victorian etiquette women don't snap back.

24

He falters, and adds, 'Quite. It must be very difficult for you. And it must be even worse for your mother, she's known him for longer than you.' Jesus Christ! It must be worse for all of us, you stupid prat!

'Look, Jasper,' I say. I am so angry I can barely speak. I am shaking and – if you want the grim details – my sphincter clenches in three sharp spasms. Probably because it's so damn amazed I'm saying what I think. 'Look, Jasper, my father has just died and I have a lot to do. And you, saying things . . . saying stuff like . . . like what you were saying, it just isn't helping.' For the first time since this fiasco started I am close to tears. 'Now, Jasper. Do you have anything else to say to me?'

He looks at the floor. Then, to my surprise, his face turns slowly crimson. 'Sunday,' he announces. 'I lied. I saw Louisa last week. And we boffed. I – I didn't mean to. It just happened.' He looks straight at me. I stare back. 'I felt bad,' he explains, 'And, seeing as your father passed away, I thought I owed you the truth.' What a fine courageous upstanding citizen you are.

'Well!' I say, 'How kind. Some good came of my father's death after all!'

Jasper doesn't get it. He looks pleased, and says, 'Yeah.'

'Jasper,' I say, clenching my fists. 'You are a wanker. Please leave. It's over.' His head jerks in surprise.

'But,' he stammers, 'but Babe, it was a mistake. An error of judgement.'

I glare at him. 'It certainly was,' I say. I say it and I don't even know if I care any more, maybe I'm just saying it because that's what you *say*.

Jasper pushes his hand through his hair and in a patronising tone says, 'Helen, you're—'

I interrupt. In a harsh voice I say, 'Jasper, you're dumped.'

The paradise blue eyes harden and he shrugs.

Then he leaves. He shuts the door quietly behind him.

Jesus. What have I done. The dizziness is back. Angry

tears start falling, fast, uncontrollably. Furious, I sniff aggressively and smear them away. I walk into the kitchen in a daze. I feel ill, headachey, exhausted.

My mother looks up. 'Helen! What a nice boy! I can't believe you never introduced us. He bought me lilies.' Pause. She sees my blotchy face and adds gently, 'Darling. Did you know that during the war they grew vegetables in the Tower of London moat?'

Chapter 4

For my fourth birthday, my father took me to see *The Nutcracker* and I shamed him by roaring, '*I* want to be a fairy too!' I have since revised this ambition, for the sad single reason that fairies wear skirts. I don't wear skirts. I refuse to wear skirts. I haven't worn a skirt for approximately five years because my legs are short and stocky and if I wear a skirt I tend to look like a dressed up bulldog. That said, I recently spied a slender, tapering *Breakfast At Tiffany's* creation in Miss Selfridge and madly, recklessly broke my rule. I wore it to work, thought, 'Actually, my legs aren't that bad.' Then I saw someone else's and I thought 'My god, what were you thinking?' The next day, I gave away the skirt to Michelle – who was pleased to accept it and said she'd get the dry cleaners to take it in for her.

Incredibly, my mother refuses to accept my no skirt rule. 'You can't wear trousers to a funeral!' she squawks.

'Why not?' I snap. 'I'm sure Dad wouldn't mind.'

When I say this, she stamps her foot. She's fifty-five years old! 'Yes, but *I* mind!' she screeches.

'But—'

Her voice starts to crack: 'Just *do* it, Helen! Don't argue with me, I'm warning you, I can't take it!' My mother could teach Elton John a few things about being a drama queen and my patience is wearing so thin it's anorexic. My father wouldn't care if I attended his funeral dressed as a fireman.

Did I mention he deemed nudity on a par with Satanism?

Well, he also deemed religion on a par with Satanism. Consequently, his funeral is to be – as I commanded Uriah – spiritual-lite. No hymns, no house of worship. And no yellow because my father hated yellow. Just a simple graveside ceremony.

'Performed by whom?' asked Uriah.

'A minister, of course!' I said. This puzzled Uriah until I explained that I couldn't think who else could perform it (although cousin Stephen offered) so a minister would have to do. But he's to keep it brisk and, if possible, avoid yellow and God references.

My mother is well aware of all this, yet blows up the skirt issue to intergalactic proportions. Suddenly, the thought of spending one more minute in her shrieky, flailing company is unbearable. 'Fine,' I say. I spit out the words like grape pips. 'You win. I'll wear a skirt. I'll wear a skirt but I've decided' – and I decide this as I say it – 'I want to drive to the funeral myself. I don't want to go in the procession thing. I think it's grim. I refuse.' Cue, world war three.

There is no *way*. Am I *mad*. Do I want to *kill* her. It's *unheard* of. What will people *think*. Boo hoo *hoo*. Happily, part of my job involves phoning experts for extra quotes to bump up dull features written by lazy, overpaid freelance journalists. So I employ a ruse gleaned from one of the many psychologists I interview at *Girltime*. The Broken Record Technique. Whatever my mother throws at me – accusations, threats, pleas, the crumpled up *Guardian* Education section – I calmly repeat the same intensely irritating statement: 'Yes, I realise that, but I've decided to drive to the funeral myself.' On the fifth repetition, she gives a deep yowl, screams, 'Shut up shut up shut *up* I can't stand it!' and runs upstairs. I take this to indicate surrender and drive back to the flat triumphant. I don't feel guilty, why should I?

The morning of the funeral dawns. I lurch into consciousness and feel the nauseating grip of fear without knowing why. Then I remember. The sky is blue but it is a cold, blustery, vicious day. The kind of day that ruins your hair even if you've moussed and blasted it to a brittle crisp. To make matters worse, Tina has been in New York on a fashion shoot until yesterday and so unavailable for consultation, and the only cheap skirt I could find on my lone shopping trip was long, black and stretchy with a non-detachable material bow at the waist. I put it on and immediately look like Alison Moyet.

The flat is silent and I bash about and slam doors to make it less silent and feel angry with my mother for not ringing. I am slightly cheered when I switch on the radio and hear that a hot air balloon containing two nerds has crashed into the sea, thus ruining their attempt to beat the boring Balloon Around The World world record. Jesus! It's their *hobby*! I am looking for my earrings and wondering what sort of needle it would take to pop a hot air balloon when I glance at the clock and realise that it is twenty-five past ten and the funeral starts at eleven.

Six road raging minutes later I am crawling through Golders Green, trying to apply lipstick in the rear-view mirror. At least twenty-five Volvos are double-parked in the middle of the road. I'm wishing I'd taken a different route when I sense a familiar movement in the blurry distance. I focus on it and I see my father walking along the pavement. My stomach flips as I watch his striding march, his confident gait, the broad square of his shoulders, and then he glances, quickly, once, behind him and he isn't my father at all and there is an enormously loud tinny bang and I jolt forward and stop abruptly, having veered – slowly but with conviction – into a parked orange Volkswagen Beetle. 'Oh nooooo!' I shout.

My first thought is to ring Dad. I could burst out crying but I'm wearing non-waterproof mascara. Instead, I leap out and run to inspect the damage. Immediately, other cars start hooting. A well-preserved woman in a Jeep Cherokee

29

whirrs down her window and says helpfully, 'You were going too fast.' Then I hear the sound of screaming.

'You've totalled Nancy!' screams the voice. The voice belongs to a tiny blonde woman wearing emphatic lip-liner and a white coat. Her face is pinchy with rage. She runs towards me until we are standing nose to nose and I can smell her ever-so-faintly rancid breath.

'N-n-nancy?' I stammer in horror. Oh God, I've killed someone.

'Nancy, my car, you stupid cow!'

The whoosh of relief as I realise I won't go to prison plus the slow-brain processing of the fact a twee car-christening stranger is calling me a stupid cow fuse into a rush of adrenaline and I roar, 'For fuck's sake stop screaming, it's a crappy little coke can car!' She looks shocked – probably didn't think someone wearing a skirt like this would use the word 'fuck'. She opens her over made-up mouth to answer back but I am *not* in the mood. I bellow, 'I'm sorry! But I am on the way to my father's funeral and—'

I stop mid-bellow. I stop because a tall dark-haired guy, also wearing a white coat, has jogged up to us and seemingly expects to be included in the conversation. 'Yes?' I say icily.

Instantly, the blonde turns coy. 'Tom!' she simpers. She's practically nuzzling his chest. The sneer in my head must have escaped to my face because she shoots me an evil look. 'Tom, *look* what she's done to Nancy!'

We both regard Nancy's crumpled backside. Then we look at Tom. She looks adoringly. I look snootily, do a double take, quickly attempt to squash it. It emerges victorious as a twitch. Tom is gorgeous. Or rather, he's got – and I know this doesn't sound terribly complimentary but you'll excuse it as a personal fetish – eyes like a husky dog. A cool, pale, piercing blue. Woof. And his teeth. Wolf teeth. I know this, because he flashes me a surprise smile. Pointy canines do it for me. What can I say? It's weird. I mean, I don't even like dogs.

'Celine, it's mainly the bumper. Stop yelling,' says Tom.

Then he turns to me and says, 'Are you okay? Do you want to sit down?'

I shake my head. 'I'm late,' I say shrilly. 'I'm late for my father's funeral, and now this!' My voice chokes up. Celine is mutinously silent.

'What!' says Tom.

'What about Nancy?' says Celine sulkily.

'I'll deal with the car,' says Tom. 'You go inside.' Celine flounces off. Tom winces. 'Sorry about her,' he says. 'You look like you're in shock. Will you be okay to drive?'

I shrug. I mean to say that I'm fine but it comes out as 'I feel dizzy.' I fiddle with my watch and realise that my father's funeral starts in less than quarter of an hour. 'I'm so late! And the Beetle!'

Tom waves away the Beetle. 'The Beetle is worth about ten pence. Forget it. You can sort it out later.' Pause. 'You look a bit wonky to drive. Can I call you a cab?'

I shake my head. 'It starts in ten minutes,' I wail. I feel weak and feeble, not to mention a great big frump. To complete this alluring package, a plop of watery snivel runs out of my nose. I wipe it on my sleeve.

'*I'll* drive you,' announces Tom. 'I've got the van.'

'The van?' I say gormlessly.

'The vet's van,' he says.

'You're a vet!' I say.

'Yes!' he grins.

'That explains the white coat,' I say. Then I decide to shut up. I stand there, gormlessly, while Tom moves the Toyota 'round the back'. His driving is, I'm alarmed to note, similar to mine. Three seconds later, he reappears at the wheel of a dirty white van with the word MEGAVET emblazoned on its side. Classy. He toots, and I clamber in. Because of my clingy student skirt it's a gawky (except fatter), knock-kneed manoeuvre.

'Don't you have loads of animals waiting to see you?' I ask, confirming my already stunning reputation for eloquent repartee and dagger wit.

31

'Nah,' he shakes his head, 'Wednesday's always quiet. Monday and Friday are the killers. Right. Where are we going?' Of course, I can't remember, so Tom scrabbles under his seat and retrieves a ragged *A to Z*. Once we escape from Golders Green, Tom speeds up. He has no qualms about cutting up police cars. I know we're in a rush but it feels like he's trying to take off.

'Alright, wing commander?' I mutter edgily.

He glances at me. 'This isn't fast!' he says. 'You don't want to be late!'

'No,' I say. 'But I don't want to be dead either.'

He slows down. 'I'm sorry about your dad,' he says.

'It's okay,' I reply.

After this jolly exchange, we're silent. Then Tom says, 'How did he die?'

I pick the skin on my lip. 'Heart attack,' I gasp, as the van squeals round a corner. Tom, rather sweetly, gives a loud tut. I want to change the subject. I need to change the subject. I wrack my fuzzy brain for information that may be of interest to a good-looking vet who I have known for not very long and produce the conversational corker: 'I've got a kitten called Fatboy.' Jesus, what's wrong with me? My command of the English language seems to have vanished. Suddenly I possess the vocabulary and articulation of a three-year-old and am forced to suck in my cheeks to prevent myself adding 'What's your favourite colour?'

Thankfully, Tom says politely, 'Oh yes? Any particular sort?'

Here at last is my chance to prove that, despite all evidence to the contrary, I do actually own an IQ. And what do I say? 'He's orange.'

I am considering an emergency operation to have my voice box removed, when Tom says kindly, 'Orange. Good sort of cat.' This inspires me to silence. I stare at my lap and imagine my father lying dead in his coffin, starting to rot.

Seven excruciating minutes later, we screech up to the cemetery gates. 'Thank you it's so kind of you, thank you,'

I say awkwardly, trying to inject some bouncy gratitude into the flat monotone. 'What shall I do about the Toyota?'

Tom waves me away. 'You'd better rush. Just stop by when you have a moment. You can sort the insurance and stuff with Celine whenever. She won't mind.'

This is the most outrageous lie I've heard since my mother denied fancying Steve McQueen. But I let it pass. 'Thank you,' I say again.

'It's alright,' he says. He nods towards the mass of cars jamming the cemetery entrance. 'Will you be okay?'

I nod stiffly, give a silly bye-bye-baby wave, and turn away. My eyes are watering. It's ridiculous. Being shouted at I can take. But *gentleness*. Spare me. Even the word makes me cringe. It's almost as bad as 'tenderly'. Blue eyes and pointy teeth notwithstanding, I go right off him. I see Luke in a too tight navy suit hovering just inside the iron gates with an impeccable Tina and a sleek Lizzy and run gratefully towards them. Tom roars away in his dirty white van, and I don't even look back.

Chapter 5

Luke is a nicotine addict. Not only does he need a pre- and post-coital fag, he has to have one during. It is, he tells me, why his last girlfriend left him. He singed her on a sensitive spot. He says he could give up any time but refuses to chew gum as 'it gives you stomach ulcers'. He smokes on the tube platform ('the no-smoking signs refer to the track'), he smokes in the bath ('for me as a bloke it's the equivalent of a scented candle'), and he smokes while he eats his thick crust pepperoni pizza in front of *A Question of Sport* ('it's a stressful programme, you wouldn't understand'). Did I mention that as well as smoking his insides to soot, Luke says what he thinks without thinking? So it's no great surprise that when I burst through the cemetery gates he grinds his toe agitatedly on one of five smouldering fag butts and shouts, 'Helen! You, mate, are *dead*!'

'I'm *what*!' I say.

He has the grace to blush. 'I mean,' he stutters, 'your mum is going mental. She's murderous. Everyone's waiting in their cars.'

I look at Tina and Lizzy. Tina flicks her fingernails, looks down at her Jimmy Choos, and mutters 'Bloody hell!' Lizzy pulls a woeful face and wails, 'Oh poor Helen!'

I take their discomfort as corroboration. 'Hang on,' I mutter, and weave my way through what looks like a staged motorway pile-up – studiously avoiding eye contact with the goggling faces inside the cars – to the big shiny black Jaguar parked behind the big shiny black hearse.

As I approach, the window shoots down. 'Where. Have.

You. Been?' spits my mother from under a great black saucer of a hat.

I'm surprised at her courteous restraint, then I realise the chauffeur is listening agog. I bend down, wave guiltily at Nana Flo who is clutching a lace handkerchief so tightly her knuckles are white, and say I got held up. 'What's going on?' I ask, to distract my mother from her fury.

'They're in the cemetery office,' says my mother in a high, hysterical voice, 'they're doing all the paperwork and [sniff] we're not allowed to get out of our cars until it's done, and – oh I've had enough! I'm getting out! I can't just sit here! Mind out!' I hop to one side as my mother leaps from the car. Immediately, hordes of car doors click open and swarms of po-faced, droopily-dressed people start plodding slowly towards us. I stiffen in fright. No offence to our family friends and relatives but it's like *Night of the Living Dead*.

I spend the next ten minutes suffocating in a blur of powdery, lavendery, lipsticky kisses, awkward nose-clinking hugs, warm breathy murmurs of 'I'm so sorry!' and 'so sudden!', a sharp assertion of 'You must be relieved he went so quickly' (oh, delighted), a shrill exclamation 'Helen! I hardly recognise you! You've lost your puppy fat!', and 'You *are* taking care of your poor mother, aren't you – such a shock for her!' I glance at my mother who is lapping it up like Fatboy having stumbled on an illegal bowl of ice cream.

'Yes,' I say grimly. 'She needs a lot of looking after.'

I spot Uriah – done up like a dog's dinner – emerging from the cemetery office with the minister. Who, I recall in a stab of panic, left two rambling messages on my answer machine which I ignored then forgot. Uriah, meanwhile, looks distinctly annoyed at the anarchic milling crowds but as I approach his lips twitch in a careful smile. 'Miss Bradshaw,' he says. 'How are you?' I tell him I'm fine. He nods quickly, then says, 'We're ready to embark on your father's last journey, if we may. Do you wish the

35

arrangement to stay on the coffin, or shall we remove it?'

I'm stumped. 'Er, what do people normally do?' I say.

'Most folk prefer to take it off,' he says. 'They often like to donate it to an appropriate hospital ward – in this case, the cardiac unit,' he adds helpfully. How jolly for the patients.

'Oh fine, do that then,' I blurt. I become aware of a dip in the noise level. During which a woman's voice exclaims, 'I hope he's not going to be buried over the other side. I hate the walk.'

I turn and my heart thuds as I see that the dark draculaesque coffin has been rolled out of its hearse and six sober-suited men are slowly hefting it on to their shoulders. I stare at it in horror. This solid, ugly, stark token of death. Jesus! My father is *in* there. Dead. Cold. Stiff. Starting to rot. How long before the rigor mortis is softened with the stink of decay and . . . I am wrenched from my rotten thoughts by my mother who storms right up to Uriah and shouts in his face: 'Morrie's Cousin Stephen wants to carry the coffin!'

Not by himself, surely, I say in my head. Cousin Stephen is about ninety-three and the height of a Munchkin. 'Mum,' I begin, glancing nervously at Uriah, 'we were supposed to sort—'

Uriah stops me with a light touch on my shoulder. 'It's not a problem,' he says grandly. After a short flurry – and when I say short I mean short – Cousin Stephen is promoted to a pallbearer. Uriah somehow organises everyone into a long straggly line, eyeballs Luke into extinguishing his cigarette, and takes his place in front of the coffin, with the minister.

My mother, Nana Flo, and I stand behind it. I glance at Nana to see if she might faint but she has a strong, angry look about her, like she's preparing for battle. My mother is trembling and her face is swollen with tears. I hug her and nearly collapse as she promptly relaxes her entire weight on to me. She clings with one arm, and uses the other to keep her hat from whizzing off her head and spinning across the white sea of gravestones. I feel as if I'm acting a part in a film. It's ridiculous! Today is a chill, blustery Wednesday morning. I should be sitting at my desk in an overheated office, slurping a double espresso and leafing through the *Sun* on the pretext of doing research. Instead, here am I, with a great troupe of people, in the bloody countryside, stumbling over the muddy earth behind a big brash coffin containing my dad, towards a freshly dug grave to bury him deep in the ground – bury my *father* – who only last week was cheerily celebrating the dropping of his handicap with fat cigars and a round of brandies for his putting pals in the Brookhill Golf Club bar. I wonder how Tina's £195 shoes are negotiating the dirt.

For the first five steps of the funeral march, the coffin is – thanks to squat Cousin Stephen – wobbly and uneven. Thankfully, Uriah's men hoick it up and off Cousin Stephen's short shoulder until he is actually standing underneath it. He is forced to be content with placing a nominal hand of support on its polished surface and our bizarre procession shuffles on. I glide forward like a zombie. Everyone is hushed and the only sound is a plane droning overhead and the wind whipping the soft, feathery branches of the elderly yew trees.

I feel sick. I am dreaming, and soon someone is going to wake me, tell me it's a mad, twisted nightmare, and I'll open my eyes and I'll be in my warm soft bed and this surreal situation will vanish. Disappear. End. Stop. '*STOP!*' roars my mother in a voice that God could have used to part the Dead Sea. Everyone – including, unfortunately, the pallbearers – jumps about a foot in the air and staggers to a hurried halt. Nana looks dumbstruck.

'Good grief,' I say rather stupidly, 'what's wrong?' My mother is sobbing and trembling so violently she can barely speak. Uriah bustles over, full of official concern. 'Okay,' I say soothingly, stroking her back. 'It's okay, just calm down. What's upset you?'

My mother is gasping and choking but eventually manages to wheeze out the word 'ring'. Ring?

'Ring?' I say. 'Ring who?'

This prompts a fresh energised burst of woe: 'Nooaaaaaaaawww!' she wails. 'We-dding ring! His wedding ring! It's still on his fi-fi-finger-her-herrrr!' My jaw drops and I gawp at Uriah aghast. He gawps back. He presses two bony fingers to his pale temple as if he has a headache. Which indeed he has.

At first, Uriah tries wheedling. 'But Mrs Bradshaw,' he intones, 'if you remember we did go through this, we filled in the form—'

My mother's sagging head snaps up sharply like a bad-tempered puppet. Her eyes glint. She is queen of the classroom and Uriah is a silly little dunce who hasn't done his homework. 'I don't care!' she hisses. 'I don't want to hear your excuses! I'm paying you! I want my husband's wedding ring! Now, get it!'

I am briefly dumb with horror and mortification. I glance nervously at Nana who says nothing but looks at my mother once, quickly, a look of unconcealed hate. I stammer, 'But you . . . you can't—' I stare helplessly at Uriah.

This is a man who knows when he's beat. He raises a thin, weary hand. 'We can,' he sighs.

And so, the rumours rumble back through the chilled, bewildered crowd until everyone present knows that the coffin containing my dead father has been wheeled behind a couple of conveniently tall headstones, the mahogany top prised off it, the gold wedding band forcefully wrested from his pink finger, polished on Uriah's black tailcoat, and presented to my sulkily defiant mother. (Luke sidles up behind them to peek and later tells me, 'Honestly, Helen, he looked really well! He didn't look corpsey at all!')

After this unscheduled interlude – during which I spy the minister checking his watch – we make it to the graveside. I try to steer my mother's attention towards the garish floral tributes propped around the hole and away from the fresh pile of earth heaped beside it and the two scruffy men standing not quite far away enough, each one casually leant on a great big sodding dirt-encrusted shovel.

The pallbearers and a relieved Cousin Stephen lower the coffin to the ground. No one is quite sure where to stand. One elderly guest with crepey skin and hair like candyfloss observes in a loud whisper, 'I would have expected more flowers. But I suppose they'll come later.' The minister approaches us and asks if there is anything we'd like him to say. My mother becomes flustered. Someone has given her a red rose to throw on my father's coffin and she has picked it to bits.

'Like what?' she says.

'Well, er, any particular tribute to the deceased,' he replies.

'No one told me about tributes!' she exclaims rudely. 'Helen, you should have said! I'd have written something down!' Talk about ungrateful!

'*Me*!' I cry. I have just about had it with her flouncing. 'How should I know! Why is it *my* fault?' A small worm of guilt niggles its way into my consciousness because possibly vaguely maybe I sort of recall the minister's message might have mentioned the wisdom of writing a short note for him to include in his address but – I'm sorry, I can't be responsible for every piddling detail!

'He was a loving, attentive father,' I lie, reading off a nearby gravestone, 'and a wonderful, kind, adoring husband,' I add in a rush to appease my mother. She sniffs approval.

'He was good at golf,' she says. 'Say that.' The minister nods, backs away, clears his throat, trots out a thin service and the speediest, tritest, most anodyne accolade I have ever heard bar the one my headmistress made at my school leaving ceremony.

The coffin is then lowered into the grave. I note Uriah nodding surreptitiously to the fourth pallbearer who grabs a rope before cousin Stephen can wimp, sorry – muscle in and make a hash of it. Is it my imagination or are those gravediggers closer than they were? Vultures. We sprinkle dirt on the coffin – Luke manages to hurl a large clod of earth containing a stone at 110mph that goes *pank!* as it hits the casket and makes a slight dent. I keep my arm around my mother on the pretext of lending her loving support, but really to prevent her throwing herself into the grave. I doubt she will, as her black Jaeger dress cost – according to Tina's informed guess – approximately £250. But after the ring episode I'm taking no chances.

Nana Flo stares silently down at the coffin, shaking her head. I'm relieved that Nana's sister has flown in from Canada although she's having difficulty reaching her as every time she takes a step, a dragonish fire-breathing relative blocks her path crying, 'Great Aunt Molly! When was the last time we saw you!'

I release my mother for one minute to comfort Nana Flo and the next thing I know is, my mother has bowled up to the minister, and declared, 'We won't be using you again! And don't think you're getting a tip!' Even Luke is shocked. And, for one unholy second, the Molly botherers stop nattering.

The blessed Uriah swoops to the rescue. 'Mrs Bradshaw,' he croons, 'you must be frozen, might I fetch you a blanket?' Her attention-hungry head swivels and I am reminded of a cartoon hero bravely distracting Godzilla from crushing a child by waving and jiggling his juicy self as a decoy.

'You may,' she says graciously. The minister sneaks off. Uriah orders a minion to fetch a blanket. Luke, and a million others, spark up and start yapping. I could almost believe that we were burying a stranger and that my father decided to stay at home, like Homer Simpson shirking church.

Then I see Nana Flo. She is standing tensely over the grave staring blindly at the mud-splattered coffin. Uriah waits a decent while before slinking up to me and saying, 'Whenever you're ready we'll take the cards off the flowers for you.'

'One second', I say. I run over to Nana Flo, touch her shoulder softly, and say, 'The funeral director asked if you would like him to take the cards off the flowers yet.'

My grandmother seems to drag herself back from somewhere far away. Her head turns slowly like a tortoise. She says in a bright hard voice, 'Yes thank you, that would be lovely.' I nod, retreat, and tell Uriah to go ahead.

Uriah's men go to work and I gaze unseeing into the middle distance. I stand as inanimate as a maypole, while a sweep of blurry faces whirl and dance and chatter around me. Eventually, a gentle hand on my arm forces me to snap into focus. 'Helen,' says Lizzy softly, 'everyone's going back to your mother's house. Do you want me to stay here with you for a little longer?'

I blink, and see that most of our guests are revving up their cars, the cards are gone from the flowers, and the gravediggers are inching towards the abandoned grave. Uriah, in the distance, is helping Nana Flo into the black limousine. Another plane drones noisily overhead and I am furious at its blithe intrusion. 'Let's go,' I say to Lizzy. She takes my arm and we walk in silence through the mass of past lives to the cemetery gates where Luke and Tina are waiting. My mother is snug in the plush car and content to meet me at the house. I squeeze into the back of Tina's yellow Ford Escort – a secret obsessively kept from her fashiony friends – and we roar off. And that is the end of my father.

'All this way for a sausage roll,' is one indiscreet but apt verdict on the after-show party. Our Canadian relatives – having secured free bed, breakfast, lunch, dinner, entertainment, electricity, fluffy towels, and hot water from my mother – have repaid her by dragging their slothful selves to Asda and spending roughly three quid on a few loaves of white bread (economy), foul-tasting margarine (economy), potted shrimp paste (which until I tasted the disgusting evidence, I assumed was a spiteful myth devised by Enid Blyton to dissuade children from going on picnics), four packs of crisps (Asda own brand) and three packs of Jammie Dodgers – which I refused to eat even as a two-year-old because of the mingy squiddle of jam they contained compared to the mouth-parching excess of biscuit.

My mother narrowly saves the day by picking the lock on my father's drinks cabinet. Everyone falls upon the alcohol like alcoholics. My mother – who has a history of embarrassing my father at cocktail parties by demanding a cup of tea – swallows four double Baileys in ten seconds then lurches up to me and sniggeringly confides, 'Cousin Stephen is so tight that when he walks his arse squeaks!'

I am secretly impressed at this stunning transformation from grief-stricken widow to gobshite, but know if I reveal the smallest sign of amused acquiescence she'll run around braying this pertinent witticism to everyone, including Cousin Stephen. So I prise her fifth pint of Baileys out of her vicelike grip, replace it with a chill glass of water, and say primly, 'At this precise moment, Mummy, you are in no position to be calling other people tight.'

I pour the Baileys down the sink and wish that everyone would leave. I don't want to talk. Not even to my friends. It's effort. I don't want to hear how much Great Aunt Molly enjoyed chatting to my father about the Canadian property market or how he and Cousin Stephen went camping together when they were boys. I don't give a shit. Trying to appropriate the lion's share of the grief and limelight when they're barely related! I don't want to be sociable. I want my father to walk into the kitchen and say, 'Helen, make me a cup of coffee, will you.'

The doorbell rings, and I sag, dramatically, like a sullen teenager and plod grumpily towards it. As I approach I can make out a familiar figure through the frosted glass. Surely not. I ping out of my slouch and curse myself for not changing my student skirt the second I returned to the house. Marcus. As if on cue, Luke wanders out from the lounge. 'Marcus said he might turn up later,' he says brightly.

'Thanks for warning me,' I say as I smooth my hair and yank open the door.

'Hell-*ie*,' says Marcus in a soothing tone. 'You poor love. I am *so* sorry I missed your old man's send-off. I *so* wanted to be there but some doll from this new girl group Second Edition needed showing round the gym. I tried to get out of it but it was no go.'

I narrow my eyes disbelievingly and purse my lips in the beginnings of a pout. 'I'm sure you were desperate to escape from the glamorous pop star,' I say.

'Oh Hellie, don't be like that,' he grins. 'I'd prefer to spend time with you any day. To be honest, she was a dog. Legs like tree trunks.' I do a token-feminist tut to disguise a large smirk. Incidentally, Marcus is the only person in the world I would ever allow to call me Hellie.

I have had an unrequited crush on Marcus for approximately nine years, ever since I spied him in the dinner queue at college. We had Luke's friendship in common but as Marcus spent every waking hour at the gym I only got to know him at close range three years ago – when he bought his flat in Swiss Cottage and needed someone, preferably more reliable than Luke, to rent a room. (Fortunately there wasn't anyone, so Luke suggested me.)

Marcus is undeniably vain and an unrepentant philanderer, but alluring even so. His job – assistant manager and personal trainer at an exclusive London health club, pardon me, health *spa* – suits him down to the ground and, not infrequently, into the bedroom. He knows that I fancy him, am humbly resigned to his romantic indifference, and that my lust is lying fallow. He therefore deduces – correctly – that I am delighted to be his friend and lodger even if he does charge slightly more than I can

43

comfortably afford (there's a surcharge for Fatboy.) And he *is* fun to be with. He's a monster bitch who is acidly critical of everyone he meets yet superb at playing the sweetly caring friend. Marcus is adept at prising juicy chunks of gossip from his celebrity clients, and even adepter at blabbing them out to me and Luke. If I were ever to think about it – not that I do of course – I'd say that Marcus is fond of me. We enjoy a flirtatious relationship which peaks when I'm going out with someone. When *he's* going out with someone it dips. When neither of us are going out with someone it drops into free fall.

But today Marcus is touchy-feely. He kisses me on both cheeks in a sincere manner, lightly resting a warm hand on the back of my neck. A *zing!* of lust shoots down my back, my sourness dissipates and my sunshiny temperament is magically restored. 'Would you like a drink?' I purr.

'G & T would hit the spot, low-cal tonic if poss,' he replies immediately. I nod, direct him to where Lizzy, Luke, and Tina are sitting, and obediently trot off. 'Nice skirt, Alison,' he calls.

'Piss off,' I shout, as I bump into Great Aunt Molly. She looks straight at me and bursts into tears. I grit my teeth. 'I didn't mean you, Auntie Molly,' I say in a saccharine voice.

'Oh no dear, I know you didn't. It's all got on top of me – *sob!* – talking to Florence. Such a tragedy, losing her baby, her baby boy. And what a funeral! You young people have very strong ideas about how you like to do things. In my day, we had respect for religion! I know it's hard for you too, dear, but losing a child, a child – no parent should ever have to bury a child—' Great Aunt Molly is revving up for a big, bosomy, tear-stained rant, breezily innocent of the fact that I am fantastically insulted and itching to slap her.

'My father was fifty-nine,' I say coldly. 'He was hardly a child.' This, I know, is a truly evil statement but I have no room in my heart for other people's whingeing grief. I can just about stomach my mother's. I squeeze past her, snatch

44

the gin bottle from a comotose Cousin Stephen, pour Marcus's drink (full-fat tonic, I'm afraid), and speed back to him and the others.

Luke and Tina are deep in conversation about lord knows what, and Marcus is baiting sweet, courteous, well-mannered Lizzy about precisely why she ditched her last boyfriend. 'Was he a marshmallow in bed?' he demands.

'No! no, I mean, I'd really rather not—'

Marcus rolls his eyes and nods knowingly: 'He had a matchstick dick!' Lizzy nearly spills her glass of Perrier. 'Really! Really, I don't think—'

But Marcus is relentless. 'So what then? Was it big? Bite-size? Medium?'

Lizzy looks down at her lap and says in a small, reluctant voice, 'Medium.'

I shove the G & T at Marcus without making eye contact, march out of the lounge, up the stairs and into the bathroom. I sit on the side of the avocado green bath, and laugh and laugh and laugh. I refuse to cry.

Chapter 6

Almost every night, from ever since I can remember to the age of thirteen, I dreamed one of three dreams. Like most of the young female population I'd attend school wearing no knickers – an omission I'd discover as we queued for assembly. Or I'd fly around our house with Peter Pan, leaping carefree over the bannisters and floating upwards as weightless and airy as Tinkerbell. Most frequently, though, I'd walk alone into our local wood, in the terrible knowledge that a family of wolves lurked in the bushes. I'd start running, and they'd chase me. The dream never varied except on one memorable occasion, when I sped out of the wood and jumped over interminable lines of parked cars to escape them. Recently, however, my dreams have taken on a more urgent note. I dream I am hiding from a group of nameless baddies, in a huge empty house. I know they will hunt me down and the dream always ends as they yank me out of the attic cupboard. I try to relate it to Marcus but he yawns loudly, blips on the TV, and says, 'There's nothing more boring than other people's dreams.'

The bastard's right so I ring Lizzy and tell her about it instead. Lizzy immediately consults a book she has entitled *Definitive Meanings Of Dreams Dreamed By People We've Never Met But Whose Unconscious We're Experts On*. Or something like that. 'Your ambition is pursuing you and pushing you towards success,' she declares.

'Are you sure?' I say doubtfully. Lizzy recommends that tonight, before I go to sleep, I imagine confronting the baddies and demanding to know what they want from me.

'Mm, okay,' I say, knowing full well I will do nothing of the sort. Anyhow, I know what my dream signifies: that I am tired of being hassled by relatives who I wish to avoid but can't escape.

Last night – after the hoi polloi finally left and the beneficiaries sobered up – our family solicitor, Mr Alex Simpkinson, read out my father's will. Maybe I drank more than I thought because all I remember is my mother sobbing, Cousin Stephen whining, and Nana Flo shouting: 'Silence!' I'm sick of the lot of them. I have two more days of compassionate leave and my mother is badgering me to 'pop round'. In other words, to share the burden of familial duty. Joyously, I have a valid excuse: my car is at the vet.

'You mean the garage,' she says.

'Yeah,' I reply, because I can't be bothered to explain.

'Get a taxi then,' she says quickly.

I tell her I'm broke and furthermore, this week I'm on half pay. 'I'll pay,' she growls. I tell her thank you, but I'm urgently busy. This isn't, funnily enough, a lie. I have to locate my car insurance details and I haven't the least idea where they are, who I'm insured with or, indeed, if I'm insured at all. My father was always instructing me to file important papers but how monstrously uncool is that? Far trendier to shove them in the nearest drawer. Only now, they seem to have vanished. Admittedly, my prowess with paperwork is mediocre. But today it is borderline chimp. A red wave of frustration floods me and before I know it I've snatched up my breakfast plate – a square of marmalade toast still on it – and hurled it at the wall. The plate (one of a garish set Marcus bought from the Habitat sale) smashes loudly into a thousand sharp pieces and leaves a dent. The marmaladen toast, of course, sticks messily to the wallpaper. Good.

Luke discovers me, thirty minutes later, hyperventilating on the bed. I whine out the tale of the horrid, spiteful car insurance papers and he gives a cursory glance around my bombsite bedroom, pokes aside a rogue pair of greying knickers with his toe, picks up a few sheets of paper festering underneath them, and says, 'Isn't this it?' I am too relieved to be embarrassed. Anyway, it's only Luke.

'Thank you,' I say stiffly.

'No problem,' he replies. 'What are you going to do now?'

I'm not sure but I *think* he's asking me less out of interest than to ensure I'm not about to smash any more of Marcus's precious plates. 'I'm going to put on a ton of mascara then call a cab and get my car back.'

Luke nods approvingly. 'Say hi to Tom,' he says.

Tom, it turns out, used to play football against Luke when Luke – fighting fit on a mere twenty a day – was a goalie in the Sunday league. I know this because as we motor home from the funeral Luke demands, 'How do you know Tom?' Not, you'll note, 'Why did you arrive at your dad's funeral in a vet's van?' But then, that's Luke. I assume Tina didn't notice and Lizzy was too polite to ask.

An hour later I am standing in the clinical-reeky reception of Megavet, attempting to be civil to Celine. Who is, pleasingly, on her hands and knees wiping up a yellow puddle of Labrador wee. But it's impossible. I apologise, again, for denting the car – I refuse to refer to it by name. Her rude response: 'Your negligence has caused me a great deal of inconvenience.'

My rude response to her rude response: 'What long words! Do you know what they mean?'

We exchange details in the same manner as, I imagine, Batman and the Joker after a prang in the Batmobile. I employ my sneeriest, snootiest, shop assistantest expression throughout then realise I need to ask her a favour. I decide to be brazen. 'Is Tom around?' I say in a bored tone.

She looks down her ski-jump nose and drawls, in an equally bored tone, 'He's busy.'

I am on the verge of leaping over the reception desk and throttling her when the surgery door clicks open, a large dough-faced woman carrying a tiny Yorkshire terrier waddles out, and Tom appears – a happy medium – behind her. I rearrange my expression to saintly.

'*Hell*o,' he says, when he sees me. He jerks his head towards the surgery door. 'Come in – I'll be one second.' Tom then turns his attention to totting up the bill, so I cross my eyes at Celine, smile nastily, and sashay in to the surgery. I sit down, and am suddenly overcome with the irrational fear that I have spinach in my teeth (unlikely as I don't eat spinach) so I dig through my bag, extract a make-up mirror, bare my teeth and peer into it. So when Tom walks in I am making a face like an aggressive baboon. I shut my mouth and the mirror about as fast as the speed of light. I *think* he didn't notice.

'How was it?' says Tom, 'if that's not a stupid question.'

I look at him blankly. 'How was what?'

'The funeral,' he says.

'Ohhhh! Oh, that. Terrible, actually.'

He wants to know why so I tell him, at length. Then I wonder if he *really* wanted to know or if he was just being polite. In the past, I've been reprimanded by Jasper for engaging his boss in a long discussion about my recurring headaches and whether they might indicate a brain tumour, after she answered his phone and asked how I was. 'Even if you're in intensive care on a life support machine, you don't *tell* people!' he'd squawked. "You say 'I'm fine thank you very much, and you?'"

I remember this gem of advice after regaling Tom with tales from the crypt for a full eight minutes. 'Anyway,' I say quickly, 'it's over now. I just really came by to get my car and say thanks again for the lift.'

Tom's face breaks into a smile and he says, 'Any time,' like he means it. He is fiddling with a pen. There is a short silence then we both speak at once.

'I think you know my flatma—' I say.

'I wondered if you—' he says. He stops, quickly.

'You say,' he says.

49

I giggle nervously, and say, 'I was only going to say, I think you know my flatmate Luke Randall. Or at least, he knows you.'

Tom wrinkles his nose. 'Luke, tactless Luke?' he says.

'Yeeees!' I say, in a disproportionate squeal of pleasure.

Tom laughs. He then tells me about the time a bunch of them went on a boys' night out to a rough East End nightclub and the screw on Luke's glasses came loose. 'So he goes up to the barman and says, "Have you got a knife?"!'

We are sniggering fondly when there's a sharp rap on the door as it is hurled open. Celine, in a voice of doom, declares: 'Mrs Jackson and Natascha Tiddlums The Third have been waiting to see you for twenty minutes and if you keep her waiting any longer she's going to be late for her charity lunch.'

Tom mutters under his breath, 'Who, Mrs Jackson or Natascha Tiddlums?' Then he smiles at me and says, 'I'd better get on.'

He looks as if he wants to add something so I hesitate. But he doesn't, so I say awkwardly, 'Okay, see you then. Bye.' As I walk towards the surgery exit I am aware of Celine's beady eye burning a hole in my back like a laser sight, so I turn round and sing in a sarcastically gay tone, 'Byee!'

I drive home in the dented Toyota, smiling.

Chapter 7

Lizzy hasn't done it because 'it has never even occurred' to her. Tina hasn't done it because she's 'never met a man who deserved it', and I've done it once, with Jasper who – ungrateful sod – didn't respect me for doing it.

I refer, of course, to sending a man flowers. Laetitia recommended the florist she uses to pacify important freelancers after shredding their copy. 'How much would you like to spend?' asked the florist.

'Um, fourteen or fifteen quid?' I replied.

There was a haughty silence, then the cool enquiry, 'Fourteen or for*tee*?'

Not wanting Jasper or the florist to think I was a cheapskate or poor, I snapped, 'Forty, of course!'

Forty quid. That's practically a foreign holiday! I kept the resentment at bay by imagining how touched – and inflamed to lust – Jasper would be on receiving the bouquet. (After all, it was two months into our relationship, a stage at which libido conquers frugality.) At 5.56 p.m. I gave in and called him. 'Did you get it?' I asked breathlessly.

'Yes,' he replied in a flat voice. 'What a surprise. I've never been sent flowers before. And certainly not pink ones.' Said in such a way that I immediately realised sending Jasper pink flowers signified to his colleagues, beyond reasonable doubt, that Jasper was gay.

You – I thought furiously, with your nautical prints and green corduroy trousers – should be so lucky. But all I said to him was 'Fine. I'll take them back then.'

51

Incidentally I sent flowers to Tom yesterday. Only this time, I took no chances and briefed the florist. 'It's got to be a manly bunch,' I said sternly. 'Can you put loads of twigs in there and stuff?' I discussed my intention with Tina and Lizzy first, in case it was a blatant gaffe. But Lizzy thought he sounded 'angelic' and agreed he deserved flowers for chauffeuring me to the funeral. Tina thought he sounded 'suspiciously nice, probably married', but agreed he deserved flowers for helping me to irritate Celine. He hasn't called, though, to say thank you. Oh well. See if I care. I'm far too busy lying on my bed staring at the ceiling to worry about men. And I've taken next week off as holiday. Inexplicably I've started waking up – head buzzing, blood jangling – at 5 a.m. *Me*, who usually has trouble rolling out of bed at 8.15.

Lizzy suggested it might be to do with my father – she insists on relating everything to my father, she's obsessed. Finally, I told her coldly, 'I don't think about him at all. I did on the day of the funeral but now I don't. There's no point.' It's not quite a lie. I'm too numb to think, and I don't have to. The death of my father is a constant, like tinnitus. It's just *there*. My edginess is probably the dread of returning to work. I'm exhausted, and I don't feel strong enough to spend nine hours, five days a week, sweating and toiling under Laetitia's manicured thumb. Or maybe I'm just lazy. Trouble was, I knew the feeble excuse 'my father just died so I'm knackered' would cut no ice.

Then Tina rang to inform me that according to the fashion director, Laetitia had had sex for the first time in thirteen months with a Count, and was in rapturous mood. So if I wanted another week off, now was the time to ask for it. I owe the Count a drink. Especially as he is – according to Tina who heard it from the fashion director – actually a plumber who used to caretake at Gordonstoun.

Thanks to Tina and the Count, I have been able to spend Friday, Saturday, Sunday, Monday and Tuesday in my bedroom. I prepared for it. On Friday morning I drove to

Pet World and stocked up on tins for Fatboy. I forgot to stock up on tins for myself which is possibly why, when I rang *Taste of India* yesterday for the fourth night in a row, the man taking my order asked me out for a drink because I 'sounded lonely'.

I have also been screening my calls. My mother has rung approximately fifty times and I know I should be with her in her hour of need, I know it's bad of me to be avoiding her, but just the sound of her petulant voice, it's suffocating, it hems me in, like she's pressing me down into a small, dark, airless box, and I want to scream at her to go away, leave me alone, stop *wanting*, I can't stand it, I can't give you anything.

Jasper and Tom, however, haven't rung at all. Meanwhile, Marcus – Luke tells me – has been giving the doll from Second Edition a series of intensive personal training sessions which, it would appear, involve him staying at her Hampstead pad five nights in a row. All I can say is, her inner thigh muscles must have been extraordinarily out of shape. Lizzy has also been calling but I'm not up to facing the full force of her good intentions.

Finally, on Tuesday evening, Tina broke the lethargy spell. She marched round to the flat (I only opened the door because I thought she was from Dominos), barged in, and bellowed, 'You old slag! Donchou look a state! You've got a day – one day – to get yourself decent! Tomorrow night we're going out and we are going to party! And you darling are going to get *wasted*!'

She was so forceful that Fatboy puffed up his tail in fright and helter-skeltered down the hallway. 'If you say so,' I replied meekly. The party is at a hip new bar in town and Tina is picking me up at eight, on the premise that if we arrive unheard-of-ly early, we can stake out the best table – and the best men. I suspect she just wants to get me out of the house. Before she leaves, she shoves a silver carrier bag at my chest. I open the bag to find she's pinched a hot pink camisole top from the fashion cupboard, the one

I was drooling after last month when these things mattered.

Wednesday lunchtime and I am wandering around the flat, peeling apart my split ends and prising the flaky bits off my fingernails, when the phone rings. I brace myself but it isn't my mother, it's a man, it's *Tom*. 'Hi, this is Tom, calling for Helen, to say thank you again for the brilliant flowers, called on Friday and spoke to your landlord, he said he'd pass on the message but—'

I snatch up the receiver – 'Hello, Tom?'

'Helen?'

'Hang on, let me switch off the answer mach, oh bugger, okay, hi!' I am garbly with pleasure and indignation: 'Marcus never told me you rang!'

Tom says, 'Yeah, well he sounded like he was in a rush, so I thought I'd ring again to make sure. Those flowers were wild! Thank you so much, you didn't need to! So how come you're at home, anyway?'

I am unable to think of a funky excuse so I say, in an attempt to sound attractively rebellious, 'Oh, you know, can't be arsed to go back to work.' Realising this could easily be interpreted as unattractively loserish, I add – may God forgive me – 'Also I've been looking after my mother.' Hmm, too spinstery. 'And seeing friends. I'm seeing my friend Tina tonight, we're going to this new bar.'

My *fwend*! I curse myself, but Tom says warmly, 'Sounds good. Where is it?'

I am seized by a burst of recklessness, 'Just off Piccadilly Circus. It's supposed to be so cool that no one talks, they just stand about. Do you want to come?' So as not to appear too keen, I add, 'Bring someone if you like.'

Pause. Tom says, 'Great! I'd be on for that. Although it'll probably just be me. I'm on call tonight, but it shouldn't be a problem.'

So I arrange that Tom will meet Tina and me inside the bar at 9 p.m. I put down the phone, and ring Tina immediately in a panic. 'Do you fancy him?' she demands.

'Not sure,' I say.

'That means yes,' she replies and tells me what to wear.

Ten past nine. Squidgy red leather sofas. Dim lighting. Retro music. Beautiful women with hair clipped up in that messy, sexy, just-got-out-of-bed-wanna-go-back? style, sleek men in slim-fit shirts and dark trousers. Feeling smug. Looking good, for me. Slinky top. Black trousers. Killer boots. Subtle slap. Trowelled on but barely there. Barky, laughing, girly talk with Tina. Sips of champagne. Half past nine. More champagne. Bigger sips. Gulk-gulk. Golden tequila. Thick golden tequila. But you don't even like tequila. Ten past ten. Don't care. Gimme a straw. That's what I want. Gimme a fag. But you don't smoke. Don't care wanna fag. Chunky glass after glass of Cuervo Gold tequila. Screechy, slurry, blurry talk with Tina. Twenty to eleven. Staggering, giggling, swaying, to the loo. Dazed, smudgy mascara, jerky check in mirror, scrunchy, clumsy, puffing up limp hair. Lurching, dizzy, teary, back to Tina. Eleven thirty. Feel ill. Whiney where *is* he the fucker bastard git wanking wanker fuck more tequila tastes gross fags making me dizzy don't care want more want more wasted Tina need more tequila my purse take it what who lemme alone tired wanna lie down tom tom Tom *Tom!* flucking buddy late you tossing tosser tissing posspot . . .

I wake up. I feel sharply awake. I am lying in my bed. The ceiling is in clear focus. But something isn't right. 'Helen?' says a male voice. I emit an involuntary whimper and stare in terror at Tom who is sitting, scruffy, fully clothed, on a chair in the middle of my bedroom debris. He looks as if he is trying to stifle a grin. 'How are you?' he drawls.

I realise several things at once. I am wearing a T-shirt and nothing else. I can't recall what happened last night. There is a curious absence of head pain. But I think it was bad. Very bad indeed. 'Wa, what? How?' I croak. As I use my voice for the first time I realise my throat is sandpaper and my chest feels at least one size too small.

Tom coughs. I suspect he's playing for time. 'Tina undressed you – you had sick on your top. She's asleep in the lounge.' He stops.

'What happened?' I whisper.

Tom looks sheepish. 'I was on my way and there was an emergency.' His voice rises as if he's asking a question. 'Emergency op. It was bad timing. I called the flat to say I'd be late but you'd already left. I'm so sorry. It's kind of my fault.'

What is his fault. He's talking in code. He sees my fearful expression and grins again. 'I haven't seen you naked if that's what you're worried about. Me and Luke stayed outside while Tina did the business. You were impressively plastered.' I manage a nod. I don't dare speak.

Tom shifts to his feet. 'I've got to go to work but I'll call you later.' He strides over, kisses me once, on the forehead, then walks out, softly shutting the door behind him. I wait until I hear the front door shut, leap out of bed, run into the hallway, remember I'm knickerless, run back into my room, scrabble through the wreckage for my tracksuit bottoms, yank them on, run into the lounge, shake Tina awake, and wheeze in a – painful but aurally pleasing – husk, 'Shit shit shit what happened now now now!'

Tina struggles upright, groans, squeezes the bridge of her nose and screws up her face, growls, 'Get me Nurofen out of my bag,' and swallows two Nurofen dry. Then, she tells me.

'Helen, you big tit. You made a right prat of yourself. He was late but it wasn't his fault. He'd tried to ring but he didn't have your mobile. I think he might've even called the bar but they're too arsey to take messages. He came straight from doing the op. I think it was an Alsatian. This Alsatian escaped from its owner and ran into the road, and this car, I think it was a BMW, a green one, three series, fuel injection, and – what? Okay, okay. Well, he got there just before twelve and we were both wasted, but you, you were something special. You'd been on the tequilas, neat tequila all night. You were storming! I've never seen you that bad. I was on the bubbly, I was way behind you. You don't even like tequila! But no, it had to be tequila. You were a right stroppy cow. And you pinched all of my fags. Anyway. So Tom turns up and excuse me but that man is fit. And you're about comatose. You were rude to him actually. Called him a tosspot except you said it teapot, so maybe he didn't realise. You were jawing on and on and on about how you're sick of gittish men and you can't stand it and this always happens to you and you just want a bloke who doesn't let you down and, like, really cringey whingey stuff. I tried to shut you up but you weren't having any of it. Then you tried to stand up to, I think, slap him, and you fell over. He caught you and then the bar staff were getting narky so we dragged you outside and you were in a baaaad way and we thought we ought to take you to the hospital to get your stomach pumped but none of the cabbies would let you get into their cabs. So I used the *Girltime* account. Then you started crying because you felt sick and then you were sick and then the cab came and it had to stop to let you be sick again and maybe that's why you don't feel so bad today but you will darling because we got back to your flat and we tried to find your keys and then you we— I mean then we rang the bell and woke up Luke and – what? No, nothing. Helen, I'm telling you you don't want to know. Alright then. You asked. You wet yourself. Easy, tiger, my head's killing me. Look, you asked, what can I tell you? I'm sorry. You pushed me. I wouldn't have said. Yes, of course he saw. What? He gave you a fireman's lift. *I* don't know if any went on him! I was wasted! Christ, woman, keep the noise down, I'm in pain here! Look on the bright side, the geezer works with animals, he's used to being pissed on! What? Ow! Take it easy, I was trying to help! So he put you on your bed and I said I'd undress you which I did and you owe me you big pissing tart, and I put you in a T-shirt but I was wrecked and knackered, I couldn't manage anything else, and then he was jawing with Luke and I said I thought you were okay, but he said he'd sit with you in case, and so I crashed on the couch and Luke went to bed and yeah, that's it. That's the end of it.'

Shall I kill myself now or later?

Chapter 8

I've lived in this red brick mansion block for three years and every springtime, as soon as the trees blush pink with blossom and the air turns hazy with warmth, they appear. They sit together, he and she, on the lawn. They have a favourite spot, a few metres from the brook that runs behind our communal gardens. During winter I'll forget them then, one bright day, glance out of the window to see the yellow daffodils and they'll be there, content in their coupledom. He's gorgeous, flamboyant, very striking. She's plump-chested, plainer, yet quietly beautiful. Sometimes, the sight of their constant love makes me smile. Other times, I hurl a few hunks of stale bread on to the grass and think, 'Helen. You're twenty-six and you have a less fulfilling relationship than a pair of puddle ducks!'

And today, I don't have any relationship at all. In fact, even daring to compare the state of our love lives is grossly insulting to mallards. I make the mistake of telling this to Tina who says, 'Stop it, you're freaking me out.' Tina is in a mood with me – and not just because she had the unenviable task of changing my nappy on Wednesday. Tina makes a huge show of her cynicism towards men to disguise the embarrassing fact that she has never lost in the mating game. Her first shag was with her childhood sweetheart aged sixteen and it was – get this – enjoyable. They saw each other for eight years then parted amicably. Since then she has had two one-night stands, leaving each lover wowed out and heartbroken, a longer dalliance lasting seven months – she ended it and they're still friends

– and has spent the recent past happily single and fending off drooling offers.

Blessedly untouched by the Jaspers of this world, she therefore sees male–female relations in pre-war black and white. Her attitude is – although she tries to hide it – if you like him, you date. If he gives you trouble, you don't. So, she cannot understand why I don't want to speak to Tom and becomes aggressive when I try to explain. Even when I tell her the man has wormed his way into my life, messed me around (Alsatian or no Alsatian), and frankly, I don't like to make a great gallumphing fool of myself in front of people I barely know.

'You mean pee your pants in front of ravishing men,' says Tina.

'Will you stop going on about that!' I shout. Having played the urination scenario over and over in my head a million mortifying miserable times I don't need reminding of it. 'Anyway,' I add sulkily, 'you're wrong.'

Tina doesn't buy it. 'Then what's your problem?' she says rudely.

I shrug. 'It's just . . . well, saying those things, you know, when I was tipsy.'

Tina snorts, '*Tipsy!*' she crows. 'That's a new one! You were ninety per cent proof! Although,' she concedes, 'you did come out with some grim and embarrassing stuff. What was it, oh yeah, "Men! They're all the same! They all piss off and leave me! I'm going to be a spinster with cats!" You prat! What a bunch of rubbish! No one made you buy a cat!'

I am about to argue when I realise The Self Sufficient One has unwittingly won my case for me. 'Exactly!' I cry. 'Grim and embarrassing! Which is why, A, I am never going to drink tequila ever again ever, and B, I do not wish to see or speak to this man ever again ever, or at least, for a very long while!'

Oddly, this seems to pacify her. 'Oh,' she says, in an irritating I-know-something-you-don't tone, 'alright, darling, if that's how you want to play it.' I wait for the catch. But all she says is, 'Ring us if you want to go out this week. Laters!' and puts the phone down.

A picosecond later, the phone rings again. I snatch it up and bark, 'Now what!'

There is a short pause then a voice says uncertainly, 'Helen?' It isn't Tina.

'Yes,' I reply shortly. 'Who is this?' In fact, I know damn well who it is and I am nursing a grudge of watermelon size.

'It's Michelle, honey!'

Oh, I say in my head. Would that be the same Michelle who professes to be a close friend yet doesn't turn up to my father's funeral, explain her absence, or bother to send her condolences? Sadly I am the Terminator in theory and Stan Laurel in practice, as pathetic at confronting friends as I am at confronting spiders. So all I say is an unenthusiastic, 'Hi.'

Michelle is oblivious. She rushes on, 'Gotta make it quick. The reason I rang is – and I guess you forgot, but never mind – it's my birthday tomorrow, and we're going for drinks and a boogie at the U-Bar in Soho.'

Jesus, she's got a nerve. I say frostily, 'Unfortunately, my father died two weeks ago, as you may recall, so I'm not really doing much socialising.'

I have known Michelle for over twenty years and in all that time I've never heard her say the word sorry. She doesn't break with habit now. There is a hammy gasp down the phone, 'I know that! That's why I haven't called – I figured you didn't want to be disturbed. I thought you'd want to be left alone! That's why I didn't mention it! I didn't want to remind you!'

A likely story. 'I'm hardly likely to forget, am I?' I say sharply.

'I realise that,' she says, equally sharply, 'but apart from anything else, it's a tradition in my family. Women don't go to funerals.' Really, I think. That will cause a dilemma when one of them snuffs it. I break a tradition of my own and am pointedly silent. Michelle, the mind game queen, bulldozes my attempt to shame her by adding, 'Helen, I'm thinking of you here. It would do you good to get out instead of moping around your apartment. Life goes on. And' – here, a slight whine – 'I'm going through a rocky patch with Sammy. I need your support. Please come.'

Hilarious. *She* needs *my* support because her gormless gimp of a man who won't drink a spritzer or eat a chocolate liqueur without permission from his mummy is in a sissy little huff. Michelle must have asked him to change a light bulb or boil the kettle. She has been going out with Sammy for five years and two months and he has been a milksop namby-pamby bore for about 1,886 days. Michelle's favourite hobby is griping about him to any friend too gutless to cut short a strident two-hour telephone diatribe but she takes outlandish offence at my free therapy sessions and considered attempts at constructive criticism ('Michelle, why don't you bin him?').

'So will you?' she demands. I give in. There is little point making a principled stand because as well as being as thick-skinned as an elderly rhino, Michelle is a hardcore grooming addict and will actually believe me if I say I'm devoting all of tomorrow night to washing my hair.

'Yes, okay,' I sigh, 'I'll be there.'

'Honey, you're the best!' says Michelle, who has read Jackie Collins' *Hollywood Wives* four times and adapted her speech patterns accordingly. I replace the receiver, slump on to the sofa and exhale crossly through my nose. Michelle and I were thrown together aged five because our mothers were determined to share the school run. As my discriminatory powers were yet to kick in, her impressive collection of Walt Disney stickers sealed our friendship. Twenty-one years later, I curse Bambi and Thumper and all their twittering companions.

I call Tina to request backup. She is looking for a reason to avoid staying in tomorrow tonight as she is trying to wean herself off *Coronation Street* and is delighted to accept.

I expected the U-Bend – sorry – the U-Bar, to be tacky but it way exceeds my expectations. For one thing, there is a purple life-size Cadillac bumper stuck to the wall. I refuse to sit under it in case it falls on my head. Michelle is resplendent in a fake leopardskin crop top and tight white jeans and appears to have modelled her hairstyle on Monica Lewinsky's.

Tina, meanwhile, is hypnotised by the heavy concentration of proudly flaunted fashion crimes and repeatedly gasps, 'What *is* she wearing?' I am dressed in bog standard black trousers and a crumpled silver shirt I retrieved from the depths of my linen basket. It had been in there for three months on the pretext that I'd take it to the dry cleaners when I had a moment, but I never did and know I'm never going to, so why bother to maintain the pretence? Anyway, silk, crushed silk, who's to know? That said, when Tina saw it she asked in a carefully neutral tone, 'Where did you get that?'

I replied, also in a carefully neutral tone, 'From the linen basket.'

She gave me a reproving look and murmured, 'I'll say no more.'

I glared at her and said, 'Good.'

My mood does not improve when – after ignoring us for an hour in favour of a stocky ginger guy whose back is shaped like a Dairy Lea triangle – Michelle sashays over for a 'quick chat'. Tina immediately excuses herself and speeds to the Ladies. I clink the ice in my Coke. Michelle glances sharply at my drink. 'Jack Daniels and diet Coke?' she says.

'No,' I say evenly, 'just Coke.' I know what's coming.

'Aren't you dieting?'

I slam the Coke on the table and squeak, 'No I am *not* dieting! Are you?'

63

Michelle laughs and pats her pancake-flat stomach, 'Sweetheart, are you kidding! Born lucky I guess.'

Born going to the gym seven days a week and eating one meal a day like a Weimaraner, more like. But, it *is* her birthday. Let's be charitable. 'So how's your sister?' I say.

Michelle flares her nostrils. 'Nightmare! On and on and on about that freakin' baby! You'd think she was the first person in the world to give birth, my God! Say what though, her tits are fantastic! Normally, she's got nothing! She's like you! Now all of a sudden, she's Dolly Parton!' I am speechless with indignation, which gives Michelle enough time to summon an oily faced man with a concave chest, press him down beside me, say, 'Helen, sweetheart, this is my cousin Alan, I know you'll just *mesh*,' and swan off.

Heart pounding, I scan the room for Tina and, to my dismay, spot her propped against the bar practically rubbing noses with a handsome blond man in a dark suit. She flicks back her hair and cups his hand as he gallantly strikes a match to light her cigarette. The brazen hussy. I'll get her for this. If Alan doesn't get me first. A few more hearty blasts of death breath and he might.

I'm cornered. He asks me a question about *me* – as all the self-help books for social lepers recommend – but as soon as I've rapped out a sentence he – as I very much doubt the self-help books recommend – ricochets it back to the glorious subject of *him*. For instance, where did I last go on holiday? I went to Spain. What a coincidence! He went to Spain when he was three, yes, he went to Madrid and saw a bullfight and decided he wanted to be a matador but, ha ha, he's settled for being an intellectual property lawyer, and he travels all over Europe, and only last week the senior partner was remarking on his singular dedication to the firm and how the drone drone drone.

I've sunk into a trance which I snap out of when Alan's woolly-jumper-clad arm snakes around my shoulder. I shake it off and snarl, 'I've got a boyfriend.'

Although this is a lie he looks greasily insulted. 'And I've got a girlfriend!' he says preeningly, 'but I presume we can still be friends.'

I shoot him a killer look and hope he dies – or at least goes away, but no. Alan's type never do. He prates on about himself for approximately eternity. Then, praise the lord, a swig of his lager and lime goes down the wrong way and he stops bragging to choke for a minute. I take this fortuitous opportunity to stand up and say, 'Bye, I'm going now.'

But, *but!* he sweatily grabs my hand and croaks, 'Can I have your phone number?' The bumptious, conceited oaf.

'I thought you had a girlfriend,' I say.

'I do, but, you know, if things start going badly in either of our relationships—'

I interrupt, 'I'm happy with mine.'

He scratches his oily nose, 'Yeah, me too, but you know, say in a month's time, I could ring you up and we could get together.' As if.

'For what purpose?' I say icily.

Alan assumes a slow nasal drone as if he were talking to, I imagine, his secretary. 'Helen,' he says, 'how old are you?'

Like a bleating fool I reply obediently, 'Twenty-six.'

He smiles loftily and – before I realise what he's doing – slides a slick paw on to my left buttock and squeezes. 'When people of our age get together, I'm sure you know for what purpose,' he leers, as I furiously knock away his hand. A frizz-haired groper and patronising to boot!

'I'm sorry,' I say in a sweetly vicious lilt, 'I don't think I will give you my phone number. But' – consolingly – 'thanks for trying.' Then I angrily elbow my way through the U-Bar's brightly attired clientele – heaven knows where Tina got to – and leg it to the tube.

Even the train journey is incensing. I don't mind the hordes of raucous, rowdy, shouty, drunken louts – after all, any other Friday night they're me and Tina. It's the pair of perniciously canoodling pensioners who sit directly opposite me holding hands and smiling soppily who make me want to scream and scream, strangle them and smash up the train with a sledgehammer.

I hate them. It's disgusting at their age. Why aren't you dead, I think. You should be dead. My father's dead, why aren't you. By the time the train pulls into Finchley Road tube station I am buzzing with a hatred so vivid I feel physically ill. I stamp home in the dark, daring any mugger, rapist or murderer to attack – just try it, matey, and you'll wish you hadn't because I don't care and by the time I'm finished with you I'll make you wish you'd never been born.

I arrive home, unscathed, ten minutes later. It's only 10.50. I quietly shut the door, take a deep, slow breath, glide to the kitchen table and, in a stiff robotic movement, sit down. Then I rest my head in my hands and think, 'Help me, someone, please help me,' over and over and over. I don't know what to do. My life is lurching, hurtling, spinning out of control. I'm going mad. 'Oh God, please help me.' I think I say this aloud because suddenly Marcus is beside me stroking my hair and saying softly, 'Hey, Hellie, my all-time favourite girl, what's up?' and I say it again, 'Oh God, someone, please help me' and burst into tears.

Ten minutes later, I'm snogging Marcus.

Chapter 9

The last time I had a leg wax was after reading a feature in *Vogue* about French women. French women are strangers to the concept of ratty period knickers, have weekly manicures *and* pedicures, and don't clear their plates just for the sake of it. I rang Tina in a flap to see what she thought.

'It's beautifully written,' she said, 'and very persuasive, but I think the writer is teasing. It's funny, and yeah, they are like that, but she *is* having a laugh.' At that moment it struck me that Tina dresses, acts, and eats like a slightly unhinged Frenchwoman even if she is from Tooting, so she would say that. I booked an emergency appointment at the hairdresser, the beauty clinic, ran round the block, then zoomed to Waitrose and bought a lettuce, five carrots, a box of tomatoes, two tubs of cottage cheese, a loaf of wholemeal bread, three tins of tuna in brine, four potatoes, and a box of peppermint tea. All of it rotted away in the fridge of course, but at least that week, my legs were bald, my bikini line straggle-free, I had no split ends, and my nails were as buff as Brad Pitt in *Thelma and Louise*.

Unfortunately, that week was nine months ago, the Parisian peer pressure since has worn off, and I have reverted to my slovenly English, plate-clearing ways. So, as Marcus licks and puffs and murmurs pretty words in my left ear, my overriding emotion is not swoony molten lust, but jumpy jittery fear. When, for instance, did I last *thoroughly* clean my ear?

Casually, I twist my head so my ear is out of puffing

range and our lips meet in an ungainly clash of teeth. 'Oops, sorry!' I giggle. I'm not entirely sure how this happened. One minute I am bawling like a red-faced baby with wind, the next, Marcus has hauled me out of my seat and into his strong (yes!) firm (oh my!) musclebound (bonus point!) arms. I cried and snotted on to his linen shirt leaving a wet, greenish slime mark which, fortunately, escaped his notice. He stroked my hair some more and whispered, 'Poor Hellie, poor little chicken, hush now, don't you cry.' Then he started kissing my head. Marcus J. Bogush! Kissing *me*. After all these barren years!

Pensioners forgotten, I clamp my mouth to his. He pulls my head back by grabbing my hair which is painful, but I don't dare ruin the moment by saying 'ouch'. We kiss long and hard but – horror of horrors – his snogging style isn't quite as blissful as his reputation with the ladies suggests. To be miserably honest, I'm disappointed. His tongue rolls wetly around my mouth like a large dead salmon in a washing machine. Then he breaks off to say cheekily, 'Feeling better now?' and I fall in lust again. He pulls me on to the sofa and, in the heat of passion (except it's premeditated) I grab at his hair too. He stops groping me for a second to pull away and say, 'Hellie, sweetest, I adore you but you're pulling my hair.'

'Sorry,' I mumble, and we slobber kiss again. This man produces an inordinate amount of saliva, I'm thinking ungratefully, when the phone rings. It clicks to the answer machine.

'Hi, Helen, Tom here! Calling to see if you fancied a tequila sometime . . .'

I freeze. Tom's timing is very, bad, indeed. Marcus lets go of me as if I'm radioactive, the lustful bleariness vanishing from his clean-cut face as if he's torn off a mask. 'So I've got competition,' he remarks airily.

'Not really,' I stammer.

'*Yes* really,' says Marcus pleasantly. 'Perhaps I should leave you to it.' He jumps up and scratches daintily at a strange greenish mark on his shirt.

I say, 'It's just that he's been—' I stop as I look at Marcus who stares back unblinkingly.

'Your choice, Helen,' he says.

I pick up the phone. 'Hi, Tom?' I say.

'Oh!' he says, 'screening your calls. And I made it!'

This – despite all my recent protestations to Tina – is going to be difficult. I glance nervously at Marcus, who crosses his arms Gladiator-fashion and yawns. 'Tom,' I say sadly, hesitantly.

He interrupts. His voice is somewhat cooler, 'This isn't going to be good, is it?'

I bite my lip. 'Tom,' I sigh, 'I like you and everything but I'm really busy right now, at work and stuff, but I'll, why don't I give you a ring sometime.' I glance again at Marcus. He looks unimpressed. So I add, 'But, huh, don't hold your breath.'

There is a short pause. Then, in a cold, contemptuous voice, Tom says, 'Message received and understood.' The line goes dead.

'Ker-bam!' says Marcus loudly as he smoothly removes the receiver from my hand and spins me round to face him, 'You tell him!' Then he grins and murmurs, 'You're a force, Hellie, you know that, don't you?' I smile and nod, although I didn't know it. 'So,' he continues – kiss kiss on my neck – 'what' – kiss kiss on my throat – 'shall' – unbutton nibble – 'we' – unbutton kiss – 'do' – unbutton slurp – 'now?'

I cling on to Marcus's broad shoulders and close my eyes in a parody of desire, but inwardly I feel weak and wicked and about as turned on as a dead bunny rabbit. I have humiliated Tom, but *I* feel humiliated. Those four words – message received and understood – fill my head and shame me again and again.

I am roused from my non-lecherous thoughts by the unwelcome realisation that Marcus is giving me a love bite. He appears to be trying to suck all the blood out of my body through the skin. Pardon me but I grew out of teenage territorial marking behaviour *at least* three months ago. My lack of enthusiasm is maybe obvious because Marcus abruptly ceases his suction pump impression and says in a solemn tone, 'Hellie, we can stop right now or we can take this further.'

I snap out of it. This is Marcus, my nine-year lust object, for heaven's sake! 'Let's rock!' I say in what I hope is a sex kittenish growl.

He smiles a triumphant smile, says, 'That's my girl!' then picks me up, grunting slightly with the effort, and lugs me into his bedroom.

'I'm quite heavy,' I murmur coquettishly, in smug expectation of the obligatory denial.

Incredibly, Marcus doesn't take the bait. Instead, he dumps me plonkily on his bed and mutters, 'You said it, darlin'!'

Six and a half unerotic minutes later, Marcus and I are lying side by side under his white duvet and I am trying to think of something to say. 'That was nice,' I lie. Amazingly, considering his cut-price performance, he believes me. He props himself on one elbow and idly twiddles a finger – I never noticed before how little his hands are – around my right breast. I glance up and, with a shock, see he has what can only be described as an *amused* expression on his face. 'What?' I say suspiciously.

Marcus wrinkles his nose. 'Nothing,' he grins, 'they're cute.'

The impudence! For the record, my bosoms happen to be size 36A, and for the record again – seeing as we're being so free and easy and judgemental about other people's body parts – Marcus's dick happens to be size AA, as in pocket camera battery size. Only it doesn't last as long. I am bristling with pique, when Marcus throws aside the duvet, announces, 'I'm going to shower,' and springs out of bed.

'Fine by me,' I murmur, snuggling down and drawing the duvet up to my chin.

'So,' he continues, a little brusquely, 'aren't you going to shower?'

I prop myself on my elbows and purr, 'Is that an invitation?'

Marcus looks embarrassed. He scratches the back of his left calf with his right foot and says, 'Hellie, I have this thing about showering? It's kooky but I like to shower alone. But you can go and use *your* shower, I don't mind.'

At first I don't understand. I blurt, 'What, and come back here afterwards?'

Marcus hesitates and says, 'If you like, although it might be awkward if Luke spots you, that's the only thing.'

I will the hurt not to show on my face. 'You're so right,' I say slowly. 'Would you mind passing me my shirt.'

He passes me my shirt. I try to look carefree. Marcus twirls my ratty period knickers around his stubby finger and pings them in my direction. They hit me in the face and he bursts out laughing. 'Lighten up, Hellie,' he grins, 'the wind'll change.' He pulls an exaggerated impression of my sullen face. I try to keep it stony but I can't. I stick out my tongue.

This is obviously the correct response because Marcus winks and says earnestly, 'You know, Hellie, I'd love to spend the night with you. But this way you'll get your beauty sleep! Another time, eh?' He delivers this cliché like it's a Perrier Award winning joke.

'Ha,' I say. He's alright. He's *Marcus*. Marcus is Marcus. With an entire body pointlessly pumped up except for that one crucial part. My resentment dissipates. 'Go and have your shower,' I say in a kindly tone, 'and I'll see you tomorrow.'

This elicits a showcase beam. 'Night, night,' he says.

He turns away (phew he's hairy!) and walks, starkers, towards his en suite bathroom and I feel a pang. 'Marcus!' I blurt.

'Yes?' he says, only a tad tersely.

As I speak I am wriggling into my worst-ever knickers.

71

'I'll make you dinner tomorrow night, if you like.'

I can't quite decipher his expression but he replies cheerily, 'Sure, yeah, great, see you then,' disappears into the bathroom and shuts the door.

I heave myself out of his bed, collect my trousers, socks, and boots, plod to my bedroom, remove my shirt, take a pair of scissors from my drawer, cut up my granny pants from hell, throw the shreds into the bin, and fall into bed. I haven't removed my make-up, washed my face, cleaned my teeth, or flossed. 'Big fat hairy deal,' I say sarcastically to the ceiling. Then I lie stark staring awake till 4 a.m.

I open my eyes at, according to my under-used alarm clock, 2.18 p.m. and for the second time that week think – without yet knowing why – 'Oh no.' My memory allows me half a second's grace before it all comes trickling back. Oh no. I churn over last night's events. The U-Bar. Alan. The pensioners. Marcus. The cocktail sausage. The shower. The dinner offer. The *acceptance*.

Maybe not so oh no after all. Then I run through what I can cook and am back to oh no again. I peek out of my room but the flat is silent and Marcus's door is ajar. He must be at the gym. Luke must be at the pub. I ring Tina at home but there's no answer so I leave a succinct message: 'Oi, slag, where are you. Call me the minute you get this.' Then I march to the untouched clutch of cookery books on Marcus's highest kitchen shelf and pull down a few.

The Italian one falls at the first chapter because I don't know what a trevise is. The English one devotes 100 pages to stodgy main meals and 425 pages to full-fat desserts. As Marcus would rather boil himself in oil than eat anything cooked in it, I'm left with the American one which lists recipes for mashed potatoes (I can do that!) and chicken pot pie. Easy! Oh bugger. It expects you to make your own pastry. Get real. I abandon the books and decide to improvise.

I'll make mashed potato (peel potatoes, boil potatoes,

72

mash them, stir in tub of margarine) and the fish dish (chop leeks, wok them, put them in baking dish, plonk block of frozen fish on top, plonk Greek yoghurt on top of fish, grate Cheddar on top of yoghurt, cover and stick in oven for as long as it takes to seduce your guest). Lizzy told me how to make the fish dish and it's delicious. And, more importantly, it requires four ingredients as opposed to ninety. Tediously, though, I now have to go to the supermarket. I check the fridge first. My section (Marcus has partitioned it to cut down on pilfering) is empty except for a carton of solidified milk, a cracked yellow rock of Cheddar, and a crumb-encrusted pat of butter. I could trim the butter but the cheese is on its deathbed.

Which reminds me. I really should call my mother. As of Wednesday she's stopped phoning which is brilliant but curious. I'll ring her tomorrow. I'll just try Tina again before schlepping to Waitrose.

This time, she answers. 'And why haven't you rung?' I demand.

She ignores the question and simpers, 'Oh Helen! Bloody hell!' Her voice oozes woozy post-orgasmic wonder.

I say accusingly, 'It's that blond bloke!'

She sighs blissfully, 'Oh Helen, it certainly is!'

At this point I'll interrupt to say, this is peculiar. Not normal. Usually when Tina meets a man – with, say, the looks of Matt Dillon, the wealth of Bill Gates, and the wit of Jerry Seinfeld – the most you'll get out of her is a grudging 'he's okay'. I am rapt. 'Tell me. Now.'

She sighs down the phone, 'We-e-ell, his name's Adrian—'

'*Adrian!*' I squeal.

'Yes, Adrian!' she says sharply. 'What's wrong with Adrian?'

I gulp, 'Nothing, nothing, it's a lovely name. Yes, so carry on.'

Adrian, apparently, is perfect. His perfection kicks all other men on this earth into touch. He is perfect from the tips of his perfect toes to the top of his perfect head and he is particularly perfect around the groin area. He has a perfect husky voice, he tells perfect pithy anecdotes, he has a perfect job as an architect, he owns a perfect bijou flat just outside Maida Vale, and, most perfectly of all – he thinks Tina is perfect.

'What, already?' I say. 'But you've only known him eight minutes.'

Tina cackles down the phone, 'I'm telling you, girl,' she says, 'this is the big one. I feel it in my . . . pants!'

I am not entirely delighted about this. I rely on Tina's eternal disenchantment with men – despite the fact it's a sham – as a reassuring romantic barometer. This abrupt disruption of the cynical status quo alarms me. Suddenly we're playing musical chairs and I'm the odd one out. Her reaction to my news about Marcus doesn't make me feel any better.

'But he wears tanga briefs!' she shrieks.

This stumps me for a second so all I say is 'How do you know?'

'I can see them through his chinos!' she shouts.

I speedily recover composure. 'So what!' I snap. 'We can't all be members of the fashion police!'

Tina chooses to ignore this jibe. 'Helen,' she says in a more serious tone, 'I don't want to rain on your parade, I know you've fancied him for years, but we're all agreed, he's even worse than Jasper. He's an enormous great plonking plonker.' If only. 'I mean,' she continues blithely, 'what about the aspirin habit?'

I am afraid she is refering to Marcus's custom of carrying a soluble aspirin in a silver pill box at all times in case he has a heart attack. 'He's not what you call hip and happening. He doesn't exactly live on the edge—' Now, she's ranting. And even though there is a seed – oh alright, a Redwood tree – of truth in what she says, her preaching from the sanctimonious altar of newfound love is really pissing me off.

'I wouldn't exactly say living on the edge of Maida Vale is living on the edge, would you?' I snap.

A frosty silence ensues until Tina breaks it with the polite enquiry, 'So how big was his todger?' I admit it is bonsai, we honk with laughter, and cordial relations are resumed. 'So why bother with him?' she gasps, eventually.

I shrug down the phone. 'It's just . . . I can't explain it. I *like* him. I feel – don't laugh – drawn to him. And he was so sweet when I was upset. And, it was the first time. Maybe he was nervous. Maybe it was cold in the room—'

'Maybe,' Tina interrupts, 'he has a needle dick!'

We chortle some more – although her chortling is rather more hearty than mine – then I excuse myself and plod to Waitrose.

Five exhausting hours later, the lair is painstakingly prepared. I've banished an incredulous Luke to the pub (he didn't take too much persuading) and tidied the kitchen. The mash is mashed, the fish is cooking, the table is laid, the candles are lit, the wine is chilled, the butter is trimmed, I've bought a large French stick to go with it although I had to fold it in half so it would fit in the bag, and *I* – aka dessert – am washed, brushed, dressed and tarted to the max. The only missing ingredient is Marcus.

I wait until ten to ten, eat the entire fish dish myself and let Fatboy feast on the mash.

Chapter 10

It's days like today I wish I'd invented Tetra Pak. Billions of quid for one minute of basic origami. To add insult to jealousy, yesterday I tried to squeeze open a Tetra Pak carton of mushroom soup and it didn't work! I had to pick and rip it apart with my nails – and instead of neatly transforming into a controlled, soup pouring lip it became a raggedy mess and the soup glooped all over the floor.

Luke suggested I was attacking it from the wrong side but I snarled, 'Since when are *you* the expert? You only ever eat out of boxes and tins.'

He looked hurt and about to argue then noticed my rabid expression and kept quiet. Luke has been tiptoeing around me ever since Marcus went AWOL. Admittedly, on Sunday morning he did exclaim, in a voice of epiphany, 'He must be staying with that pop star from Second Edition!' That apart, he's been a model of sensitivity and tact. I, meanwhile, have been a model of sourness and temper. Partly because of Marcus, partly because of Tom, mainly because – thanks to my non-innovative mind – I have to return to work today.

I slink into the office, trying to avoid attracting attention. There is a barely perceptible hush as I walk in, almost as if I'm wearing last season's trainers. Which I am. Tina breaks the silence by shouting, 'Bradshaw! Welcome back!' Lizzy rushes over to give me a fierce hug and *three* kisses (left cheek, right cheek, then just as I'm backing off – a surprise swoop on the left cheek. I think it's a continental thing). 'Helen,' she says bossily, 'take it easy today. If it gets too much go for a walk. And here, take this. It'll help you sleep better.'

She presses a small object into my hand before running back to her desk. It is a bottle of aromatherapy oil. 'Lavender Green Absolute', it reads – and underneath in smaller letters for the more intellectual users – '*Lavandula officinalis*'. I'm touched, although the last time I had trouble sleeping (I was worried about failing my A levels, with good reason as it turned out), herbs, roots and blooms had sod-all soporific effect. My doctor – who, for reasons best known to himself, hates to prescribe medication – dared to suggest I turn off the television three hours before bedtime and drink a soothing cup of camomile tea! I had slept a total of three hours in two weeks and was crazed with exhaustion so this blathering hocus-pocus did not go down well.

I *am* grateful for Lizzy's gift though, because – contrary to myth – when you are features assistant on *Girltime* magazine you receive one freebie a year which is inevitably a piece of tat no one else wants, like a fluorescent orange mobile phone case.

Some colleagues – after wary observation of my apparently stable exchange with Lizzy – trundle up to say they're sorry about my dad. Others send me kindly e-mails, and a few look shifty and treat me as if I have Ebola. Laetitia doesn't know *what* to do. Our wonderfully brusque agony aunt has sent me a sweet letter (no whimsical lily sketch sympathy card for *her*) advising me not to feel bad about the difficult times nor sad about the good times and that my father will always be with me. I turn pink with annoyance – people seem determined to distress me with sentimentality.

Laetitia mistakes my displeasure for a mewling-alert and murmurs, 'Stiff upper lip, stiff upper lip.' Then she dispatches me to fetch her breakfast (one slice of wholemeal toast with peanut butter, *no* butter, and a cappuccino with cinnamon, *no* chocolate). I buy a double espresso and a blueberry muffin for myself, which I eat guiltily while Lizzy's back is turned ('Muffin is just a sneaky word for cake!').

The day isn't too bad. I spend it transcribing readers' letters and other yawnsome copy on to the computer system (our octogenarian film critic insists on writing his reviews manually!). I ring freelance writers to remind them of the impending features meeting (the layabouts never send in ideas otherwise). I call a rent-a-quote doctor to get him to detail the symptoms of chlamydia (answer: barely any, so unless you strike lucky with discharge the first thing you know about it is, you're infertile). And I collect Laetitia's trouser-suit from the dry cleaners. The one advantage of being back at work is that I have less time to brood about Marcus. Or Jasper who – I realise – hasn't rung me for over two and a half weeks. The one disadvantage of being back at work is that when Lizzy, Tina and I go out for lunch I am forced to listen to the wonder of Adrian for sixty minutes. Even Lizzy stifles a delicate yawn. It looks like being an uneventful week.

Wednesday evening. I slouch home and slam the door. As I expect, the flat is empty. Luke is probably at the pub – he divides his time between bar work and bar play, and selling advertising space for a car magazine. The bar work I can understand, the selling of advertising space confused me. Luke tried to explain. He doesn't meet his clients. He sits in a stuffy room in a crumbly building full of scruffy men and tired women and old telephones. No one wastes time saying hello. They come in, sit down, and plough through *other* car magazines containing lists of second-hand cars for sale. Then they ring the contact numbers in the other magazines and persuade whoever is trying to sell their car to cough up again to advertise with *this* magazine. As he is freelance, Luke is paid entirely on commission.

A few months back, I tried to establish how, with his infamous diplomacy skills, he makes any money. 'I only phone people from Wales,' he replied. 'What!' I said. According to Luke, the Welsh are the most friendly and least shouty people in the UK. They often take pity on him and pay up. I smile to myself as I recall this conversation then I hear a noise and stop smiling.

The noise is a seductive giggle and it comes from the lounge. I curse myself for slamming the front door and start to creep to my room. Too late. Marcus – last seen retreating butt-naked into his bathroom – pops his head round a corner and says in a jolly voice, 'Hellie, meet Catalina!' A pretty woman with bright red plaits and huge green eyes bounces into the hallway. Interestingly, she is wearing a peasant smock and a woollen hat with ear flaps.

'Hey Helen,' she says.

'Hello, Catalina,' I reply. I suspect that while she looks like a Bosnian refugee she is actually a pop star. She is chemically friendly which makes it even worse. This must be Marcus's inimitable way of telling me he doesn't want a relationship. What a coward. I fix him with a steady look of disdain.

'Hellie,' he cries, 'why so stern!' He addresses Catalina. 'When I first knew Hellie she was such fun! But now she's so stern!'

Catalina rattles out a machine-gun laugh and squeals 'Rearlleee?' as if she's just been told her abysmal record has sensationally reached number ninety-four in the charts.

'My father just died,' I say for dramatic effect and to make Marcus look stupid. 'It tends to make you less fun.' I give Marcus another sour look and shut myself in my room. I feel sorry for myself and, amazingly, for Catalina.

On Thursday morning I notice that Fatboy is – for the first time in his well-fed life – off his food. He opens his pink triangle mouth and miaows loudly, slinks around my ankles – leaving a fine dusting of orange fur on my black trousers – leaps on to the kitchen surface (Marcus would freak but he's still in bed with Catalina) and butts my arm affectionately with his head. But when I open a tin and empty the gunk into his blue china bowl, he sticks his tail in the air like a mast, and swaggers off. Then he starts howling. This is a truly terrible noise. It starts as a deep groan and ends as a high-pitched wail. I feel I have failed as a mother. 'What?' I say in exasperation.

'*Ma-uuaaaaaaaa-w!*'

'I'm sorry,' I say crossly, 'I don't understand.'

He then – and this is the worst part – goes and sits, like a Sphinx, on the windowsill. And sits and sits, nose facing the garden, bum facing me. When I kiss his head he gets up irritably and relocates further along the windowsill. To be honest, he hasn't been eating much all week, but I thought it was because the summer has suddenly turned summerish and he was hot. Possibly he's sulking because he doesn't like the fact I've abandoned him for work. 'I work to keep you in Whiskas, you lazy pig,' I say before realising I'm late and running out the door.

I brood all of Thursday morning about Marcus and Fatboy until the afternoon when I call my mother. There's no reply. So I start brooding about her. Since the funeral day, I haven't been very attentive to my mother. That is, I haven't seen or spoken to her. I should have. But I didn't want to. I feel as warm and compassionate as a block of ice, I'd have been no good to her anyway. I won't feel bad, I refuse. Why can't I cut off for two, three weeks without it being a bloody great issue? Fuck it. I call her mobile. It's switched off. Please try again later. Where *is* she? I call the house again and let it ring and ring and ring until finally it clicks on to the answer machine. I almost drop the receiver as a voice intones, 'You have reached the home of Maurice and Cecelia Bradshaw. We are not available to take your call. Kindly leave a message after the long tone.'

My heart is hammering at such a rate I expect it to explode out of my chest – *my father's voice*. I replace the receiver and dial again. Then I hunch over my desk, close my eyes and relish my father's deep, powerful voice. '*We are not available . . .'* Mesmerised, I visualise him sitting in his favourite armchair in his study, blithely ignoring the ring-ring because he hates answering the phone. He could still be alive. I listen to his message one more time.

Finally, I leave a message. 'Hello, Mum, it's me. Hope you're okay. Sorry I haven't called. I've just been mad at work. Give me a ring. Okay. Bye then.' Maybe she's out shopping with her friend Vivienne. Or gone swimming. This is what I tell myself. But I don't believe it. I am sitting at my desk and Laetitia is ordering me to ring the book critic to remind her that her copy is a week late and all I can think is that my mother is dead and it's my fault. She's had a stroke and is rotting away at the bottom of the stairs. She's had a car crash and suffered fatal head injuries. (I inherited my driving genes from her.)

I am choked with dread and I just *know*. I am reminded of a story I skim-read in the *Daily Telegraph* about a man who was stabbed to death on a business trip to Switzerland. His girlfriend, in Sussex, had rung his mobile and he hadn't answered. 'I knew he was dead,' she told the reporter. 'At that moment, I knew it, without a shred of doubt.' I read this tale when both my parents were alive and well and annoying and my reaction was 'Huh! She knew indeed! Lucky chance!' Now, that woman is me. My mother is dead. I need air.

'I'm sorry,' I gasp to an amazed Laetitia and rush out of the office and into the street. I look about wildly, having no clue what I'm doing or where I'm going, run across the road, flop on a wooden bench – *In fond memory of Anthony Bayer, who loved London* – oh God, and try to breathe. I feel hot and cold and sick and faint. Five seconds later, Laetitia appears.

'Helen,' she says twitchily. 'What ever's the matter? Did you have a tiff with whatzisname, Jason?' I notice Laetitia stands at a distance so there is no danger of bodily contact.

'My mother is dead!' I whisper.

'You mean your father,' she says.

'My mother. I know it.'

Laetitia clears her throat. 'Helen,' she says, 'your mother just rang. She asked me to take a message.'

Shit. Laetitia never takes messages. Ever. How excruciatingly embarrassing. I breathe slowly, deeply, and sit up straight. 'Thank you, Laetitia, very much,' I say hurriedly.

Laetitia adds briskly, 'She said, if you're free, you could visit her tomorrow evening.' If I'm free? My mother, thinking of someone other than herself? Amazing. I nod and – panic over – meekly follow Laetitia back inside.

When I arrive home I brace myself for Marcus playing doctors and nurses with Catalina. I am most surprised when Marcus rips open the door as I jiggle the key in the lock, a ferocious expression on his face. Still smarting at the dead dad jibe, I trust. 'Your! revolting! animal!' he snarls, 'has! shat! all! over! my! BED! *AGAIN!*' He looks as if he wants to hit me.

'Oh no,' I breathe, proud and delighted at Fatboy's impressively pertinent social comment. Marcus marches me to the evidence. Fatboy evidently has what my mother refers to as a 'runny tummy'. I tut. 'Don't worry,' I say, smiling broadly, 'I'll clear it up.' I skip to the kitchen to fetch rubber gloves and paper towels and wonder how to reward Fatboy. Tuna juice? The coat game? (The coat game is the most tedious game in the world ever and involves me poking an umbrella or a stick under my coat and Fatboy pouncing on it ad infinitum until I die of boredom.) Retching, I scoop up the diarrhoea, leaving brown streaky smears over the white cotton. I spy my hero licking his paw from the safety of my bedroom. I am transporting the pooh-towels to the bin when the phone rings. Marcus answers it then holds the receiver out to me wordlessly.

I wrench off the gloves. 'Hello?' I say. Marcus ponces out of the room.

'Helen,' weasels a voice which I recognise with a heavy heart as the oily Alan.

'How did you get my number?' I say icily.

'Michelle,' he replies happily. I'll kill her.

'I assume this isn't a platonic call,' I say in a bored voice. At this point, Marcus stamps back into the kitchen holding his stinky bundled up duvet at arm's length and stuffs it angrily into the washing machine. He can hear every word I say. So, when Alan asks me if I'd like to join him for 'a spot of supper then on to a disco' – a *disco!* – even though I'd rather shave off my eyebrows and eat a rat sandwich – I say with a loud enthusiasm that must convince Alan I'm schizophrenic, 'I'd *adore* to go out with you on Saturday night.'

As soon as Marcus is out of earshot I press 1471 and inform Alan I've changed my mind and our meeting will consist of a quick coffee. Then I call Michelle to give her the biggest, scariest, buttock-clenching earbashing she's ever experienced in her privileged north-west London life. I start off snapping, 'Michelle, I'd prefer it if you don't give out my number to men I'm not attracted to,' and end up simpering, 'No, you're right, thank you. Yes, a night out with Alan *will* take my mind off Marcus. And Jasper, yes.'

I tell you. Sometimes, I really hate myself.

Chapter 11

As I see it, if you're a man in your twenties, your friends live to make life hard for you. They tell you you're ugly. Your job is sad. Your car is shite. Your girlfriend is going to leave you. It's their way of being supportive. But. *I* am a woman. And the entire point of being female and having female friends is that however hideous, stupid, or unwise you look, act, or behave, they are biologically programmed to tell you you're wonderful, your hair looks fab, and that you did the right thing. It's their job!

So when I tell Tina about my 'date' with Alan, I am amazed and aghast when she dares to be unsympathetic. 'If you didn't want to go, you should have said no,' she says flatly. I explain it was a ploy to make Marcus jealous. 'But Helen,' she replies, 'Marcus doesn't give a toss.'

I'm outraged. Not even the courtesy to humour me? 'Tina,' I snap, 'it's scientific fact that men always want what they can't have.'

She replies smoothly, 'And women, apparently.'

I scowl. 'And what's that supposed to mean?'

Tina snorts: 'You *know* what it means. Marcus is, at kindergarten level, a laugh. He is, if you're into the Incredible Hulk, fit. But he's also a prat, with a dick the size of a weevil. You're in a state over Marcus because he doesn't give a toss. And, because of him, you're about to waste an evening of your life with some creep. It's mad.'

Mad? It's incredible. It's incredible that one of my closest friends – who I rely on to confirm that yes, I did make the right decision to trim my fringe with nail scissors in a fit of boredom/spend two weeks' salary on a pair of shoes so high I wore them once and suffered severe backache for five days/sleep with Jasper on the first night even though he then asked 'Do you *always* sleep with a man on the first night?'/tread heavily on a man's toe on the tube when he whacked me with his briefcase before realising he was blind – isn't agreeing with me!

I ignore her and don't bother consulting Lizzy for a second opinion because I have a sneaking suspicion she'll be just as male about it as Tina. In a form of silent protest, at 1 p.m., I eat my tuna sandwich and Dime Bar at my desk while browsing through the *Daily Mirror*. Then I realise Tina's out on a fashion shoot, Lizzy's attending a perfume launch, and I've done myself out of a lunch hour. I spend the rest of the afternoon trying to keep up with Laetitia's unstoppable flow of 'little tasks', and feeling irritably conscious that my breath smells of tuna. I leave work at six on the dot and go straight to my mother's.

I ring the doorbell. No reply. I ring again. Most unusual. I ring again. Finally! A figure glides slowly down the stairs and approaches the frosted glass. Clank! clank! and the front door is slowly heaved open. 'Since when have you bolted the—' I begin as I step inside. Then I look at her, I *see* my mother. And I am frozen with shock. She looks like death.

She has always been slight (I take after my father) but in the three weeks I haven't seen her she has shed at least a stone in weight. Her hair hangs in clumps, filthy and lank, her wan face is devoid of make-up and her skin is dry and papery. This! A woman who scours the beauty pages of *Cosmopolitan*, *Marie Claire* and *Vogue* every month (she doesn't bother with *Girltime*) and can differentiate between Berry Kiss and Crimson Shimmer at a glance! Who cleanses, tones, and moisturises religiously, flosses after every meal including lunch (she keeps a toothbrush and other equipment in the staffroom), and showers once in the morning and again before bedtime. And what is she wearing? A knitted brown jumper five sizes too big for her and saggy black leggings. She looks like a student.

'Oh my God!' I say, when I recover the power of speech. 'Oh my God look at you! Mum, you look terrible, *terrible*! You're a skeleton! And that horrible jumper! It's summer! You look like a tramp!'

She stares back at me dully. Her eyes are blank. Then she says, 'It belonged to your father,' and starts to weep. Huge, gulping, hiccoughing, gut-wrenching sobs. I grab her and, in an awkward half-hug, carry her to a chair. Jesus! She's lighter than Fatboy! Which admittedly isn't saying much but you get my point. The sight of her, weak and emaciated, is so repellent I find it hard not to cry myself.

'Oh Mum,' I whisper, 'what have you done to yourself? When did you last eat for Christ's sake! The state of you! Shit! Why didn't you call me?'

She is sobbing so hard the words are swallowed almost as she says them. But while they are indistinct I hear them and her answer is like a knife slashing at my heart: 'I did.'

She starts to cry again. I crouch and rock her and stroke her flat greasy hair and the sobs become deeper and more savage until she is yowling like an animal in pain. 'Owww,' she howls, 'I can't re-mem-berrrr . . .'

I gulp, 'What can't you remember, Mummy?' I'm terrified. I don't want to know.

'I – I can't remember him, just the hospital. I want to remember him alive but,' – now screaming – 'I can't! I can't! Why can't I? I can only remember him dying, oh god oh god it's so bad, how can anyone bear it?'

I close my eyes. I have goose pimples and a hard painful lump in my throat. 'Oh Mum,' I whisper. The tears are pricking at my eyes, but not out of grief – out of guilt. I picture myself necking tequila, lolling in bars, rolling around naked with Ape Boy instead of calling my mother, and the pain is acute – I shudder and shrink from my thoughts as if they are blows.

And yet. I feel a fraud. Separate. Untouched. The feeling

is like an out of body experience – as if I'm watching my mother and myself, dispassionately, from another place. The yowling continues until my mother exhausts herself then it subsides to a whimper. I keep stroking her hair and its greasiness is sticky on my hands. I also notice that she smells. Unwashed. Stale. My mother stinks. I clutch her shoulders – ugh, I can actually feel the bone sharp underneath the skin – and give her a little shake. 'Mummy!' I say in a stern voice as if she were a small child. 'Listen to me! I am going to run you a bath and if you like, I will help you wash your hair. I'll even wash between your legs if you can't manage it yourself. What do you reckon?'

My mother stiffens in horror – rather as if her own daughter has just offered to give her a naked botty massage. 'Certainly not!' she squeaks in a voice so high and loud it would deafen a bat. 'How could you suggest such a thing! Disgusting! I'm perfectly capable of washing myself!'

Thought that'd snap her out of it. All the same, I escort her to the bathroom, turn on the taps, pour in a litre of bubble bath, and alert her to the whereabouts of the shampoo. 'I want you to stay in there for half an hour and get your hair squeaky clean,' I say. 'I am also going to put some clean clothes for you to change into on your bed.' My mother hovers uncertainly on the bathmat. Wafty as she is, I give her a gentle hug. 'You just relax in that nice warm bubble bath,' I say, uncomfortably aware that I sound like Lizzy at her preachiest health 'n' beautyist worst, 'I'll get you a clean towel from the airing cupboard. Take your time. I'll be downstairs if you need me.'

I leave my mother to undress, dig out a towel from the airing cupboard, and march to her wardrobe. I select white knickers and matching bra, a light blue cotton blouse, a beige belt, and a navy pair of what I believe elderly people call slacks. Sunny, tasteful, but not too garish in the face of death. I am laying this outfit on her bed when I catch a whiff of the sheets.

Now I don't mean to boast but I am not overly pristine. I keep as many cheesy green fluffy mould-filled coffee cups under my bed as the next woman. But when one's sheets reek of stale sweat and mature Brie, even I recognise that it is high (and I mean high) time for a spin in the Zanussi. I strip the bed of its top sheet, bottom sheet and pillow cases – an old nightshirt flies out so I grab that too – punch the whole lot into the washing machine, pour in a generous slug of Persil, and twist the dial to boil wash. Then I plod downstairs to the kitchen.

My priority is to force my mother to eat. I open the fridge – the fridge that I always make a beeline for whenever I visit my parents in the secure knowledge that it will always contain: A, chocolate mousse, B, smoked salmon, C, exotic fruit, D, expensive cheese, E home-made vegetable lasagne, F, pure pineapple juice. In other words everything my own deprived third world fridge never contains. Today, however, my parents' corporate fat-cat fridge is bereft of its bounty. Its contents: A, one tub of peach yoghurt (a week past its sell-by date), B, one wrinkly tomato, C, a micro-portion of Edam cheese, D, a small bar of Dairy Milk chocolate, E, a packet of Cornflakes, F, a copy of *The Firm* by John Grisham. Jesus. (I don't mean Jesus is *in* there, I mean . . . goodness me.)

I place the Cornflakes in the larder and *The Firm* on the bookshelf. I don't know what else to do. Should I run to the twenty-four-hour Tesco for supplies? Or should I vacuum the lounge? I reason, if my mother has starved herself thus far, she can go hungry for a few more hours. I'll tidy up the hallway and work my way through the house. I am, to be honest, fearful of what I'll find. And my fear is justified.

I peer into a plastic bag minding its own business by the umbrella stand and discover that it is stuffed full of envelopes. Brown, white, envelopes – all unopened. With a sinking heart, I snatch one out. It is addressed to Mrs C. Bradshaw. On the back, in small green print, it reads 'If undelivered, please return to:- John Lewis plc . . .'. I rip it open. It is a statement of my mother's account, as of a fortnight ago. She owes £43.00 for a Philips kettle.

Frantically, I tip the plastic bag upside down and shake its contents on to the floor. Gas bills, telephone bills, credit card bills, electricity bills. There is also a letter from our solicitor Alex Simpkinson – dated fifteen days ago – stating that my father's assets, debts and liabilities need to be ascertained in order to complete the probate papers, that my mother should forward any demands she doesn't wish to deal with on to him, that he'll be in touch as soon as he is in possession of all the relevant details, but in the meantime, should she require any advice she shouldn't hesitate to get in contact. I am trembling with – I don't know what – stress? shock? sadness? But I grimly, methodically open every envelope and place each communication in one of three piles according to status. I don't have the strength to tackle my mother on this subject right now. And right now, I don't think she has the strength to be tackled.

The rest of the downstairs is, thankfully, reasonably tidy. It is in the lounge that I make my next shock-discovery: a crisp pink pristine stack of the *Financial Times*. Twenty-four copies to be precise, including today's, neatly stowed behind my father's easy chair. His reading glasses and a heavy wood humidor of Cohiba cigars are on the side table, his red velvety slippers underneath it. I feel like Hercule Poirot. And my mother has mutated into Miss Havisham. This gloomy suspicion is confirmed by an earsplitting shriek from upstairs.

I gallop up to the master bedroom, two stairs at a time. What now? My mother, wrapped in a towel, hair dripping, screeches, 'You stupid girl, what have you done?'

I bite back my instinctive response which is 'You ungrateful mad old witch' and say – gallantly attempting to keep my voice even – 'What *have* I done?'

What I have done is to commit the most heinous, mindless, criminal act of vandalism in the history of the world.

I have washed my mother's bedclothes and my father's nightshirt in a Zanussi washing machine with lashings of Persil at the extremely high temperature of ninety-five degrees, thus exterminating the immeasurably treasured lingering scent of Maurice Bradshaw for ever.

I spend the rest of the evening apologising, tidying, cajoling, consoling, and force-feeding. I make an emergency dash to Tesco and buy spinach soup, strawberries, avocados, cottage cheese, bananas, wholemeal bread, butter, fresh pasta, ready-prepared fresh tomato sauce, salad in a pack, fresh salmon, and a packet of brazil nuts. Most of this is on Lizzy's advice – I call her on my mobile while overtaking a truck on the A1. Apparently, my mother needs oodles of vitamin B6 which, says Lizzy, will 'cheer her up' – which I doubt – and is found in 'meat, fish, nuts, bananas, avocados, and whole grains'.

I am too embarrassed to admit I don't *totally* know what a whole grain is, so I buy everything else. I also use my initiative and purchase Sugar Puffs and toilet paper. I am less than thrilled when my mother manages half a carton of spinach soup, one slice of buttered toast then announces she's 'full up'.

I growl, 'At least you ate something' and vow to work on her tomorrow. I make her eat a vitamin pill, send her to her freshly laundered bed, and tell her I'll return to check on her first thing in the morning.

When I finally stagger into the flat, it's nearly midnight. I smother a cross, wriggly Fatboy with unwanted affection, then march to the phone and ring the oily Alan. 'Hello?' His voice is groggy as if I've woken him up.

'Michelle's friend Helen here,' I say in a sharp, assertive tone.

'What time do you ca—' he bleats.

I interrupt: 'I'm calling to say I won't be meeting you tomorrow night, or any other night. We have nothing in common so there's no point.'

I am about to replace the receiver when he butts in,

sounding wide awake and spittle-flecked with fury, 'You ring me up, at this ungodly hour! To announce that you in your infinite wisdom are writing me off! And I suppose you're also going to inform me that it isn't me, it's *you*—'

I override his reedy petulance with loud disdain: 'This is a courtesy call to say please don't contact me again. I asked you not to at the U-Bar but, in your infinite arrogance, you did. And no, Alan. It isn't me, it's *you*.' Then I take the phone off the hook and fall into bed. I am buzzy, dazed and dizzy with unease about my mother. But even so, after calling Alan, I feel a teeny, tiny, weeny bit better.

Chapter 12

My most hated school subject was music. I loathed it even more than I loathed maths. I was a music illiterate. No matter how long and loud I was shouted at and made to squawk 'doe ray me far so larrrr tee doe!' the notes remained a collection of mystifying black squiggles on the page. To me, a quaver was a type of crisp. Yet, aged seven, I was still bullied into learning to play the recorder. During my lunch hour! I dreaded those lessons even more than I dreaded The Child Catcher in *Chitty Chitty Bang Bang*. All I remember is cowering in the music room with a huddle of fellow unfortunates while they played '*Frère Jacques*' and I mimed it.

Then, one fateful day, I was asked to play solo and the fiasco was up. I was brandished in front of the entire class as a tone-deaf fraud. I wanted to disintegrate with shame. However. The following morning I awoke feeling different – light, excited, and wondrously free. No more recorder lessons. Ever. And when I look back on my life's greatest traumas – recorder lessons, not being allowed to have my ears pierced – I see that each one has something in common. No matter how life-shattering they felt at the time, there was an end to them. The trouble with death is, there isn't an end to it.

It goes on and on and on. Sometimes, I'll forget it's happened. Or I won't believe it. But then I'll remember. And I can not believe it as much as I like, but it won't go away. My mother pores over photo albums obsessively. As if – because the image of my father is evident in glorious

Fuji technicolour – he *can't* be dead. I, meanwhile, am at a loss. I don't know if my mother is in such a state because she loved my father or because she is on her own.

She certainly perks up when I tell her Jasper and I are no longer together. Until I reveal that I am single – ridiculous phrase! every person in the world is *single*, even Tina who has been sensationally outed as a my-husband-and-I type – my mother is sullen towards me. As if my father's 'passing', as she terms it, is my fault! Well excuse me, but *I* didn't cook the final cholesterol-laden straw. She continues to make barbed comments like, 'He was my one soul mate. It's alright for you, you've got your support network.' And what 'support network' would that be? Luke telling me to keep my chin up? Michelle berating me for being 'a bitch' to Alan and asking me if I'm 'losing it'? Laetitia who declares – when I explain I'm late because I had a huge fight with my mother over cancelling the *Financial Times* – 'Shame. But you *must* be relieved he went so quickly. You wouldn't have wanted him to suffer.'

But when my mother snipes I don't snipe back. I don't, for example, say, 'He was my one father. It's alright for you, you can re-marry.' Instead, I spend the entire week fussing and fretting and trying to make her eat more. I buy the *Good Housekeeping Recipe Book* – an oppressive 576 pages – and decide that from now on, I shall devote every Sunday *plus* Monday and Wednesday evenings to fattening up my mother and distracting her from widowhood. Unfortunately, this plan necessitates me forfeiting my social life and learning to cook.

I also ring the local estate agent who called my mother this Wednesday (I persuaded her to start answering her phone on Tuesday) and announced he'd heard 'she was thinking of moving'. Translation: he'd heard her husband had stiffed it, presumed the widow would downsize to a cottage, and decided to procure himself a nice fat profit by browbeating her into selling up through him.

Traditionally, I welcome confrontation as I welcome a

Jehovah's Witness to my dinner table. But strangely enough, I enjoy the call. The elation of out-pompousing Alan must be addictive. I ring Rodney & Carter, having jotted down a few venomous notes in advance. I stand up (Lizzy swears this promotes assertiveness) and demand to speak with Mr Rodney. Then I assume the voice of Linda Blair in *The Exorcist* and snarl, 'My father died thirty-six days ago and my widowed mother is numb with grief and *you*, you ambulance chaser, ring her up and try to make money out of her! I hope you're proud of yourself! You disgust me – you grave robber!' Judging from his servile, cringing bleat of an apology, even estate agents fear demonic possession.

I also ring a few of my mother's friends. According to my mother, they have 'abandoned her'. From what I can gather, this is not strictly true. I play back the string of ignored messages on her answer machine and discover that her old pal Vivienne has called nine times. Nana Flo has called fourteen times. I cringe as I listen to her cracked, splintery voice. She sounds lost. 'Cecelia, are you there? Hello? Hello? Is this machine broken? Hello?'

I'd forgotten about Nana Flo. Oh alright, I'd forgotten about her in the way that you forget about a dental appointment. I'll ring Vivienne first. Vivienne's early messages are along the lines of 'Cessy, it's Viv. I do hope you're bearing up, give me a tinkle when you have a moment. You know I'm here if you need a shoulder to cry on. Call any time, day or night.' Her later messages are along the lines of 'Cecelia! Vivienne here. I'm very concerned. Why haven't you called? Have I done something to offend you? Do call. I'm dying to – I'm desperate to see you. We should do lunch.'

It emerges, when I quiz my mother, that Vivienne *did* visit her twice, three weeks ago. The first time, she popped round to invite my mother 'for a casual bite, Monday lunch' and to disinvite my mother to a dinner party, Saturday night, arranged five days before my father selfishly popped his brown Church's lace-ups and put out Vivienne's table plan.

On her second visit, Vivienne brought my mother a sponge cake, a shiny copy of *OK* magazine, and a complimentary ticket to a fringe theatre production of *Hamlet* that her Rupert Everett wannabe son Jeremy has a minor part in (he plays Rosencrantz). Her exact words: 'You won't be needing more than one, will you?' I tell my mother that while Vivienne has done ill, she means well, and to give her another chance. Meanwhile, I tell Vivienne – I catch her on her mobile between Harley Street and the hair salon – that my mother has no intention of pinching anyone else's husband *just* yet and furthermore, Sainsbury's now sell chicken breasts in single portions. So, the odd hussy out won't be a problem and on that basis, I trust her dinner invitation is reinstated with immediate effect.

Vivienne is flustered and blustering. 'Helen, she's more than welcome, you know that,' she trills. 'But you have to know I was, first and foremost, thinking of *her*. We're going to be five couples! Us, the Elworthys, the Williamses, the Schnecks, and the Struthers! The last thing I wanted was to rub salt into the wound.' I overlook the glaring fact that at least three of these guests are having affairs and explain, while it will certainly be painful for my mother to sit amid these shiny prototypes of married bliss, she would doubtless prefer it to sitting at home on her own eating a piece of Edam cheese in front of *Casualty*. The upshot? My mother – dressed in black from obstinate head to defiant toe – goes to the ball.

I meanwhile, sit at home on my own eating a piece of Edam cheese in front of *Casualty*. It is a joy and a pleasure. The only bluebottle in the ointment is Fatboy who picks at his food like a sixth-form girl on a diet then hoity-toits off to the hallway where he yowls, miaows, and scrabbles furiously, remorselessly, pointlessly at Marcus's beige carpet. 'Shut uuuuuuuup!' I screech from the sofa. I am drained of the resources needed to pacify a problem child.

Five minutes later, I plod into my bedroom to get a cardigan and see Fatboy squatting in my underwear drawer. For a split second, I'm confused. Why? A hissing pissing sound makes the enigma rapidly and unpleasantly clear. 'You little shit!' I mutter, as I realise that – unless I want a hysterical abstract wee scatter all over my bedroom floor – I can do nothing but wait until he's finished. I slink towards the drawer and stealthily move my lacier, frillier, sexier lingerie away from the target area under his peeing bottom.

As a responsible pet owner I am aware that companion animal behaviour counsellors strongly advise against any form of 'punitive technique'. Too bad. As Fatboy leaps triumphantly from my urine-soaked drawer I see him on his way with a medium-sized wallop. He speeds off, crouches like a furry Nemesis at the far end of the hall, and remains on hunger strike throughout Sunday. On Monday morning I ring work, explain to a frosty Laetitia that I have 'toothache', and take my cat to the vet. Megavet. I am jittery with anticipation and fear. I wince as I recall my recent shameful exchange with Tom. Maybe another vet will be on duty. And yet . . .

Tom waves me into the surgery without a glimmer of recognition or warmth. 'What's the problem?' he says as I empty Fatboy from his Pet Voyager – he clings frantically to its vertical side like a passenger on the sinking *Titanic* – on to the surgery table. 'Well,' I say nervously, 'he's lost his appetite. And he's blanking me. He's also had diarrhoea.'

Tom's expression turns even more disapproving. 'How long has this been going on?' he says coldly. Isn't that a line in a song, I think but don't dare say. I am desperate to beg Tom's forgiveness but too certain of being rejected.

'Well, I'm not entirely sure,' I say, squirming with guilt, but [*gulp*] 'maybe a week, two weeks.'

Tom raises an eyebrow, 'And have you tried to make a previous appointment?' he says in an incredulous tone.

'No,' I begin, 'I didn't think—'

96

Tom interrupts. He seems to have turned into a crankier version of my old junior school headmaster. 'No, you didn't think,' he snaps. 'Is there anything else? Vomiting? Is the diarrhoea ongoing?'

I shake my head miserably, 'Just one bout, I thi— I'm pretty sure.'

Tom glares at me. Then he says, 'Describe it.' How very romantic.

'Well,' I say in a slightly condescending tone, 'it was brown and runny. Rather like diarrhoea in fact.' Jesus, what does he want from me? Tom looks disgusted, and I'm not entirely sure this relates to my poetic description of liquid pooh.

He snarls, 'In a young cat, symptoms like these can be the first signs of leukaemia, Feline Aids, or FIP – a horrible disease which starts with diarrhoea and snottiness about food and ends with respiratory problems. There's no vaccination against it.'

I am stunned – 'Leukaemia, Aids, or FIP?' I whisper, unaware that FIP existed until a second ago but now certain Fatboy has it, Aids, *and* leukaemia – and it's all my selfish, neglectful fault.

Tom nods grimly. 'So,' he says, 'if it's not too much trouble, I want to know, did his faeces contain any traces of blood? Was it stringy? Bile-like? And has he been drinking and peeing more than normal?'

I shake my head to the pooh question and whisper, 'I'm not sure about the peeing.'

Tom continues, 'I'm going to have to run some bloods. A young cat like this should not be having problems in these areas, he should be eating, drinking, peeing, poohing as normal. If a cat has diarrhoea you don't hang about. If he reaches twelve to fifteen per cent dehydration he's dead.'

I gasp, 'Oh no!' and, in a small piteous voice, add, 'Fatboy won't, he won't, die, will he?' I am near tears and about to report myself to the RSPCA.

97

The side of Tom's mouth twitches and he says, 'We'll get the lab results tomorrow.'

I am weak with remorse and shame and terror. I watch in silence as Tom feels Fatboy's lardy abdomen, prises open his jaw and peers down his throat, and pushes his lip into a sneer (Fatboy's, I mean – Tom's own lip is already in a sneer). Then he gently presses Fatboy into a crouch, restrains him in a firm hug and – to loud, hissy indignation – slides a greased thermometer up Fatboy's bottom. 'Alright, big chap,' he murmurs in a soft, low voice.

My heart flips. Eventually, he removes the thermometer and says sharply, 'He has a slight temperature.' I nod sadly. He then summons the vile pouting Celine, trims a tiny square of fur on each of Fatboy's front legs, swabs each shaven patch and – while Celine holds down Fatboy who I will to bite her and if he does have Aids, transmit it – takes a squiddle of blood from each vein. He then squirts it into two transparent tubes, one pink topped, the other orange.

Considering his rollercoaster ordeal, Fatboy isn't as outraged as he should be. He emits a deep, low, angry growl but doesn't attempt to bolt. The traitor even allows Tom to weigh him while I, the evil abuser, choke back my tardy tears of penitence. Tom leans down, strokes Fatboy's head, and plops him back into his Pet Voyager.

He glances at me, seems to hesitate, then says – in a firm, but not *terribly* hateful, tone: 'That cat is taking on the proportions of a boudoir madam. But I'm sure he's fine. He probably just ate something crappy. Or picked up on a recent upset or stress. Any change in lifestyle, even moving a sofa, can send the most stable cat into a huff. Often conveyed via the distinctive brown letter of complaint. I want you to starve him for today, and I'm going to give you three days' supply of special bland cat food. Then, providing he's okay, I'm putting Fatboy on a weight reducing diet. And I'll let you know when we get the lab results. But if he pukes or squits again, bring him in immediately.'

I nod meekly and whisper: 'So there's a sliver of hope for Fatboy?'

Tom turns away – I think, to cough – then says sternly, 'More than a sliver. You want to know his real problem? He's a mummy's boy!' With that, he tots up the (extortionate) bill, hands over the 'recovery pack' and nods in his next client. He says 'Bye' but looks a fraction past my ear as he says it. I go home, groom Fatboy, and feel ashamed of myself.

I award myself compassionate leave for the rest of the day and stay awake all of Monday night praying. Tom rings me at work on Tuesday at 11.39 a.m. to inform me – in a brisk tone – that Fatboy is fine apart from a small increase in his red blood cells indicating he may have worms. I rush to Megavet straight from work. Tom briefly appears to hand me a worming tablet and a quarter (because Fatboy is so fat) in a blue and white envelope. 'If he pukes within half an hour it hasn't been digested,' he says, sounding about as warm as a deep frozen polar bear. 'If he pukes any later it's worked, it's just upset his tummy.'

I spend a good forty minutes before managing to poke the pill down Fatboy's throat. Then I spend twenty minutes dabbing my wounds with antiseptic. I am angry and upset. I call Tina. She's out. I call Lizzy. She's out. So I call Michelle. Who has run up an almighty overdraft whinge-ing about Sammy, so she owes me.

First I pander to her lingering indignation on oily Alan's behalf – 'Michelle, to be honest, I'm in such a volatile state at the moment I didn't think it was fair to, you know, burden him?' Bullshit over, I progress to my true agenda – ranting and raving about Tom. I am not quite sure how I want Michelle to react, but she puts on a satisfying show. Boy does he sound like a piece of work! You owe him nothing! What a deadbeat! Messing with your head like that! But don't sweat it! He should lighten up! He's way intense! Etc!

I am inflamed and inspired to consult her on a matter that has been niggling for some time. I miss Jasper. I keep thinking about him. I want to call him. Again, Michelle obliges. He's a cool guy and I should go for it. Encouragement and permission! So I do.

To my disbelief and delight, Jasper is 'chuffed' to hear from me. It would be 'ace' to meet up sometime. 'How are you fixed for tomorrow night?' I say (an hour of listening to Michelle and even Luke would start talking like a Hollywood Wife). 'I'm around,' drawls Jasper. 'Why don't you stop by?'

I squirm with coquettish pleasure and purr into the phone, 'I could do that . . .' I replace the receiver, head swirling. Jasper Sanderson & Helen Bradshaw. The return of! To borrow a favourite Jasperian phrase: Michelle – you played a blinder. I make a beeline for my (de-defiled) underwear drawer and start choosing knickers.

Chapter 13

If ever Tina and I want to irritate Lizzy, which we frequently do, we call her Mogadon Girl. This is because Pure Unadulterated Elizabeth is petrified of flying and before she'll set even her littlest toe in a Boeing she has to pop a great fat horsepill of a Nitrazepam. Of course she tried hypnotherapy, acupuncture, and peppermint tea first but – to our private glee – they didn't make the tiniest dent of difference and the Wholesome One was forced to resort to legalised drugs. We weren't that mean though. A while back, we spent an exhausting twenty minutes in the office trying to reassure her that God *did* mean humans to fly.

'Lizzy,' said Tina patronisingly, 'I fly so often I don't even think about it. A plane is like a bus to me.'

Feeling left out, I added soothingly, 'All the statistics show you're more likely to die in a car crash.'

We even demonstrated – with an emergency plane constructed from a circular on illegal use of company cabs for social purposes – how air pressure *forces* the aircraft to stay at 33,000 feet rather than drop like a three hundred and sixty thousand kilo stone from the sky.

'Unless the wings snap off,' interrupted Laetitia, who hates me to be distracted from toil. 'Then it plunges to the ground like a large sausage.'

Unfortunately, Lizzy is always discovering new hazards. 'What about clear air turbulence!?' 'What about uncommanded slats deployment!?' 'What about sparrows in the engine!?' When we crush these fears, Lizzy always comes back at us with her trump card: 'But you don't know. Plane crashes happen. It could be you. There's no guarantee.'

Until four months ago when my father died, I couldn't comprehend Lizzy's fears. Before my father died I was invincible. I'd read about a honeymoon couple whose plane erupted in flames over a turquoise sea, a woman stabbed as she walked home from work, friends blown up as they sat in a pub drinking on a warm summer's night, a young man shot at a bus stop, and I'd feel pity and turn the page. I knew that kind of thing happened to other people.

Now, I read about other people and they are me. I am tearful, angry, and obsessed. I imagine their last carefree minutes before the end. I wonder if they comprehended the actual moment of death. I ache for their poor, bewildered families, the stricken mother saying, 'Why him? Why do they always take the best?' The fiancé, face pale, eyes red, whispering, 'She was my life. I can't believe this has happened.' I want to comfort them but my tenderness is vampirical. I feast sorrowfully on their pain with the self-loathing and monomaniacal compulsion of a bulimic devouring chocolate cake.

These days, my mouth is dry with fear. I get out of bed in the morning and I think, 'This could be the day I die.' I feel my heart beating and I think, 'This could stop at any moment.' Of course, I reason to myself, 'Get a grip, you silly silly cow.' But then I think, Princess Diana didn't get out of bed on 31 August 1997 and know that this day was her death day. And people *do* just drop down dead – people who, might I add, eat fewer Dime bars than I do and exercise more regularly than once a month. There's no guarantee. I'm jittery. Snappy. Tense. Unless I'm engaged in a specific and enjoyable task – namely, watching *Xena: Warrior Princess*, reading murder books, or sleeping – I feel hollow and detached from the world and in the absence of anything better, my default emotion is terror.

For instance. Last weekend Tina drove to the Lake District for a shagfest with that prototype of man Adrian – who I have so far managed to avoid because I feel unable to summon up the requisite awe that befits our premier meeting – and her Escort conked out on the motorway at two hundred mph. She recounted her brush with early violent death as if it were a fairytale! Something like: 'We're doing eighty down the middle – and there's this bang on the underside of the car. Like something had dropped off. And we're hurtling along in this bloody box! No acceleration, no engine, no gears. Adrian was shouting but I coasted it to the side of road. Didn't flap. It was just, "Bang, bloody hell, the car's gone." And the brakes worked. Turned out the timing belt had snapped. Cost me a bugger to replace.'

And that was her last, carefree word on the subject! I said, 'Tina, promise me you'll be careful,' and she looked at me in a funny way and said 'I'm on the Pill.' *I* meanwhile, lie in bed six days later, dry-mouthed, shaking like a geriatric, playing the scenario over and over in my head like a weaselly tune from the Eurovision song contest. My pulse races and I think, 'Tina, you could so easily be dead. There are so many reasons why you could so easily be dead. I could have walked into the office on Monday and heard Laetitia say, "Did you hear about Tina? Tina's dead. She died in a car crash at the weekend."' Death is so random. Tremble, sweat, wheeze . . . what if?

As I struggle in my neurotic pyschotic phase, my mother graduates from what ifs. Possibly, the What Ifs are infectious and I've caught hers. Because, in the weeks following my discovery of the pink paper mountain and literary fridge, she became obsessed. What if she'd forced my father to economise on his egg intake? What if she'd ordered him out for a brisk walk after dinner? What if she'd bought him Allen Carr's *Easy Way To Stop Smoking*?

To which I could only reply, in my head, 'What if my father was another person – specifically, one who didn't come from a family riddled with heart disease?' To her face, I said, 'Mum, please don't torture yourself. You did everything you could. If it was going to happen, it was going to happen. And anyway, you know Dad wouldn't have listened.' As these lumbering platitudes were as novel and astonishing as a model dating a rock star – what can I say that isn't a cliché? – my mother sped on with the verbal self-flagellation.

What if she'd postponed plucking her eyebrows and was watching my father eat lunch? What if she'd made him a salad (no dressing, obviously)? What if his indigestion after Thursday night at the Harrises wasn't down to the high density of Leila's bread pudding? What if it was a warning sign of an impending coronary? 'Mum!' I shouted. 'Now stop it! If you'd made him a salad he'd have thrown it in the bin and booked a table at the Dorchester. What if you were a specialist cardiac nurse for god's sake?'

I intended this retort to be ironic but – and I should have known – she took it seriously and embarked on a fresh and superfertile woe-is-me route. What if she *had* chosen a medical career rather than the teaching profession? To which the honest answer was: there'd probably be at least ten more dead people in the world. So all I said was, 'Mum. You were a brilliant partner. You made him very happy. You have nothing to feel guilty about.' This made her cry and I realised, with annoyance, that I had expressed to my mother practically the exact trite sentiments that, not so long ago, Lizzy had expressed to me.

However, after three cosseted cocoony months (you didn't want to be there) my mother has perked up. Though I fear her fridge will never be the same again, she appears – as Leila Harris puts it – to be 'coping better'. And Vivienne observes, 'Your mother's lucky. She's young. She can find someone else. If they'd been married for fifty years it would be different.'

Happily for my mother, who is napping upstairs, Vivienne makes this draconian observation to *me*. Unhappily for Vivienne, she makes it when I am feeling – ooh, let's pick a mood out of the mood-swing hat – snappy.

'You what!' I snarl, banging my coffee cup on to the table and narrowing my eyes to slits. 'That's a fucking outrageous remark! *Lucky!* You don't grieve according to a, a mathematical chart! You don't grieve less because you're fifty not ninety! Don't you presume to know the measure of her loss! Her life will never be the same again. And I tell you something. If she—' at this point, mortifyingly, my face crumples like a pink tissue – 'if she should ever, as you put it "find someone else" she will be *making do*. Because for her, my father was The One. And if she knew he was coming back in thirty years,' – now I'm sobbing like a footballer – 'she'd wait.'

I am shaken and stirred by the violence of my own rage. I feel like a Molotov cocktail. Vivienne – who is equally shaken and stirred – jumps back like a startled cat and whispers, 'Helen, Helen. Calm down, I'm sorry, I didn't mean to, oh how awful of me, I've so upset you, I feel ter—'

Here, I interrupt my own blubbing to shout, 'You haven't upset me! This isn't about me! It's about her!'

Wisely, Vivienne clams up, nods, and says nothing. I feel a teeny bit guilty because, despite her limitations, Vivienne *has* been attentive to my mother. After the sympathy-surge subsided (halfway through month three as I recall) Vivienne continued to visit regularly, issuing tea invitations, doling out gossip, and bearing cake. I'd go as far as to say that Vivvy has vyed with me to keep my mother afloat.

I win though. I've become such a social worker it's a constant surprise to me that I haven't started wearing a smock.

I started off by cooking for my mother. I made vegetable risotto from the recipe on the back of the risotto rice pack (on the fifth attempt I stopped writing off saucepans and burning the rice), Tina's coriander chicken recipe (chop and fry onion and garlic in olive oil, chop and add chicken, then coriander, white wine, and half-fat crème fraîche – in deference to my father) and – because I can – potato wedges. After our fourth potato wedge dinner in a row my mother screeched, 'I'm *sick* of potato wedges! They're junk food!' and threw her plate across the room. At this point, I would have happily left her to starve.

Instead I hissed, 'Alright, Wiseguy. You're so clever, you show me how it's done!'

This rashly thrown gauntlet heralded the start of phase two – an unenjoyable period in which I spent every Monday and Wednesday night in my mother's kitchen spoiling the broth and being shouted at. She had fun, though. I think she misses overfeeding my father. Our Monday and Wednesday night liaisons continue – breaking them off isn't worth the aggravation – but gradually I've managed to wean her on to the odd takeaway. And Lizzy has been a sweetie.

During an extended session on soufflés (I tried to dissuade her), my mother confided that one of the worst things about widowhood was 'the lack of human touch'. I wanted to say, 'Try being me,' but restrained myself and said 'Oh.' But when I told Lizzy she nearly choked on her aduki bean stew. 'I've just had my first attunement!' she trilled, 'I've got the perfect plan!'

Three days later Lizzy started performing reiki on my mother. 'What *is* reeky?' she demanded, when Lizzy arrived, brimming with positive chi.

'It's an ancient art, a way of sending universal love and energy to heal people,' replied Lizzy.

'Do I have to be naked for it?' said my mother suspiciously.

'Oh no!' tinkled Lizzy. 'You just lie there, and I act as a channel for the life force energy that will unblock your auras and chakras, and balance the left and right hemispheres of your brain and enable an emotional release.'

My mother looked startled so I explained, 'You lie down, fully clothed, and Lizzy pampers you.'

After the first session, my mother leapt up and cried, 'Am I unblocked now?'

Lizzy's face fell so I said hastily, 'Mum, it's not like a plumber clearing a drain.'

Lizzy smiled stiffly and said, 'Didn't you feel floaty or tingly, Mrs Bradshaw?'

My mother shook her head and said, 'I didn't feel a thing!'

Lizzy replied, 'Well, you might develop diarrhoea and a rash—'

At which point I interrupted with, 'Lizzy, she *loved* it, she's just overwhelmed, no no, of course you won't, Mum, Lizzy was joking, yes you were, say thank you now, alright, Liz, thanks so much, see you tomorrow . . .'

The last four months haven't been easy. Maybe I shouldn't have shouted at Vivienne. I return to the flat and have a lie down.

With the benefit of hindsight, two Valium, and a cold*ish* shower, I ascribe my hissy fit to the fact that yesterday – three months after I renewed my biblical acquaintance with Jasper – he suggested we 'cool it'.

I was stunned. 'Why?' I said, gnawing at the skin on my lip. 'I thought we were getting on really well.' This, crazily, isn't a lie. We only met occasionally. And when we did, we had proper conversations. Jasper told me about going to boarding school and being unfavourably compared to his brilliant elder brother. I told Jasper about *wanting* to go to boarding school. Jasper told me about his parents moving to Singapore and seeing him once a year. I told Jasper about my parents living in Muswell Hill and seeing me once a quarter. I thought Jasper and I were having fun. Admittedly, the sex wasn't quite as fabulous as before, but that was mainly because I worried my father was watching.

'We *were* getting on well,' said Jasper, 'we *do*. Babe, I really like you. You're a great girl. And one day, you'll make someone a great wife. But, don't take this the wrong way, I think you need a break.'

Oh here we go, I thought – the wife jibe upstaged by the 'I really like you' alarm bell – he's not binning me because he wants out, he's binning me for *my* sake. 'Jass,' I replied crossly, 'don't give me that! I do not need a break! If you want a break, say so.' I raised a combative eyebrow. 'Is this because of my mother?' I growled. Jasper hesitated. I said coldly, 'You know she's got no one else. And you can always join us on our Sunday visits to the zoo and Kew Gardens and bloody Leeds Castle. Open invitation.'

Silence. 'Well?' I demanded.

'Well,' he replied, 'it's partly this thing you have about spending time with your mother, but er, you remember my ex-girlfriend Louisa . . .' This is not a question.

'Yeeees,' I said, 'if she's the same Louisa you've been slagging off for the past twelve weeks. What about her?' The penny dropped like a wingless plane. 'Oh my God,' I shouted, 'not again!'

Jasper waggled a finger to silence me. 'Helen, shussh, it's not what you think.'

I spun round in one of those uncool I-don't-believe-this circles. 'What then?'

Jasper coughed. 'I'm broke, the lease is up here, and Louisa's just bought a two-bedroom flat and needs a lodger.'

To which my witty riposte was: 'Bollocks.'

But Jasper widened his paradise blue eyes and insisted. 'She's seeing someone, there's nothing between us, Babe, hand on heart.'

You don't have one, I thought. Then I had another thought: 'So if you're not shagging Louisa,' I enquired cunningly, 'why should *we* cool it?'

His risible excuse? 'It's a single room.' He started to waffle about 'time out to reflect', but I held up a stiff hand in protest and he shut up.

My parting shot: 'Actually, Jasper, if you'd cared to ask you'd know that I'm also buying a flat. And *my* second bedroom will be a double.' Okay, it wasn't a whipcracking touché but nor was it a turkey. At least it wasn't until I bristled out of the door with my nose in the air and tripped over the step.

This morning, before work, I relate the outrage to Luke in florid detail. My disappointment at his response reminds me of how I felt, aged five, when my scoop of ice cream fell off its cone, plopped to the pavement, and was instantly devoured by a large dog. Luke's first bathetic comment: 'But you had nothing in common.' Luke's second bathetic comment: 'So *are* you buying a flat?'

I roll my eyes in despair. Some men have truly no idea about how to talk to women. 'Luke,' I say patiently, 'I don't want you to make unhelpful comments and ask silly questions. I want you to say "oh dear", "what a bastard", and tut a lot.' He looks hurt so I add quickly, 'I'm sorry. I didn't mean to snap. But, no. I'm not buying a flat. Me and Fatboy are staying right here.'

What I don't tell Luke is that as of two days ago, I *could* buy a flat. That is, I could put down a deposit for a modest pad in a reasonably un-crime-ridden area. The reason for this is I have, to put it bluntly, profited from Dad's death. To cut a boring tale short, a month ago, our solicitor, Alex Simpkinson, informed my mother – as executrix and main beneficiary of my father's will – that the probate papers were ready to check and sign.

My mother rose to the occasion. She's progressed. After the first hear no evil see no evil month, Mr Simpkinson *had* – in desperation – offered her the option of renouncing her legal responsibilities to another beneficiary, i.e. me or Nana Flo. My mother considered it. Then, as she declared to me over a TV dinner – brandishing her empty fork in emphasis – 'I told myself, "Cecelia, if that's what Morrie wanted, you do it."' I think she needed an excuse to renew the FT subscription. And the kindly attention of tall men in tailored suits never went amiss. Another factor is that she suffered a financial fright after his assets were frozen (my mother only afforded her lifestyle because my father topped up her account).

But most importantly, my mother realises that Maurice Bradshaw entrusted the fruits of his working life to his special princess and, like a good royal, she takes her duties seriously. She scrutinises the share prices each morning without fail. She has also become a devout fan of the *Sunday Times* Money section and plagues my father's broker every Monday to ensure he's investing in the latest tip stock. I'm not saying Cecelia Bradshaw has turned into Gordon Gekko. But, she may have turned a corner. Her return to school last week – she spent the first half of the autumn term at home on sick leave on full pay – has also helped.

I think even she was impressed at the joy with which Mrs Armstrong, the headteacher, welcomed her back. Even if her boss's delight *was* financially related. Consequently, when probate was granted fourteen days ago, my mother shared a cab with Nana Flo to the freeze-dried offices of Messrs Pomp, Simpkinson & Circumstance and – as she told me proudly – 'Alex went through everything again and I understood every word.'

She'd suggested we meet afterwards for tea but her offer clashed with a features meeting. Anyhow, I didn't dare ask Laetitia if I could leave work early because I sense she is bored to and beyond death of the bereavement saga and approximately one millimetre away from firing me. 'But it was a matter of life and death!' squeaked Lizzy.

I shrugged and misquoted some dead person Luke likes to rave about: 'Features are more important than that.'

Anyway, it didn't matter. I got a cheque in the post. As I opened the envelope, details of the will being read aloud on my father's funeral day loomed into focus after months of blurred forgetfulness. Specifically the short paragraph, boomed out by Mr Simpkinson, beginning: 'I bequeath the sum of £20,000 to my daughter Helen Gayle' – (Dad *knows* I hate my middle name!) – 'which I hope she will invest wisely, for instance, in property . . .'

I held the cheque in my hand and grimaced: 'Post-humous parental guidance!' Any other time I'd be straight down the shops but right now, I don't have the life in me to spend spend spend. Nor the strength to beat off estate agents. So despite my words of bravado to Jasper, when I tell Luke I'm staying put, it's the truth. I also find myself paralysed by Nana Flo's short verdict on the final account: 'My son, reduced to a few bits of paper.' I wish she hadn't said it in front of me. I act against my better judgement and tell Luke.

He says 'Oh dear!' and tuts. Then adds, 'I suppose it's another nail in the coffin.'

Chapter 14

The key to maintaining a fabulous relationship with the one you love is, according to *Girltime*'s agony aunt, to learn something new about them every day. So imagine my joy at discovering I possess a skill I didn't know I had. I realised it this morning after breakfast.

I'd just kissed Fatboy goodbye and was bolting out of the door when Marcus stopped me with a loud, crabby 'Hoi!'

I paused for a cool second, turned on my heel, and said with forced born-again sunniness, 'Good morning to you too, Marcus.' I smiled patiently as he struggled – and failed – to control his temper.

'I've just about had it with you—' he began.

'Oh I agree,' I exclaimed, 'that's how I'd describe it too.'

When Marcus got the insult his face turned scarlet. He stepped closer and hissed, 'Don't push it, Helen.'

I played innocent: 'What have I done?'

He glared, 'What haven't you done. You haven't paid rent, you haven't washed up, your sodding pasta pan has been soaking on the sideboard for two weeks, you haven't—'

I interrupted, 'Easy, Marcus, keep your hair on' – Marcus is paranoid about balding – 'I'll pay you and tidy up tonight. But hush. Puce doesn't suit you.' I grin cheekily, skip down the path and out of sight.

Then I allow my expression to revert to its customary blank. But as I plod along I think of Marcus and feel the shards of hate sharp inside me. How I ever fancied him I do not know. To think I thought he was *funny*! He's as funny as being mown down by a truck. Not only that, he's as shallow as a puddle and about as thick. He's full of smart remarks yet lacks the wit to dump me with courtesy. And I live in the same flat as him! And his hair *is* receding, now I've been close enough to check. He should transplant some off his back. The loathing churns and shifts, and I realise. I have a gift. I am a genius! I am superb at needling Marcus. The remainder of my journey is altogether bouncier.

Lizzy, who has just been promoted to Beauty Editor, is not impressed when I tell her about it. 'It's not a very positive way to live,' she says.

'But I feel deceived by Marcus,' I bleat.

'How?' demands Lizzy.

I sigh. 'All his sharking about, for a start,' I say. 'I assumed it reflected his prowess, when in fact, it reflected his lack of it.'

Lizzy giggles and says soothingly, 'Well you weren't to know.'

I add, 'And he's such a gossip – which is all very amusing when he's yakking about someone else, but less amusing when he's yakking about you. My tiny bosoms are going to be all over Swiss Cottage. If they aren't already. So to speak.' I glare at Lizzy so she doesn't laugh.

Lizzy makes a sympathetic face, so I say grumpily, 'And there were other things.'

'Oh?' says Lizzy politely.

'His neatness for one,' I blurt. 'I thought it was sweet. Proof he didn't expect a woman to tidy up for him. Now I think it's grotesque.'

Lizzy is silent. Then she says, 'But Helen, why does that matter?'

'Oh Lizzy,' I say, foiled by her generous nature and trying to sound jolly rather than spiteful, 'You're such a' – I want to say 'Pollyanna' but I know it will seem bitter – 'so sensible,' I finish lamely.

She shoots me a look. She knows. 'I hope you're not

113

upset about my new job,' she says mildly, 'I worked hard for it.'

I feel small. 'And you deserve your promotion,' I say with real warmth. 'I'm delighted for you. I really am. Sorry to be such a grouch. The truth is, I suppose, I'm jealous. But I have no right.'

Lizzy pats my arm. 'It's been difficult for you, Helen,' she says. 'You've had too much on your mind to, to focus on your career. You're practically a full-time carer! And ah, I'm a year older than you. It's about time I was made a deputy!'

This, as we both know, is an irrelevance. Lizzy has been promoted because beneath that soft, shimmering exterior is a determined, ambitious woman who is great at her job. I make a mental note to send her a congratulatory card. When Lizzy joined *Girltime*, fourteen months ago, my first impression was that she was weak, silly. She's neither, although I still think she's naive because she doesn't understand people who are nasty for fun, like Marcus. She doesn't expect deviousness because she would never behave cruelly herself. I used to look down on her for it.

And then, one night, she came round to help me dye my hair red and afterwards we chatted with Luke. The next morning Luke said, 'She's cool. I like her.'

I pounced like Fatboy on a shoelace. 'Oh ho!' I crowed. 'Luke fancies Lizzy! Join the queue!'

He shook his head. 'No,' he said – and from the way he said it I believed him – 'she's gorgeous but she's too confident for me.' He grinned and added, 'I like my women damaged.'

I beamed back, 'You mean,' I said teasingly, 'you need to be needed. You big sap!' Then his verdict on Lizzy sank in. 'You think she's confident?' I squeaked in surprise. 'But she's so quiet!'

He shrugged. 'If you're happy inside you don't have to convince everyone else.' From that day my regard for Lizzy *and* Luke blossomed. Despite the fact that when I pressed him for a compliment on my newly auburn locks, he fidgeted for a picosecond then blurted, 'You look like a mangy old cat!'

So, while I have intrinsic respect for Lizzy's opinions, I vow to continue my anti-Marcus crusade. After all, in the absence of Jasper, I lack focus. Apart from pandering to my mother's every whim – I'm beginning to admire my father for what he put up with – I have no life. Occasionally I go flat-hunting with Lizzy who is determined to buy before Christmas. That's it.

And anyway it's a pleasure to irk someone who's as catty as it's possible to be without actually being a cat. Which reminds me. Fatboy is due to return to Megavet for another worming session this week. Actually, it doesn't remind me at all. I've been thinking about it all day and trying, without success, to picture Tom's face. (Of course, I can picture oily Alan's in spotless – sorry – spotted detail.)

Tom's rudeness last time we met deeply offended me but, in retrospect, I'll grudgingly admit I deserved it. Although I partly blame Marcus. What I cannot blame Marcus for however, though I'd like to, is Fatboy's stern refusal to lose a single pound on Tom's diet. When I went to collect the worming pills, Tom enquired how many times a day I was feeding Fatboy. 'Er, five,' I said, cringing in anticipation of yet another reprimand. He saw me off with a snide lecture and some puritan low-fun cat food.

Now, Fatboy eats two and a half, maybe three times a day, but bigger portions. I also suspect he sneaks through other people's catflaps and pilfers. 'Poor angel!' I croon later, forking a large chunk of lamb and rabbit pâté into his blue bowl. 'It's not *your* fault you're big boned.' He snarfs the lot in twenty seconds flat and stretches, elongating his torso and dragging his back legs. He looks like a warped reflection in a fairground mirror. I brim with pride. Fatboy is, at the risk of sounding like a big sad loser, the cheeriest part of my existence. And when the cheeriest part of your existence pukes a great lake of brown purée on to your carpet *just* as you drop into bed, your existence isn't terribly cheery.

Fatboy's appointment with the doctor is at the ungodly time of 9.45 a.m. on Saturday. As I do not wish to arise one moment earlier than 8.45 – and even that's cutting it fine – I plan my wardrobe in advance. Towering black boots, black trousers, plain white scoop-neck T-shirt, and black cardigan. Minimalist, classical, elegant. Especially as I intend to trowel on a good thick inch of subtle make-up. Tina would be proud. If, that is, she could stop dribbling and mooning over Adrian long enough to notice. She is *shameful*! A lesson to us all. Well, to me anyway. I pray I was never ever like that. Even with Jasper. She rarely sees us outside work and when Lizzy suggests a girls' night out she looks uncomfortable and makes a weak excuse such as 'I promised Adrian I'd make him dinner that night.'

To think I used to admire her untameable free spirit. Envy her level-headed approach to romance. Wish for a wisp of her immunity to infatuation. Initially I put it down to her growing up with three brothers. *She* put it down to her growing up with three brothers. She never said so of course, as she was too busy masquerading as Mae West. But now and again – usually after an alcohol glut – unguarded comments would slip out. Such as 'They're not another species for chrissake!' All highly impressive at the time.

However, in regretful hindsight, I am forced to conclude that her brothers had diddly-squat to do with her bold invulnerability. Not that they didn't help her learn to understand men, to get along with men, to get along on her own. Doubtless they did. Yet I think the simple truth is, that until she met Adrian, she had never fallen in love. Not even for one mad minute, blissful hour, or whirlwind day. So my admiration is cancelled out.

I awake on Saturday at 8.45 a.m. feeling groggy. Is there no justice? I went to bed at ten! I bolt to the mirror and my

116

worst fears are confirmed. I'm piggy-eyed. My peepers are as puffy and bloated as if the five Dime bars I ate this week – tiny little things, can't possibly be fattening – went straight to my eyelids. I snatch up the phone to call Lizzy then remember it's practically the middle of the night. I'm sure she's up, all shiny hair and glowing face, running round a meadow or something, but if she *is* living dangerously and lying in till half nine I'd hate to disturb her.

So instead, I creep to the fridge and steal two slices of Marcus's cucumber, replacing it in an upright position to give him an inferiority complex. If I was him I'd stick with baby sweetcorn. Then I lie on my bed, with cucumber eyes, for five tedious minutes. When I can bear it no longer I jump up and rush to the mirror. As puffy as Puff the Magic Dragon after a birthday blow-out. And my skin is as scaly. Bugger. I slap on about twenty quid's worth of moisturiser, use eyelash curlers to disguise the eyelid bloat, then spend a full fifteen minutes tweaking and fluffing my hair in a vain attempt to stop it lying flat on my head. I end up looking like David Bowie circa 1972. Let's hope Tom is a fan of Space Oddity.

I arrive at Megavet – Fatboy wailing and clawing inside his Pet Voyager – in bad humour. It is not improved when I see Celine. She blanks me. I return the compliment and assume the expression of one who has just smelt a decaying corpse. I pretend to be engrossed in *Dogs Today* and am wading through a three-page feature on mange, when the surgery door swings open and a deep, resonant voice shouts 'Next!' I nearly faint with nervous tension and look hesitantly into those blue eyes. 'Hi,' says Tom, not quite smiling. 'Won't you come into my parlour?'

'Delighted,' I whisper, trundling into the surgery. I spend a full minute coaxing Fatboy out of his Voyager in order to compose myself. Then I lift my wriggling cat on to the table and mutter – in a pre-emptive strike – 'He hasn't lost much weight, but he seems happy. It must be his metabolism. I don't want to give him a complex.'

Tom looks sceptical and declares, 'I'm going to have to pull you in on that one. Madam! Please blow into this bag of shit!' But his tone is friendly.

'Tom,' I blurt before I can stop myself. 'I just wanted to say, I mean, I've been wanting to say for ages, I' – Fatboy chooses this delicate moment to emit a silent but poisonous fart – 'I, that wasn't me by the way, I swear, he always does that when he's nervous, but the point is, well, I just wanted to say that I'm sorry. You know? I'm sorry that I was so rude to you on the phone and I still cringe about it.' As the words jumble tumble out it hits me that they sound arrogant. As if I assume Tom has spent the past three months withering away in his room because of my childish telephone snub.

So I blather on, 'Not that, I'm sure, you care or you've thought about it much or anything but' – I am about to explain I was under stress because of Marcus, my mother, my father, oily Alan, the Toyota, but realise they are all monstrous excuses so I finish with – 'but *I* have thought about it and' – Jesus, I'm making a hash of this – 'I wouldn't want you to think badly of me.' I stop. Oh God, that sounds self-centred! I add in a rush, 'I didn't want to hurt you.' So presumptuous!

'I mean, not that you *were* hurt but it wasn't nice and I really regret my behaviour. I still feel terrible.' I dig my nails viciously into my palms to prevent myself bleating out even one more brain-dead syllable. Why doesn't Tom speak instead of gazing at me like that? Finally he grins.

'Apology accepted. And I don't think badly of you. Not *that* badly.' He grins again to indicate that this is a joke. Fatboy parps out another evil fart. I'll kill him, the spiteful orange git.

Tom gives the windbag the once over, skims his medical notes, and says casually, 'And *I'm* sorry if I scared you about Fatboy's health. I went a bit over the top.'

I shake my head, jumping at the chance to be magnanimous. 'I deserved it,' I say. If Fatboy could find it in his heart and bowels to withhold any further farts, I'll play the coat game every day for a week, I pray silently.

'He's got a good colour' – it takes me a second to realise Tom is referring to Fatboy's gums and eyeballs rather than his fur – 'and a nice shiny coat. He's still a podge but otherwise healthy. I'm just going to give him his worming pill. If you hold him like that, while I prise open his jaw. Good. Alright, big chap' – *grraowwww* – 'There! That wasn't too bad, was it?' As Tom strokes a glowering Fatboy I think to myself, 'No. It wasn't bad at all. We were standing so close I could breathe in the clean smell of your hair and it's having an extraordinary effect on my knees. And, if I'm being crude, higher up as well.' I force my face into a non-leery expression.

'Thank you,' I say, lifting Fatboy into the Voyager. I am reluctant to leave but I don't want to loiter foolishly like an infatuated schoolgirl. My thoughts bypass my brain and whirr into speech without permission. 'You probably won't but—' I begin.

'Don't if you—' Tom starts.

We both stop. I giggle. 'You first,' I say.

He rakes a hand through his dishmop hair. 'Do you want to go for a drink sometime? Orange juice even?'

I beam as widely as it's possible to beam without straining a face muscle. I squeak joyfully, 'I'd love to.' Fatboy immediately farts again but my delight is such that frankly, my dears, I don't give a damn.

Chapter 15

People who quote other people do so because they're too stupid to think of anything clever to say themselves. That's what I used to believe. As of five minutes ago I've changed my mind because I want to quote W.C. Fields who once said, 'If at first you don't succeed, try, try again. Then quit. No use being a damn fool about it.' Sensible man! I'm about to employ his advice with my mother.

I've tried with her for over four solid months, and now – feeble though it sounds – I'm quitting. I give up. Why? Because I'm tired. I don't understand her. I don't know what she wants or how her mind works and nothing I do for her makes her happy. If only Dad were here, *he'd* know what to do. He was, I think, terrified of being a father, but he made a brilliant husband. He managed my mother beautifully, and in the tender light of his gruff adoration, she shone. She enjoyed being bossed by him, it made her feel centred. Without him she is dull and incomplete, like a book with pages missing. I can't compensate for what she's lost, I can't compete with my father. I never could. Not that I mind, I love my mother but I don't particularly *like* her. I like my Mary Poppins role even less.

Oh don't misunderstand me. I'll still be events manager, organising reiki, forcing my friends round to eat her food, and prising her out of the house on zoo visits (although on the last outing she got upset because so many of the animals were in pairs). It's just that I am, in my head, still eighteen, and used to looking after myself and only myself. I am *not* used to parenting and protecting other, helpless people. It's not as if my mother set a stunning example. She is the epitome of egotism. Yet she expects me to pick up where my father left off – just like that! How the hell do *I* know what to do? No wonder she's frustrated. And the more I do for her the less she'll do for herself.

She frets and stresses about work, even though I practically sacrificed my own job to save hers. While my mother wailed like a banshee with a stubbed toe, *I* called Mrs Armstrong, the headmistress, to inform her of my father's death so she'd know to organise cover for the last few weeks of term. When my mother afforded herself the luxury of going on mental strike, I called Mrs Armstrong again – interrupting her summer holiday in Umbria – to warn her that her most treasured staff member had flipped and I had a doctor's certificate to say so.

While my mother rocked on her bed in a tight ball, I explained that she'd been signed off work by her GP for, well, for as long as it took. Yes, of course I understood that Mrs Armstrong wasn't being unsympathetic in asking if there was any indication how long it *would* take. Absolutely. I'd keep her informed. And I did. My mother drifted along with all this, without a word of gratitude. She took the medication but refused to see a counsellor. Then, mid-October, forty minutes after an upbeat lunch at The Bank with Alex Simpkinson, she abruptly declares herself fit, well, raring to return to work. Thus, bang after the half-term break, the supply teacher's reign ends and the prodigal mother is reinstated.

And yesterday – a piffling four weeks later – she rings me to say she thinks she no longer has the strength to 'hold it together'. My heart sinks and I ask if she's mentioned this to Mrs Armstrong. My mother replies, 'Mrs Armstrong makes it quite plain she doesn't want to know.' I say that Mrs Armstrong's attitude is understandable – after all, she's been forced into breaking her measly budget to accommodate your needs, what more do you want? I make this reasonable if innocuous comment and my mother just about bites my head off. Do I think she doesn't realise this? Do I think she isn't frantic about disrupting her class? Do I think she isn't aware of her colleagues' resentment? Do I think she doesn't feel a sense of responsibility? Do I think she isn't distraught about unsettling the children? Do I think she'd be complaining if she wasn't at her wits' end about it?

Er, yes. However, I ride out the verbal assault and say, 'Mum, it's difficult for me to advise you because I don't understand how the school system works. You must have *one* colleague you can confide in.' I know I am passing the buck but I am also at my wits' end. I thought she was getting over it!

My mother replies in a flat, zombified voice, 'I suppose so,' and puts the phone down. I can't deal with this! It's not my job! It's my father's job. I am furious with him for deserting us. How dare he go! How dare he? My mother needs him. I can't believe he didn't have some control over dying and I feel that being dead is no excuse for abandonment. If he was alive, he'd think his behaviour shocking. How inconsiderate can you get? I feel a niggle of angst and – for lack of anyone better to bother – call Vivienne. What does she think?

Vivienne, who is reluctant to share her thoughts after the Molotov cocktail episode, says hesitantly that my mother *does* seem subdued but it's probably because she's realised 'life goes on'. I quash the ripple of irritation (do I never learn?) and assure Vivienne I'm grateful for all that she's done for my mother. I say this to flatter her into doing even more. Because I intend to do a lot less. Call it selfishness or self-preservation – I'm too shattered to care. I feel terrible about it but I have nothing more to give. The exertion of continually buoying up my mother is slowly drowning me. And of course I've disappointed my father yet again. So I seek refuge in the words of a dead actor. Or was he a cricketer? I'm not sure. Whatever, I've tried and tried, failed and failed and so I'm quitting. No use being a damn fool about it.

I am fantasising about being involved in a non-fatal car crash so I can spend a week in hospital watching talk shows and being fussed over, when the phone rings. Every time Laetitia wants to avoid someone she orders *me* to take the call. Unfortunately, it's a one-way deal. I adopt a 1950s BBC clipped telephone voice in the hope that, if it is my mother, she won't recognise me.

'Helen?' says the person at the other end. 'Are you okay? You sound funny.'

I clear my throat hurriedly and cry, 'I'm fine! fine! It's just, er, it's just a bit mad here today. How's it going?' And guess what. As of a minute ago, it's going well. Tom has called to ask me out on a date. Not a vague, hopeless 'we'll speak sometime next week to arrange something' half-promise, but a real, solid, write this down in your diary *date*. The date is in thirteen days' time as he's off to Manchester tomorrow to attend some vet association congress – or as he says – 'a ten-day piss-up with a ball at the end of it'. But he's looking forward to seeing me. I restrain myself from asking any giveaway questions like 'is Celine going?' And I refuse to consider that Tom will meet a beautiful, intelligent female vet who drives a BMW Z3 and specialises in saving bunny rabbits' lives, and instead concentrate my mind on the facts. Fatboy's peach of a doctor has asked me out – me, Helen Gayle Bradshaw, a stumpy, grumpy dogsbody who drives a Toyota and kills spiders without a twinge of regret. Here is my chance to make it right!

I replace the receiver smiling and I only stop when Laetitia says sweetly but in a voice that brooks no argument, 'Helen, the writer who infiltrated the brothel doesn't want to pose for the picture so I need you to go along to the shoot – they've got the costume, it's all set up – if you leave now, you'll be there by two.' I stifle a sigh and get my coat. As Marcus said the day I had to stand outside the

Houses of Parliament, disguised as a giant tampon, in protest against tax on sanitary protection, 'Helen, you're so very lucky. You have such an *interesting* job.'

The second jolly surprise of the week is that Lizzy has finally pinned Tina down to a girls' night out. 'Wot no Adrian?' I joke to Tina.

'He's got a stag night,' she says curtly.

'Oh right,' I say. In truth, I feel hurt. As if Lizzy and I are a stop-gap. But I force myself not to take it personally. (Michelle says I 'take everything personally'.) I don't own Tina. It's *her* life. She's not obliged to see me. It's not like we're related. Mini reprimand over, I am able to brush the hurt to one side and say, 'Well, it'll be nice to see you properly, out of work, you old slag.'

After the recent downturn in our relationship, the endearment sounds false and awkward. For a second, I worry I've insulted her. But Tina seems to collect herself, and replies cheerfully, 'You too, you big tart.' The evening in question is this Thursday. On Wednesday Lizzy informs us 'Bring some loose-fitting clothes for tomorrow night.'

Exsqueeze me? To my and Tina's mutual horror, Lizzy has decided that beer, bars, and batting eyelids are not on tomorrow's agenda. She has taken it upon her do-gooding self to snap us out of our alcohol-quaffing, poky bar-propping, fast-food stuffing, suffer in the morning, rut. To me, she says in a firm tone, 'I've been watching you and you've eaten nothing but junk for weeks. You've got black rings round your eyes. You look like a racoon. You need to do something for *you*.' To Tina she says mysteriously, 'This will calm you.'

We stare at her suspiciously. 'What?' we chorus. (Me, still wondering if racoons are svelte creatures. I mean, she *could* have said 'panda'.)

'We are,' says Lizzy – in a voice as pretty and munificent and autocratic as Glinda the white witch – 'Going to my health club to do a t'ai chi class. It's booked and paid for.

Afterwards, we're eating in the juice bar. Oh my! I'm late for my lunch appointment! See you tomorrow!' Of all the rotten low-down cheatin' tricks.

'Does the juice bar sell fermented grape juice?' I shout after Lizzy, as she speeds out of the door. The coward.

Tina and I regard each other in dismay. I say grumpily, 'Do you even know what t'ai chi is?'

Tina makes a face, 'It's a martial art.'

At this I perk up. 'It's not aerobic?'

Tina shakes her head, 'Nah.'

I pause for a second, recall every James Bond film I've ever seen *and* a leering feature in a men's magazine about a blonde, beauteous television presenter who in her spare time, kickboxes. I decide that women who do martial arts really impress men and it's about time I became one of them. 'I'm quite looking forward to tomorrow,' I tell Tina.

'Me too,' she says vacantly.

I'm stunned. I feel like Little Red Riding Hood duped by a wolf disguised as a pink lacy grandmother. Lizzy deserves to be frogmarched to McDonald's and force-fed five Big Macs in quick succession. I should have trusted my instinct and scarpered the minute I clapped eyes on Brian, our t'ai chi instructor. He had long hair, wore purple trousers and his first word was 'basically'. Tina and I, loitering at the back of the studio, exchanged a snide look. For the 'newcomers' – here, a lingering smile at Lizzy and a meaningful glance at Tina and me – he began with a short introduction to t'ai chi. T'ai chi is an ancient Chinese art, a slow pattern of movements constructed thousands of years ago to promote vitality and inner harmony.

I nodded briskly, in the hope that he'd hurry up and show us a few karate chops. To my disbelief, he droned on for eight further minutes – during which I lost the will to live – then announced, 'I'm going to teach you how to walk.' As I learned how to walk a quarter of a century ago, I presumed this was a joke. Sadly, no. We spent eighty-five minutes walking in slow motion. Bend the back knee, lift up the other foot – you know, *walking*. To my delight, Tina looked like a junior clerk from the Ministry of Silly Walks, but it didn't compensate. I wanted to scream with boredom. It was sooooooo slooooooooooooooow. Like being in detention.

I stifled forty yawns and didn't dare look at Tina because I knew we'd both keel over laughing. Afterwards in the juice bar, Tina and I – hysterical with relief that the nightmare was over – mutated into a pair of fourteen-year-olds who found everything in the world rude and/or funny. When Lizzy politely enquired of the etiolated teenager behind the bar 'Is your juicer working?' we hooted and howled with raucous mirth. When Tina quipped, 'I'm gonna beat you up – it's going to take me ages,' we nearly wet our loosely fitting trousers. When I ranted about Brian's pointing foot – 'The way he pointed his foot at stuff! His slowwwwwly pointing foot, pointing for what seemed like daaaaaays . . . !' – we snorted and sniggered until our stomachs hurt.

Then Lizzy did a very unLizzylike thing. She swore. She snapped, 'Will you two bloody shut up!' Our mouths champed shut in surprise. '*Bloody*' from the woman whose expletive of choice is 'Fiddlesticks!' Fiddlesticks, I ask you!

'Why?' said Tina, shocked.

'We were only joking,' I added, stifling a giggle. Lizzy looked murderous. 'It was lovely of you to arrange it, though,' I continued hastily. 'It just wasn't our thing.'

Lizzy glared at me. 'I'd prefer it if you didn't take the piss' – 'the piss'? good lord, this is unprecedented! – 'out of Brian.'

Annoyed that my pink laughter bubble had been popped, I was about to blurt, 'But the man's an ageing hippy moron,' when a tiny, but blessed, brain cell of common sense prevented me.

Alas, it didn't stop Tina who squawked, 'Ah come on, Lizzy, leave it out! Brian's an arse!'

126

Lizzy's face tightened. She placed her fork neatly at the side of her bowl of walnut, avocado and leaf salad and said sharply, 'He is also, as of one week ago, my boyfriend. So' – and her next words were much more Jane Austeny, much more reassuringly Lizzy – 'I'd thank you to keep your horrid opinions to yourselves.'

Oops.

Chapter 16

My two least favourite words in the world are: moist, and gusset. My third least favourite is *should*. As in Helen, you should smile more. Helen, you should know what eight times six equals. Helen, I'm confiscating *Cosmopolitan*, you should be revising. Helen, you should do stomach exercises. Helen, you should ask for a raise. Helen, you should get a sensible job. Helen, you should visit your mother on days of the week that matter, like Fridays. Helen, you should go out tonight, even though you'd rather chop off your head, because you might meet your future husband or even this month's shag.

All these nagging shoulds, imposed on me by my parents, my partners, or myself. I block them out yet they claw at my conscience, shaming me, dragging me down. The latest should: Helen, you should spend three hours making merry with Lizzy and Brian in the juice bar to prove your regret at insinuating that t'ai chi is less than wondrous and Brian has a silly pointy foot that he points for what seems like days. Obviously, Tina isn't as wracked and hounded by shoulds as I am because shortly after our monster boo-boo, she excused herself on the grounds that she told Adrian she'd be home by ten. Liar, liar, pants on fire. (I've loved that rhyme, ever since I saw a wife say it to her cheating husband in a film then set a pile of his clothes alight in their front garden.) And so *I* was left – a great green pulsating gooseberry – with the mammoth task of coaxing Lizzy into forgiveness and persuading her that I thought Brian was a truly fabulous guy.

As Lizzy is incapable of bearing a grudge for longer than fifteen seconds, the first bit was easy. But as for persuading her I liked Brian. Try: excruciatingly difficult, nay, impossible. He was so repulsively, new-mannishly earnest. And the way he stared when you talked! Like Fatboy stalking a pigeon. Admittedly, these were minor sins. But despite his friendliness to me and his glowing adoration of Lizzy, I couldn't warm to him. I kept thinking, ugh but you're so *old*. Old enough to be her father. It gave me the creeps.

'He's forty-five if he's a day!' I screech to Michelle, who has ditched Sammy and couldn't give a rat's ass about other people's boyfriends.

'Some women like older men,' she says blandly, to stifle the line of conversation so she can bring it round to the more interesting subject of her. 'Sammy and me were about the same age,' she adds wistfully. (She's sixteen months older than he is.)

I make sympathetic noises and wish the doorbell would ring so I'd have an excuse to get off the phone. It's Friday night and Luke has got *Die Hard* out on video. Marcus and I are barely talking but as neither of us wants to gratify the other by retreating to our room, we are about to watch Bruce Willis be macho together. According to Luke, Catalina left Marcus a few weeks back after 'falling in love' with a record producer. Like, wow, it must be fate.

'So how are you fixed for tonight?' says Michelle suddenly.

'I'm watching a video with Luke and Marcus,' I say, trying to make my company sound as unappealing as possible. There is no way I am driving to Crouch End to entertain Michelle. I am exhausted and plan to drink myself into woozy oblivion.

'Sounds wild! I'll be round in thirty!' *Pank!* Gobsmacked, I wait for the phone to ring again, and twenty seconds later, it does. 'Uh honey, gimme your address again . . .'

I'm impressed. It appears that getting rid of Sammy

129

signals the dawn of a new era. Because in all the time I've lived here, I am embarrassed to say that Michelle has never once graced me with her presence. Admittedly, until eight months ago she and Sammy were residing in New York. (Sammy's father, who emigrated after his divorce, is something big in bagels and wanted his son to join the family business.) Michelle – seeing the move as a step nearer Hollywood – browbeat Sammy into taking up the offer, escorted him out there, and found work in a beauty salon.

They stuck it out on the Lower East Side for a glorious twenty-six months before Sammy ran away home on the pretext of undertaking crucial research into the UK bagel market. (Translation, he missed his mummy.) I suspect that on forcing Michelle's return to quaint north London, Sammy unwittingly signed his relationship's death warrant. Hooray. But the point is, Michelle has had two-thirds of a year to visit my shambling abode and hasn't. I'd say her excuse is she's been too busy setting up as a freelance beautician and/or she prefers to meet in town but she hasn't ever *offered* an excuse. If I do suggest she pops round, she's suddenly 'dead on her feet', or has 'shit to do at her place'. Only once did I dredge up the courage to bleat, 'But you've never seen where I live,' and she drawled, 'Honey, I can imagine it.'

I do some imagining of my own. And it takes me approximately twelve seconds to work out that Michelle is making the journey to Swiss Cottage because the long-hours, no-perk position of Michelle's Boyfriend is now vacant and she wishes to fill it. I stomp to the bathroom and scowl into the mirror. Will the victim be Luke or Marcus? She hasn't met either and I wonder who will appeal most.

Luke? He's not *my* type – too kind and easily intimidated – but Michelle thrives on bullying. And, if you aren't privy to Luke's odious, malodorous bathroom habits, he *is* beguiling. Messy blond hair, green eyes, winsome smile, clumsy manner. A human Labrador. The only problem I can foresee is Luke's tendency to speak the bald truth. Please God Michelle never asks him his opinion on her recent DIY switch to peroxide blonde. I dismiss the thought that I am concentrating on Luke's potential because I suspect Michelle and Marcus will get on – will get *it* on.

I do not want this to happen – I know Marcus would see it as a triumph against me – but I have a bad feeling about its inevitability. A small stone of nauseous fear in the pit of my stomach. At the risk of sounding disloyal, Michelle has been out to trounce me ever since I made the rash error, twenty-one years ago, of beating her in the egg and spoon race. And she isn't stupid. She knows that my recent hate campaign against Marcus isn't born of indifference. As for Marcus. Whatever else he is, he isn't choosy.

Consequently, when Michelle arrives fluttering under such a weight of mascara it's a miracle she can keep her eyes open, I brace myself. I march into the lounge where Luke and Marcus are slumped on the sofa. 'You two, this is Michelle,' I mumble, hoping her entrance will go unnoticed. Their necks jerk round like ventriloquist's dummies. Michelle wiggles her fingers in a cutie-pie wave and is treating Luke to an appreciative once over when he emits a loud, involuntary belch. 'Pardon me,' he says politely, but he's blown it. I curse him as she transfers her predatory gaze to Marcus. He looks her straight in her come-hither (and anywhere else you fancy) eyes, and pings from the sofa and across the room.

'Charmed,' he says, taking her hand and gently pulling her towards him to kiss her cheek.

'Me too,' she replies silkily. I flare my nostrils in disgust. A millisecond in and they're like a pair of baboons flashing their arses. Except more blatant. I can hardly bear to watch.

The remainder of the film is ruined as Michelle pretends girly mystification at the plot – it's *Die Hard*, for God's sake! – and keeps whispering at Marcus to explain.

131

Needless to say, the sleazebag is thrilled to oblige. 'Does anyone mind if I turn on the light?' I snap as I notice Marcus patting Michelle's lower arm to emphasis a point. 'Watching telly in the dark gives me a headache.'

Luke looks concerned, 'I've got a Nurofen somewhere if you want,' he says.

'Forget it,' I say miserably, 'it's probably a tumour.' I walk to the kitchen and pour myself a mug of red wine. I knew this would happen. But I didn't know it would feel quite so bad. I try to feel good about bringing Ken and Barbie together. Michelle needs compensation after dumping Sammy. And while she's insensitive, it's not as if she's swiping my current squeeze. Meanwhile Marcus hates me so it would be churlish – and pointless – to try to keep him to myself. Anyhow, he's soiled goods. This pep talk has no effect. I still feel like crying.

The tears are pricking at my eyelids when Michelle sings, 'Is that wine you're guzzling, you greedy girl? Are you gonna hog the whole bottle or can we guys have some?'

Self-pity is engulfed by violent rage. I casually rest one hand behind my back and tense it to a claw. This alleviates tension and allows me to reply in a fond tone, 'Ah Michelle! I forgot – it takes more than a man to keep you off the booze! Help yourself!'

She darts me a look reminiscent of Nurse Ratched in *One Flew Over The Cuckoo's Nest*. I quake inwardly, keep the smile pinned to my face, and make a mental note to avoid being left alone with Michelle ever again.

The rest of the evening is excruciating. I do my best to crush the sweet bloom of romance without success. My first bout of psychological warfare is to order four large pepperoni pizzas, 'On me!' Luke is thrilled beyond belief. Marcus and Michelle are – as planned – livid. Michelle faces a dilemma. She hates to eat in front of men – 'it looks gross' – but loves to maintain that she gorges herself daily on chocolate and pizza as all self-respecting supermodels do. Ha ha ha.

Marcus is equally torn. Pizza and all its fatty cohorts – curry, kebabs, burgers – are purgatory to Marcus. He hails from a genetically obese family and is so afraid of nature taking its pudgy course, he observes the eating habits of an anorexic sparrow. His mother and his two elder sisters weigh, at a conservative estimate, seventeen stone apiece. Marcus has so far warded off fate by exercising manically and eating healthily, but he lives in fear of the big bloat. (If I want to infuriate him I say, 'Hey Marcus, just roll with it.')

He is painfully aware of the unmacho nature of his obsession and – as I've repeatedly witnessed – part of his seduction routine is to starve himself for two days to make room for a staged 'I'm a regular guy' blowout in front of his intended. Sadly, as Michelle is a surprise bonus, he's pitifully unprepared. He'll eat his pizza so as not to appear unmanly, but every bite will be poison (and a five-minute IOU to the running machine). I chomp away happily and watch the lovebirds struggle.

'That was really kind of you, Helen,' says Luke with his mouth full.

'My pleasure,' I reply smugly, ruffling his hair.

Michelle pouts a small 'pouff!' indicating she's stuffed after just two slices. 'I guess I shouldn't have chowed down that burger and fries on my way over,' she sighs. Yeah right. She'd rather sew up her mouth.

Marcus gawks longingly at her cleavage. 'So don't you feel hungry?' he murmurs coyly. I nearly regurgitate my pizza on the spot. All further attempts at sabotage fail.

Michelle is wearing sparkly gold sandals, which gives me the chance to exclaim, 'I never noticed! You've got such long, elegant toes!'

Gratifyingly, Luke cranes his neck and cries, 'Let's see!'

Marcus also looks but – rats rats rats – his verdict is: 'They're stunning toes!'

Michelle squirms with victorious pleasure. Towards the end of *Die Hard 2*, she snuggles closer and closer to

Marcus until she is practically sitting in his lap. Their conversation becomes increasingly whispery and secretive. At midnight, Luke announces he's knackered and trundles off to his room. The deserter. I bid him a cold goodnight and remain stiffly, stubbornly in my chair. I'll stay up till dawn to foil their lustful plans!

At ten past twelve Marcus and Michelle start snogging in front of me. I concede defeat and go to bed.

Chapter 17

Did you have a nickname when you were little? When I asked my friends this question, nearly everyone said yes. Marcus denied it at first but later admitted that his adoring mother called him 'Ver Likkle Chubbly'. Luke's despairing parents dubbed him 'Trouble'. Lizzy's unofficial name was 'Jellytot'. Michelle's astute parents referred to their daughter as 'Madam'. Tina's mother re-christened her 'The Squeak'. Laetitia's parents – it goes without saying – stuck grimly to 'Laetitia'. And my father? His nickname for me was 'The Grinch'.

Never a great one for reading books in which no one dies, I forgot its origins and often skipped to infant school squawking a sophisticated home-made song to myself: 'I'm the Grinch! Little Grinch!' As I grew up, my father stopped calling me the Grinch and started calling me Helen. Only when scribbling my annual birthday card did he revert to the teasing familiarity of 'Dear Grinch'. As signs of affection were rare in our house, I accorded 'Dear Grinch' the same degree of symbolism that most patriotic citizens reserve for their national flag. And then I found out.

I was in the pub with Tina one Friday, a few months before my father died, indulging in a fond whinge about Jasper. He'd dismissed The Divine Comedy (my favourite band) as 'poncy shite' and had forced me to listen – on *my* car stereo, mark you – to Daryl Hall and John Oates. Secretly I admired his nerve, if not his taste in music. Tina exclaimed nastily, 'He's a grinch, that one!'

I started and said, 'A grinch? What do you mean by that?'

135

She gave me an odd look, 'You know! Mean. Petty! Fun crushing!'

I smiled weakly and said, 'Is that what grinch means?'

Tina hooted, 'You're having a laugh! Didn't you have Dr Seuss in north London? *The Cat In The Hat*? *How The Grinch Stole Christmas*? No?'

I shook my head, muttered 'No, no' and ran to the bar to buy the next round. The next day I sped to the library and asked the librarian to help me find a children's book. She smiled a collaborative smile.

And I discovered that a grinch was not – as I'd imagined – a cute, furry little love bundle but a spiteful, red-eyed, cave-dwelling creature with a heart 'two sizes too small'. Sure, he turns into a sweetie at the end. But right up to the penultimate page, the Grinch is a vicious, ugly slimeball with no friends.

I didn't want Tina to laugh at me again so I decided to share my life-shattering news with Lizzy. *She'd* give it the sober consideration it deserved. After my tenth bottle of Becks I boohooed out the shocking tale in a wetly incoherent ramble. And she laughed at me! 'Helen,' she tinkled, 'it's a pet name! I'm sure he didn't mean anything by it! It's just a nice word, like . . . pumpkin! My dad still calls my sister Pumpkin – and she's thirty-one and as thin as a whippet!'

I staggered to bed tear-stained and woke up feeling foolish. Lizzy, the voice of reason, had spoken. My father dubbed me the Grinch because it was a nice word. Nothing sinister. In fact, I should count my blessings – after an unfortunate accident during assembly Michelle (then aged four) spent the rest of her infant school life under the moniker 'Stinky-Pooh Pants'. And that was just the teachers!

I'd blocked out the hurt when, a few days later, Lizzy approached. She hoped I didn't mind but she'd been discussing grinches and pumpkins with a pyschologist friend and *he'd* said, 'What these names mean is less important than how they make you feel.' Had I thought of confronting my father? Certainly. Like I'd thought of painting myself green and running down Oxford Street butt-naked. I hate shrinks. Ferreting out issues where there are none. I shoved this irksome exchange to the back of my mind, where it stayed. Only occasionally does it drift back into consciousness.

Such as this morning when I wake from a restless sleep and cringe at what a fool I made of myself last week, trying to stop Marcus shagging Michelle. At times like these, I am the Grinch. Mean-spirited. Petty. Fun crushing. My father was right. Can't confront him now though! Meanwhile, I haven't seen bronzed hide nor coiffed hair of Michelle or Marcus. I presume he's staying at her place. He always disappears after scoring. I swear he does it to convince his conquests he's infatuated. One realisation about Marcus – his utter lack of spontaneity. Even Jasper had his spur of the moments, bless him. But Marcus's every move is premeditated.

I wish them luck. I say this not because I'm nice suddenly but because I have a date with Tom tonight. Michelle is welcome to Marcus Microwilly. In all fairness, they're beautifully suited. Long foodless days pounding the treadmill, steamy passionate bitching sessions, hours of mutual grooming, hot sizzling nights on twin sunbeds . . . It's mid-afternoon and I am wondering if I'll be invited to the wedding when the phone rings. Michelle!

I don't say 'Funny, I was just thinking about you,' because nothing would please her more. 'How *are* you?' she squeals as if she hasn't spoken to me for a decade.

'Fine, how are you?' I say cautiously.

'Great, great. Honey, I have a favour to ask.' Oh yes?
'Oh yes?'

Michelle pauses, 'It's kinda good news and bad news. Marcus has asked me out. But I won't go if you don't want me to. I don't want to upset you.'

Ooh she's a pro. I keep my voice light, 'Michelle, it's

great news. I'm so happy for you. And I can't imagine why you think I should mind. Marcus is' – I search for a searing phrase – 'a small blip in my past. Small being the operative word!'

I can hardly believe my own daring, and neither can Michelle. She snaps, 'God, you're bitter,' and bangs down the phone. I take a deep breath, inform Laetitia that I'm popping out for a double espresso, and I'll be back in five minutes.

'Get me an almond slice and a still mineral water,' she shouts after me. 'I'll pay you after I've been to the bank.' After *I've* been to the bank for you more like, I think. I rewind that last thought and brood on it.

Am I bitter? Of course I am! Who wouldn't resent Laetitia's infinite list of demeaning chores? I'm a journalist not a butler! In theory. And why am I even friends with Michelle? Because seventeen years ago we shared an interest in Japanese pencil cases and *The Sound of Music*? I am storming along the pavement, throbbing with rage, my face crunched into a scowl. I must look like a bull mastiff. I try to breathe through my nose, and relax the frown. Passers-by are regarding me warily and dodging out of my path. I see myself as they must see me and feel sick at heart. I don't want to be like this . . . this bitter person.

I force my frenzied mind to calm, more pleasant subjects like Tom. Those eyes. His mouth. My heart starts racing again and I smile inside. Pathetic! But it worked. We are meeting tonight outside Covent Garden station at 8 p.m. (My mother – unwillingly placated by the promise of a day at a health farm – has relinquished a Monday night. A hard bargain as limited access to food panics me and I hate being prodded.) I'm wearing black trousers, black boots, and a grey V-neck top. For a change.

I purchase the almond slice, the mineral water, and – in my newfound spirit of zen – a double decaffeinated espresso. I hold the door open for a smart elderly man. The kind of man who makes my insides shrivel with pain because he didn't die of a heart attack at fifty-nine.

It's not personal. It's not his fault. It's not personal. I bite back the swell of resentment and force a smile. The man winks and says in a cut-glass accent, 'You're *so* kind!' I beam, and look away fast as my eyes fill with stupid tears. I'm kind. I bask in the glow of a stranger's praise as I puff up the stairs to *Girltime*. Maybe, if Tom could see me now, I wouldn't disappoint him.

I march back to the office and recognise the tone of my phone ringing. Laetitia, of course, is reading the *Daily Mail* and ignoring it. Please don't let it be Tom cancelling. 'Hello?' I say fearfully, snatching up the receiver.

'Helen!' says a quavering voice, 'it's Vivienne! And I'm afraid, I'm sorry to tell you, oh it's shocking news—'

My voice is hoarse with terror: 'Tellmenow!'

Vivienne wobbles out five words before bursting into tears: 'Your mother's slit her wrists.'

Chapter 18

Once, aged six, I was walloped and sent to bed at 5.30 p.m. for saying in front of Michelle's mother, 'Daddy, isn't it true we can't pay our mortgage?' Admittedly I didn't actually know what a mortgage was, but it was an impressive phrase I'd overheard somewhere and was desperate to use. I was also accustomed to my mother – never a great listener – absent-mindedly agreeing with everything I said even if it was a humungous fib.

Alas, Mrs Arnold's eyes lit up like Beelzebub's and my father blamed me for what he predicted as the certain ruin of his financial reputation. As I snivelled myself to sleep I prayed that my father *and* my mother – who hadn't dared tiptoe upstairs to console me – would die in a tornado. At that moment I considered Orphan Annie the most glamorous creature in the world and wished fervently that I were her. Miss Hanigan was a pleasure compared to my evil parents! Scrubbing floors would be a privilege! The delight of being *made* to sleep on a bunk bed! And I'd get to sing 'It's a Hard Knock Life!' in an American accent.

But twenty years later being an orphan patently doesn't appeal to me quite so much because when Vivienne tells me that my mother has slit her wrists, my legs go numb and I sink to the floor with a moan that Lizzy later terms – in a whisper of hushed awe – 'feral, primeval, chilling, like a wild animal writhing in pain'.

As the most savage noise ever heard in the *Girltime* office is Laetitia snarling because the Dunkin' Donuts assistant put too much milk in her tea, my impression of a tiger with earache gets noticed. Lizzy and Laetitia leap towards me, crying, 'What's wrong?' Their faces are indistinct as if we're underwater and it's hard to breathe and I gasp to the blurriness, oh please not my mother not my mum oh please don't take my mummy oh God not her too, and my head swims and I choke the words oh please not my mummy over and over until they form a seamless shroud that shields me from reality.

Meanwhile, the receiver dangles, faint hysterical squeaks emanating from it. Lizzy snatches up the phone while Laetitia takes this – perfect – opportunity to slap me hard and stingingly across the face. By the time I've said 'Ouch,' and glared at her, Lizzy is crouching and gripping my trembly, clammy hands.

'Helen,' she says in a clear, firm voice, looking straight into my dazed eyes. 'Your mother is okay. She's not dead. Okay? Can you hear me, she's fine.'

I stare helplessly at Lizzy. I don't understand. I feel like a five-year-old. 'She's slit her wrists,' I say doubtfully.

'Only superficial cuts,' insists Lizzy in the kind of loud, emphatic voice my father used to use when addressing foreigners. 'Grazes. Vivienne was phoning from the hospital, they're in Casualty but it's not serious. Your mother is fine, she's fine, okay?'

I nod and say, 'Okay.'

I am shaking like an elderly poodle in a cold bath. I don't know what to do. Happily, Lizzy makes an executive decision: 'I'll call you a cab to the hospital right now. Won't I, Laetitia?' she adds.

Laetitia – who doubtless relieved some long pent-up tension with the slap – nods once and says, 'Absolutely.'

Lizzy helps me to a chair and sits me down. She rushes to the kitchen, returns with a bag of brown sugar, and tips at least half into my double decaff espresso. 'Drink that,' she orders.

'You wouldn't,' I grumble, and take an obedient sip.

Fortunately the cab arrives within minutes and rescues

me from Turkish coffee hell. Lizzy, who has packed my diary and other debris into my bag, helps me into the cab. But first, she sweeps me to her in a warm, solid hug, and says, 'It's going to be okay, I know it. And . . .' – she pushes me back a little to look at me – 'Oh Helen, I've been a neglectful friend. I—'

I stare at her, confused. 'Lizzy, don't be mad! You're a great friend. All that wasted reiki! *I'm* the bad friend.'

I'm thinking of t'ai chi and pointy feet but Lizzy is shaking her head, 'No, Helen. I should have looked after you more. I could see you, festering, and I should have said something but I didn't want to—'

Festering? Bring back 'racoon', all is forgiven! 'Lizzy,' I say, 'I'm honestly fine, I just had a shock about my mother but, as you say, she's okay, she's not hurt. And I'd better rush.'

Lizzy seems reluctant to let go of me. 'Do you want me to come with you?' she says. I shake my head. 'Be kind to yourself,' she says, giving me a little shake.

I sit in the cab. Kind. That word again. I'd like to be kind. Although, when I see my mother I am going to kill her. How dare she pull a stunt like this, the selfish cow! My heart pounds with the terror of it and I lean back and grip the seat. Jesus, what possessed her?

When I run into A & E it's *déjà vu*, it's *Groundhog Day* meets *Amityville*, it's that vomitous, surreal whirl of impending doom all over again. It doesn't help that Casualty stinks of wee. Stinks! I look wildly around and see – oh thank God – my mother and Vivienne huddled in a corner surrounded by people who look as if they've been there for years. Vivienne's bright orange fake fur coat (she bought it after being attacked in Islington while wearing her mink) shines out amid the drab defeatism like a bad taste beacon.

I bound towards my mother and my anger dissipates as I see her weary chalk-white face. She is wrapped in a grey blanket. Grey, I decide, is all very well on the catwalk as a clever foil to your skinny wealth and muted sophistication, but it is shit shit shit in hospitals and funeral parlours because it's for real – all shabby poverty and lacklustre hopelessness.

'Helen!' whimpers my mother. Her spindly wrists are wrapped in makeshift dressings. I bend and hug her tight. Vivienne swiftly vacates her seat so I can get a better hold. My mother sobs in my arms and I rock her like a baby.

'Oh Mummy, promise me, never never, terrible, Daddy would be furious, you know I'm here, what would I do? okay, looking after you.' While this isn't exactly a coherent sentence, it makes perfect sense to my mother who nods and sniffs and burrows closer to my chest. I glance past my mother at Vivienne who I can tell is gagging for a Marlboro Light. I indicate with my eyes to the exit. 'I'll join you in a sec,' I mouth. She draws her orange coat around her, smiles tensely, and teeters off.

My heart twists as my mother bawls silently, her fingers digging weakly into my lap. I wait and wait, hug and hug, until the crying subsides and try not to think that I could have avoided this by meeting Tom on a Thursday. Then I say sensible things like, 'How long have you been here?' and 'Do you want a hot drink?' and 'Is the pain bearable?' She answers, respectively, 'Ages,' and 'Had one,' and 'Not too bad.' When I suspect she has no more tears left, I ask her if she minds if I see how Vivienne is. 'It must have been a shock for her too,' I say gravely.

My mother nods dumbly and looks at the floor. 'I'll be back almost *immediately*,' I say, 'so stay right there and don't move. Promise promise?'

My mother recognises the phrase I'd squeak while bargaining for treats when I was five and we were a family. She manages a sad smile and replies, 'Promise promise.' I kiss her on the forehead, and run off to find Vivienne.

Vivienne sits on a wooden bench and lights what I suspect is her fortieth fag of the day. She breathes the smoke slowly, lovingly out of her nostrils before speaking. 'She knew I was coming round at four thirty, after school and my Italian class. We were going out for coffee. Oh God, it was frightening. I think she'd only just done it.' Vivienne's scarlet mouth trembles.

'I rang the doorbell, and she didn't answer. I rang again. Still no answer. I thought she must have been held up at school. I was just turning away to go and wait in the Jag when she opened the door. She looked as weak as water and so pale – like a Scotch person!' – Vivienne is so agitated that my wince at her blithe prejudice goes unnoticed as she rattles on – 'She held out her wrists, said "look what I've done" and burst into tears. It was horrific. She'd used a pretty blunt razor blade – she'd pushed it backwards and forwards, but not thank God, deep.

'There were masses of scratches, and welts of blood. I was so shocked, Helen, I nearly fainted on the spot. She seemed fine on the surface – quiet, but fine. Back at work, busy with the children, on top of your father's finances – imagine! Cecelia! I, I never thought, not in a million years, that she'd do something like this. It's been, what, five, six months, I thought, surely, she should be over it by now . . . er shouldn't she or ah maybe not?'

Vivienne, who has been talking more to herself than to me, glances at my face and stutters to a halt. I don't shout at her even though I want to. Even though, at this precise moment, I'm busting for an excuse to shout at anyone. If Johnny Depp sauntered past and accidentally trod on my toe right now I'd *crucify* him – brooding designer stubble or not, that man would be pulp!

But to Vivienne I keep my voice steady and say, 'Vivienne, I, I, you know, I, thank God you found her, you, I, no, I'm thinking, five months, it seems ages, maybe, to you, but to her, and, I mean, to me also, it's no time. No time at all. I, also, stupid, I thought she was, well, getting better, but it's a, not right. She isn't over it. I don't know how long it'll take. Longer. Maybe she'll learn to live with

144

it. I hope. But, sorry, I'm burbling, go on.'

Vivienne takes another drag on her cigarette. She sucks so hard I'm surprised it doesn't shoot down her throat. 'I took her to the kitchen and wrapped her wrists in damp tea towels, and drove her straight here. She said she'd done it in the bathroom and she'd "lost a lot of blood" so I ran upstairs to see, and it didn't look *so* bad – I couldn't *see* any blood – but I'm not an expert in these things, and she'd put towels down to, I expect, protect the carpet, but there wasn't any blood on them, so I rushed down again, and called an ambulance and they – outrageous! – said *I* should drive her! I've a good mind to write to my MP! Whoever he is.

'So I brought her here, and they assessed her for, *sniff*, suicidal intent, and from what she said they said it was probably a cry for help rather than a serious attempt to, you know, and they patched her up "for now" and, but, what gets me is, when they asked her why she did it she said, she said . . .'

Vivienne – who I thought would only ever cry if Gucci's flagship store in Sloane Street was wiped out in a freak thunderstorm – sniffs and dabs at the corner of each eye with her thumb pad.

'What?' I whisper.

Vivienne swallows hard and adds, 'Your mother said, "There's no point. Not without my Morrie." She said, "The world keeps turning and I can't see any point." Oh Helen. I didn't realise before, how much she loved him.'

I pat her trembling hand and suspect, meanly, that Vivienne is so overwrought because if *her* husband died she'd crack open the Bollinger, maintain he wouldn't have wanted her to mourn, and continue to prey on impressionable young men with even more gusto than she does already. But I shake my head and sigh, 'Neither did I.' Privately, I wonder to what extent today's dramatics relate to my mother's feelings for my father and to what extent they relate to her feelings for herself.

145

We go back inside. My mother has fallen asleep in her hard orange plastic chair. She looks about ten years old.

We sit and wait to be called and suddenly I realise. Tom! My date with Tom! Shit. A large notice forbids use of mobile phones inside the hospital so I grab mine and run outside again. It's 6.37 p.m. I ring Megavet and – a plague on my house or what – Celine answers. It's supper time and today's special is humble pie. 'Celine,' I say in my most winsome tone, 'it's Helen Bradshaw, the one who—'

'I know who you are,' she says in a sharp voice. Bugger.

'Is Tom there?' I say.

'He's busy,' she snaps. I refuse to freak out because I know that's what she wants. I decide to play it straight.

'Celine,' I say, 'I was supposed to be seeing Tom tonight but I can't because my mother has had to go into hospital suddenly, it's an emergency, very serious, and I've got to be with her. I'd be so grateful if you could pass on that message to Tom,' you sour bitch, I add silently.

I am amazed and grateful when Celine summons a shred of humanity from the air and says, in a serious tone, 'I'm sorry to hear that. Of course I'll tell Tom. Go and look after your mother and don't worry about it.'

I'm stunned. 'That's really kind of you, Celine,' I say.

'My pleasure,' she replies.

I beep off the phone. Wow. What did I do to deserve that? Maybe she's found a suitor for Nancy – a well-to-do Mercedes named Charles, with alloy wheels and leather trim. More likely she's thrilled that family tragedy has scuppered my date with her beloved boss. I hurry back to Casualty. My mother has woken up and is complaining that her 'wrists hurt'. You don't say. I bite my tongue to stop it flapping out something facetious.

Approximately three years later my mother's name is called and she, Vivienne, and myself are ushered out of the godforsaken waiting room and into what appears to be a corridor separated into tiny little cubicles. 'Did you bring your swimming costume?' I joke feebly to my mother who doesn't laugh. The duty psychiatrist – who has deep purple rings under his eyes and looks like he's been in a fight – glances at me as if to say 'prat'. I assume a meek expression and shut up. We can't all fit into the shoe-box cubicle, so Vivienne offers to wait outside.

I don't blame her. In the shoe box to our left a man is shouting and in the shoe box to our right a woman is weeping. How relaxing. I glance nervously at my mother for signs of mental instability but she sits quietly on the cubicle chair and allows a nurse to dab a clear liquid on her wounds. I may need new glasses because I have to squint to see the cuts. 'This is saline solution so it's going to sting – but only a little,' says the nurse kindly. My mother nods. She is uncharacteristically docile while her wrists are wrapped in a big sticky tapey plaster and a thin bandage, and remains silent even when she's given a tetanus injection. 'Just to be on the safe side,' says the nurse cheerfully. I smile gratefully at her. As soon as she leaves, Nasty Cop – alias Dr Nathan Collins, according to his badge – begins an interrogation.

How has she been sleeping? What's her appetite been like? Has she found it hard to concentrate? Has she had thoughts of wanting to join her loved one? Thoughts of wanting to go to sleep and never wake up? Why did she do it? Has she ever done this before? Was it on the spur of the moment? Did she write a suicide note? Does she wish that she were dead? Did she want to be found? What did she think it was going to do? What does she want? Has she felt suicidal before? Has she ever taken an overdose? Has she ever tried to harm herself in the past? Has she been seeing things that aren't there? Or hearing things? Has she a support system?

I am agog at these bold, prying questions. I quake in anticipation of each answer and half expect my mother to break down and run out of the shoe box. But she doesn't. The hot tears run down her face as she replies. I hold her hand and study my feet. And she tells Dr Collins she's been sleeping a lot and eating a little – 'A little!' I think, 'we've chomped through Prue Leith's entire repertoire, twice!' – and found it impossible to concentrate and she's had no thoughts of joining her loved one but some thoughts about sleeping for ever and she did it because Morrie died and she misses him so much she can hardly breathe and no one understands and everyone thinks she should have bounced back and she hasn't and she can't and it's all too much and she thought it was getting better but it's getting worse and she feels as if she's going mad. No she hasn't done it before. Yes it was spur of the moment, she just wanted everyone to 'sit up and take notice'. No she didn't write a note. She doesn't truly wish that she were dead – she wishes that Maurice was alive. Yes she wanted to be found. Make people understand. To make people understand. No. No. No. Not really, although she makes a point of talking to Maurice each night before she goes to bed, just a chat really, like yesterday, the new Tom Clancy came out and she knew Morrie would have been irked to miss it and so she told him she was going to read it for him. She couldn't *see* him but she felt a presence. It was just chitchat really. Occasionally she thinks she spots him in the street but it always turns out to be some stranger.

(Incidentally, that was an edited account as she burbles on and on like a babbling brook, each answer as long as the Bible, until Dr Collins snaps, 'I want a yes or no answer!')

He watches her closely then says, 'Mrs Bradshaw. You've suffered a terrible loss. The pain of bereavement is always far worse than you can possibly imagine. And you're right – people don't understand. It's hard for them to see you in pain. What they don't understand is that pain is part of the grieving process, and you have to go through it in order to heal. And five months is nothing!

'It can take twenty years to come to terms with the death of a loved one. Your reaction is not mad in the least, it's normal. It's very common for the pain to hit around now. In the early stages, you're in shock. And that's your body's way of taking care of you. You couldn't deal with all that grief at once. And you still have the sense, the familiarity of your husband's presence to buoy you up. But now the penny's dropped because you know he isn't coming back. And that, Mrs Bradshaw, is the real bummer.'

My mother stares in awe at Dr Collins as if he's the Oracle, then wraps her skinny arms around my waist, and sobs piteously into my jumper. Dr Collins nods at me as if to say, 'She'll pull through.' I'm stunned. I don't know whether to hit him or hug him.

Chapter 19

I've never reacted well to being told off. Once, after a piggishly large dinner, I was reprimanded by Jasper for suggesting he 'untighten' his belt. (Apparently I should have said 'loosen' – there's no such word as 'untighten'.) I felt most aggrieved and sulked for the next hour. After five grouchy 'What's wrong?'/ 'Nothing' exchanges, I confessed my gripe. Jasper explained that he was only trying to save me 'from sounding thick', so I reluctantly forgave him. But inside, the resentment churned. As I see it, constructive criticism, however constructive, is still criticism. It's being told off in thin disguise.

Which is why, when Dr Collins took me aside and said that my mother had 'been a bit neglected recently' and politely but firmly suggested that 'it might be wise to keep an eye and ear on Mum until we can organise some support for her' it was hard not to feel hurt. I *did* keep an 'eye and ear' on my mother, I protested in my head. As far as it was feasible. Short of quitting my job and my home – I've already quit my social life – and tailing her like a stalker, how close an eye was I expected to keep?

But I tried to play down the sting of his remark. In my heart I knew I'd dismissed her recent attempts to communicate her desperation – no excuse could justify it – so promising to shadow her was the least I could do. As for the ear. I assume Dr Collins meant I should listen to her talk. Eek. Hiding knives and Nurofen and spying on my mother like a pervert would be a joy and a pleasure, compared to listening. I didn't say this to Dr Collins but I loathe listening to my mother talk.

It's wretched to hear her spew out her emotions like she's a friend or an American or someone my own age. When she rattles on about the sweet things my father did for her like kiss her in the mornings or run her a hot bath in the evenings, I feel like a voyeur. A crap one though because I don't know where to look. Call me a prude but it feels inappropriate. It's like – not that I ever did thank God – overhearing my parents having sex. And, if you must know, I envy her. Listening to her talk is, as Dr Collins said, hard. Yes, because I hate to witness her pain. But also because it makes me wonder what's wrong with me, what kind of a daughter am I, that *my* pain is so fucking wishy-washy, sporadic, and inferior to hers?

Yes, I tell Dr Collins, of course I will keep an eye and ear on my mother. For as long as she wants.

Vivienne drops us home. I thank her, tell her she's been wonderful, and wave her off. She departs at 90 mph and I don't blame her. My mother is subdued so I keep talking. Dr Collins has given her two anti-depressants, prescribed her more, arranged for another doctor to see her in a fortnight, and for a 'CPN' to call her tomorrow. When Dr Collins said the pills were Prozac, my mother visibly staggered backwards. He then had to convince her that they wouldn't make her suicidal. She also made a fuss when he mentioned seeing another doctor.

'What for?' she demanded.

He replied: 'You've been through a dreadful time, Mrs Bradshaw. You need some support, and the doctor will manage and regulate your medication.' My mother was so mesmerised by her blue and white capsules in the little bottle, she forgot to ask what a CPN was. So, when she trotted off to show Vivienne her spoils, *I* asked. 'The community psychiatric nurse,' replied Dr Collins.

I stared at him in horror and shouted, 'But she's not mental!'

Dr Collins rubbed his bloodshot eyes and said in a

scarily soft voice, 'My priority is to avert disaster.' To avert being struck off, more like.

'Dr Collins seems like a nice man,' I say brightly, as I fuss aimlessly around the kitchen. 'So you'll probably go back to the hospital in a few weeks. Do you want me to take you?' I add, still brightly, hoping against hope that she'll say no.

'No,' says my mother, surprisingly.

'Are you sure?' I say suspiciously, wondering if she's planning a bunk.

'If I wanted to say yes, I'd have said yes,' snaps my mother.

I glance at her tired face and change the subject. I am trembling suddenly and feel an urge to grip my mother with both hands and prise an untouchable promise out of her. I want a written guarantee that she is going to remain alive and chipper for another sixty years. That's what I want, please. Because otherwise, otherwise . . . I don't want to live like an ant, scurrying about my futile business until one day like any other, I'm crushed pointlessly, indiscriminately, under the black-booted foot of fate. I feel sick with disgust at life's haphazard nature. It's about as orderly as my underwear drawer.

'Mum,' I blurt, grasping her wrist.

'Yes?' she says.

I want to say, I'm so afraid, so fucking afraid that it's killing me, but I can't. So I say, 'I wish you'd called.'

My mother replies shortly, 'You were busy.'

I feel clueless. I want to scream. I want my dad back. He'd shake some sense into her. I want control and I hate not having it. Should I make a to do list? I'll make a to do list. I make a to do list.

To Do List
1. look after Mummy – indefinite – maybe Thursdays too?
2. go home and get clothes and toothbrush

152

3. phone Laetitia
4. phone Mrs Armstrong
5. ask Luke to feed Fatboy
6. phone Tom to apologise again
7. phone Lizzy for moral support
8. listen to Mum talk

I don't dare leave my mother alone while I collect my stuff from the flat, so I ask her along. I am apprehensive about driving her silver Peugeot 206 – never having driven a car I'm not ashamed of before – but I refuse to squander even one more penny on cabs.

'It'll be nice for you to see Luke, Mummy, won't it?' I say enticingly. I don't mention Fatboy as – both being loud, egotistical attention seekers – they can't stand each other.

Before we go, I suggest my mother 'freshens up' – which is code for 'change into a long-sleeved jumper so the public doesn't realise you've just tried to top yourself'. I select a mint-green sweater, she obligingly pulls it on, and we speed off. The first noise I hear as we troop through the door is not Fatboy demanding dinner or Luke playing the Verve – and, no doubt, air guitar – in his room. The first noise I hear comes from Marcus's bedroom and it is 'uuuh! uuuh! uuuh!' and 'oh! oh! oh! my! *God*!' Oh my God indeed. I invite my mother to my flat for the first time in about a year – I thought it would depress her – and she discovers it's a bordello.

Thus stabbing home the painful point that her darling is dead and everyone else is dancing and bonking on his grave (so to speak). I curse Marcus and Michelle for picking *now* to rut like rhinos. I bet they hardly ever have sex! Marcus hasn't got the necessary equipment and Michelle hates friction. Why else did she date Sammy for five years?

I start speaking loudly and incessantly to drown out the shrieks of Michelle faking orgasm. 'Mum, come and sit down in the lounge and switch on the telly there might be something good on and would you like another cup of tea I'll put on the kettle anyway or would you prefer to listen

153

to the radio in the kitchen yes come into the kitchen and let's turn it on anyway oh look here's Luke, Luke you remember my mother don't you, yes Mum you remember Luke he was so helpful at the hospital last time and he played the cheesecake-in-Lizzy's-bag joke at the supper party, ah Luke would you mind terribly feeding Fatboy tomorrow morning as I'm staying at my mother's tonight and maybe for the rest of the week?'

I pause for breath. Luke and my mother look at me as if I'm a nutjob. 'Are you okay?' says Luke.

'Fine, fine,' I say, jerking my thumb towards Marcus's room and pulling an I'm-repulsed face.

'Oh yeah,' nods Luke, immediately. 'Marcus and your friend shagging. They've been at it like rabbits for, I dunno, ten minutes. Can't hear myself think.'

Oh hooray. Luke the dufus goofs again. I glare at Luke, say, 'Sorry, Mum, Luke's just joking,' and wait for the cloudburst.

Instead, she starts giggling. 'Helen! Don't be such a priss! I do know what sex is! I have had it!' Said in a jovial patronising lilt and with a coy glance at Luke to indicate that she and he are the real grown-ups and I am the silly little girl who can't cope with words like 'bottom'. I'd forgotten how she mutates into a coquettish Judas in the presence of any man over twelve.

'Well I don't care if you don't,' I say sulkily, as Luke and my mother laugh at me. Traitors.

'So *will* you feed Fatboy?' I say to Luke, in an attempt to recover some dignity.

'Love to,' he replies. 'Fatboy's my mate.'

I smile and tease, 'That figures, what with your similar hygiene habits!' Fatboy, unlike normal cats, isn't overkeen on washing. He always smells – as Tina puts it – 'a bit particular' behind the ears. As for Luke. He regards baths with the same affection as vampires regard garlic.

I expect Luke to laugh, but he doesn't. 'Thanks,' he says coldly.

'That was a joke!' I stutter.

'Well it wasn't a very nice one,' pipes up my mother who I will strangle if she offers one more unwanted opinion. I give up.

'Sorry, but I didn't mean it,' I say crossly. 'I'm going to make some calls,' I add as I stamp into the lounge. Luke and my mother are already gassing and ignore me. Unbloodybelievable!

The answer machine is blinking. Maybe Tom? I press play. 'Helen, it's Laetitia. Calling to see if all is okay and to remind you there's a meeting about the Get Rich Quick supplement tomorrow at nine thirty sharp. I need oodles of ideas and I'm counting on you!' This is Laetitiaspeak for 'I don't give a damn if every member of your family has stiffed it because I am paying you (just) to be my maid-servant, so be there or be unemployed!' Needless to say, I have *no* ideas for the supplement – I'm the poorest person in the office. The work experience girl earns more than I do. What do I know about Getting Rich Quick?

Actually, here's a good one: Wait For Your Dad To Croak – Hey, It Worked For Me! Ooh, now Michelle would call that bitter. Calm down, Helen. I breathe deeply, and refer to my list. Phone Tom. I leaf frantically through my diary to find his home number. I ring it and hold my breath.

'Hello?'

'Tom?' I squeak, 'it's Helen! I'm *so* sorry!' There is a pause.

'What's the excuse this time?' he says icily. *What?* I am horrified.

'You mean, you mean' – I am practically speechless with indignation, that sly lipliner-abusing witch! – 'You mean Celine didn't pass on my message?' Pause.

'So you bothered to leave one.'

Am I paranoid or does everybody hate me? 'Yes I did, actually. To tell you that my mother slit her wrists earlier today and had to be rushed to hospital.' Take that, Ice Boy!

Pleasingly, my underhand strategy has the desired effect.

'Shit! Christ, Helen, that's terrible! God, I'm sorry! Is she, er, how is she? And how are *you*?'

I say, in a conciliatory I've-got-the-moral-upper-hand tone, 'She's alright.' I feel like adding, 'But it was touch and go'. (A, I've heard this said on *Casualty* and B, I want to punish him for being unfriendly.) However, I restrain myself. First, it's a lie, and second, I'd be playing into Celine's over manicured hands.

'And how are you?' says Tom again.

I nod down the phone before whispering a strangled, 'Fine.' I can't tell him the truth – that I am rigid with fear and seriously considering keeping my mother in a padded box at the end of my bed to avoid further fatalities. Instead I tell Tom an abridged version of the gory story and an elongated version of my phone call to Megavet. 'She's such a liar!' I shriek, adding, before I can bite off my tongue: 'She fancies you, you know!' The second I say it I regret it. Why don't I just shout 'I fancy you, you know!'? It's tantamount to the same thing.

'Oh yes?' says Tom coyly. 'Why do you say that?'

The bastard! 'I say it,' I reply in a cute, flirty sing-song tone, 'because she guards you like a hyena guards an antelope carcass.'

Hm. That didn't come out the way I meant it to. But Tom's good humour is patently restored because he says drily, 'You flatter me.'

I giggle. 'I'm sorry about tonight,' I say. And I mean it. I am sorry. I'm also concerned that, this being the second time I've screwed up, a third offer won't be forthcoming. Do I dare ask him? It's not like I'm asking him to lend me money. Lizzy would ask a man out. Why am I the *Rules* girl?

'Would you, are you free sometime later this week, or maybe next week?' I blurt, cleverly making it sound as if my life is a friendless void.

'Definitely,' says Tom, 'but maybe next week is better?

Things might have calmed down a bit.' We fix on the Tuesday.

I put the phone down and straight away start analysing the conversation like a bad psychotherapist. By suggesting next week as opposed to this week, was he hinting that I was selfish? Neglectful of my poorly mother? (Who, as I ponder this, I can hear cackling in the kitchen). Does it mean he doesn't like me any more? Not that he said so, at least, not *consciously*. And Tuesday – that's a worky, plodding, got to get up early tomorrow, good excuse to scarper at 10 p.m. sort of day. Does that mean he . . . ?

Enough. Enough already, you dork. The minute I start caring is the minute he'll stop. I give a quick shake of my head to emphasise this cessation of caring, and phone Lizzy. She picks up and in the background I hear what sounds suspiciously like monks chanting. So before I inform my friend that my sole remaining parent is at no immediate risk of death I address a more pressing issue: 'What the fuck's that you're listening to?'

She ignores the question and demands, 'How's your mum?' I tell her. And, eventually, she confesses that her CD is entitled *Gregorian Moods* and she'll tape it for me if I like.

'No ta,' I say.

'Well, maybe for your mother then?'

I pause. It is a matter of principle that I automatically write off all Lizzy's spooky chanty health-freaky bean-munching willow pod worthiness as twaddle. That said, I want to help my mother in any way I can and I cannot see her yapping away with a shrink. I really can't. She has chosen *me* as her shrink. She'll see the nurse once to humour Dr Collins but I reckon that'll be it. She doesn't want to speak to a stranger. My mother doesn't want people listening because they're paid to. She wants people to listen because they care about her. It's all highly inconvenient and I need all the help I can get.

'I'll pay you for the tape,' I tell Lizzy. I can't bring myself to speak the words 'Yes, I'd adore a copy of *Gregorian Moods*,' aloud.

'I can't wait to tell Tina,' says Lizzy happily.

'One word and the feng shui plant gets it,' I reply sweetly.

I have rescued Luke from my mother and we are trotting down the hall towards the front door, when Marcus emerges from his room wearing a small white towel round his trim waist. His face falls when he sees a grown-up. 'Hi,' he stammers, 'I just, er, got out the shower.' My mother ogles him, I'm ashamed to say, like a bird eyeing a plump worm.

'We heard,' I say chirpily as I push my gawking mother out of the flat. 'A fifteen-minute shower – must be a record!' The recall of his speechless fury keeps me smiling all the way to the Peugeot.

Chapter 20

When I started work at *Girltime*, I suffered from an affliction known as Fone Fear. (Okay, Phone Fear, but Fone Fear makes it sound less like an excuse and more like a syndrome.) Anyway, every time I had to make a call I'd put it off and put it off until it was 6 p.m. and the person I needed to speak to had left the office. My illness lasted approximately three days before a verbal thrashing from Laetitia scared it out of me. Alas, the virus was cowed but not defeated. Because this morning I rang my mother's boss at the brisk hour of seven to tell her about her little relapse and it took me from 3.13 to 4.36 a.m. to perfect my lines, and another forty-five minutes to summon the courage to dial the number (I started lifting and replacing the receiver at 6.17 a.m.).

Mrs Armstrong's first *overt* concern was for my mother's health. 'Shocking news . . . rest and recuperation . . . best wishes for a speedy recovery . . . spring back to her old self.' Yet the undercurrent of strained patience and fretful guilt soon burst – gasping for atonement – to the surface.

Only last week, it emerged, Mrs Armstrong had 'had a quiet word' with Cecelia about 'organisation'. Not a reprimand, goodness no, just a reminder that the Christmas concert was fast bearing down upon us and the programme, rehearsals, costumes, scripts, timetable, ought really to be well underway. She hoped Cecelia hadn't taken this suggestion as a slight. Cecelia was an excellent teacher, a true professional. Only that if one staff member wasn't

159

firing from all cylinders, it placed a burden – no, wrong word – rather, it affected everyone.

I reassured Mrs Armstrong that her 'quiet word' had in no way prompted my mother to slash her wrists, although privately I bloody well thought it had. I told Mrs Armstrong I'd report back on an approximate date for my mother's return to work (again) after consultation with the hospital. But from Mrs Armstrong's artful response – 'It's easier for us to plan if we know someone is going to be absent for a while, than if we expect them to be there and they're not' – I suspected that Mrs Armstrong would prefer to rely on alternative cover until Christmas at least. For the sake of her own sanity, if not her budget.

At 8.30 a.m. – after a long hot shower that I'd have happily stood in for the rest of my life – I wake my mother with a cup of tea. And not by throwing the cup at her head. She rubs her eyes, does a little double-take on seeing her bandaged wrists, and slowly, gingerly heaves herself upright. 'How are you feeling?' I say.

'I don't know,' she replies flatly. Damn.

'Mum,' I say, 'I've got to leave for work in three minutes or I'll be out of a job. But I've spoken to Mrs Armstrong, and she sends you her best and says don't hurry back until you're "right as rain". Now what are you going to do today? Shall I ring Vivienne and ask her to come round? Would you like to meet me for lunch? What would you prefer?'

My mother wrinkles her nose and says, 'Vivienne has her batik class on Tuesdays.' Inwardly, I'm starting to panic. I can't leave her alone already – blowing about aimlessly like a wisp of tumbleweed. She's got a great cavernous yawn of a day stretching endlessly before her. She might have another pop. An unwelcome idea begins to form in my head. I don't want to voice it. I'd rather ignore it until it retreats. Unfortunately it is now 8.33 and I have precisely no minutes to think of an alternative plan.

'Mum,' I blurt, 'I know you don't see each other that

160

much, but what if I call Nana Flo?' The mere chattery sound of her name sends an ugly dart of remorse shooting to the pit of my stomach.

The truth is that since the funeral day I've spoken to her twice. Once, on discovering my mother had become Miss Havisham. It occurred to me that, for all I knew, my grandmother had turned into Darth Vader and it was my duty to investigate. Her woolly stream of phone messages increased my trepidation. It took me four days to approach the telephone. When I explained that my mother hadn't returned any of her calls because she was – according to her GP – 'suffering from grief, resulting in a depressive illness', Nana Flo was silent. Then she said, 'Ah well, gotta get on!' I was about to argue: my point being that when you have a depressive illness you *can't* get on, but realised I'd be banging my head against a seventy-eight-year-old brick wall. And then it occurred to me – if Nana Flo was so rigidly in favour of getting on, why ring my mother every other day for an entire month, bleating like a small lamb mislaid on a mountainside?

So I said, cleverly, 'Talking of which, how are *you* getting on, Nana?'

She replied, 'I'm managing.'

At this point, I was ready to let it go. But – spurred on by the real live spectre of my closest relatives dying or zombifying one by one – I blundered on: 'You have been calling Mum a lot, er, recently. Are you lonely at all?'

Nana Flo gave a mirthless bark and retorted in an unpleasant tone, '"Lonely" she says! "Lonely!"' – then in a snitty one – 'Your mother always did like to play helpless.'

What could I say to that? After a stunned pause, I said, 'I'll get Mummy to call you when the doctor says she's strong enough.'

The second time I spoke to Nana Flo was when I actually saw her – the day probate was granted. After work I drove round to see my mother and my grandmother was sitting

161

in the kitchen reading the *TV Times* through a magnifying glass which distorted her eye and made her look like the Hunchback of Notre-Dame. We had a short, civil conversation about her blood pressure ('can't complain') and that was about it. Since then we haven't exchanged one word. And, not wishing to overdramatise my feelings on the situation, I'd rather jump off the top of the Empire State Building than speak to her now.

Although if I know my mother, I suspect she'll feel the same way and I won't have to. I am incredulous when my mother says, 'You go to work, I'll call her.' At first, I don't believe her.

'Really?' I say shrilly. 'But you never call her!'

My mother shoots me a snide look: 'And what do *you* know?' she says rudely.

'I know,' I say huffily, 'that you call Nana Flo about as often as *I* call Nana Flo.'

My mother regards me haughtily and replies, 'Then you obviously call her at least twice a week.' Do I believe my ears?

'Mummy, you're joking,' I say.

My mother looks as smug as it's possible to look when you've recently tried to unhand yourself with a razor blade. She says: 'We see each other every Thursday. She's not that bad when you get to know her. Actually she's good company – for a grouchy old crone!'

I am so delighted I smack my mother's leg playfully through the bedclothes. It's only as I'm puffing down Long Acre towards the office that it strikes me: I've been squandering about sixteen hours a week with my mother for the last five months. Why the hell didn't she tell me before? Needless to say, I skid into work ten minutes late for the supplement meeting.

When I slink out of the supplement meeting exhausted but relieved (having winged it – or is it wung it?) there is an illegal copy of *Gregorian Moods* sitting on my desk and a note from Lizzy: 'Lunch?' She's so sweet but I know she'll expect a gritty account of my mother's progress and today, I'm not up to sharing with the group. My head is swirling. Why didn't Mum tell me about her and Nana Flo? Her concealment is as offensive as Tina's sudden, hypocritical refusal to divulge intimate juicy details about her sex life with Adrian. When Lizzy and I are her closest friends!

I make my excuses, then pounce on the phone and ring my mother. She picks up and I rattle off about fifty questions: 'How are you? How are you feeling? Is Nana with you? What have you been doing?'

My mother, to my infinite relief, is calm. She's 'tired but feels better than yesterday'. Christ, I should think so with all those jollifying drugs inside you. My mother also tells me that Nana Flo came round although she only arrived at 11.30 because she took the bus. Nana Flo has been showing her pictures of Morrie as a small boy. He looked serious in all of them.

While I am impressed that Nana Flo is – for the first time in her life – doing the old person thing and hoicking about dreary aged photographs, I suspect my mother is keeping something from me. I can hear it in her voice. I ask a very stupid question: 'Mum, are you okay?'

She chirps, 'Fine! Nana Flo is moving in for a while.'

At first I don't believe her. I'd find it easier to believe that Santa Claus is shacking up with the Tooth Fairy. 'You're kidding!' I squeak. But she isn't. 'But why?' I say.

'Because Dr Collins said I need a support system,' she retorts.

'Well, that's great,' I say slowly. 'So you won't need me to stay over then.'

My mother replies happily, 'No.'

This news should delight me, but it doesn't. It makes me growly for the rest of the afternoon.

By the time I get home to the flat I'm feeling as snappy as a shark with a tooth infection. I slam the door and am promptly assaulted by a guttural cacophany: 'Uuuuh! Uuuh! Uuuuh!' and 'Oh! Oh! Oh!' *Please*, not again! It's

163

obscene. I hurl a frenzied volley of V-signs towards Marcus's room, then blow a long, loud raspberry. Bastard bastard bastard. The anger pulsates. Every grunt and moan is a personal affront. I stomp to the kitchen, viciously grinding my heels into the carpet. (A typical Marcus refrain: 'Can you take off your shoes in the house, please? That carpet cost £24.95 per square metre.')

I yank a stick of French bread out of the freezer and wish I was a certified psychopath so I could burst into Marcus's room and beat him about the head with it and not be sent to prison. Hey, maybe I could bribe my mother to do it. I shove the baguette into the oven, thunder back to my room, and flop on to the bed. Normally I'd play the Beastie Boys to reinforce my wrath, but this mood is too dark and malevolent for tunes. It demands silence. Abruptly, I'm gripped by a surge of hate so vivid I can taste its sour potency. Suddenly I'm thumping and pummelling my pillow – bam! bam! bam! – and my fists are bashing Marcus's face to a pulp and I'm screaming and screaming. No words, just a long shrill blast of sound.

I only stop screaming when Luke, Marcus, and Michelle burst into my room on the assumption that I'm being murdered. Luke is blinkily anxious while Marcus and Michelle are as breathless and pink-faced as I am. Michelle is wrapped in Marcus's red velvet dressing gown and Marcus is wearing black silk boxer shorts. 'Bad day at work,' I explain, forcing a smile.

Marcus glares at me.

Michelle affects concern and croons, 'You've burst a blood vessel under your eye – loads of funny red dots! Do you want me to get you some ice?'

I sit on my hands to stop them clawing her face. 'I'm fine, thank you,' I say, although my voice is now as hoarse as a stallion, 'you can all go away now.'

Marcus treats me to one last glance of disdain before exiting. Michelle curls her fingers in a queenly wave and follows, shutting the door behind her. Luke remains, his arms dangling awkwardly. He scratches his head and says, 'Do you want a hug?'

I don't, but it would seem churlish to refuse, so I say, 'Yes please.'

Luke clumsily clasps me to him. My nose is squashed into his armpit which makes it difficult – and probably unwise – to breathe in. Eventually, I am forced to snuffle loudly for air. Luke obviously mistakes the snuffle for a sniffle because he kisses my hair, pats my back (nearly winding me) and exclaims, 'Don't cry!'

I disentangle myself and croak, 'I'm not!' Then I add gruffly, 'Thanks for, um, worrying though.'

Luke beams and says, 'What happened at work then?'

I consider telling him the truth then decide against it. He'd blurt it out to Marcus by mistake. 'I got told off for being late, this morning,' I whisper.

'Maybe you should set your alarm earlier,' says Luke immediately.

'Mm,' I say, trying to hide my irritation. I've already lectured him on offering solutions where they're not wanted. There is a silence which is cut short by a distant roar. We stare at each other, intrigued.

'Maybe Marcus had a bad day at work today too,' says Luke. I do hope so.

We jump up and run into the kitchen, where Marcus is dancing from toe to toe like a hobgoblin and frenziedly flapping at the oven with a dishcloth. The room is thick with grey smoke. I peer into the haze and see the French bread burning to death. 'Shit! I forgot about that,' I say, carefully avoiding any mention of the word 'sorry'. Marcus speeds across the room, holding the French bread – a blackened corpse with glowing red innards – at arm's length. He drops it into the sink, twists the cold tap, and the charred remains of my dinner hiss and sizzle.

Michelle coughs pointedly. Luke watches, gob agape, entranced by the spectacle of Marcus in a tizz. I suck in my cheeks to stop myself laughing but don't entirely succeed.

Marcus hurls the dishcloth to the floor like a gauntlet, and shrieks, 'My Poggenpohl is a *ruin*! I am so sick of you and your slovenly ways, you, you, you *slut*!'

I have never been so insulted, not even by Jasper. 'Takes one to know one,' I reply, and stalk out. Before running into my room, I yell from the hallway, 'And if I were a bloke with a Poggenpohl like yours, I'd bloody well keep quiet about it!' Childish, I admit, but the best I can do at short notice.

Chapter 21

British weather is famed for its sneakiness but this year, throughout August, it disgraced itself. The entire month, I'd pull open the curtains at 8.15 to the soporific sight of a baby blue sky. I'd scurry to the station in T-shirt, flimsy trousers and open-toed sandals, and feel the sun shine seductively warm on my skin. Before starting work I'd flap around exclaiming to colleagues, 'Isn't it *hot*!' Then at 12.45 I'd glance out of the window, wondering whether to get lasagne or a baked potato for lunch (answer: whichever looked bigger in the shop), and behold a monsoon!

The sky would loom as dark and baleful as doomsday and someone would inevitably rush in, shake the cold droplets from their hair, brush off their thin cotton shift dress, and proclaim it '*Freezing* outside.' This climatic spite would persist until the day I'd painstakingly haul in a raincoat and extra jumper. Then there'd be a twenty-four-hour heatwave. The only consolation was, everyone got caught out. Except Lizzy.

'Are you telepathic or something?' I grumbled one lunchtime, huddling under her umbrella to save my hair from water damage.

'No,' she replied, 'I watch the weather forecast before I go to bed.'

Despite the rain, I stopped in the street. 'By God you're a genius!' I exclaimed. 'What a brilliant brilliant novel idea!' But while admiring her guile, I knew I'd never have the patience to follow her example.

So I got wet. I always do. I'm like Fatboy in this respect

– I regard forward planning as a yawn. (Fatboy's favourite pastime is to creep into Marcus's newly washed duvet as it dries over a chair, even though he always gets lost and trapped in it. But he'd rather embark on the duvet adventure now, and miaow piteously for help later.) I also rarely think ahead, then suffer the consequences.

And so, it never in a trillion years occurred to me that my mother and Nana Flo might be driven to pal up, and that I'd feel spurned and foolish and jealous when they did. Lizzy, though, has more foresight than I do and has realised – in retrospect – that their friendship was a certainty.

I tell her all about it over lunch on Friday, as by then I am able to sound nonchalant. She nods wisely and sips at her Evian. 'I suppose they have your father in common, if nothing else,' she says.

'Yes, but they've always had my father in common,' I say, with my mouth full of tuna mayonnaise, 'and it made bugger all difference.'

I pause, fascinated, as Lizzy daintily extracts the capers from her olive pasta sauce and lines them up neatly at the side of her plate. 'Why didn't they get on?' she asks. I frown. 'Don't frown, you'll get wrinkles!' she cries.

'Sorry,' I say. I try to think without frowning. 'I get the impression Nana Flo disapproved of my mother.'

Lizzy gasps: 'Why? Your mother's lovely!'

I shrug. 'Well, although Nana worked herself, she doesn't really approve of women working. Not married ones.' Lizzy rolls her eyes. I add: 'Less time to devote to my dad. And she was never a great housewife.'

Lizzy giggles. 'So that's where you get it from,' she says.

'I have other talents,' I grin. 'Talking of sex, how *is* Brian?' (I still think the man's a berk but for Lizzy's sake I'll feign interest. Anyway I am interested. In a repulsed sort of way.)

Lizzy blushes, 'Really well. We're getting on brilliantly.'

I widen my eyes and lean towards her: 'Specify.'

Lizzy beams, 'We were chatting recently and I happened to mention that I liked fresh figs but they're really expensive. And last night he came round to see me and he'd bought me a great big bagful! In November!' Not being a massive fruit fanatic I am unappreciative of the lengths one has to go to in order to obtain fresh figs in November. Don't you just walk into a shop?

Lizzy misreads the dim expression on my face and adds, humbly, 'He's not traditionally romantic, like Adrian is to Tina – all those bouquets – but I've never really cared about flowers. Not that it isn't lovely for Tina, of course. But the figs! I was so touched. It was such a thoughtful gesture.'

I jump to correct her: 'Oh no, I didn't think anything bad, it was a lovely thing for him to do . . . if you want your girlfriend parping away all night like a foghorn.'

Lizzy reddens again and giggles. Suddenly she stops laughing, and taps the table as if to re-direct our attention to the business of the day. She says, 'So how come Nana Flo approves of your mother now?'

I have no idea. 'I have no idea,' I say, 'I don't even know if she *does* approve of her.'

Lizzy replies, 'But she must, if they've started meeting up all of a sudden!'

God knows. 'She's weird,' I say. 'I think, she's never taken to my mother but she's always tried to be friendly.'

Lizzy nods, 'For your father's sake?'

I nod too, 'Yes, I suppose.'

Lizzy pauses. 'So maybe, now your father has . . . passed on, she's still being friendly for his sake.'

I wonder. 'Yeah, maybe.' I say, 'Maybe it's because he's no longer there to fight over. But I think it's down to my mum too. She never needed Nana Flo. And now, perhaps, she does.'

Lizzy looks excited: 'And maybe,' she exclaims in a breathy I-love-it-when-a-plan-comes-together whisper, 'now Nana Flo has lost a son, she needs a daughter! Now I think about it, it makes perfect sense!'

Blimey, I wouldn't go *that* far. 'Nana Flo,' I say, 'is the least maternal woman I've ever met, apart from my mother. She's not what you'd call sympathetic. She didn't stop my mum slashing her wrists, did she?'

Lizzy purses her lips, 'No, but that's not what I'm saying. How could she stop her? No one could.'

I say, 'Except my father bouncing back from the grave, alive and well and not a ghost, shouting "tricked you!"'

Lizzy turns down the corners of her mouth, dismayed at my irreverence. 'Oh Helen,' she says, 'no one can replace your father. But even if your grandmother isn't sympathetic – I'm sure she cares.'

That's the problem with Lizzy. She thinks everyone is as goodly as she is. Even me. I sigh and say, 'Yeah. I suppose Nana's better than nothing.' I think of my efforts to care for my mother and a small defensive voice inside me says, 'But *you* weren't nothing. You were something. Your cooking was vile but you weren't *nothing*.' Aloud, I say cautiously, 'Funny how my mum didn't tell me about seeing my grandmother, don't you think?'

Lizzy tilts her glossy head to one side and considers. Then she says, 'Maybe she forgot.' And maybe the earth is flat and the moon is a large piece of cheese. Time to change the subject. The conversation has turned maudlin and, frankly, after Monday I've had maudlin up to my eyeballs.

'You know when you do that body brushing thing?' I ask slyly.

'Yes,' says Lizzy, sitting to attention.

'I always forget: you brush towards your hands and feet, don't you?'

Lizzy looks aghast: 'Oh heavens, no! You brush towards your heart! It's essential!' She embarks on a ten-minute lecture about exfoliation and friction and massage and on a deeper level improving microcirculation and removing toxins and excess fluid and – Nana Flo is forgotten. Mission accomplished. I am relieved that when we next convene for lunch Tina deigns to join us and therefore serious conversation is banned. In fact, almost *all* conversation is banned. I start off on what I assume is a safe topic: Adrian.

Me: *[jokily]* 'So Tina, how's lover boy?'

Tina: *[coldly]* 'What do you mean by that?'

Lizzy: *[diplomatically]* 'She, Helen, means Adrian – he seems mad about you. We wondered how he was.'

Tina: *[shiftily]* 'Well, thank you.'

Me: *[offended]* 'I don't see why you're so touchy about a simple question. It's not like I asked the size of his dick.' *[thinks]*: Anyway, back when this relationship wasn't such a holy relic you told me, so I know anyway.

Tina: *[snappish]* 'Some things are private. We're not fucking fifteen.'

Me: *[goading]* 'What's wrong, are you premenstrual?'

Lizzy: *[hurriedly]* 'I'm sure Tina isn't but I've got some Evening Primrose Oil if she is. It's superb, really effective. I swear by it.'

Tina: *[furious]* 'I haven't got PMT! Bloody hell! You wouldn't ask a man that! And don't give me that flower oil crap! I swear by it too – it's fucking shite!'

Lizzy: *[shocked]* 'Tina, I'm sorry, I didn't mean to upset you.'

Me: *[sullen]* 'Me neither.'

We fall silent. Lizzy fiddles nervously with her steamed noodles, I prod sulkily at my baked potato, and Tina scowls at her baked beans on toast. I chant: 'Beans, beans, good for the heart, the more you eat the more you f—'

Tina slams down her fork and roars: 'Shut it!' If you ask me, she's been watching too many re-runs of *The Sweeney*. And this may sound contrary, but the snarlier Tina becomes, the keener I am to annoy her. So I move away from flatulence jokes and on to personal jibes. Tina has a scabby cold sore by the side of her mouth. I rip off a piece of brown potato skin and stick it on my lower lip: 'Who's this?' Lizzy stifles a giggle. I catch Tina's stricken expression and collapse. I am wheezing with laughter at my own

171

gag when Tina leaps up, scraping her chair, and rushes out.

I freeze. 'Do you think she's okay?' I ask Lizzy.

Lizzy looks perturbed. 'I'm not sure,' she says.

I sigh and throw down my napkin. My potato is as hard as granite and as tasty. 'Wait here,' I say. 'It's my fault. You finish your noodles.'

We both run out of the café and chase after Tina. 'Tina! Stop! I'm sorry!' I shout. But she keeps running. Happily, she is encumbered by her Prada shoes and pencil skirt and we soon catch her up. It takes four minutes of five-star grovelling before she agrees to let us buy her a coffee. This time, Lizzy and I restrict the conversation to *our* love lives. Or, in my case, lack of one.

Lizzy: *[shyly]* 'I'd love you both to meet Brian properly. Are either of you free tomorrow night?'

Tina: *[stiffly]* 'Ta for the offer, but I'm busy I'm afraid.'

Me: *[proudly]* 'Me too.'

Lizzy: *[after consideration]* 'Oh. What are you doing, Helen?'

Me: *[coy]* 'I'm seeing Tom actually. You know, the vet. You remember Tom, Tina?'

Tina: *[more relaxed]* 'I certainly do, Tequila Girl!'

Me: *[suddenly keen to change subject]* 'Anyway Lizzy, let's arrange to meet Brian another time.'

Tina:*[getting even]* 'So! Tom is on again, is he? I didn't realise he was into watersports.'

Me: *[incensed]* 'Shut up! Don't be disgusting!'

Lizzy: *[clueless]* 'What? I don't get it.'

Me: *[quickly]* 'Never mind. Where are you going with Brian tomorrow then?'

Tina: *[butting in]* 'So Helen, tell us more about Tom. How far have you got?'

Me: *[glaring at Tina]* 'It's not like that. Anyway, "some things are private."'

Tina: *[spitefully]* 'In other words you've got nowhere.'

Me: *[defensive]* 'Who said I wanted to get anywhere anyway?'

172

Tina: [sarcastic] 'So it's platonic? Oh I believe you.'

Me: [angrily] 'I only split up with Jasper about a minute ago! Why do I always have to be shagging someone?'

Tina: [nastily] 'You tell me.'

Me: [hurt] 'Thanks for that.'

Tina: [not that sorry] 'I'm sorry, Helen, but you're always splitting up with Jasper.'

Lizzy: [finally able to get a word in] 'We just want the best for you. That's all. And Jasper, well, Jasper isn't always that thoughtful.'

Me: [embarrassed] 'Blah blah blah. Leave Jasper out of it.'

Tina: [triumphantly] 'We did until you brought him into it!'

Lizzy: [desperate] 'Why don't we all go out later in the week? I'll bring Brian, and you two can bring whoever you like or it can just be the four of us? How about Friday?'

Me: [subdued] 'Okay. But it'll probably be me on my own.'

Tina: [rubbing it in] 'I'll see if Adrian has any plans.'

Between the two of them I am relieved to get back to the office. Which is a first. Laetitia promptly sends me out again to buy her some non-perfumed deodorant. 'As you wish!' I chirrup and rush off. When I return, Laetitia asks me to call an expert for a quote on 'domestic violence' and I start ringing around immediately. Usually I faff around scrunching up bits of paper on my desk for at least half an hour in preparation. I know Laetitia is impressed by this afternoon's uncharacteristic enthusiasm because when I cry 'Done it!' ten minutes later, she replies, 'Good.'

She's only ever said 'good' to me twice before (the first time when I passed on the message that the *Girltime* astrologer was threatening to resign and the second time when I told her that someone called Oliver Braithwaite had called 're the hunting weekend'). I beam and reply, 'My pleasure.' I need every Brownie point I can scrape. I am also trying to distract myself from dwelling on the fact that on Thursday morning my mother has her first appointment with the Nut Nurse. (The nurse is coming to the house as my mother refused to go to the clinic.)

I decide that from now on I'm going to be ultra-efficient until Laetitia is forced to promote me to junior features writer. She won't want to, of course, but she'll have no choice. The thought of my imminent ascension to grandeur and the wealth and kudos it will bring cheers me. Maybe I'll be trusted to write the *Happening* page and conduct interviews with minor soap stars, and some poor keen innocent will unwittingly replace me as Deodorant Monitor. I'll need a trouser suit, of course.

By 5 p.m., I have been promoted (in my head) to Editor in Chief. I decide to take my mother out to dinner to celebrate. Brrg brrrg! 'Bradshaw residence!' croaks the Queen. Or rather, Nana Flo in her telephone voice.

I recover speedily enough to say in a friendly tone, 'Hello, Nana, it's Helen. How are you?'

She replies: 'Can't complain, Helen. What can I do for you?' Helen? She never addresses me by name! Could be the onset of senility. That or she's been watching *It's a Wonderful Life* and the euphoria hasn't yet worn off. Next thing she'll be calling me honeychil'.

Bemused, I ask to speak to my mother. 'How is she?' I ask quickly (best to be forewarned).

'Not so bad,' says Nana Flo briskly. 'We're keeping busy.' Oh?

'Like how?' I say, intrigued.

'Clearing out cupboards,' she replies tartly. I squeeze my nose between my thumb and forefinger to snuff the laughter. Let justice be done!

'Actually, Nana,' I say, when I regain composure, 'I er, don't have to speak to my mother, I can ask you.'

There is a pause. 'Yes?' she barks.

I clear my throat and say, 'I'd like to take you and Mum out for dinner this Thursday, if you're both free.' (That last bit was a courtesy.)

When Nana Flo replies her voice is as stern as ever: 'You sure you've got the money?' Of all the ungracious cheek!

'Yes,' I say (not a total lie, as I will have it when Barclaycard lend it to me).

'Then,' intones my grandmother plummily, 'I don't see why not.'

I grin down the phone and crow: 'Sorted!'

'What?' replies Nana Flo.

Chapter 22

I have more embarrassing moments than most. One of my earliest occurred when I was four – my parents had dragged me out for a bracing walk in Regent's Park one Saturday morning and they were so engrossed in each other they didn't notice I'd lagged behind, transfixed by the huge orange fish in the ornamental pond. When I looked up my parents were gone and the park was full of tall terrifying people. I ran among them, stumbling in panic and scuffing my black patent shoes. At last, I spotted my father from behind, and slipped my hand into his. He looked down, and I looked up – into the bemused face of a stranger. Thankfully, because I was four and cute the stranger found it funny and helped me locate my real dad.

Alas, my latest embarrassment occurred this morning and as I'm no longer four and cute, the witnesses showed me no mercy. I'd eaten breakfast and was perfecting tonight's persona in the bathroom mirror. I wasn't sure how to present myself to Tom so I was experimenting. The bubbly: 'Hiiii!' and a sparky hello kiss on one cheek ('mwa!')? Or the more sophisticated: 'How *are* you?' accompanied by a closed mouth smile? Or possibly the sexily smouldering: 'Hello, Tom,' plus enigmatic twitch of the lips?

I was earnestly acting out these possibilities when I became aware of what I believe thriller writers call a Lurking Presence. I spun round and there at the bathroom door – which, in my enthusiasm, I'd forgotten to close – stood Luke and Marcus, stuffing their fists into their mouths to stifle their glee. 'Piss off!' I roared as they bent over laughing and lisping witticisms like, 'How 'bout smearing ma lipstick!' I slammed the door screeching 'I did not say that!' then sat on the toilet seat, head in hands, rocking back and forth, moaning 'Nooooooo!'

My mortification reverberates throughout the morning, overshadowing my new efficiency resolution. I can't concentrate on my work because I keep recalling their rapt faces, shuddering involuntarily and mewing 'no!' to myself. Finally I can bear it no longer and am forced to unburden myself to Lizzy. 'I've got post-traumatic stress syndrome,' I say grumpily, as Lizzy tries not to laugh.

'Helen,' she tinkles, 'you mustn't worry about tonight. Just be yourself!'

I roll my eyes and trundle back to my desk. The phone rings. I don't want to answer in case it's Tom cancelling but as Laetitia tuts and huffs if I let it ring more than twice, I snatch it up. 'Hello?' I sing. 'Features desk!' (This is an attempt to make myself seem a pacy, high-flying career woman instead of a risible, plodding bottom-feeder.) Sadly, my efforts are wasted as it's my mother. What gripe now?

'Hi, Mum,' I say cautiously. 'What's up?' I brace myself. Could it be Nana Flo has stripped my father's wardrobe and packed all his clothes off to Oxfam? Or is she driving my mother madder with 'If Onlys'? Might she be forcing her to watch *The Antiques Roadshow*? Or berating her as a spendthrift because she won't buy tinned sausages?

'I'm exhausted,' she says petulantly.

It emerges that last night my mother felt sick and padded downstairs at 2 a.m. in search of some anti-nausea pills. She was rifling through the First Aid box when the kitchen door was thrown open – 'I nearly died of fright!' – and the pill bottle was whipped from her hands by a triumphant Nana Flo. Apparently, my grandmother quavered: 'As long as I'm in this house there'll be no more nonsense from you!' I suspect my mother is both irritated *and* touched. She ends the conversation by saying stiffly, 'I haven't been taken out to dinner since our last wedding anniversary. Where are we going?'

I haven't a clue but I say quickly, 'There's a Thai restaurant near Islington I thought would be nice. They do jasmine tea.'

My mother pauses. 'That sounds nice,' she says. 'I don't think I've ever had Thai before.'

I whisper, 'I'll pick you and Nana up at eight,' and put the phone down. I stare at my desk, and the front page of the *Mirror* blurs. I blink and it looms back into focus. I can't be sure but in all the months we've chopped leeks together I don't think my mother has ever expressed – pleasure is too strong a word – *positivity* at the prospect of my company. That said, this is the first time I've ever taken her out to dinner.

The afternoon drags by. Laetitia cripples it by ordering me to sort out the invoice file. Even though I am bored out of my skull I try to maintain an aura of zeal. Eventually Laetitia peers over her computer, regards me suspiciously, and says, 'Helen, did they up your medication?' She peals with laughter.

'Ha ha,' I say, unamused. Laetitia's jokes are as rare as tax rebates and as funny as cancer. I wonder how I am going to uphold the work ethic charade when I intend to leave on the dot of six. (It is essential I reach home at six forty, in order to allow myself a moderate eighty minutes to beautify.)

Laetitia cuts short my dilemma at five thirty by grabbing her coat and walking out. None of that 'goodbye, see you tomorrow' nonsense. Laetitia is enviable – although personally I can't stand her – in that she doesn't give a toss about being liked. I don't carry it off with the same conviction. Laetitia is liberated. I'm still struggling. For instance, I hate and despise Marcus but it matters to me that he hates and despises me back. And as for Jasper. I feel murderous but *fond*. He reminds me of Prince Philip. He's

178

a git but he can't help himself. Though I haven't heard from him (Jasper, not Prince Philip) since he moved in with Louisah, I need him to admire me. This puerile confetti swirls around my head until I unlock the flat door. Then I veto all thoughts of Jasper and Marcus and turn my attention to the Herculean task of washing and crafting my hair into a socially acceptable shape.

Tom rings the doorbell at 8.10. His timing is suspiciously perfect and I wonder if he arrived early and waited in his car. I feel a twitch of irritation – not too early, not too late, but just right. Like Goldilocks and the porridge. And she was a little prig. I bet Tom is one of those men who asks for the bill with a squiggle flourish of one hand and a flat palm of the other. Like Marcus. Oh! Enough about Marcus. Jasper, as I recall, raises a languid hand and the waitress comes running.

I walk to the door and pinch my arm to exorcise my silly frilly killjoy thoughts. What's the matter with me? I hope Tom isn't wearing anything frightening, like a waistcoat. I yank open the door to face my doom. Tom grins at me, and I sigh with relief and grin back. He's wearing jeans, a khaki green shirt, a white T-shirt under that, and brown loafery shoes. In the old days I'd have made a mental note of each item and reported back to Tina so she could assess if he was cool or if I should run for the hills. But as Tina has silently relinquished the position of my personal fashion advisor and Tom looks ravishing, I don't bother.

'You look nice,' says Tom, kissing me on the cheek. I think two things. A, did he practise his greeting in the mirror too? and B, I should damn well hope so after one and a half hours of preening, primping, and plucking. For which I have Lizzy to thank. This morning, after bleating the party line: 'just be yourself', she told me it might be wise to pluck my eyebrows. Her exact words: 'Eyebrows are *so* important – they're the clothes hanger on which you hang your face. If you don't pay attention to your

179

eyebrows you can apply as much make-up as you like and you'll still look fuzzy. It's a beauty basic . . .'

I took the hint, flicked through a copy of *Glamour* until I came across a pair of enviable eyebrows, then tried to copy them. I'm not sure I succeeded fully, but Tom says I look nice. It worked! 'Thank you,' I say, 'so do you.' (Lizzy has also briefed me in the importance of accepting compliments: 'If you don't it's insulting the person who gave it to you.')

However she obviously didn't brief Tom because he looks bashful, pulls at his shirt, and says jokily, 'What, this old thing?'

I giggle. Suddenly, I'm tongue-tied. I say, 'So er, come in, um, do you want a coffee or' – I nearly say the immortal dollybird phrase 'something stronger' but manage to stop myself – 'or a beer or something?'

Tom waves the plastic bag he's carrying and says, 'A client gave me a bottle of red this morning. We could open that if you like.'

I blurt, 'What, a hamster went and bought you some Pinotage?'

Tom says mock-huffily, 'No actually. It was the hamster's Mummy.'

I realise I'm hovering, so I beckon Tom towards the kitchen. There's a rattle as Fatboy beats it through the cat flap. Tom trots obediently along behind me. 'So, how is your mum?' he says dutifully.

'She's okay, thanks,' I say, deciding that my mother is *not* going to hijack tonight.

'Yeah?' says Tom, encouragingly.

'My Nan is looking after her,' I say shortly as I uncork the wine and glug glug at least half of it into two huge green goblets. (I bought them specially as Marcus's wine glasses are tiddly. In keeping with the rest of him, boom boom.) Then, being me, I break my vow immediately and tell Tom the Curious Tale of the Secret Granny Meetings.

'I was seeing my mum three times a week. Why didn't

180

she tell me?' I squeak, hating myself for caring.

Tom looks puzzled. 'It's a weird one,' he says. 'I might be wrong, but it sounds manipulative. A power thing.'

I am silent. I take a large slug of wine. Call me naive but to this second I've imagined that I've always done mostly as I pleased, despite my mother. But. Now Tom mentions it, the possibility dawns that I've always done as *she's* pleased – and if I haven't she's brought me sharply to book by, ooh I don't know, slicing her wrists.

I say slowly, 'Do you think so?'

Tom scrutinises my face and says quickly, 'I don't know your mother, it's just a guess.'

I pause. Then I say falteringly, 'She does love to be the centre of attention. But maybe she just didn't think. Or thought I wouldn't be interested.' Then I realise Tom and I have been sitting at the kitchen table discussing my attention-loving mother for a full twenty-eight minutes. Foiled again! 'Anyway, enough about her,' I say brightly. 'Tell me about your parents.'

Tom shifts in his chair and says teasingly, 'I'm not sure you want to know.'

I didn't but now I'm intrigued: 'Tell me!' I say.

So he does. In about three seconds flat. Tom's parents divorced when he was five. His mother re-married three years later and he regards his step-father as his real father. His mother is 'a diamond' and his stepfather is 'a great bloke'. He doesn't see 'Mum's first husband'. The way he says it, I know he doesn't want to discuss it further.

'Why?' I gasp.

He shrugs and tells me that they never got on.

'What!' I exclaim. 'Not even when you were four? What's not to like!' I see Tom's discomfort and add quickly, 'You don't have to tell me.'

Tom laughs and says, 'It's nothing sinister! He just wasn't too keen on kids. It wasn't just me. He was the same with my brother and sister. Mum was, has always been I suppose, liberal. You know, all for girls playing with tractors and boys crying, and her husband was the opposite. Girls should wear pink and dress their dolls and boys should wear blue and dress as cowboys.'

I pour myself another vat of red. Tom has hardly touched his, but I top up his goblet anyway to make myself seem less of a wino. 'So,' I say – desperate to know the answer but aware I'm treading on Jerry Springerish ground – 'did you like to' – as the words form I remind myself that tactful restraint is of the essence – 'wear pink then?'

I wince at my own crassness. Tom laughs. 'And what if I did?' he says, raising an eyebrow.

'Nothing, nothing. Nothing at all,' I blabber, thinking – I should have known. He's gay. The nice ones always are. If they're not married. Or both. I knew there was a catch. And now I've offended him. I am so preoccupied with my narrow, booze-confused train of thought that I don't hear Tom's next comment and have to ask him to repeat it. And it turns out that four-year-old Tom loved painting until the day his mother's first husband snapped his brush in half and smacked him round the face and then he went off painting and hasn't painted since.

'That's terrible!' I gasp, the gothic tragedy of the situation intensifying in direct proportion to my alcohol consumption.

'Not really,' grins Tom. 'My mother booted him out two days later, and we all lived happily ever after. Shall we go and get a pizza?'

I nod and say demurely: 'We could even splash out and get two.'

We hail a cab to Pizza Express because Tom reckons there's no way I can walk in those shoes and the conversation progresses to the certainty that Scooby Doo was much better off without that upstart Scrappy and that even if you can't do an accurate impression of Scooby Doo – or indeed any other cartoon or TV character – the fact that you've devoted the valuable time and painstaking effort makes you worthy of much respect. Tom does a superb

Scooby Doo which I force him to repeat about nine times. And he concedes that my Marge Simpson is second to none. My prowess wins me the last dough ball.

I notice that Tom doesn't talk with his mouth full and when it's time to pay (the staff start stacking chairs on tables) he doesn't do an air-squiggle. We clatter noisily back to the flat and I know it's going to be a good night.

Chapter 23

I've never believed that what goes around comes around. To judge from personal experience, the Wheel of Fortune has a flat tyre. So I don't entrust retribution to a medieval caprice. I implement it myself. This is why I recently tore a helpline number out of the *News Of The World*'s problem page and pinned it to Marcus's noticeboard. As soon as he emerged from his room last Sunday morning, I scampered into the kitchen, drew up a chair, and feigned absorption in the *Spectator*. Marcus took one glance at my reading material and became instantly suspicious. Fifty seconds later he spotted the 'Manhood Too Small?' cutting, ripped it from the wall, and stuffed it in the bin.

I was hoping for histrionics but instead he leant heavily against the sink, folded his brawny arms, and stared at me in menacing silence. Although I knew this was an intimidatory technique he'd filched from a Robert De Niro film, it worked. I was starting to squirm when Michelle marched in, cake-faced and big-haired, mewling for black coffee. I legged it, puffing with relief. But I puffed too soon. Because Marcus too is the live and let die type. And he chose to wreak his grim revenge on Tuesday evening.

Tom and I had stumbled into the flat, squabbling over the relative merits of Cadbury's and Galaxy chocolate when I clapped eyes on the least welcome sight I'd seen since Fatboy's last puke (from a shelf, as it happens).

Marcus, sitting at his oak veneer table, flicking through the latest issue of *Musclebound* and sipping a banana milkshake. I stopped dead in shock, elation shrivelling.

Tom veered to a halt behind me. Marcus smiled like a shark. 'Well, well, well,' he said in a portentous tone, 'so *this* is Tom.' I half expected him to cackle and add, 'Hello, my pretty!' I was petrified.

'Tom,' I said trying to sound calm, 'this is my landlord Marcus.'

Tom, the innocent, grinned and said, 'Hi!'

I – the guilty – twisted my hands and said, 'Marcus, you're up late.'

Marcus smiled another hammerhead smile. 'Couldn't sleep. But hey' – spreading his hands wide helplessly – 'everything's for a purpose! Now I can chinwag with you two.' *Chinwag.* What is he, an eighty-year-old woman? He continued, 'I've heard all about you, Tom.'

What! No he hasn't! I looked at Marcus in horror, 'I don't think I've mentioned Tom to you,' I said. The edge in my voice made Tom glance at me.

Marcus laughed. 'Playing coy,' he chortled, nodding at Tom. 'She always does this with her men! Every week!'

This was serious. I blurted: 'Marcus, stop teasing. Please!'

The please hurt and Marcus knew it. He gazed at me blankly for a second before adding, 'Only this morning she was in the bathroom, practis—'

Tom and I interrupted him at the same time. Tom began: 'I'm not sure I want to—' but I spoke loudest: 'Marcus, much as I'd love to stay and chat over your Tums And Bums magazine, I'm feeling exhausted and I've got to get up in, oh, five and a half hours' time, so, Tom's just about to leave so ah, say goodbye to Tom.'

I manhandled Tom out of the kitchen. What else could I do? Wrestle him into my bedroom? Although I'll admit that until Marcus made me sound like a slapper, that *was* the plan. 'My men' indeed! As I steered Tom into the hall I whispered, 'Sorry about him, he must have OD'd on the steroids. He pops them like Smarties.' This was – as far as I know – a lie, but I was desperate.

Tom replied solemnly, 'Must have.' He paused, then said, 'Hyper, isn't he?'

I nodded vigorously, 'God, yes.' There was another awkward pause during which I cursed Marcus to hell. He must have had tuition from Michelle. Not that he needed it.

I smiled stiffly at Tom and said, 'Well, thanks. It was really nice to see you.'

Tom smiled back, 'And you. I enjoyed it.' Pause three. 'I'd better go. I'll give you a ring, sometime.'

Sometime? That means never. 'Definitely,' I said, drooping.

Tom bent and kissed me swiftly on the cheek. Miles away from my mouth – practically on my ear. I kissed him back, feasting miserably on the scent of his aftershave, and waved him out of the door. Then I went straight to bed, pulling the duvet over my head to block out the sound of Marcus whistling the *Pretty Woman* theme tune.

Lizzy refuses to believe that anything is amiss. 'I'm sure Tom realised Marcus was joking,' she says, making me want to strangle her.

'He said I bring home a different man each week!' I shriek. 'That's not a joke! That's libel.'

Laetitia, who is listening, snaps, 'Slander! Unless it's true. Rah ha ha!'

I smile sweetly at her and curl my hands into claws under my desk. One day, when I am rich and successful, I will sponsor a tarantula at London Zoo and name it Laetitia Stokes. I confide this ambition to Tina who is in a rare sunny mood and says brightly, 'I bet it only costs a tenner, you could do it tomorrow.'

This cheers me up so when Laetitia pops out for a cigarette, I ring London Zoo and am put through to lifewatch membership and adoption enquiries. To my dismay, a 'whole tarantula' costs £70 although I can have shares in one for £35. I'll save up.

'And could I *name* it?' I ask slyly.

'I'm afraid not,' is the polite reply, 'because you're adopting the species rather than the individual. So no name would appear on the board. You could name it privately though.'

What's the point in that! I thank the zoo man for his time and replace the receiver.

The rest of Wednesday comes and goes and Tom doesn't call. I am tempted to call him on Thursday but can't as I am out of the office for most of the day accosting women in the street for an eight-page section Laetitia has commissioned entitled 'The Worst Way I Dumped Him'. I know exactly why she's commissioned it. Counts are in short supply and Laetitia has been stepping out with a banker. His family bought their own furniture and – even though Laetitia's did too – it grates and she's looking to punish him. Poor man. I'm stuck with doing her research. I skid back into the office at five thirty. 'Did anyone ring?' I enquire hopefully.

'Your mother,' replies Laetitia shortly. 'How did it go?'

I nod, 'Fine, fine, I got some great quotes.' Laetitia ignores me. I trundle wearily to my desk and call my mother.

'I saw my *male* nurse from the clinic today,' are her first words. Heaven help him, so she did.

'How was it?' I ask warily, then add, 'Actually, don't tell me now, tell me later – I've booked the restaurant for twenty past eight. Are you and Nana still up for it?'

My mother replies in her best teachery tone: 'Good thank you, and if by "up for it" you mean are we still planning to join you for dinner, the answer is yes.'

I giggle and say, 'Don't be pompous, Mummy. I'm not one of your children. I'll see you later.'

I'm about to put the phone down when she squeaks, 'Is it smart? What shall I wear?' I pause and recall that I told her the restaurant was in 'Islington' when to be accurate I should have said 'Holloway'.

'It's smart-casual,' I say evasively. 'See ya!' I sigh with relief and dig out my tape recorder.

I am looking for an excuse to postpone transcribing when – hallelujah – the phone rings. 'Hello!' I say merrily, praying it isn't my mother again.

'Helen?' says Tom.

'*Hiiiiiiiiii!*' I say. When he asks how I am I can tell from his voice that he's grinning. Wolf teeth. Rrrrr! 'Fine,' I say, wondering if calling a woman two days after a date classifies a man as wet. 'And you?'

He tells me he's well, and he wondered if I was free sometime over the weekend. This is annoying. Can't he be more specific? I mean, if I say I'm free on Saturday night and then he says actually he meant Sunday, what kind of a loser does that make me? But, at the same time, he's so patently keen. It detracts from his allure. I can't help but find it offputting. I am hit by a brilliant idea.

'Are you free tomorrow night?' I say. 'A bunch of us are going out for a drink. Tina will be there. You remember Tina, don't you?'

I can hear the smile again, as Tom replies: 'Tequila Night. How could I forget?'

For the second time in five minutes I replace the receiver, relieved. Safety in numbers. But I am also disappointed. Why didn't he have the decency to wait a few more days and make me sweat? It's highly unsettling and I brood about it until I realise it's six thirty and way past going home time. I lock my tape recorder in my drawer. 'I'll start transcribing first thing tomorrow,' I shout to Laetitia on my way out. She ignores me.

I pull up to my mother's house bang on eight and see Nana Flo nosing from behind the net curtain. I hoot and wave. A good ten minutes later she and my mother bustle out. Nana is wearing a faded purple coat that may well be made from thistles. Her grey hair is high and brittle under her thin headscarf. My mother is powdered and lipsticked and

188

carrying a shiny black handbag. I wonder how long it's been since my grandmother ate in a restaurant. 'You both look nice!' I say, hoping to set the tone.

Nana grunts. My mother says 'Do I?'

I tell them the place we're going to is called Nid Ting. 'What kind of name is that?' says Nana Flo.

'A Thai name,' I reply, wondering why I bother. I park round the corner.

'Grotty round here, isn't it?' says my mother loudly.

'But wouldn't it be boring if everywhere was like Muswell Hill!' I say cheerily, through gritted teeth.

We plod in and – to my relief – are given a cosy table in the corner. Nana Flo looks at the red patterned carpet and the pink tablecloths and the windowsill buddhas and purses her lips. When the waitress offers to take her coat, Nana clutches it to her and snaps 'No thank you!' She sniffs suspiciously at the complimentary bowl of prawn crackers. 'They're Thai crisps, Nana,' I say, 'prawn cocktail flavour.'

My mother munches away happily and says, 'Do you know, I think I'll have a glass of wine!'

Nana surveys the other diners and tuts, specifically at a skinny man sporting a pierced chin and baggy jeans. 'Ruffian!' she hisses. 'It's a disgrace! And would you look at his trousers. I wouldn't mind but I never saw such a waste of material! Puts me in mind of that ragamuffin who showed up this morning, Cecelia.'

Refreshing though it is to hear Nana Flo's radical opinions I seize at the chance to shut her up. 'What ragamuffin?' I say, addressing my mother.

'My nurse!' she replies.

'Ohhhh!' I say, which is all the encouragement she requires to embark on a monologue as long as the history of the world. My mother's nurse is not *at* all what one would expect. In fact, when he rang the doorbell she assumed he was 'a thug'. Only after inspecting his ID and ringing the clinic to check his authenticity did she let him in. (Luckily for him, when he arrived Nana Flo was at Asda.) But you could hardly blame her. A goatee and long sideburns! An earring in his ear! A rucksack! Army trousers! How was she to know! She'd expected a lady in a white uniform! And his name was Cliff!

Surprisingly, Cliff was 'charming'. Extremely chatty, very concerned, sorry to hear about the razor incident and interested to know what happened and how my mother feels now and to see the wound and inspect the special box she bought to keep her pills in. Eager to be shown photographs of Morrie, intrigued at how they met (Cliff knows people who met at a dance too – at a dance hall called The Ministry), and so understanding about the horrors of car maintenance (Cliff also knows nothing about cars, prefers to cycle, lets his partner deal with all that, how *does* one manage when that person is gone?).

Cliff can't imagine how hard it is for my mother to cope on her own, tell him, how *did* she manage before she met Morrie? Captivated to hear about the tiny room she rented after leaving home and how she painted it herself – quite a thing in those days, although these days, absolutely, anything goes. He suspects she's being modest – she sounds so resourceful! Totally impressed to hear about her newfound financial prowess – what an achievement! But still, must be difficult not to feel resentful towards someone for dying – how *does* she feel? Asked to be shown around—

When my mother says Cliff asked to be shown around, Nana Flo – who has been quietly yumming down her steamed fish and plain rice while affecting huffy dislike – snaps, 'Casing the joint!'

My mouth drops open. 'I'm sorry?' I say.

'Florence watched *Starsky & Hutch* on satellite this afternoon,' explains my mother. 'You enjoyed it, didn't you, Florence?'

Nana Flo shrugs and says grudgingly, 'Not bad, compared to some of the modern rubbish.'

All of which keeps you pinned to the sofa, I say in my

head. Aloud, I say, 'He does sound a bit nosy, Mum. Are you sure he's okay?'

My mother is most defensive. Cliff is a lovely boy.

'He smoked drugs in the house!' bawls Nana Flo.

I frown at my mother who says pityingly, 'Florence, they're called *rolos*. They're normal cigarettes, but home-made. And he asked my permission.' My mother looks beseechingly at my grandmother but – to quote my old form teacher – no answer is the stern reply.

So we hear more about Cliff. He is what you'd call headstrong, now she considers. Rushed her, when she was talking about how it's harder for a young woman to meet a young man at an organised dance nowadays, it's all raves and lap-top dancing, isn't it? – he hurried her along at that point – but otherwise, a pleasant young man. Keen to hear about *you*, Helen. He said it would be nice to have a chat with you so I gave him your number. He's not suitable as a boyfriend, although if he shaved and removed the earring and ironed his shirt perhaps—

'What!' I shout, loudly enough for the couple at the next table to start eavesdropping. 'Why should this do-gooding trendy wendy want to call *me*?'

My mother looks uncomfortable. She twiddles her noodles round her fork and says, 'To talk about *me*, probably.'

I sigh and say, 'Oh, okay,' although secretly I'm not convinced.

There is silence while my mother clears her plate. Then she says, 'He said he imagined that one reason I'd want to stay well was because you depend on me.'

I nearly spit out a prawn: 'That's a laugh – he doesn't even know me!' I squeak.

My mother replies excitedly, 'Exactly! That's what I said! I said you were very independent.'

I nod, pleased. My mother takes a sip of water and clears her throat. She carefully blots her mouth with her pink napkin. Then she says shyly, 'Helen, if you need any money you know you can ask.'

Two hours later, I drop them off and heave a sigh as Nana's purple coat disappears into the house. In my grandmother's own words, the evening 'wasn't so bad, considering'. At one point I tempted fate by observing, 'I see you've eaten all your fish and rice, Nana.' To which she replied tartly, 'I don't like to see food go to waste.' She then gave me a look which said 'even if it is foreign muck' but I appreciated the effort it took to stifle the words. My father was mentioned once. My mother cried suddenly, 'Wouldn't it be nice if Morrie was here too – then we'd be a family!' I didn't like to say that if my father was here too, we'd all be out the door and up to the Savoy Grill in a shot. Or, more likely, we wouldn't be out together in the first place. So I said nothing.

Nana Flo said curtly, 'Please God he's looking down on us' – a curiously sentimental comment. No one mentioned him again. I am so surprised at having enjoyed myself – even if it was in a masochistic way – that when I return to the flat I slam the front door and wake up Marcus. I know this, because as I stand in the bathroom wiping off the layers of make-up, he bursts from his bedroom and storms pettishly down the hall to get a glass of water (I hear the furious whoosh of the tap.) The perfect end to a not so bad considering night.

Chapter 24

Some days I think I may as well be fifty. I'm constantly tired. I haven't been to a club in about twenty years. And I've gone without sex for so long I wouldn't be surprised if it's closed up. I see Friday night as a chance to remedy two of these complaints.

The evening kicks off when Tina, Lizzy and I pile out of the office and into the loos to tart up at 6.01 p.m. 'Strictly speaking,' I say to Lizzy who feels guilty about quitting on time, 'we did an extra thirty-one minutes, so I'd feel good if I were you.'

Tina regards me smugly: 'The rabid ambition wore off then,' she says.

I retort, 'It's not what you do, it's what you're seen to be doing. And when Laetitia left the office at five forty-five I was slaving over my desk.'

I smirk and dig my eyelash curlers out of my hotch-potch of a make-up bag (my eyelashes are unnaturally straight and if I don't curl them I look bald.) Lizzy opens a metal case that looks like it might contain a gun, retrieves a paintbrush from one of its compartments, and fluff-wuffs a waft of powder all over her face. Tina starts from scratch – carefully wiping off the day's shine with cotton wool pads and cleanser. A mere touch-up isn't good enough for our lord and master Adrian, I think sourly. I know it's mean of me but she's so *precious* about him.

'I'm looking forward to meeting Adrian,' I say, in an attempt to combat my own nastiness.

'Good,' says Tina. She adds lightly, 'Do try not to say anything offensive.'

I widen my eyes as far as they'll go and say, 'Cheeky cow! How about *you* try not to say anything offensive to Tom. No weeing jokes, okay?'

Tina smiles, says 'deal!' and turns back to the mirror.

'*You'll* like Tom,' I say, addressing Lizzy, 'I'm sure you will.'

Lizzy beams into the mirror and says earnestly, 'I can't wait to meet him, he sounds lovely.'

I smile my gratitude, finish my patch-up job and am instantly bored. 'How's the new flat?' I ask Lizzy, who has just bought an airy loft apartment in Limehouse.

'Oh!' she says, 'wonderful! The view of the Thames! I could look at it for ever. It's so beautiful.'

I was under the impression that the Thames was a stinky brown river, but I simper, 'How lovely.' Maybe it looks picturesque from a distance. And anyway, what am I carping about? *My* bedroom overlooks the driveway and Marcus's metallic blue RAV 4. I wonder if there are any flats for sale in her block. 'Aren't you nervous about having a mortgage?' I say.

Lizzy tilts her head to one side and says, 'Not really. Mum's a financial advisor. She helped me plan for it.' Of course she did.

'And have you got much furniture?'

No, not yet. Lizzy wants to take it slowly. She'd rather build up a select number of 'signature pieces' (whatever they are) than a hoard of clutter. Last weekend, she tells us, she saw a brilliant 'Line chaise' (again, search me) for £650 from the Conran Shop.

'Six hundred and fifty squids!' shouts Tina. 'Are you mental?!'

Lizzy knows it's a tad indulgent but it is '*So* sleek.' And it would look sensational against the maple wood flooring.

I tell her if she wants a line chaise she should go for it and skimp on other luxuries – a bed, for instance. 'And what are the neighbours like?' I say.

Lizzy pulls a funny face. *Some* of the neighbours are friendly, she tells us. She had a long chat with Number 28 only yesterday. Number 28 told her that Number 26 was 'a dealer'. 'Oh!' tinkled Lizzy, 'an antiques dealer?' No, replied Number 28 kindly, 'a drugs dealer'. By the time Tina and I have stopped sniggering, we're at the pub.

Brian is the first man (if he qualifies) to arrive. He dutifully pecks Tina and me on the cheek and then turns to Lizzy. He gazes on her like an art lover looks at a rare painting and lifts her hand to his lips and kisses it. Lizzy giggles and tucks her hair behind her ear. I can't help smiling, even though the gallant gentleman is wearing a patterned jumper and grey shoes. Tina also looks. She obviously regrets the 'Brian's an arse!' remark because she leaps up and asks him, 'What can I get you?' But Brian insists on buying. He walks to the bar to purchase a still mineral water, a Becks, and an orange juice ('Tina, aren't you feeling well?').

I look at Lizzy and she seems visibly to swell with pride. 'Aw!' says Tina – lighting her fifth cigarette in ten minutes – 'young love!' I shoot her a fierce glance – Brian's knocking on eighty! – but neither she nor Lizzy notice the blunder. Brian returns from the bar and I am limbering up to despise him for being teetotal when I see he's bought himself a pint. I glance at Lizzy for signs of disapproval but there are none. She strokes his arm lovingly. 'You two!' says Tina, 'get a room!'

Brian laughs. To my surprise he has a deeply dirty boyish laugh. He settles down close to Lizzy and addresses the table in general: 'So, how's work?'

Happily, we are whisked from small talk hell by the arrival of the Messiah, aka, Adrian. Tina jumps up to greet him so fast she spills her drink. 'That's a first,' I say snidely. She ignores me.

'Everyone,' she announces formally as if she's

introducing him at an AA meeting, 'This is my boyfriend Adrian. He's an architect.' Adrian smiles a shiny white smile and shakes everyone's hand. Mine is suddenly sweaty so I wipe it on my trousers before my turn.

'Hello,' I say, thinking, wow. I take it all back. He *is* the Messiah.

Adrian is exceptionally easy on the eye. Exceptionally! He is wearing a tailored navy suit, crisp lilac shirt, and deep pink tie. His golden blond hair is as curly as a cherub's and you expect blue eyes but his are brown with long, girlish lashes. His smile is bright and wide against his light tan. 'Oh Tina!' I say approvingly, 'I believe the hype!' Adrian laughs and so does Tina. She then speeds off to fetch him a red wine.

Lizzy nuzzles closer to Brian and chirrups, 'We've heard *so* much about you!'

Adrian smiles at her and says, 'All good, I hope?'

Lizzy giggles and says, 'Aha!'

Tina rushes back with Adrian's red wine which she places lovingly before him. Jesus, it's like *The King and I*.

'So,' jokes Adrian, slapping a hand on Tina's Miu Miu clad thigh and giving it a fond shake, 'what have you been saying about me?'

Tina looks up startled and says, 'Nothing! Why?'

Adrian replies teasingly, 'Apparently, you've been telling your friends all manner of secrets – and I'd very much like to know what they are.' He lifts his hand from her lap and starts gently massaging the back of her neck and she shivers with pleasure. I don't wish to sound like Mother Superior but it's obscene. Flaunting themselves! Can't they wait? I decide to cut short the public foreplay session.

In a firm loud voice I say, 'She's told us you're handsome, successful, witty and all, but she's been most disappointing and hasn't revealed anything in the least bit private. So you're safe!'

I expect Tina to be irked at my grinchlike behaviour but she beams at me. So does Adrian. He rewards Tina with a kiss and murmurs, 'The truth will out!' Cultured too, it's sickening.

'Alright,' I say, 'enough of that!'

By the time Tom turns up – soon after seven thirty as promised – the conversation has turned to Lizzy's bizarre biscuit habit. Lizzy doesn't like to eat 'empty calories' (even though I reasonably argue that you could justify eating 'empty calories' by substituting them for 'boring calories' – just replace your green salad with a chocolate Hobnob and large multivitamin). Oh, no, Lizzy would never do that. Although she does surrender to the occasional craving. In which case she goes to the remarkable trouble of 'breaking a plain digestive into eight pieces and eating one piece per hour'. We are agog. 'What, *on* the hour?' asks Tina, fascinated.

'But then you're thinking about this one mingy biscuit all day!' I squeak. 'Doesn't it make you obsessed? Wouldn't it be better to wolf it down and get it over with?'

We erupt into loud debate about our own biscuit habits. Tina can have a packet of biscuits sitting on her bedside table for literally weeks and not even feel a twinge as biscuits 'do nothing' for her. If she has a weakness it's for smoky bacon crisps and (inexplicably) 'they're good for you'. *I* can devour fifteen biscuits in one fell swoop and still have room for pudding although to be fair, it does depend on the individual biscuit. And no I do not feel guilty. 'I'd feel guilty if I killed someone,' I say sternly to Lizzy who is gasping and shuddering like a landbound halibut and obviously needs the crime to be put in perspective.

Adrian laughs at this and says, 'So we're discussing biscuit eating as a moral issue!'

Brian – the earnest old goat – pipes up with 'You say that, but in fact there are many women, and indeed men, who *would* describe themselves as feeling "bad" for eating a biscuit, even "terrible" – and wouldn't you say, the use of such highly charged emotional language is enormously significant in terms of their self-judgement and in consequence, their self-estee—' No doubt he would have rambled on forever if Tom hadn't picked this perfect moment to walk into the pub. I greet him joyously (apart from anything he looks gorgeous) and Brian is forced to terminate his diatribe. Adrian, for one, looks relieved.

I introduce Tom to everyone – 'and you remember Tina but we'll leave it there, shall we?' – he smiles, kisses, shakes hands and insists on getting the next round.

'You know Tom already, I take it,' says Adrian to Tina, quickly, before Brian can resume his lecture.

'I only met him once,' says Tina nervously – aware that I am monitoring every word and am willing to douse her in beer if she even dares to *hint* at a urine joke – 'we went out with Helen for a quick drink.'

Adrian is intrigued. He narrows his gorgeous eyes and says, 'So why do we have to "leave it there?"'

I have no intention of allowing Tina to blurt out the hilarious tale of my alcohol-induced incontinence so I interrupt: 'Because I drank too much and got a bit tipsy.'

I stare at Tina in a way that I intend to appear benign to everyone else and threatening to her. It works. Instead of declaiming me as a drunken liar, she says meekly, 'Helen was embarrassed. She doesn't like to be reminded of it.' I beam at her.

Adrian suggests, 'Then it can't have been *that* quick a drink,' but Tina insists – as poker faced as a guard at Buckingham Palace – 'Helen's like me, she doesn't drink much so her tolerance is low.' Frankly I am surprised her nose doesn't grow to Concorde size and smash through the pub window. I feel the rise of a giggle fit so I smirk gratefully at Tina and gabble that I'm going to the loo.

When I return, Tina and Adrian are deep in touchy-feely conversation, and Tom is chatting to Lizzy and Brian. My heart lurches in fear, *please* don't let Lizzy be ranting on about yurt weekends and Jungian psychoanalysis. Please let Tom like her, and please let her like Tom. (Brian is on his own.) Happily, they turn out to be discussing Cornwall.

Brian was born in Morwenstow – right on the coast – and although he's lived in London for twenty years he misses the tranquillity.

'Doesn't t'ai chi compensate?' I say wickedly.

He smiles and replies, 'A little. But above all I find t'ai chi extremely useful if you suffer from pointy foot syndrome.' He bursts out laughing as that flap-mouthed ratbag Lizzy glides to the Ladies and I cough-splutter into my drink.

In a very small voice I say 'I am *so* so sorry.'

Brian waves away my apology and says, 'Forgiven, forgotten, just teasing.'

I know Tom is about to cry 'What?' so I say quickly, 'Do you do, er, any sport, Tom?' It's a nerdy question but it's also an emergency.

'I run. And box,' he says obligingly, 'although I'm not that good.'

I exclaim, 'Rubbish, I'm sure you're brilliant!' mainly to sweep the conversation way and beyond the pointy foot episode.

'Oh?' says Tom, bestowing me with a sunshine smile, 'and why are you so sure?' He is looking at me in a way that would melt chocolate.

I jiggle my foot to stop myself blushing. Then I return the look, playfully squeeze his upper arm, and purr, 'You look quite hard – ooh you are hard!' To be honest, I'm useless at playing the vamp. I'm invariably thwarted by loose paving stones, dogs on heat, and stubborn revolving doors. But tonight I am shameless. I bite my lip suggestively (I hope) and say under my breath, 'Mm, *very* hard' and pray to God that Tom doesn't burst out laughing at me.

Tom puts his mouth to my ear and mutters casually, 'Try me.'

My heart does a massive thump – either there's a rabbit's foot lodged in my chest or I've got palpitations and need to see a doctor. I hold his ice-blue gaze and my cheeks burn and I murmur, 'Try and stop me.' By this point, Lizzy and Brian are tactful enough to be talking amongst themselves.

I move closer to Tom until our thighs are brushing and my heart hammers. It *is* lust but not pure lust, there's something else in there too. I can't work it out. We sit in the pub and flirt disgracefully till chucking out time, we go to a poky little club in Soho and shout above the music and touch hands and still I can't work it out. Tina and Adrian go home because they're exhausted and Adrian's working tomorrow, Lizzy announces she's got to be up early to do her Christmas shopping (only three weeks to go!) and I still can't work it out.

Tom and I roll into the street and hold hands and eat revolting kebabs and my heart is still racing and I still can't work it out. And then I spit my kebab into a bin and he pulls me to him and we kiss and kiss and clutch at each other and the rabbit foot is thumping at ninety miles an hour and we kiss and kiss and we're kissing and kissing and then I realise and I pull away for air. It's fear. I don't know why and I don't know if Tom knows but he doesn't say anything. He kisses me slowly and strokes my hair. Then he hails a taxi.

And then he hails another one for himself.

Chapter 25

When I was at college and a stranger to grim reality, I briefly suffered from a surfeit of confidence. This had much to do with escaping my parents. Also, the majority of students were present to extend their sex education so if you wanted action you could usually find it. Jabba the Hutt would have pulled. Indeed, I snogged him myself on several occasions.

So it was a shock when I went on the prowl with a girl named Beatrice who was as plain as a blank wall, and the guy I'd set my night on bought us both drinks but asked *her* to dance. The next morning Luke visited and – planting the seed of my misplaced passion – brought Marcus along. I decided to chew over the riddle in his presence. I was, no doubt, hoping that horniness was contagious. 'Do you think,' I said as I spooned peanut butter out of the jar, 'that he was playing hard to get? Using Beatrice to make me jealous?'

Marcus followed the spoon's progression to my mouth with fascinated revulsion, and declared (the first and last words he spoke to me for five years): 'Sweetheart, there's no mystery – he fancied Beatrice! If a bloke fancies you, he'll do you!'

I am reminded of these poetic words at 3 a.m. on Saturday as I pay the taxi driver and walk to the front door, alone. Yes, I pulled away from Tom first. I'm not sure about him anyway. But why did he have to follow *my* lead like a thick puppy? Hasn't he got a mind of his own? I flounce into the flat and am about to karate kick open my

201

bedroom door when I see a note stuck to it: 'Flat Meeting, lounge, Sat morning, 10 a.m. Attendance compulsory.' And I think, living with Marcus is like living under martial law. I scrumple up the note and set my alarm for 2 p.m.

I fall asleep and dream the empty house dream. I am still being pursued by baddies, and still hiding in cupboards, but having been there forty times I am now used to it. I'm hunched in a wardrobe and someone, something, is thumping up the stairs, thump! thump! and now they're banging on the wardrobe door, bang! bang! louder and louder. I wake up with a start, sweating, and hear bang! bang! Marcus is banging on my door and singing 'It's nine forty-five! This is your wake up call!' I hurl a boot at the door and pull the pillow over my head. Marcus keeps banging, bang! bang!

'All *right*!' I scream, 'I'm coming to your frigging meeting, leave me alone!'

I drag myself out of bed, muttering. I pull on my dressing gown, plod to the kitchen, and make myself a coffee. There's no milk in my section of the fridge (there's nothing in my section of the fridge) so I steal from Marcus's. There are *two* milk cartons in his section and propped against them is a note reading 'I have put bleach in one of these cartons and only I know which one.' I am tempted to replace it with a note reading 'Fatboy has peed in both of these cartons . . .' but then I realise one of the cartons is unopened. Berk.

Luke has also been turfed out of bed to attend. He looks rumpled and tired. 'Do you want a coffee?' I say.

'Please!' he says.

'Okay,' I say, 'the mug's on the shelf, the coffee's in the jar, and the milk's in the fridge.'

He looks crestfallen and says 'Oh!' so I pinch his cheek fondly, sing 'only joking!' and make him a coffee. Fatboy is also up, stretching and yawning and prrrp!ing for break-fast. We're used to Marcus's Flat Meetings. He always hauls us in for a bollocking when our slobbiness reaches a

202

crescendo and we always say that we're sorry and we won't do it again and continue exactly as we were.

So it's a shock when Marcus tells me he wants me out of the flat by the end of the week.

'But I've got nowhere to go!' I bleat.

'Not my problem,' says Marcus coldly. I stare stonily at a black hair poking out of Marcus's nose – I refuse to cry or argue as nothing would please him more. Luke tries to stand up for me but I don't want him to be booted out too so I shush him.

'Marcus,' I lie, 'you're doing me a great favour. And you've got a black hair poking out of your nose. It's like a hamster's tooth.' And I stalk out of the lounge, into my room, and flop on the bed.

I don't believe it. I don't believe it but I should. Of course this was going to happen. How could it *not* happen? Marcus may be a grasping tightwad but he's also as proud as, well, as a man with a ripply back. I know this. And yet, ever since he rebuffed me I've been kicking him where it hurts. Although it does require careful aim with a target that small. See what I mean? Did I expect him *not* to retaliate? I suppose that I was so caught up in personally effecting his eternal punishment that the consequences didn't occur to me.

I look back and I don't think I could have stopped baiting him even if I'd wanted to. I have this stagnating pool of hatred for him that kills rationality, and I don't know why. If I'm honest – something I'm not very good at – what did he really do wrong apart from trying me for size and deciding I didn't fit? (And likewise.) Marcus's brittle ego was bound to snap one day, and it has. I should be steeled for it, but I'm not. I'm scared. Again. A timid little girl-mouse. I should rejoice in my enforced freedom but I can't. Living with Marcus may be purgatory but it's safer than striking out alone. Living with Marcus is like being stuck in a job you hate. You know you should stop bitching about it and resign and find something better but the terror of what's out there constrains you. But now Marcus has made me redundant so I have no choice.

I call Tom.

I didn't intend to. After the meeting I think about last night and decide that the fear I felt was instinctive. A warning. You see, I like Tom. I feel drawn to him like a sailor to a mermaid on a rock. Tom's all fuck-me eyes and silvery tail, his siren promise drawing me slowly in. He's so squarely there for me, how could I resist? Thing is, I'm unsure if I'd despise him more if his eagerness was real or an act. At least I know where I am with the likes of Jasper. There's no pretence. Men who behave willing and artless and forever yours are myth. Maybe I want to be deceived. But I paused and Tom ran away. Slipped into the Soho sea and vanished. What kind of forever is that?

I think all this, and then I think bollocks and call him anyway.

And the bastard isn't in!

I call my mother instead. 'Nana Flo wants a word with you!' she says, before I can utter a syllable. I am about to ask why, but am handed over to my grandmother on the 'w'.

'Hello?' she shrills.

'Hello, Nana, how are you?' I say.

'Well thank you. I saw a very interesting programme on the television last night.' Hm. Where's this leading.

'Oh yes?' I say politely.

'About freezing your eggs,' says Nana. Odd. She doesn't know what I eat and has never betrayed any sign of caring.

'But can't I just buy them when I need—' I start, but my grandmother interrupts:

'Freezing *your* eggs! Putting your eggs on ice! You're not courting! You've not settled down! You're not getting any younger! Your eggs are dying inside you! It looked a very simple operation on the television!'

I thank Nana for her concern, tell her I'll consider it, and ask to be put back to my mother. My mother's first words are, 'Nothing to do with me!' Aided and abetted though, I'll warrant. But I let this pass as I have a more pressing matter to discuss.

My impending homelessness. 'You can come and stay with us!' she cries. I can just imagine it. Three witches and an orange cat. It would be like living in a tin drum. I tell her it's a sweet offer but no thanks. I spend from noon till five moping and grizzling and grooming Fatboy – who is desperate to escape and claws at the door – and hoping that a passing fairy godmother will save me from being turfed on to the street or (worse) being forced into cohabitation with Psychomum and the Eggwoman.

At 5.05 there is a loud toot-toot! in the driveway. I peek out of the window and see Ivana Trump emerging from a red Golf. Her hair is as big as a barn. She and Marcus must be going somewhere swish tonight like the Hard Rock Café. How *could* he? Choose her over me? Even though I now hate him and wouldn't shag him for practice, it smarts. Michelle's betrayal pales in comparison. I squeeze out a tear and, for lack of anything better to do, look side-on at my stomach in the mirror. I stick it out as far as it will go – eight months pregnant, the virgin birth!

I stroke it in fascination and remember once, before I knew better, telling Marcus that I wasn't sure but I thought I'd gained weight on my *feet*. I said it as a 'wonder of the world' type statement and he snapped: 'If you eat shit, you look like shit!' I pull my dressing gown together, and slump on my bed. I must have fallen asleep because the next thing I know, Luke is shaking me awake and brandishing the phone in my face. 'Phone!' he shouts, unnecessarily.

'Who?' I mouth.

'Tom!' he shouts.

I snatch it from him. 'Thanks, Luke!'

Tom is friendly but says nothing about last night except he had a good time. Well what's *that* supposed to mean? He enjoyed his kebab? He asks how I am. I start off airy and defiant but the confusion and envy and self-pity merge and, to my absolute mortification, my voice cracks. 'Basically,' I sniffle – a word I usually veto on principle – 'me and Fatboy have got nowhere to go!'

Tom is silent. Then he says, 'What are you and Fatboy doing tonight?' I consider spinning him a glamorous lie.

'Nothing!' I bleat.

'Do you want me to come round?' he says.

I know I should say no to, if nothing else, reclaim a sliver of dignity. But as I've mentioned before I hate the word should. 'Yes!' I say.

'Don't move,' he says, 'I'll be with you in a couple of hours.'

I stand dazed for a picosecond before leaping into action. My first port of call is the fridge where a trusty cucumber – labelled 'this belongs to Marcus' – awaits me. I cut off two generous slices to place over my red puffy eyes and, as a symbolic gesture, stick the rest of it down the waste disposal.

Chapter 26

I've always fancied being psychic – forgo the crystal ball and tasselly skirt and it's a darkly glamorous talent. And I could always hide Fatboy in a cupboard and buy a sleek Burmese with golden eyes and warm chocolate coat to complete the mystical allure. But as I've failed repeatedly to predict the weather or what shoes Michelle is going to be wearing on a certain day, I've had to get over my big-earringed fantasy and resign myself to mental banality. Anyhow, I'd rather be burned at the stake than exchange my orange yob for a pedigree. But hope springs eternal so when the phone rings as I storm around trying to transform my room from a fleapit to a boudoir, I guess: *Tina*. It's Lizzy.

I ask her how the Christmas shopping went. 'All done!' she replies.

'You're amazing,' I tell her, 'amazing. What did you get?' Lizzy reels off an ingenious list of perfect presents. I'm duly admiring. 'I can never think of what to buy people! At least' – and here, I say 'huh' to indicate this is a joke – 'I won't have to worry about what to get Dad this year. Nightmare! Even when I got him a golf book he never read it!'

Lizzy tuts. 'I'm sure you're mistaken! Although Christmasses and birthdays *are* the worst! How are you feeling about all that, Helen?' she says. 'You never talk about it.'

I'm touched, but feel obliged to correct her. 'Lizzy!' I say, 'You're so sweet but stop asking! I'm fine. Mum loves the

Gregorian Moods tape. And Vivienne's told everyone the dramatic tale of how she single-handedly saved my mother from a bloody and violent death so all her ghoulish friends are paying her masses of attention at the moment. And what with Nana Flo, she can't move for people fussing. It's great.'

Lizzy pauses. 'Yes, but what about you?' she insists.

I frown. 'Have you been talking to your psychologist friend again?' I say.

'No!' she says so fast I know it's a lie.

'Liz,' I say, 'I know this is hard for you to understand, but me and Dad, we were never that close. I know you mean well and please don't take this the wrong way, but to be honest I don't feel that much any more so it makes me uncomfortable when you keep asking. Do you see?' There's silence on the other end, so I assume she's nodding.

'Okay,' she says finally, reluctantly. 'But please talk to me if you need to!'

I say, 'okay okay' and then 'I wouldn't chuck Adrian out of bed!'

Lizzy giggles, and says, 'Personally, I prefer Tom.'

Delighted, I reply, 'Oh do you indeed!'

Lizzy says, 'Yes, actually, I do. And I can see he's quite in love with you!' Bless her. Only Lizzy would dare to use the phrase 'in love' without irony. I do adore Lizzy but it amazes me how she manages to breeze along impervious to harsh reality and, furthermore, succeed at every turn. She's a Jane Austen throwback, she really is.

I tell Lizzy what happened. Partly because it's so soul-cleansing to listen to her pretty rose-tinted view of the world instead of my ugly bog-coloured one. Her theory is that maybe Tom wanted to wait until he felt sure *I* was sure. Spare me. 'But he's a man!' I squeal. 'If they fancy you they do you!'

Lizzy says 'What!' in a loud voice. She sounds severely agitated. 'Do you truly believe,' she snaps, 'that you as a woman have no choice in the matter? That you're a passive

208

object? That all men are brutes? Or should be?'

Brutes! Hang on a sec, she's the girly one here. *I* didn't cry at *Sleepless in Seattle*. 'No,' I say defensively, 'you're twisting my words. You're being defensive.' (This is an excellent ruse to win arguments, derived from an e-mail I was sent from someone in the advertising department. Other tips: Make up direct quotes. Say 'You're arguing against yourself.' Or 'Adolf Hitler voiced a similar sentiment.')

Infuriatingly, Lizzy doesn't fall for it. She says calmly, 'You are allergic to being treated with the respect you deserve.' To prove her wrong I inform her that Tom is coming round in approximately twenty minutes, so there. 'So you'd better stop talking nonsense and get off the phone then,' she retorts cutely before saying goodbye. I replace the receiver and then I think, wait a minute, she rang *me*. I smile to myself. She's learning.

The doorbell rings and I freeze. He can't be early. That's cheating! I bite my lip in the hope it'll swell into a fetching pout and, in kamikaze mindset, heave open the door. 'Surprise!' exclaims my mother, throwing her hands wide like the young Shirley Temple. Nana Flo lurks po-faced behind her. 'Aren't you going to invite us in?' cries my mother, blind to the fact that my face has fallen about ninety foot.

'Of course!' I say, recalling my promise to Dr Collins and forcing a smile. 'Come into the kitchen. Nana, would you like a cup of tea?'

(In times of doubt I resort to clichés. It gives me time to think. Although when I rack my brain for inspiration it's napping and won't be disturbed.) I have just poured a cup of PG Tips for Nana, a camomile tea for my mother, and retrieved half a packet of biscuits from my room, when the doorbell rings again. 'I wonder who that is!' chirps my mother, who is very obviously still taking the pills.

'I think it may be a friend of mine, Tom,' I mutter.

209

As I walk into the hall I can hear my mother squawking 'Tom! Tom? Do I know Tom?' and my grandmother growling, 'Tim, Tom, who knows any more?'

I squeeze the bridge of my nose between my fingertips, paste a smile to my face, and open the door. Tom is brandishing a wilting bunch of garish blue marigolds in what appears to be a doily. 'Garage flowers!' he declares, 'the finest and the best!'

I gasp and take them, exclaiming, 'The rare and priceless turquoise marigold! You shouldn't have!'

He grins and says, 'I pawned my Ferrari.'

I reply sweetly, 'Not your Ferrari *poster*?'

He nods, and says 'Don't be too sad, my 911's still on the wall!'

I feel an inexplicable surge of joy and – before I have time to reconsider – step towards him and kiss him on the mouth. I am about to pull away but he wraps his arms around me and kisses me and so I close my eyes and kiss him back and my heart does a delirious dance and I feel the firm warmth of him pressed against me and 'Helloo-ooo! Anybody there-ere!'

My mother's brisk schoolmarm tone kills the moment stone dead and Tom and I spring guiltily apart. 'Surprise visit from my mum and grandma,' I explain hurriedly. Tom swoops and sucks gently, briefly, on my upper lip causing a lightning strike to the groin. I grasp his shoulder for balance and think, good grief! Show me the way!

'What are you waiting for?' he murmurs. 'Introduce me!'

Dazed and grinning like the village idiot, I lead Tom into the kitchen and introduce him. 'You took your time,' says Nana, grouchily. 'What lovely blue flowers!' says my mother. I will her not to say anything akin to 'Is this your boyfriend?'

'Is this your boyfriend?' she asks, eyes wide.

'Tom and I are just good friends,' I say, trying not to sound panicked.

Tom says helpfully, 'I'm Fatboy's vet.'

My mother ogles him and says, 'I see.'

Nana Flo says snappishly, 'No need for it! In my day, a dog was a dog and that was that!'

Tom says politely, 'I see what you mean.'

I say under my breath, 'I'm glad someone does,' then louder, 'Tom, would you like a coffee and a biscuit?'

My mother, who keeps staring at Tom, says in a loud show-offy voice, 'Helen, haven't you got something more substantial to offer him?' I am tempted to say, 'my body?' to shut her up but the question is rhetorical. She adds, 'You can't expect young men to survive on *biscuits*' – at which point Nana Flo joins the fray with – 'A man needs a good solid meal inside him!'

Whereas a woman, I presume, can survive on sweetness and light. A plausible supposition slowly dawns in my head. And although my dearest wish is that the pair of them vanish in a whiff of sulphur (at least until tomorrow) I say casually, 'Mum, Nana. If I were to nip down to the corner shop to buy something nice for Tom to eat, would you like to join him, us, for supper?'

Nana Flo speaks up so fast her false teeth nearly fly out of her mouth: 'If you insist but don't go to any trouble!'

My mother says, 'I don't see why not. But no onions or red peppers. Onions and red peppers give me a migraine.'

More like the incessant yapping of your own voice gives you a migraine, I think but don't say. I turn to Tom who, to his credit, hasn't run away. 'Tom,' I say, hardly daring to meet his eyes, 'Would you like to come to the shop with me?' There's no way I'm leaving him to the mercy of the Munsters.

Tom – and I can hear the mischief in his voice – says, 'No no no, *I'll* go to the shop, *you* stay here and keep your mother and grandmother company. It would be rude to leave them alone.'

Nana Flo nods at this and mutters, 'Quite right!'

'I'll see you to the door,' I say acidly. As soon as we're in the hall I try and whack him but he dodges me and, as he shuts the front door behind him, grins at me tauntingly, all teeth, like an ape.

'Well brought up!' remarks Nana Flo on my return, glancing at me dismissively as if to say 'unlike you'. Please, I reply in my head, don't put me off him.

'Where's that nice boy Luke?' trills my mother. She's insatiable!

'I think he's gone to work,' I say.

'What, on a Saturday night!' she replies.

'He works in a pub,' I say. Nana Flo's mouth shrinks in disapproval. 'Luke works very hard,' I say, irritated.

'I dare say,' says Nana.

'I *do* like Luke,' purrs my mother, 'he's *so* charming.' In her hormonally charged state I suspect she'd find Frankenstein's monster charming and am wondering if I could bribe Luke to paint his face grey and stick a bolt in his neck to test this theory, when Marcus sweeps into the kitchen.

He is wearing smart cream chinos, a yolk-yellow shirt, and his hair is as springy and bouffant as an expertly baked soufflé. (And, let me tell you, I should know.) His haughtiness turns to dismay on seeing my relatives. 'Hello,' he says awkwardly.

Nana Flo peers at him. 'Is this the one?' she says loudly. The distress on my face is reflected on Marcus's.

'No, Luke is blond,' I say desperately.

But Nana is not to be deterred. 'No!' she bellows. 'Is this the one who's turning you out!'

I say quickly: 'He's not turning me out! I'm glad to be going!'

At this, my mother appears confused. 'Oh,' she says, 'but I thought you—'

I interrupt her with the first piece of trivia I can think of: 'Marcus is going out with Michelle, Mummy. You know Michelle.'

My mother shrugs and in a flat voice says, 'Vaguely.' (As she has known Michelle for the best part of two decades this is intended as a slight. As I haven't told my mother about the Michelle/Marcus perfidy, I know it's nothing personal. It's just that Cecelia's enthusiasm for young women is less than her enthusiasm for young men.) She gives Marcus a cursory glance, starts, then stares. She is staring at him like a miser staring at a pot of gold.

Marcus pats his hair nervously and scratches his shin with the toe of his moccasin. 'Well, I'd better—' he begins, but my mother stops him.

'Sit down!' she orders. I stare at her in fury but she doesn't notice. Marcus sits, stony faced. She pulls her chair towards his, and says suddenly, 'Florence, doesn't he remind you of Maurice?'

'Nothing like!' bleats Nana. Her eyes bore into Marcus, and then she looks away and back again and says, quietly, 'nonsense.' But she doesn't take her eyes off him.

'Don't talk rubbish!' shouts a voice, which turns out to be mine. The doorbell goes and I race to it.

Tom lifts a heavy plastic bag and says, 'I got some eggs. I was thinking of your Nan's teeth.'

I smile wanly and say, 'Brilliant.'

He frowns and mouths, 'What's up?'

I clutch my forehead, roll my eyes, and say, 'Don't ask.' We troop into the kitchen where Marcus and his hair are still trapped.

My mother is grasping his wrist and exclaiming, 'The mouth and eyes are identical, identical! Helen! It's uncanny!'

I keep my temper with difficulty. 'No it is *not* uncanny,' I say. 'Please.' My voice sounds shrill, panicked. She's mad. Everyone reminds her of my father. Next it'll be Fatboy. ('They've got exactly the same appetite although' – girlish tinkle – 'your father didn't have a tail!')

I am about to command her to free Marcus when Ivana flounces in. 'Markee! Wher— Oh hello, Mrs Bradshaw! And Mrs Bradshaw Senior!' she cries.

'Hello,' replies my mother dourly.

Nana actually recoils. 'Who are you?' she says rudely.

'I'm Michelle!' says Michelle. 'You remember me!'

Nana scowls and says, 'All young women look the same to me.'

Michelle turns the full beam of her automated allure upon Tom. 'I don't think we've met,' she husks, lashes lowered.

'Tom,' he says briskly, extending a hand, 'I'm with Helen.'

The smile dies on her lips, to be briefly resurrected as she spies the blue marigolds. 'How sweet,' she croons, 'so the flowers must be from you! I'm always telling Markee that a gas station bouquet will do me fine but the angel *insists* on Paula Pryke!' and in the next breath: 'Markee darling, a black tea before we go out.' Tom glances, amused, at me. Marcus leaps up gratefully.

'Right,' I say, 'Mum, Nana, I'm making scrambled eggs. It's that or nothing.'

My mother pouts. 'I can't eat scrambled eggs!' she cries. 'You should know that! It's too painful!'

I say hurriedly, 'Sorry, Mum, I'll do omelettes instead, is that better for you?' My mother nods regally.

Michelle's eyes bulge at the prospect of intrigue. 'Why?' she says breathlessly.

'Scrambled eggs killed my father,' I say tonelessly.

'*Woh!*' says Michelle. Her brain tries to assemble the clues and fails. 'How?' she gasps.

My mother's love of attention overcomes her dislike of Michelle and she embarks on the tragic tale. I start yanking pans out of drawers and Tom says, 'Why don't you sit down and I'll make the omelettes.'

Marcus says coolly, 'Not for us, we're eating at the new Conran restaurant.' Tom starts cracking eggs into a bowl. Tom has already been to the new Conran restaurant, which irks Marcus. He says rudely, 'But you're a vet!' My jaw drops.

Tom swallows a laugh and says, 'I know! Can you

214

believe it! My coat was the glossiest it's been!' Marcus scowls.

I collapse into a chair. 'What time's your reservation? Shouldn't you get going?' I say to Michelle.

She glances at her thin gold watch, 'No rush,' she says to me, and 'Yes, go on!' to my mother. I suppress a sigh. My neck is so tense it aches. By the time Tom starts placing omelettes in front of my mother and Nana, the tension has spread to my shoulders and jaw.

Marcus hovers by the table. 'Michelle,' he says tightly, 'we ought to set off.'

Michelle sticks out her lower lip and says, 'Five seconds, honey! Mrs Bradshaw's at a really exciting bit!'

Marcus slumps into the chair next to Tom. I can see Nana gazing at him. 'Same height,' she says, 'I'll give her that.' Marcus smiles an unhappy smile. I grit my teeth.

Tom winks at me. 'Ketchup, anyone?' he says.

'Yuck,' sings my mother.

Nana shakes her head, 'Not for me, dear.'

Pardon. I don't wish to be picky but I, her grand-daughter, am rarely accorded the courtesy of being addressed by name whereas Tom, a man she didn't know existed until an hour ago, is '*dear*'?

'Helen,' says Tom, 'ketchup?' I shake my head.

'Just me then,' he says cheerfully. He holds the bottle upside down, gives it a hefty whack on its bottom, and a large red gloop shoots through the air and lands 'splat!' on Marcus's yellow shirt. 'I am sorry,' says Tom happily – as Marcus leaps up with a bellow of dismay – 'can't take me anywhere.'

I clamp a hand over my mouth and swallow a bit of omelette faster than I meant to. Michelle's mouth is a perfect scarlet O of dismay. My mother and grandmother gaze mesmerised at Marcus, as he shouts, 'You *idiot*!' at Tom.

Michelle escorts him to the bedroom to change. 'We are going to be *so* late!' she spits at Tom on her way out.

215

Nana Flo pats Tom's hand – don't tell me she fancies her chances too! 'My word, what a fuss about nothing!' she snaps. I grin weakly at Tom. Much as his ketchup trick makes me want to hug him, I feel unable to rise from my chair. Because at the moment Marcus's mouth and eyes thinned in anger, a sickening jolt of perception hit. Why, how didn't I see it before? It's undeniable. Not so much the features as the posture, the temperament, the volatility. My father, the very image.

I run to the toilet and throw up the omelette. I've only eaten two bites but I can't stop retching.

Chapter 27

Lizzy endears herself to me in many ways, but the sweetest thing she ever did (in my opinion) was to fall asleep bang in the middle of a romantic evening with her then boyfriend – before any actual banging had occurred. She'd just returned from a family holiday in France and the poor man was desperate to welcome her home in, as he termed it, 'traditional fashion'.

('That really put me off,' confided Lizzy later.) He'd cooked a vegetarian dinner, lit scented candles, bought a bottle of non-alcoholic wine, washed the sheets, and – get this – sprinkled rose petals on the bed! He carried Lizzy upstairs, nipped into the bathroom to clean his teeth, and sprang back into the room to find his sweetheart unconscious on the pillow. 'I was so tired I hadn't even taken off my make-up!' she exclaimed – expecting me to say, 'Oh my gosh, *that* tired!'

She added, 'He was so sulky about it. It was the final straw. And I don't like people tearing up flowers.' As I said, the poor man. But I was impressed that Lizzy was so relaxed about the prospect of sex that she could conk out before her darling had even stripped off. I'm usually so chuffed to be considered I'm a human Martini – any time, anywhere. Or is that a Bounty bar?

Anyhow, soon after I spew up my omelette, Michelle and Marcus vroom off in the RAV 4 for a showcase meal, and my mother and Nana Flo depart in the Peugeot to catch a Clint Eastwood film on Channel Five. Before she leaves, my mother tells me, 'You needn't bother coming round tomorrow, I'm going shopping with Vivvy!' and my grand-mother wags her finger at me and says, 'You're over-excited! You need an early night.'

I nod and say, 'Okay, Mum,' and 'Yes, Nana.'

When they've gone I lean against the door and shudder at Tom. And the turncoat says, 'I'm with Nana Flo!' What is this, a conspiracy?

'There's nothing wrong with me,' I lie. I've got to be fine. Tonight, I am blearily certain, we're seeing some action! I should clean my teeth and floss. Tom suggests I lie on the sofa for a few minutes while he stacks the dishwasher. 'Alright,' I say, 'but only as a favour.'

I wake up four hours later when he carries me to bed.

Never in my life did I imagine that exhaustion would overpower my libido. I feel drugged. I can't even move a leg. 'Stay,' I murmur sleepily, as Tom lowers me on to the bed.

'Here?' he whispers.

'Mm,' I breathe.

I lie unfetchingly limp as Tom wrestles off my boots. A dilute fear washes over me – what if he sniffs them? – but I'm too comatose to care. He leans close and whispers, 'Can I undress you?'

I reply – and I swear I wouldn't have said this had I been conscious – 'Yeah.' Which is how I wake up on Sunday morning at 10.22 starkers and squashed right up against Tom's naked – I'll say that again – n-a-k-e-d – chest.

My eyes ping open and I marvel at him sleeping. His hair is even more tousled than normal and his cheeks are flushed and he is breathing deeply. Broad shoulders. I lift the duvet a little to inspect his chest and whew, I've seen worse. Not too muscled but defined, *solid*. Nice nips. And not scarily hairy like Marcus. I wonder if he's naked all the way down. I also wonder if it would be possible to sneak into the bath-room – which would entail clambering over him knickered but otherwise nude – and brush my teeth. I run my tongue over them. They feel like suede. Should I chance it?

I glance at Tom to check he's still asleep and he snorts gently through his nose so I reckon it's safe and I am lifting the duvet higher so I can peer lower when a hand shoots out and grabs mine and he shouts 'gotcha!' and I scream. He grabs my other hand and rolls on top of me – at this point I realise he's wearing boxer shorts – and pinions me to the bed. 'So!' he says, blue eyes boring into mine. 'Thought you'd sneak a preview!'

I am writhing and squealing – part shock part horror – not least because my own chest is on full wobbly view and we haven't even *slept* together yet. In the rude sense, I mean. This is wrong! I envisaged a slow, tantalising striptease, my prize lace Wonderbra teasingly unpeeled, his trembling hands caressing my skin, me unbuttoning his shirt to reveal his beautifully toned torso, his taut sinewy biceps, slowly undoing his belt buckle, feeling his, ah, arousal bulging beneath his Calvin Kleins (pref, grey cotton, unfussy). Damn and damn again.

'Do you mind!' I shout primly, trying to obscure my breasts with my shoulders (don't bother trying – it's physically impossible). 'I need to brush my teeth. They're filthy!'

Tom laughs and murmurs, 'But I like filthy,' and he bends and brushes his lips on my left nipple and a great whopping thud of desire whips through me and I arch against him and we're kissing and I say 'woof!' to excuse my dog breath and he says, 'Helen, you're fucking gorgeous, God you're sexy' and I think, *me*. Are you talking to me? I don't see anybody else around here . . .

And you know what, I do feel sexy, very sexy, the sexiest woman in the room, and suddenly I'm grabbing at him and kissing and sucking and licking and he's kissing and sucking and licking – I haven't been so delirious since I discovered that Dime bars occur in mini form and I'm attacking Tom in the same greedy passionate must-have way and he's grabby and ravenous and all over me too and when I pull at his hair and nibble at his neck he groans and runs his fingers down my back and over my stomach and down, and oh God that feels promising, 'get these off!' I hear myself saying – and he's yanking off my black knickers and I'm pulling at his boxers – navy but would I care if they were orange pantaloons, well maybe for a second but not – woho!

And I make no apology for our appalling lack of originality, I say 'oh God that's big!' and he gasps and says 'oh Helen! you feel so good!' and it's wonderful and I hope my father isn't listening in and Tom and I are so desperate to – as I think I say – 'get it in!' his penis boinks against my inner thigh and we snigger and he says 'ow!' and I giggle 'nearly snapped!' and then, oh. my. God. it tastes it feels indescribably delicious and I'm oohing and ahing fit to burst and we're kissing and moving together and we're so together I don't want it to end and even when I do a loud fanny fart and squirm with embarrassment he grins and says 'wahey!' and kisses me harder and I think in all my slapping around and in all my practising alone (and until Dad died may I say I was fairly studious) – I never thought it could be like this.

So of course I have to ruin it.

I come first ('ladies first!') jokes Tom before joining me five seconds later and the soaring rapture drowns in a fierce, inexplicable wave of sorrow. I bite my lip to stop the sobs. Tom flops out like a starfish, one arm flung warmly over my stomach, and says plaintively, 'Can we do it again?' – and I start laughing and say, 'It's like all my bones have been removed!' and he grins and rolls over and kisses the nearest bit of me – my chin – and says, 'Gorgeous Helen.'

He looks into my eyes and it's not the sweep of desire that's killing me, it's the ugh ugh I hate this word – *tenderness* of our connection – it's new and stupefying, it makes me recoil, so raw and exposed like an open wound. Then the weepiness is back with a vengeance and the tears start falling until they fall out of control and, stupid stupid girl, I'm blubbing and whimpering and wailing like a great big baby and Tom looks horrified and says, 'It wasn't that bad, was it?' and I laugh but I'm still crying. I'm crying so hard my teeth are chattering. He hugs me and rocks me and says, 'Tell me, Helen, *please* tell me what it is.'

Tom shouldn't have asked, he really shouldn't. It's nothing to do with him. But he does and it all pours out. Stuff I didn't even know was in there. It gushes madly out like sewage out of a burst pipe. And he lets it happen. He just listens while I rant.

'Hes gone hes not coming back, oh god i cant believe it and no one understands im so alone i don't know who i am any more who am i in the world and why is it like this we werent even close i never understood him he hardly knew me who i was and now its too late too late to make it right and we never talked and i never asked why didnt you care i just couldnt and i don't know why i feel like this and no one understands its all her its all about her and how she is and she never thinks about me and i thought i was over it i didnt cry at the funeral i was numb i felt nothing so out of place and even lizzy cried and i couldnt cry i didnt deserve to cry and i failed him and i wasnt good enough and he died and i never said i loved him and he never said he loved me he said i was a grinch oh god i cant bear it i need him back and why wont he come back i want to see him again i hate him i hate how he makes me feel i feel so bad adrift its the worst its worse than i ever imagined im a fraud im so angry the anger wont go how can i feel like this i dont even know what i should feel and i feel scared im so scared what if mummy dies too and nana shes on the way out and tina and lizzy and luke and fatboy and now you and im so scared they will and i cant say because they wont understand and oh god i cant believe it hes my dad its so not fair im so tired i cant even dream about him other people dream about dead people and they come back and hug them and smile and say its okay and be happy and they love them and theyre in a fucking white room and i cant even do that he wont appear in a single dream he wont even tell me how hes doing its all too late its so fucking typical hes never there for me hes never been there so why do i miss him oh god help me its all my fault . . .'

Beat that for embarrassing.

Chapter 28

I'm so mad and distraught the horror of it doesn't dawn on me till later. When the words run out Tom rocks me and hugs me. He doesn't tell me to shush, he rubs my back and he listens. All he says is, 'Helen, don't you think, you've got um, stuff that needs sorting?'

I shake my head because I don't know. I feel ashamed. 'Please pass me my clothes,' I say stiffly. Tom leans down, grabs a baggy shirt lying on the floor, and helps me into it. I am sapped. 'Sorry,' I mumble, 'I don't know what happened.'

He replies, 'Doesn't matter. But Helen, I just, maybe, Lizzy, Tina, me, we're not going anywhere. And you mustn't think you're not good enough. I don't know what to say – you're great and' – at this point Tom's voice becomes fierce – 'and your dad should have let you know that.'

This is kind of him. Although I'm not sure I appreciate him slagging off my father. I feel tired and teary again and I say, 'Do you mind if I have a quick nap?' Tom kisses me and then I curl up. Every time I think of what I said my heart bobs in my chest like a gull on a rough sea. I was nothing with my father and I am nothing without him. What is the point of me? I am not a positive force. What is the point of anything? I want to shrivel up and cease existing. I could cry but there aren't enough tears in the world to extinguish this pain. I shrink into the smallest ball that I can and sink into a deadening sleep.

When I wake up it's twenty past two and I'm starving.

I've also got a cracking headache. The craziness of the day seeps back into my consciousness and I cringe. I can't begin to think about the sex because I can't stop thinking about the blathering. I prefer to keep my basest instincts to myself. Deep dark Daddy emotions included. They are personal, too intimate, too infernal to share. How *could* I let Tom tease them from me? I feel like I've vomited up my soul.

I lie still for a long time. The room is empty except for Fatboy who's perched on the windowsill. He hears me rustling, says 'prrt!' and trots over. Must want something. I lie flat on my back and stroke Fatboy and think oh Jesus what did I *say*? I feel woozy as if I've drunk too much wine and oddly flat. I wonder if Tom has gone, and I half hope he has. But no. I can hear a bark of laughter in the lounge. I tiptoe to the door, open it a crack, and realise he's talking to Luke. The conversation appears to be about the longest they've ever driven their cars with their eyes shut.

Tom managed three seconds before 'bottling out'. Luke trumps him with seven. From what I can gather they were both teenagers at the time but even so! I pull on some tracksuit bottoms, tiptoe in, and say 'How *could* you!' They both jump and start bleating 'it was the middle of the night' and 'there was no one on the road' and 'I was only doing twenty' until I hold up a hand and say crossly, 'I don't want to know. You could have killed someone!'

I can't bear to look Tom in the eye. Not because of his irresponsible driving but because, as of this morning, he knows me stripped bare in every sense and it's too awful to contemplate. So I focus on Luke instead. This is a mistake because he peers closely at me and says, 'Why are your eyes so puffy?'

I snap, 'No reason!' To deflect further interrogation I say, 'Is there anything to eat?'

Tom jumps up and says, 'Let's go out and get something!'

I look withering and say, 'What, with me like this?'

224

He lifts a hand, tilts my chin, and says, 'But Miss Bradshaw – you're beeoootiful!' And then, in a more serious tone, 'You are though.'

I wrinkle my nose and say, 'Hang on while I get some shoes and sunglasses.' Ten minutes later (after a detour to the bathroom to try and make myself look less like a gargoyle) I am ready.

'Can I come?' says Luke.

'No,' says Tom meanly, 'it's a boy girl thing.'

Luke's eyes saucer. 'What!' he says. 'You and Helen!'

I'm not sure if I should be impressed or insulted that Tom hasn't told Luke about balling me. So I joke, 'Why are you so surprised, Luke? Is Tom out of my league?'

Luke shakes his head frantically and says, 'No, mate – you're out of his.'

His delightful compliment is tempered by the appellation 'mate'. I don't wish to set feminism back but I'd rather be called 'darlin'. But I say gallantly, 'Luke, that is very sweet of you', even though I'm tired and hungry and sick of banter.

Tom repeats cheerily, 'Luke, that is very sweet of you.' Luke gives him the finger. It's a relief when Tom says, 'Ready?'

It's a freezing winter's day but we speed to Golders Green, buy four cream cheese and smoked salmon bagels, and drive to the heath extension. I eat my first bagel in Tom's rusty old Honda Civic EX. 'You don't have a name for it, do you?' I say suspiciously.

'No I do bloody well do not,' he replies. 'It would be like naming your willy!'

I giggle. We discuss our ideal cars. 'I'm not really a car person,' I say, 'but if I had the money I think I'd have an S-type Jag. A car with cheekbones. The only thing is, they look a bit claustrophobic.'

Tom says, 'So you're not hard to please or anything?' Tom is fond of Jags too but was put off them when his thirty-two-year-old cousin got an XJ8.

'What's that?' I say.

He says, 'You know, the big luxury wood interior sort. He was boasting about the "front suspension" and my sister suddenly said dreamily, "*faaa-ther* drives a *Jaag-uarr*"! She's hilarious like that! She just says things! I love it! My cousin went quiet. I think she ruined the moment for him.'

I giggle and say, 'Well, the big sort is for fifty-year-olds really, isn't it?'

Tom hum-hahs: 'Yeah, but it's still class.' We fall silent in brief contemplation of the unobtainable.

'Which do you think is worse,' I say, 'a Honda Civic or a Toyota Corolla?'

Tom shrugs and says, 'They're two rats eating out the same chip bag!' We are snorting with laughter (even though I pat the Honda's dashboard and say 'poor car!') as Tom pulls up.

The heath extension is a higgledy assortment of green fields plonk in the middle of smart north-west London. I love it because it's mostly scruffy and overgrown and has a less commercial feel than Hampstead Heath. We walk to a wooden bench, clutching our bagels and discussing our ideal cars. The sky is pale blue with skeins of cloud and our breath fogs in the dry air. There are frozen puddles along the path and I dig my heels into them to crack the ice. We sit on our bench and eat our bagels and watch people walking their dogs – one brown dog makes us laugh by dragging his bottom along the grass while his owner shouts 'Brandy!' and pretends not to know him.

'It's so peaceful,' I sigh.

'Mm,' says Tom with his mouth full of bagel. 'Gissa kiss.' I kiss him chastely on the cheek.

'Your nose has gone pink,' I say.

'It's so cold I can't feel it,' he replies.

I finish my bagel and he hugs me to him. We look at the view. Pale sky, bare trees, frosty ground, silence. Stillness. I sigh. A boxable moment of happiness. I begin to think that maybe I *did* need to tell someone about my dad and I am marvelling at how easy it is to be with Tom, how undemanding, how effortless, and what a bloody miracle he is in bed, when he spoils it by saying, 'Helen, about what you told me about your dad. I know it's hard for you to talk about your grief but you were, are, were so sad and I thought that maybe you were punishing yourself – for something that wasn't your fault and maybe it would help to—'

No no no no no no no. 'No, don't,' I snap, more sharply than I mean to. Tom stops. I hesitate. Then I say, 'It's kind of you but—'

This time Tom interrupts me. His tone is annoyed: 'Helen, this isn't me being *charitable*, this isn't some holy, po-faced exercise in making myself feel good – it may sound stupid and incredible to you but I like you and I'd like you to be okay but I don't think you'll ever be anything but miserable if you keep on denying what you feel about your father and how he was, and keep pissing around with wankers like Marcus, it's pointless, why be a martyr, wh—'

I jump up from the bench and shout, 'Stop it! Stop it! You don't know!'

And how the hell does he know about Marcus? Tom shuts up. He looks thunderous. I take a deep breath, sit down again, and pat his leg. 'I'm sorry,' I say. Then I say grumpily, 'How did you know about Marcus?'

Tom snaps, 'You'd have to be stupid not to.' I chew my lip.

Then I say, 'It was ages ago and just once. A mistake. I'm sorry I shouted. Forgive me. I'm fine, I don't know what got into me – hah! – I mean, I don't know why I got so upset this morning, or rather, I do know' – and here I whip out my heart for a second and shove it on my sleeve to show the extent of my sincerity – 'I got upset because my father died and it's weird, but it was mainly because, in fact, I'm sure it was because, well, I'm being turfed out and

I've got nowhere to go. And it's just another stress on top of everything.'

This, I admit, is a bad habit of mine. I don't state what I want, bluntly, like Laetitia. I hint. Hinting is not, I know, the bravest way of asking. But at least if you hint and are rejected the rejection is blurable rather than blistering. Whereas if you ask outright and are refused, the humiliation is as stark as a streaker on a football pitch. Anyhow, unless Tom is an imbecile he surely will take the hint and if he likes me as much as he claims, he will sweep to my assistance like a guardian angel and ask me and Fatboy to come and live in his flat. I pause. Tom says nothing. What is he, dumb? Then he says – and do I detect a hint of coldness – 'Didn't your mum say you could live with her until you found somewhere?'

I reply crossly, 'Yeah, but you've met her – she's a nightmare! And I'm twenty-six! I can't live with my mum and my gran for chrissake!'

I expect Tom to understand but he plays obtuse. He snaps, 'It's better than being homeless. Can't you look for another place to rent?'

When he says this I lose my temper. 'Take me back to the flat!' I shout.

'Fine, if that's how it's going to be,' he growls. We stomp back to the car in silence. All that blarney and he can't even bail me out when I need him. He knew what I meant. We don't talk apart from once when Tom blurts out, 'If you ask me it'd do you good to shack up with your mother – you could tell her some of what you told me.'

I roar, 'I did not ask you!' He screeches to a halt outside Marcus's flat. I jump out, spit 'Bye!' and slam the door. Tom clenches his jaw and roars off with as much haughtiness and speed as a Honda Civic EX F-reg can muster. Which, I am spitefully thrilled to note, isn't much.

I get in, shut the door, shout 'bugger!' and see Marcus storming towards me. He roars 'That's *it*! That's it that's it that's it!'

I watch his tempestuous approach with detachment. This, I think to myself, is a truly remarkable day. I feel no emotion at all. I scream at the top of my voice (and in this respect I'm my mother's daughter) '*What's* it, you great big twittering ninny?'

Marcus's face turns purple. He bellows, 'You *dare* speak to me like that, you vicious little cow! Your fucking cat brought in a pigeon! A great big frigging pigeon flapping round my kitchen, shitting on the surfaces!'

Even though I loathe Fatboy's bird-catching habit, I roar, 'Don't you know anything, you big fat fool, a pigeon from a cat is a present! He bought you a present!'

Marcus is screeching so loudly his voice cracks: 'It took me two hours to catch it! Two hours! I was meant to be at the gym!'

I yelp: 'For what! To make your pecs bigger and your pecker even smaller?' This strikes me as funny and I start laughing.

Marcus shakes a hammy fist in my face and snarls, 'I want you out tonight! Do you hear me, tonight! And that fat slug of a cat – because if I catch him do you know what I'm going to do? I'm going to step on his fat orange head and crush it to a pulp!'

I say in a voice dripping with sarcasm, 'Hey, big man!' and then, in my normal voice: 'Marcus. Guess what. You don't scare me. You and your threats. Shout as much as you like. You're powerless. Impotent.'

It's true and he knows it. He can't touch me any more. I march past him. Then I retrieve Fatboy from Luke's wardrobe – his favourite hiding place because it's full of warm, soft, dirty clothes – and carry him to my bedroom. 'Angel Baby,' I say, 'pack your things, we're moving out!' Fatboy catches sight of himself in the mirror and hisses. I hate to say it, but he's as thick as a brick. I suspect he's a warning that I should never have children.

I ring my mother and ask if she minds if I move in

tonight. She says, 'Oh. Okay. I don't know where you'll sleep though. There's no bed in the study and Florence is in the guest bedroom.'

I reply, 'I can sleep in the lounge on the sofa.'

She pauses. Then she says, 'But me and Florence are watching *The Horse Whisperer*.'

I sigh and say, 'Well I won't go to sleep until you're finished then, will I?'

Pacified, she replies, 'No, good.'

I put down the phone. I rest my head in my hands and think, if only my mother had owned a cat we'd have all been spared a lot of grief.

Chapter 29

What if my obituary states to the nation that I had a knack of failing at almost everything I did? I start fretting about this on reading about Mr Cane in the *Daily Express*. 'The prosecutor said Mr Cane, who had not been reported missing, was a shy, introverted loner who appeared to have a knack at failing at almost everything he did . . .' I sit on the train and I can't get the sentence out of my head. A knack at failing at almost everything. What a terrible legacy. It churns me up because I feel that I'm heading the same way.

I now live with my mother and grandmother, both of whom prefer Robert Redford to me. I'm too feeble to live on my own. I'm still Deodorant Monitor. And Tom hates me. I haven't got a capsule wardrobe. We've destroyed the ozone layer. I've got an itchy spot on my stomach which may be a flea bite. A forest fire somewhere hot has just decimated millions of trees. Which negates the fact I recycled all my newspapers last week. A meteorite is probably going to smash into Earth. And I can't stand what I'm wearing. Someone is poisoning dolphins. I have a fear of estate agents so am doomed to live with my mother for ever. My hair is as flat as if I'd pasted it to my head. And no one even noticed that Mr Cane was missing. By the time I get into work I'm feeling a bit low.

So it doesn't help that when I return from the toilet, Laetitia screams across the office in a voice as loud as Concorde taking flight, 'Helen – private call for you – it's your Community Psychiatric Nurse!' I freeze and stare, as does the entire office. Laetitia trills sweetly, 'Shall I transfer him to you now?'

I stare at her in dismay and say, 'If you must.' She smirks. I decide to intercept her invitation to the Has-been Debutantes' Christmas Ball and amend the dress code from 'Black Tie' to 'Beekeepers'.

I snatch up the phone. 'Yes?' I hiss, cupping the mouth-piece.

'Helen Bradshaw?' says a warm voice. 'Sorry to hassle you at work. Cliff Meacham – your mother's CPN. Hope she warned you I was going to call!' I swallow. I am bubbling with rage at his indiscretion when he adds, 'Your colleague wouldn't pass me on unless I identified myself. But we can schedule the call for another time if you prefer.'

I forgive him and make a mental note that Laetitia's invitation will also read 'Please Bring Own Hive'. I sigh and say, 'Could you call back at lunchtime?' Infuriatingly, he can. And he does.

Thankfully, Laetitia is lunching 'a contact' at the Ivy, and so the office is deserted. I expect Cliff to leapfrog the pleasantries and land on the point, but he seems determined to chat.

'So you're a journalist!' he begins. 'How exciting! Do you interview lots of famous people?'

'Masses,' I reply, trying not to laugh outright.

Cliff is so enthralled by his glamorous vision of my profession that I invent three celebrity exclusives so as not to disappoint him. His interest is beguiling, and I am explaining why Demi saw fit to confide in *me* about her marriage difficulties before she told, ah, Bruce, when I realise I'm a mile out of my depth and should bail out now.

'Anyway, enough about her. She's a very private person. What can I do for you?' I say politely.

Cliff drags himself back to mundane reality and tells me it's important for him to understand my mother, her relationship with my father, and how she's changed since my father died.

'But I thought you asked her all that,' I say. He tells me it's useful for him to hear my impression of events as well as hers. I say, in the understatement of the year, 'She's been a bit up and down.' He doesn't say anything so I add, 'I've tried to look after her but she misses my dad.' I stop. Nothing.

Then Cliff says casually, 'And how do you look after her?'

I tell him about the cooking and the gallery trips and the reiki and the supper party and the listening and the forcing Vivienne to invite her to dinner.

Cliff says, 'Wow.'

I'm puffed from talking but Cliff doesn't notice. He asks about ninety more mother questions. He wants to know who I think is the strong one in our relationship. He wants to know whose needs I think take priority. He wants to know everything I'd prefer not to tell him.

Then he asks, 'And what happens when you need looking after?' I'm stumped.

'I don't follow,' I say.

'Well, when *you* need mothering, what happens then?'

A question which would have been more appropriate when I was four. I say brusquely, 'It's not really like that.'

I hear Cliff take a deep drag on his home-made cigarette. 'I see,' he says in an indefinable tone. He coughs, excuses himself, then says that as from tomorrow, my mother has a weekly appointment at the clinic, and ideally, he'd like me to attend at least one session with her.

'I'd love to,' I lie, 'but I'm afraid I can't.' Cliff pauses. 'Work,' I explain. He suggests that maybe I could think about it. 'Yeah sure,' I say briskly. 'Anything else you need?' I say this as a shooing ploy but he ignores it. He explains that it's helpful if he understands the family 'as a whole'.

233

I'm nodding and saying 'mm,' and wondering what Cliff does for fun, when he asks me how my life has changed since my father died. Spaghetti in my head. I think of my post-orgasm outburst and my insides float with panic. I itch to slam down the phone and bolt. After a full minute, Cliff says, 'I sense you're having difficulty in talking about how you feel.' He must have *The Ladybird Book of Psychiatry* open on his lap at page seven.

I reply tartly, 'I'm not feeling anything.' It's nearly true. Cliff is disbelievingly silent. I blurt, 'I've been too busy at work and looking after my mother.' Cliff remains silent. It's like talking to a stone. Hey, maybe he *is* actually a cliff. 'She's been very upset since, you know,' I say.

'What?' he says.

'My father's death!' I snap. What did he think I was talking about? Her team's relegation?

'She cut her wrists!' I exclaim. Cliff seems to expect elaboration so I tell him what happened, even though I'm sure my mother has told him at rambling length. I make it plain to Cliff that the wrist-cutting night was the only Monday night I'd missed and of course, after that, I'd never ever miss one again. I don't want to be accused of parental neglect a second time.

But when I've finished Cliff says, 'You've been devoting a lot of your time to your mother.'

I nod and realise he can't see me nodding. 'Well, she needs me now,' I say. Cliff goes silent again. Jesus, I'd hate to be his girlfriend. I joke, 'I turn my back for one minute and bam! She's whittling at her wrists!' It's not one of my best jokes and Cliff doesn't laugh. He says it sounds to him as if my mother was trying to force me to look after her. 'But I *was*!' I squeak. I bloody knew we'd get round to this.

Then he says it sounds as if she was trying to punish me for not being there. 'Well you got that right,' I say sourly.

'But Helen,' he says, 'what about *your* life?'

I am speedily tiring of our conversation. It's like an

234

extremely dull quiz show without the cash prize incentive. 'What about it?' I say sharply.

'You can't be living it totally for your mother,' he replies.

'No, but—' I start and then stop. 'I'm not. She needs me. Anyway, I've got nothing better to do. She's got no one else,' I say crossly.

'She's got herself,' he replies.

I am about to remark on the fatuity of this comment when Cliff adds that it isn't healthy or normal for a mother to be so dependent on her child – *child*! I'm older than he is, the little schnip! Cliff says the higher I jump every time she pulls a strop, the worse it will get. 'It's just not helpful,' he concludes.

Oh, so it's my fault. 'No it is *not* your fault,' says Cliff quietly. 'You are not responsible for your mother's behaviour. Only your own. The most helpful thing you can do for yourself and your mother – in that order – is to let her learn to manage her own grief.' Easy for him to say, sitting in his clinic, smoking his stinky cigarettes, never having experienced the wrath of Cecelia Bradshaw Upon Not Getting Her Own Way.

'And so I just ignore her, do I, until she leaps from a window?' I say sarcastically.

Cliff – who is turning out to be as charming as halitosis – admits that resisting my mother's demands is a gamble. But he also says if I'm always available to bail her out, neither of us will 'move on'. I'm not sure I like the all-inclusive nature of that last statement.

'What do you mean by that?' I say haughtily.

Cliff coughs and says, 'If you can't deal with pain, the easiest thing to do is to put it back in its box. If a person spends all their time worrying about someone else's pain they distract themselves from their own.'

I feel uneasy so I say stiffly, 'I don't know what you're talking about.'

Cliff hesitates, then changes the subject. 'Okey-doke,' he says. Bet he doesn't say that in front of his right-on friends.

'Helen, tell me a little about your relationship with your father,' he says in a melty-honey tone.

I say sourly, 'What's to tell.'

Cliff waits. Does that classify the situation as a cliff-hanger? 'Well, for instance, what did you like to do together?' he prompts.

'Not much,' I say. Analyse that up your bum. My shoulders are so hunched they're level with my ears. I look at the clock. Christ, I've been on the phone to this man for thirty minutes! Hasn't he got a life to lead? I pick at a mystery green crust under my left thumbnail and say, 'Look, I've got to go. I need to get a sandwich. Anyway, I thought this call was about my mother.'

Cliff pauses. I can hear him flicking his lighter. I suspect he's about to say something pompous. I'm not disappointed. 'Helen,' he says. 'When someone dies, a door opens into a room where there's grief. There may be more rooms. If you have the courage you can look further. Some people shut the door again.'

He then starts wittering about 'closing' and asks if there is anything else I want to say but there's nothing.

I stare into space for ten minutes then start calling estate agents.

Chapter 30

I rounded up all my favourite memories this morning. They have one thing in common. Food. Being taken to a grown-up party and asking the hostess for fruit salad 'but only the cherries', and getting them. Eating a boiled egg on a ferry and not being able to finish it – a magic bottomless egg that went on for ever. Michelle's grandma buying us comics and a Curly Wurly each. A peach in Spain as big as a ball, my skin smelling like toffee in the sun. Reading the words on my mother's cottage cheese pot – 'low fat cheese' – and asking, 'Mummy, how can cheese be low?' and making her laugh. All delicious.

But my best edible memories revolve around Christmas. Helping my mother make a currant-filled cake for her class and scraping out the bowl. Baking gingerbread men at school with cut-out shapes. Stuffing myself with Quality Street (except the purple ones) until I felt sick. Asking for six roast potatoes and leaving three and my father being too merry to boom, 'Your eyes are bigger than your stomach!'

My father was fun at Christmas. He'd creep into my bedroom late on Christmas Eve and plop a Terry's plain chocolate orange into my stocking. (I prefer milk chocolate but he wasn't to know.) We'd drive to the garden centre and choose a tree and I'd breathe in the smell of fresh pine and and he'd say, 'Daylight robbery!' or 'Peculiar shape!' And he'd buy himself a cigar and me a pack of sugar cigarettes and we'd smoke them in the car on the way home. Naturally, this tradition came to an end when I turned seven, but I think of it today and I want to drag him out of his grave.

I am dreading Christmas without him and so is my mother.

Understandably, Vivienne's benevolence does not stretch to inviting Cecelia round for Christmas dinner. Especially now she comes with the unseasonal condition of Nana Flo (who is to parties what myxomatosis is to rabbits). I know my mother perceives this as a slight because at breakfast she declares, 'I'm not doing Christmas this year, I'm staying in bed. So don't expect any presents!'

I pause from feeding Fatboy his Turkey and Giblets Pâté and exclaim, 'But Mummy, we can't *not do* Christmas! Even Michelle does Christmas!'

My mother snaps, 'Michelle's father is still alive!'

I am about to say, 'Look, I know it's hard for you,' when I think of Cliff flicking his lighter. I say calmly, 'I'm still alive. Nana's still alive. Just. What about the cake we made together?'

My mother slams down her tea cup. 'I don't care about the stupid cake!' she whines. 'It's not the same without a man in the house!' Indeed it isn't. There are no willies lurking under trousers.

'Oh, Mum,' I say sadly, 'I know it isn't. But why can't we have a quiet Christmas, just the three of us?' She sticks out her lower lip. She must have learned it from one of her kids. It's so comical – a four-year-old's expression on a fifty-five-year-old face – I have to bite my tongue to stop myself laughing.

'I can't be bothered,' she says defiantly.

'Mum,' I say, 'is this because you're going to the clinic today?'

My mother snorts and says, 'No. It's because I want nothing to do with Christmas and I refuse to go Christmas shopping. I shun it!' Fine.

'Alright, Scrooge,' I say sternly, 'then Nana and I will have to celebrate it ourselves. Won't we, Nana?'

Nana Flo, who has just shuffled in carrying her hot water bottle, shrugs and mutters, 'Nothing to celebrate.'

I feel foolish for thinking that Nana would help me out. She doesn't go a bundle on helping people. Not even herself. I remember last Christmas when, in a burst of benevolence, I bought us tickets to see *Les Misérables*. (I wasn't sure what it was about but it sounded perfect. And I felt guilty for not visiting her in six months.) As I was working that day I suggested that we meet in the foyer. She rang me at 5.45 p.m. and announced she couldn't make it, as 'if you haven't the time to come and fetch me what's the point?' This from a woman who's been travelling on buses ever since they were invented!

I look at Nana Flo in her ugly black shoes and beige tights and drab frock and the opal brooch at her neck holding it all together and I wonder if she has ever been happy. And I'm not just saying that. Really, I wonder. 'Nana,' I say, 'when do you think you were, ah, when do you think you were happiest?'

Nana Flo's pinched face seems more colourless than usual. 'On my wedding day,' she says.

'Of course,' I mumble. 'Well, I'm going to work now, see you both later.' I scurry out of the door, berating myself for my gabbering stupidity. Nana Flo married Grandpa Gerald on her eighteenth birthday, a fortnight before Hitler invaded Poland. A week after war was declared, Grandpa Gerald was conscripted. Two months after that Grandpa Gerald was blown to smithereens by a shell during training.

I think Nana Flo put her grief back in its box.

I am still brooding about my grandmother being robbed of her sweetheart *before* he had the chance to be very brave and fight the enemy like a lion when Michelle calls to inform me that she and Marcus are engaged. Her exact words: 'I guess you were his final fling!' And I guess I'm thinking about the shreds of my grandfather strewn across

Salisbury Plain because – when I regain the power of speech – instead of saying 'Would you like me to recommend a quack specialising in penile augmentation?' I say I'm pleased and I hope they'll be happy. My voice sounds high and thin but not, I hope, hysterical. Michelle – who has obviously psyched herself up for a flouncy row – sounds taken aback. She says 'Oh!'

Then she adds, in a deflated tone, 'Oh sure! Thanks. And I, uh, I hope you'll be happy with that guy, even if he is a complete jerk. He ruined my fiancé's shirt. It was an Armani!'

I say before I can stop myself: 'Michelle, I know that shirt and it was a present from Marcus's mother who bought it from Bhs. And Tom is not a jerk and anyway, I'm not with him.'

Ker-ching! Michelle's ears prick up like a Dingo's. 'Oh?' she says, 'Why so?'

Me and my yapping mouth. I say shortly, 'It didn't work out.' The carcass of my ill-fated romance is not going to be picked over by the spindly fingers of Ivana the Terrible.

'No way! Why?' she demands.

'Michelle!' I squawk, 'I'm not discussing it.'

She huffs down the phone, 'Okay, chill!' There is a pause before she asks in a whisper, 'Did he beat you?'

I shout 'Beat me! Are you mad? He's a vet!'

Michelle is put out. 'What happened then?' she wheedles. The tenacity of the woman! She's like a bloodhound sniffing at a crotch.

'I said,' I say in a hard voice, 'I don't want to discuss it.'

Michelle snaps, 'There's obviously something you're not telling me!'

I grimace and say slyly, 'So has Marcus given you an engagement ring?'

She replies joyfully, 'I'm taking him, I mean, he's taking me to Tiffany's this afternoon.' I smile as I imagine a house falling on Marcus's wallet.

'Ooh,' I say, 'lucky you.' The scenario reminds me of my

father's favourite joke: the one where Mrs Goldblatt gets on a plane and the man sitting next to her admires her enormous diamond ring. Yes it *is* beautiful, says Mrs Goldblatt, but sadly this beautiful diamond ring comes with a curse. Mr Goldblatt. Personally, I never thought it was funny, but now it seems apt. I know Michelle will take this question the wrong way, but I still ask: 'Michelle, are you in love with Marcus?'

Silence. Then a tinkle of merry laughter and the gloating words, 'You're jealous!'

I say evenly, 'Not really,' but Michelle insists and I'm too indifferent to argue so I let it be.

'You could always go back to Jason,' she says gloatingly.

'Jasper!' I gasp – my goat finally gotten – 'Michelle, I am not going back in that muddy puddle. Give me credit! Anyway I'm fine by myself.'

Michelle brands me a liar and adds that the wedding will be a 'select affair' so if I don't receive an invitation I shouldn't be offended.

'Michelle,' I say – before cutting this cancer off and out of my life for ever – 'let's end it there.' I complete the purge with a double espresso.

None of the four estate agents I called has got back to me. This isn't a huge surprise. When I rang JI & Sons in Kentish Town the yob at the end of the line said, 'So what you looking up to?' I told him and he said, 'Have you tried our Surrey Quays office?' The response from Wideboy Estates was: 'The cheapest we've got at the moment is two hundred thousand,' and Gitfinger Properties enquired, 'Is that per week for letting? Oh! To buy!' By far the most courteous was Snatchit & Co. who declared, 'Let me put you through to my colleague who deals with flats – I only deal with properties over three hundred thou,' then put me on hold until the line went dead.

So when Lizzy – who was on a shoot all day yesterday and is 'bursting' to hear my 'news' – suggests I join her for lunch I grab the excuse to postpone flat hunting. Only after accepting the invitation do I realise I don't feel like talking.

'Tell me everything!' demands Lizzy. 'No skipping!'

I pick at my lip. 'You're going to be disappointed,' I say.

Her face drops. 'Why?' she cries, brimming with genuine concern.

I wrinkle my nose and say, 'Tom and I had an argument and I shouted at him. Really shouted.' I cringe, remembering my frenzied rage.

Lizzy blurts, 'Oh no! Why? What about?'

I tell her. Or rather, I tell her the bits I want her to know. I don't tell her about the woe-splattered gunk that spewed from me like blood from a slashed artery. I'd prefer not to believe in it until it fades away. So I gut and dissect the truth and present Lizzy with the leftovers. Lizzy is torn. Partly, because she can't bear to speak ill of anyone. But also because I give Tom a lousy write-up.

Eventually, she says sorrowfully, 'What a terrible shame. He seemed so nice. Maybe he didn't mean to interfere. Although I must say, it's not nice to criticise someone else's parent. Especially as your father was *such* a nice man.'

My conscience – which spends most of its life asleep – pokes me at this point and I mutter, 'It wasn't all Tom's fault. I did moan about Dad. Not very loyal of me, was it?'

Lizzy brushes away my gloom with an airy, 'Don't be so hard on yourself! Everyone complains about their parents occasionally – I know I do all the time!' (Lizzy only ever speaks of her mother and father in glorious glowing hyperbole.)

I sigh. 'You're right,' I say. 'You don't tell people what to do. It's intrusive.'

Lizzy – scrabbling desperately for a happy ending – says, 'Are you *sure* he wasn't just interested?'

I recall Tom's snub over the flat and I'm too mortified to confide in my close friend.

'Positive!' I growl.

Lizzy is silent. 'Are you sure you can't patch it up?' she says.

I reply, 'This wasn't a silly little tiff, Lizzy, it was a serious disagreement.'

She says dejectedly, 'Maybe it's best to leave it for a while then.'

I nod, keen to switch subject before Lizzy assails me with further questions. But every topic I consider is barred by a large 'Don't Go There' sign. I'm loath to discuss living in Muswell Hill because it may lead to smithereen grandfathers or psychiatric nurses. I'm reluctant to ask about Brian because we may edge back to Tom again. I'd prefer not to mention Michelle because my skin crawls when I think of Marcus and the phantom father syndrome. My head is one huge roadblock. I blurt, 'Liz, do you think I smother my mother?'

Instead of answering Lizzy clutches my arm – I assume to show me my question is on hold – and cries, 'Tina! Tina!' I follow her gaze and see Tina ducking into a shoe shop. 'Let's ask her to have lunch with us!' exclaims Lizzy, skipping after her.

If only the Faraway Tree was real, I think. Sugarspun Lizzy would fit in *so* well. 'I'll wait outside,' I say. Seconds later Lizzy emerges with Tina in an armlock.

'Jesus! What happened to your nose?' I gasp.

Lizzy answers for Tina: 'She was getting a tin of baked beans off the top shelf and it fell on her. Poor thing!'

I say, 'Does it hurt?'

Tina shakes her head. I sense that she isn't overjoyed to be having lunch with us. Lizzy also feels uncomfortable because she tries to lighten the mood by joking, 'Well, it just proves that tinned food is bad for you!'

No one laughs. And from this low point the mood goes into free fall. Tina appears to have taken a vow of silence, and I am nervous to ask Lizzy about her weekend in case she boomerangs it back to mine. So – foolishly – I whip a shred of beetroot from Lizzy's plate, stick it across the bridge of my nose, and say, 'Who's this!' Lizzy is quiet. Tina looks at me. I stare back and I'm shocked at the revolt in her eyes. I remove the beetroot from my nose and mutter, 'Bad joke, sorry.'

Tina says coldly, 'You always say that but you never change, do you? You're like a fucking broken record.'

My mouth drops open. 'Shit!' I squeak. 'I didn't mean anything by it, okay? What *is* it with you? You're so aggressive. I can't say anything any more without you leaping down my throat.' Tina's expression is molten rage but I rant on: 'Ever since darling Adrian came on the scene – Adrian! Adrian! – we're not good enough for you now!'

Tina bangs her fist down on the metal table making Lizzy and the plates jump. 'You, girl, are out of line!' she snarls. 'Vicious! What is it this time? Tom? Jasper? Marcus? Oh sorry, I lose track.'

I feel hot with anger and I spit, 'No actually, it's not about a man. It's my father.' For once I am telling the absolute truth.

I expect it to silence her but she snarls, 'And the rest!' Then she jumps up and hisses, 'Don't use your dad as an emotional crowbar on *me*, Helen. You never liked him! You've strung it out long enough! Have some respect – let the bloke rest in peace!'

This is without doubt the nastiest thing anyone has ever said to me in my life. Michelle, in her wildest dreams, hasn't come close. Marcus calling me a slut – chickenfeed! The fury is so fierce I want to hit Tina in the face. Luckily for her she flees the café before I've organised my fist. I'm so aghast I can't look at Lizzy. I sit trembling. I crush my napkin into a tight ball, and wonder how it came to this. I suck in huge gulps of air but find it impossible to catch my breath. Eventually, I feel a soft touch on my back and Lizzy says gently, 'Are you okay?' I nod and shake off her hand. She whispers, 'Tina didn't mean it.'

This rouses me from petrification and I snap, 'She did though. And she needn't think I'm running after her this

time because I bloody am not. That's it with her and me.'
The unwelcome thought occurs to me that I'm shedding
friends and acquaintances at a rate of four a week – and
there's Wednesday, Thursday, Friday and Saturday still to
go.

Lizzy takes a breath. Then she says, 'I don't think Tina's
happy. Despite Adrian. Or I can't believe she would have
said those things.'

I shrug, 'Whatever.'

Lizzy perseveres: 'About what she said about your dad,
well, firstly – it's your right to feel what you feel. Even if
you weren't that close, which I can't believe. And, er,
secondly, well maybe reiki could help?'

I giggle. And I wonder, if a madman hacked off my leg
with an axe, would Lizzy offer to kiss it better? I force
brightness into my voice and say, 'Lizzy, you know I dislike
people fiddling with me.'

Lizzy replies, 'Well, I don't know . . .'

She is reminiscent of myself tempting Fatboy out of the
boiler cavity with a bowl of tuna juice. And I must say, it's
working. I feel one degree calmer. I mutter, 'I just said the
dad thing to make Tina feel bad. She's right. I'm in a foul
mood.'

Lizzy sighs and says, 'Why though? If it's not your dad,
is it Tom?'

I knew this lunch was a bad idea. I throw my napkin on
the table and say, 'Tom puts his hand up dogs' bottoms
and his car is worse than mine. It isn't Tom.'

Lizzy says crossly: 'Helen, you don't give a fig about
cars! And he gets *paid* to put his hand up dogs' bottoms!'

I mumble, 'What – and that's supposed to make me feel
better?'

Lizzy purses her lips and says, 'Maybe it'll be good for
you to be on your own for a bit.'

I tut loudly and say in a bored tone, 'Why?'

Lizzy dabs her mouth with her napkin (her perfect
lipstick remains perfect) and like an archbishop delivering

the punchline to a televised sermon declares: 'You've got to be happy alone before you can be happy with someone.'

I sit back, fold my arms and try to look agnostic. 'Liz,' I say, 'Did you read that in *Girltime*?'

'I might have done,' says Lizzy airily. 'So?'

I reply sternly: 'I wrote it.'

Chapter 31

It takes two hundred thousand frowns to etch a line on your forehead. I look at the deep furrows on my mother's brow and wonder how many of those 200,000 sorrows and puzzlements were down to me. I'm doing my best to be impassive so I'm not pitying – just curious. I can't think of anything more stressful than being a parent. It must be even worse than having Laetitia for a boss.

Being responsible for the health and happiness of a live person. Scary. I spent forty-five quid on cat books and another fifty on cat tat before I dared purchase the orange orphan from Battersea, and I still regard his lardy survival as a miracle. All the plants I've ever bought have perished within a fortnight, even the cactus. My mother is the same. There's no greenery in her house and never has been. She buys flowers for herself but that's different – they're *expected* to die after a week. So how she managed a smelly, crotchety baby I don't know. Actually I do – she hired an au pair.

Isabella was scared of the vacuum cleaner and wore fabulous white stilettos that made grooves in my mother's polished wood floor. I liked her very much. Once, at the skinny age of five, I moaned to Isabella that I was fat because I'd heard Vivienne moan it to my mother. Isabella hoicked up her orange T-shirt to reveal bunched up rolls of brown flesh and declared happily, 'You not fat! Zees eez fat!' I was mesmerised and after that, fat was no longer something to be feared. Thank God for Isabella. She saved me. Without Isabella and her cack-handed exuberance – 'I

247

look Helen, Meeseez Bradshaw, you go shop!' – I think my mother would have suffered a breakdown. And possibly I would have done too.

As it was, thirty pounds a week plus meals (which probably made it up to £130) released my mother from the slave labour of parenthood and she fled it. So her attempt to sidle back up to it twenty-six years on is amusing. Bless her, but she's rubbish at it. I slink in from work and she hijacks me in the hall. The first thing she says is 'Florence wants to move out!' and the second is 'I'm losing all my family!' and the third is 'I've made you tea!' I drop my bag on the floor and try not to look alarmed. I also try to respond fairly to all her statements.

'Is Nana moving out because of *me*?' I say.

My mother flaps her hands as if to ward off the idea. 'Sort of,' she says.

I knew it. I bleat, 'I didn't think! Christ, where is she, I'll go and explain!'

My mother looks confused. She says, 'I don't know what you're talking about! It was the sardine pilfering!'

I squeak, 'What sardine pilfering?'

It emerges that this morning Nana placed her favourite lunch – three sardines and a slice of white bread – on the side to 'air'. Ten minutes later she discovered Fatboy, whose motto is 'Finders Keepers', crouched next to the plate chewing at his third sardine. This confirmed her every prejudice about living under the same roof as 'vermin' and as a direct result, Nana is returning to her stringbeans first thing tomorrow morning.

'Sorry,' I mutter, 'I'll try and stop her if you want.'

My mother shakes her head and says cheerfully, 'She's in her room, packing! Don't bother! You're here now! And I've made you tea!'

'But I don't drink t—' I begin as I walk into the kitchen. To my surprise and dismay the table is heaped, *heaped*, with sandwiches and little cakes – concoctions I didn't think existed any more like chocolate Wagon Wheels and pink and yellow Fondant Fancies. There is even a Battenburg Cake.

'I made it for you!' she repeats, like a six-year-old who has fashioned a monstrous pom-pom at school with card and wool and expects her mother to attach it to her smartest hat.

'That's er, very kind of you,' I say as I sink into the chair she yanks out for me.

She sits down excitedly and watches eagle-eyed as I reach for a Marmite sandwich. I hate Marmite. I take a small bite and wonder what the hell's going on. 'How are you?' asks my mother.

'Fine,' I say, trying to swallow the sandwich without retching.

She sighs pointedly as if this is the wrong answer and snaps, 'No, how are you *feeling*?'

I hear this sentence and it all becomes clear. The dastardly Cliff!

'Mummy,' I growl, 'what has Cliff been saying to you?'

She looks guilty and says sulkily, 'Nothing! Nothing at all!'

I point a finger. 'You never ask how I'm feeling! He must have said something! What did you discuss this morning?'

She wriggles crossly in her seat and says, 'That I don't like going to the clinic because everyone in the waiting room is mad!'

I allow myself to be sidetracked. 'Oh! How come?'

My mother leans forward and shrieks, 'It was positively Kafkaesque, I've never seen anything like it! Psychotic, the lot of them! I couldn't believe I was there! So drab! And dirty! It was disgusting! Worse than school! This woman, this woman wearing a plastic bag on her head, mumbling to herself and shouting at the ceiling, her bag was full of carrots and she, she, she asked me for money!'

Poor thing. To be mentally ill enough to think that my mother – with her neat bob and tightly clasped handbag – would relinquish even fifty pence without receipt of a cut-glass 'Please.' I say, 'She was probably desperate, Mummy. I hope you gave her something?'

My mother shakes her head and says, 'I told her to go away and leave me alone. She smelt funny.' I sigh. To think that the moral education of thirty impressionable children is in this woman's soft yet brutish hands. And they consider her their best teacher!

'So what else did you talk about with Cliff?' I demand.

'He wasn't so nice this time,' she replies. 'I didn't like him as much.'

I place my Marmite sandwich on my plate. 'Mum,' I say, 'the clinic is not a dating agency. You don't have to like him. So what did he say?'

But my mother is determined not to tell and becomes agitated. 'It doesn't matter!' she insists. 'Just tell me how you feel! And don't stop eating!'

I grab a Fondant Fancy, peel away the pink icing, and lick a glob of cream off its top. If my mother is treating me like a toddler I might as well make the most of it. 'How I feel about what?' I gasp, as the nerves in my teeth revolt against the sugar.

'I don't know!' she cries. 'Everything!'

I take a sip of lemonade (she's bought that too) and try to think. What can I say that won't upset her? That I don't mind about Christmas? That the additives are delicious? That she shouldn't worry about Nana Flo? That I won't move out until she wants me to? That I'm glad she's returning to school in January? All these thoughts are anodyne, inoffensive, and safe. Feelings are trickier. But feelings are what she wants. And if I don't tell her, she'll never learn. She has no imagination and if this silly tea is anything to go by, no common sense. Fine. She asked. I realise my mother is staring at me at the same time I realise I'm rocking in my chair and nodding like a little old lady. But it's hard to speak. I am terrified that the ache I want to think of as a fading bruise will be diagnosed as gangrene.

Finally I blurt, 'How I feel is that I miss Dad.'

My mother claps her hands and exclaims triumphantly, 'That's how *I* feel!'

I conceal a smile. My mother is fifty-five and never going to change. Cliff is fifty years too late. I *was* going to add, 'Yes, but you have the right. You loved each other,' and see what – on the crest of her new empathy fad – she made of it. But I decide I'd be better off working out the answer for myself.

When the phone rings and I hear Luke's voice at the other end of it I practically deafen him, such is my joy at being whisked from Fondant Fancy & Feelings Prison. 'You sound pleased to hear from me,' he says delightedly.

'I *am*!' I squeal. 'How *are* you! I miss you!'

Luke says bashfully, 'I miss you too. It's not the same without you.'

I suggest, 'It's tidier?'

He laughs, 'Much.'

I beam. 'So what's up?' I say.

Luke pauses, 'You heard about Michelle and Marcus?'

I reply, 'Yeah! I don't know who to feel more sorry for!'

Sounding surprised, Luke says, 'So you're not upset?'

My tone is shrill: 'God, no!' I squeal, pressing the tip of my nose to stop it growing.

I can hear the smile in Luke's voice, 'Great! So uh, how's Tom?'

It's my turn to pause. 'I haven't seen him since Sunday,' I say shortly.

'It's only Tuesday!' says Luke. 'Give the man a chance!'

I feel obliged to set the record straight. 'We're not seeing each other,' I say. 'We fell out.'

Luke replies, 'Oh. Well can you give us his number? I'm going out with the lads on Friday, thought I'd ask him along.' I am divided between fascination (how is it possible to be so interested in football and so uninterested in human relations?) and admiration (so sweet natured yet so acutely insensitive – surely the pinnacle of self-preservation?).

'Hang on,' I say, plodding into the hall, emptying my bag

on to the floor, and sifting through the rubble. Eventually I find my phone book. I read Luke out Tom's number and try not to sound miserable.

'So what you doing for Christmas?' says Luke. His knack of hitting the nail on the head when it has a migraine is uncanny.

'I'm not sure,' I say. 'How about you?'

Luke replies, 'The usual. Going to my parents' where there'll be too much to drink and a monster family row.'

I say, 'How lovely,' and mean it.

Then I trot back into the kitchen where my mother is staring forlornly at the Battenburg. 'Leave it, Mummy,' I say, 'I'll clear it.'

She replies crossly, 'You barely ate a thing! I'm going to wash my hair!'

I shout after her, 'I'm taking some up to Nana! It won't go to waste!' I listen to myself. I sound about ninety. The sooner Nana moves out the better.

I knock timidly on her door. 'Who is it?' she shrills.

'Fatboy!' I feel like shrilling back, but don't. 'Helen!' I bellow.

She shuffles to the door and pulls it open. 'Yes?' she demands.

I wave about the cake plate at nose level. 'I brought you up some cake.'

She sticks out a hand and takes it. 'Thank you,' she says and tries to shut the door!

I stick my foot in the gap. 'Nana,' I say in a clear voice, 'I know you're busy but could I come in for a second?'

She shrugs and says, 'If you must,' and doesn't open the door any wider.

I suck in my stomach and squeeze through. Her few clothes are neatly folded in a stiff battered suitcase which is lying open on the bed. Her purple thistle coat is hanging neatly over a chair. Nana herself sits in the chair and starts guzzling the cake. I notice that her swollen fingers are dry and cracked at the joints and suddenly I feel like crying.

252

'Nana,' I say in a rush, 'I'm so sorry about my cat pilfering your lunch, and—'

She interrupts me: 'I told your mother it was unhygienic to have that filthy creature in the house, but would she listen?'

Privately I think that letting sardines 'air' is marginally more unhygienic than Fatboy but – as I accept it's unpleasant to have one's lunch munched by an animal – I keep my opinion to myself. I apologise again. Then I say, 'And Nana, please forgive me for reminding you about Grandpa, I didn't mean to. And I do hope you're not leaving because of it.'

Nana makes a noise in her throat and for a nasty second I think she's choking to death on cake. When I realise it's a gurgle of disdain, I'm relieved. For a couple to die, respectively, in smithereens and from cake would be too cruel. My grandmother says, 'Not a day goes by when I don't think of my Gerald.'

I'm thankful – so I didn't remind her! – but unsure of how to react. I'd like to ask her all about him but I'm scared of upsetting her. So (as per programming) I say, 'I'm sorry.'

Nana replies, not unkindly, 'That's life and you have to face up to it. I make the best of things.' She nods towards the door. I take this to indicate dismissal and head towards it. I don't dare answer back but I wonder about what she says. Do you? I think.

My way of making the best of things is to run away from them. And I don't care what anyone says – I stand by it as a basic human right. I wake up on Wednesday, become aware of a nasty sinking sensation inside, and remember that Tom and I aren't shagging and I wish we were. I get to work and confess to Lizzy who says, 'Call him then.'

I have a better idea: 'Let's get wasted!' Lizzy pouts. 'On orange juice!' I add, knowing that the chance of getting Lizzy to put alcohol to lip is remote. 'Wasted from a surfeit

253

of vitamin C! Hooray!' I exclaim, to tempt her and to stop myself sagging. Lizzy looks unconvinced so I say, 'Brian's in Hong Kong at the t'ai chi convention, you went to the gym yesterday, the day before, and probably the day before that. Too much exercise is bad for you! You'll grind away your hip bones! Ugh! Think of the arthritis!'

I fold my arms and wait. 'Did I tell you Michelle and Marcus are engaged?' I say, in a sly bid to further my cause.

'What! No! When? Ohmigod!' says Lizzy. 'Alright,' she adds reluctantly, 'but don't think I don't know it's blackmail.'

I say, 'That's a double negative but good,' and start plotting.

The prospect of luring Lizzy to drink is so uplifting that I'm inspired to call an estate agent. To my surprise Adam has two properties to show me. They're both in Kentish Town and within my price range. One flat he describes as 'well located for all the local amenities'. The other is 'spacious and well positioned'. I tell him that I'm busy tonight but maybe tomorrow and he has a fit. 'There's lots of people viewing!' he screams. 'Are you serious about this or not! There's nothing else around! They'll disappear like that!' I hear a snapping of fingers and suspect that Adam is what Michelle's grandmother would call a 'meshuggener'. But I agree to view the flats tonight anyway.

I break the news to Lizzy at six and she doesn't mind at all. 'It'll be fun!' she says. We take the tube to Adam's office and announce ourselves. Adam is busy talking on the phone and gestures for us to sit down. Four minutes later he leaps up, manfully jangles a huge bunch of keys in our faces, and ogles Lizzy. I can tell he's impressed by her, and she and I are knocked out by him too – or rather by his foul industrial strength aftershave. 'It's Joop!' whispers Lizzy, when Adam goes to pick up his Mondeo, 'but you're not meant to put that much on.'

I wipe my stinging eyes and murmur, 'You don't say.'

A second later, a white banger with a dented passenger

door swerves to a halt in front of us. We jump back to avoid losing our toes. 'Lizzy, you can go in the front,' I say sweetly but she demurs. So *I* get to sit next to Adam who – with his gelled French crop and gold signet ring and outsize ego – is speedily becoming irresistible. Joke. I shift my feet and try not to disturb the car's delicate ecosystem of cans, cartons, and copies of *FHM*. For lack of anything to say I bleat, 'Oh dear! Your stereo's been stolen.'

He replies, 'Yeah, wank, innit?' and lights up a fag.

Although it's midwinter, he winds the window right down and clutches at the roof – presumably to stop it flying off. Happily for all concerned, Adam's mobile phone rings. Adam spends the next ten minutes shouting stuff like: 'Nah! Donna! Nice one! Yeah! Well stacked! The Harvester! Sorted!' and I shiver in my coat and say to Lizzy, 'I can't believe I'm doing this.'

She coos, 'Why not! It's brilliant living on your own! I love it! Imagine! Not having to share a bathroom!'

I nod and say, 'I suppose,' then the car lurches to a halt and Adam jumps out.

Fifty-nine seconds later we are all sulkily hunched in the car again. I glower at Adam's black leather shoes (each fetchingly adorned with a metal bar) and squeak, 'Well located for all the local amenities! It's above a fish and chip shop!'

Adam can't see the problem. 'Sweetheart,' he says, 'for your money that's whatchure gonna get around here. And you'll never go hungry!'

I say suspiciously, 'Does that mean the other is next door to an all-night petrol station?'

Adam is impressed. 'Howge know?' he says.

'East Finchley's nice,' says Lizzy comfortingly, as Adam races off. 'Maybe you could look there?'

I wrinkle my nose. 'It's too near my mother,' I say. 'Let's find somewhere to sit.'

Fifteen minutes later we are perched at a table in front of

255

a bottle of red. I am glugging and Lizzy – having been persuaded 'just this once' – is sipping. She is keen to hear the inevitable tale of Marcus and Michelle and shrieks, '*No!*' whenever I try to skip bits. We empty the wine bottle extremely fast. Or as Lizzy says – after two small glasses – 'fasht'. She's a cheap date, I'll say that much. I order a second bottle and Lizzy hiccoughs. 'I never do thish in the week!' she giggles.

'You never do it at the weekends either!' I say.

The conversation veers on to Christmas. I announce that I'm doing 'bugger all' and Lizzy says she's 'helping out at a koup sitchen'. We hoot with laughter. 'Wow. Good for you. But doesn't it make you sad?' I say when we calm down.

'No,' says Lizzy, 'ish great. Ish uplifting! Ish what Christmas ish all about!'

I pour us each another glass. 'What – hassling the homeless so you feel smug *and* avoid your family?' I say. Lizzy looks dumbfounded so I add hastily, 'Only joking, but aren't you seeing Brian?'

Cue an hour-long ramble about Brian, during which *Lizzy* orders another bottle and I think 'but Brian's so old'. 'But Brian's so old!' I declare and I clap my hand over my mouth.

Lizzy smacks me playfully on the arm and yells, 'I heard you! He's not old! Well he's old*er* but sho what!'

I shriek, 'But it's like going out with your dad!'

Fortunately Lizzy chooses to find this funny rather than slap my face. She whacks the table, peals with laughter, and squeals, 'He's nothing like my dad! You freaky! He's old*er* but sho what!'

Possibly the volume of alcohol swishing round my insides has pickled my brain because I feel unable to contest this assertion. 'Yeah! Sho what!' I repeat.

Lizzy takes a gulp of wine and tosses her hair back from her face and giggles, 'You're funny! You're in denial! That's what my shycol, shycol, that's what my friend says!'

Lizzy is so busy flicking shiny hair and trying to pronounce the word 'psychologist', she doesn't notice my startled expression.

'About what?' I say, the laughter dying in my throat.

'I don't know!' she roars, lolling in her seat. 'Tom probly!' she sniggers.

I snigger too and shout 'Cak!' Then we snigger at the word 'cak'. I'm reluctant to stop laughing so I wheeze, 'But he, but he—' Lizzy teetle-heetles and gasps, 'puts his hand up' – we chorus together: 'dogs' bottoms!'

And then I say something that seems like a good idea when I say it. I suggest we go to Tom's favourite bar. 'He lives near here! It's just down the road!' I say.

'If ish just down the road,' says Lizzy, 'lesh go!' We pay and totter out. 'My legsh are like rubber!' sings Lizzy as we lurch along clutching each other for support.

'You don't have to shout,' I bellow, 'I'm right next to you!' When you catch yourself thinking 'I'm dull when I'm pissed' *when* you're pissed there's no doubt you are very dull when pissed. 'This is it!' I exclaim. 'Let's look in the windows.'

Lizzy is already jumping up and down. She looks like Zebedee in a wig. 'I can't shee!' she complains. 'Lesh go in!' and with that she boots open the door and yanks me in.

My life falls off a cliff and splinters in a second. We see Tom. Tom is grasping the hand of an elegant woman. Lizzy shouts, 'There he *ish*!' and falls over. Everyone in the pub, including Tom and the woman, stares at us. I become instantly sober and pull Lizzy off the floor. She uses one hand to stop wobbling, the other to point, and roars, 'Helen doeshn't like you any more Tom cosh you put your hand up dogs' bottomsh!'

It is small consolation that as I hurl Lizzy and myself out the door, everyone in Tom's local is staring at Tom.

Chapter 32

One of my most useful habits is blaming other people. Giving yourself a hard time is *so* tedious and I'm sure it weakens your immune system. But sadly, when I wake up dribbling on Lizzy's bony designer sofa at 7 a.m. and wince through the tragedy of last night, there is no denying that the Dog's Bottom Disaster is entirely my fault. Alcohol and lunacy aside, what possessed me? What's it to me if Lizzy drinks cranberry juice? Aren't I big and bad and ugly enough to get drunk on my own? And what *was* I on to suggest we ferret around Tom's pub? What must he think of me? Why did I do it? Am I mad? Have I no shame? What a prat. I'm coming down with a cold.

I stare out of Lizzy's bay window, watch the pale winter sun glisten on the Thames, and wonder how long Tom has been seeing the woman. Even the fact that my fears and cynicism are justified can't console me. If *I* was Tom I'd be seeing her too. She looked sharp, glamorous, and together. As opposed to blunt, berkish, and cracking up. I feel a lump of pain heavy inside me but I'm too tired to fight it. Anguish washes over me and I let it. I'm defeated. I contemplate emigration to New Zealand then clench my teeth and hiss defiantly, 'So what!' Might as well be a man about it. When Lizzy shuffles into the airy lounge wearing a white towelling robe and a woeful expression, I'm picking my nose.

I can tell she's revving up for a long apology. I hold up a hand. 'Don't!' I say. 'It was my fault. And you were very funny.'

Lizzy doesn't smile. She looks near to tears. She blurts, 'I can visit him at work and explain! I *will* visit him! I—'

I interrupt: 'No you won't! Jesus, that'll make it even even worse!'

Lizzy strikes a Madonnaish pose (and I don't mean the Material Girl, I mean Christ's mother) and lifts the back of her hand to her smooth forehead. She's incredible. Even hangover chic suits her. 'I can't believe what I did!' she wails. 'I don't drink! I'm not like that! I feel terrible! I'm going to have to detox!'

I giggle nervously – I've led the Virgin Mary astray – and wheedle, 'But Lizzy, you only had four glasses – in your whole life! You go into detox when you're drinking vodka for breakfast!'

Lizzy perches her small behind on a large glass-top table and patiently details the difference between detoxing in a drying out clinic and detoxing on a three-day juice diet. The drying out clinic sounds jollier and I silently vow that if I ever find myself eating raw cauliflower for lunch and six dried apricots as 'a treat' I'll turn to drink immediately in order to increase my self-esteem.

Lizzy plods mopily into the kitchen and makes a peppermint tea for her and a double espresso for me. She is distraught at having to skip breakfast ('the most important meal of the day') because she feels nauseous, but tries to be brave. I refuse her offer of a shower and/or low-sugar muesli and collapse on the bottom-bruising sofa again until Lizzy suggests we leave for work. 'I think you should pull a sickie,' I say, studying her fashionably wan face.

'I couldn't!' she whispers, as if her chrome halogen lamp is bugged.

I shrug, retrieve my mobile, and ring my mother.

'Yes?' she says in a bleary voice.

'Mum? It's Helen!' I say. 'I stayed at Lizzy's last night.' She sounds confused, 'So?'

I pause then say, 'Well I didn't want you to worry, I thought you might be wondering where I was.'

She replies, 'Oh! Oh. I hadn't noticed. I dropped Florence home yesterday. I was very tired so I went to bed early. I was sleeping. You woke me up.'

At this point I lose the will to continue the conversation. I say, 'Mum, it's practically midday. Will you feed Fatboy when you do eventually get up?' She says yes and cuts off.

'Is she okay?' enquires Lizzy.

'She's lazy is what she is,' I say.

Lizzy doesn't know how to respond so she changes the subject. 'I wonder if Tina will be in today,' she tinkles. I am silent so she adds, 'Do you think she's okay?'

I bark, 'Don't know, don't care.'

Lizzy sighs and says, 'I know she was terribly rude to you but I'm sure she was sickening for something – she wasn't in yesterday. If she's not in today I'll ring her.'

I nod. I'm not sure what to think about Tina. I know this much: she isn't sadistic like Michelle. I decide that if she grovels I'll forgive her. She's as chippy as a French fry but she's ultimately a true friend and I don't want to lose her. Although what she said stung, I'm trying to rationalise it. Possibly I *am* a raging hypocrite. But I can't help what I feel. Even if it doesn't make sense and is more of a surprise to me than anyone. At least Tina was ranting – I'd have been more upset if she'd said it while in control. Maybe I'll ring her later.

'So when's Brian back from Hong Kong?' I say to Lizzy who is desperate (I can tell by the look of ravaged purity) to absolve herself of last night's sin by harassing Tom.

'Soon,' she replies miserably, and then '*please* let me explain to Tom!'

I clutch my forehead and say, 'It doesn't matter! Anyway, there's no point. You saw he was with someone.'

Lizzy wails, 'But she could have been a friend! Or his sister! You don't know!'

I grimace and say – as if addressing a very stupid child – 'Liz, he was holding her *hand*.'

Lizzy starts, 'Yes but holding hands can mea—', sees my

260

thunderous face, and stops. She is, in her see-no-evil way, disappointed in me. She pouts and wrestles a small brown bottle from her bag. She twists it open, presses its pipette top, and squeezes two drops of liquid into her mouth.

'What's that?' I say, sniffing.

'Bach Rescue Remedy,' she replies shortly.

'It smells like whisky,' I growl.

'Well it's herbal,' she growls back.

'Hair of the dog more like,' I mutter.

'What?' says Lizzy.

'Nothing,' I say sweetly, 'just remind me never to get you drunk again.'

'You won't have to remind me,' she snaps.

I glance at her cross face. She's wearing a red coat, brown suede gloves, and looks exactly like a sulky china doll. Only the ruffles are missing. 'Aw!' I say. 'You know the best hangover cure?'

Lizzy regards me hopefully. 'What?' she breathes.

'A fried breakfast,' I say sweetly. She says nothing but gives me a small – but remarkably painful – pinch on the hand. 'Geroff!' I squeak, and we both giggle. We then lapse into weary silence until we reach the office.

I collapse at my desk and decide to call Tina tomorrow. I have far too much work to do today. I have estate agents, mothers, and vets to harangue. Laetitia is in a meeting so I spend thirty minutes scrounging broom cupboard details off young men with names like Richard and Costas who are insulted at the piddly sum I have to spend and reluctant to waste their sharking time on a minnow.

Then I call my mother. This time she's awake. 'Hello?' she trills.

'Mum,' I say, 'could you do me a favour?'

There's an alarmed pause before she says unwillingly, 'What is it?'

I scratch around for a trigger phrase and produce, 'I need some support.' I wait to see if a neurone picks it up. Silence. I continue, 'I need you to take Fatboy to the vet.'

My mother replies, 'Tim, the vet?'

I say, 'Yes, Tom.'

She says, enthusiastically, 'Such a charming boy! Clumsy but so charming!' I wonder how to play it.

'Mum,' I say eventually, 'Fatboy is unwell. He's sleeping a lot and I'm concerned that he has, er, sleeping sickness. So he needs to see Tom, urgently, preferably today.'

My mother is unconvinced. She declares: 'But cats sleep sixteen to eighteen hours a day! Sixty-six to seventy-five per cent of every twenty-four hours! They have light sleep periods lasting about thirty minutes, which is where we get the term "cat nap" from, and then, unless you pull their tail, a deeper sleep phase, which is an essential biological function! They—'

I cut this lecture short by shrieking, 'Mother!'

She stops mid-sentence then says sulkily, 'We did a project on it last term.' Just my luck.

'I'm sure you're right,' I say, trying to remain civil, 'but I'd like Tom to check him over anyhow.'

My mother says quickly, 'Why don't *you* want to take him?'

I squeak, 'What do you mean?'

She replies, 'I'm not daft, Helen! I'll be a go-between if you like, but I'm not daft!' An unfair and highly inconvenient statement. The woman plays Clouseau for the whole of my life but picks now to play Sherlock! This trait – call it the IQ Swing – is just one of the many which make my mother so exquisitely annoying.

'Alright,' I say reluctantly, 'but promise you won't say anything to embarrass me?'

She booms, 'Of course not! Tell me why you're not taking him!' I have no choice but to tell her.

'Tom and I had a disagreement,' I say carefully. 'Tom made *me* feel bad when I'd done nothing wrong! Anyway, Lizzy and I went out last night and bumped into him, and er, well, Mum, please don't repeat any of this, but Lizzy insulted him because he was with another woman.'

My mother gasps and I expect a long, ranting tirade about the loose morals of the younger generation but she exclaims: 'So what's wrong with that?'

I shriek, 'What's *wrong*?! Mum! He gives me all this flack and then it turns out he's cheating on me!'

She replies snappishly, 'Is he sleeping with you?'

Her bluntness floors me and in a bid to protect her from the sordid truth, I bleat, 'Er, no!'

My mother snorts loudly in my ear and barks, 'No! Why not? What's wrong with him? Is he gay?'

I nearly swallow my tongue (trait no. 2 – the Anomaly Opinion) and whimper, 'No!'

My mother is confused. She says briskly, 'So if he isn't sleeping with you, what's the problem? When *I* was your age I dated three men at a time and they liked it or lumped it! All's fair in love and war until someone proposes!'

Interesting. I don't argue. I merely say, 'I just want you to get an idea of how Tom feels about me right now, and if possible, find out who the woman is.' I add solemnly – wishing I had a gadget to press into her hand – 'I'm depending on you.'

My mother gasps again and says proudly, 'It all depends on *me*! Give me the address! I feel like a detective!'

I roll my eyes and say jokily, 'Great, just don't forget to take Fatboy.'

There is a pause and I brace myself for laughter. But she says, 'Fatb—? Oh yes, of course!'

I put down the phone and wonder, what's the worst that can happen?

I'm distracted for two minutes because Richard rings with a 'fantastic bijou property' he wants me to see. 'What's wrong with it?' I say.

'Nothing!' he says in an injured tone.

'Something must be,' I say.

He confesses that it 'needs a bit of work'. But it isn't above a fish and chip shop so I agree to see it tonight. As I

263

replace the receiver I hear him hiss 'Yesss!' Then I pick at the skin on my lip and pray that my mother doesn't do anything foolish at the vet. I mean, did I just give a handgun to a chimp? I wait and wait, spend an hour trawling supermarkets in search of a vegetable called 'purslane' for Laetitia's dinner party (when I return folorn and empty-handed she shouts, 'Are you completely useless? It's an ethnic vegetable!'), wait and wait, take a prank call from a pervert who wants me to read out *Girltime*'s coverlines to him (this month one of them contains the word 'orgasmic'), wait and wait, type in a feature on celebrity cellulite ('It contains tips you could make use of!' sings Laetitia as she plonks the 3,000 word piece in front of me), wait and wait, and when I can wait no longer, ring my mother.

She picks up. 'Mum!' I squeal. 'Why haven't you rung?'

She says huffily, 'I've only just stepped in the door. *And* I sat in that waiting room for hours! The inconvenience! It took me ages to find the cat! He was out hunting. I was on the doorstep calling him for twenty minutes! I got a funny look from the postman.' I suspect this is because she refuses to call Fatboy by his name and insists on calling him 'Pussy'. But I don't say so because I'm desperate to hear about Tom.

'So did you see Tom?' I say.

'Fuff!' replies my mother – who savours power to the extent that she'd make a fabulous Bond villain – 'That cat weighs a ton! Let me catch my breath! No, he wasn't there. Someone else saw to the cat. He hasn't got sleeping sickness but he has got fleas. And Tom's on holiday with his girlfriend.'

Chapter 33

As people who've never had anything bad happen to them always say, something good comes out of everything. So when I drive to the video shop on Saturday evening and see a young man crossing the road with a copy of the *Sun* and a four-pack of toilet rolls I grin because I'm reminded of Luke and how much closer we've become in the six days since Marcus evicted me. *Six* days since I saw Tom! It seems like an age. Anyhow, Luke is a lot more fun now we aren't living together. For the first time in years, the two of us spent three hours together without scrapping.

Vivienne had invited my mother for Saturday tea – 'A sympathy tea! To make up for not inviting me for Christmas. But it doesn't make up for it at all!' – so I called Luke and suggested he come round. My excuse was that Fatboy was demanding that Luke exercise his visiting rights (a lie as Fatboy's affection for anyone evaporates the second he swallows the last lick of pâté).

The truth was that while I did want to see Luke, I was more impatient to know if Luke had seen Tom the night before, on his lads' night out. Just to be sure. But Luke sounds so pleased to be invited – 'should I bring a tin of tuna in brine or pilchards in tomato sauce?' – I feel instantly ashamed of my duplicity. 'Just bring yourself!' I exclaim guiltily and rush out and buy two tubes of Cheese & Onion Pringles. (Luke's motto: 'Crisps, crisps! Food of the gods!')

When Luke arrives bearing pilchards *and* tuna, I hug him hard and feel chipper for the first time in days. I make

265

coffee, present the crisps, and retrieve Fatboy from his new napping spot (the blue metallic bonnet of next door's Volvo). I watch Luke watching Fatboy who bolts the pilchard juice, yawns pinkly, and stalks off to lie in a shaft of sunlight. Then I ask casually, 'So how was last night?'

Luke scratches his ear deeply and wipes his finger on his crumpled blue shirt, leaving a waxy yellow smear. His face breaks into a wide smile. 'Yeah! It was great. We had a great laugh.' He embarks on a long story which begins with ten pints apiece in a functional no-frills pub and continues with a boisterous meal in an Indian restaurant where Luke's mate Gobbo (who sounds like a sweetie although I've never had the pleasure) leans back in his chair and tells the bloke on the next table to 'Shut your mouth you nobber or I'll stick that table up your fucking pooh hole' and continues further with Gobbo punching Luke in the kidneys and Luke about to leave it until Luke's mate Parky says, 'You're not going to let him get away with that, are you?' and Luke doing this move he learned from a Jackie Chan film and he flipping Gobbo over his head and Gobbo landing on his back like a turtle and Parky killing himself laughing and Gobbo all red in the face and saying it was a fluke and that Luke knows 'SAS – Shit About Shit!' and Parky laughing and Gobbo thinking Parky's laughing because Gobbo just said something clever when in fact Parky's laughing because Gobbo *thinks* he said something clever and—

'Was Tom there?' I say after twenty minutes' yarn.

Luke stops mid-sentence. 'No.' He seems surprised at the question.

I try to act relaxed but my head jerks forward involuntarily and the words slide out in a sharp tumble, 'But I thought you were going to ask him.'

Luke's response is to wedge seven Pringles into his mouth and a short battle ensues between his jaw joints and the mass of crisp and until Luke gains control and his cheeks revert to their normal shape I am forced to wait.

266

Luke swallows and replies, 'I spoke to him but he was going away.' He looks at me nervously.

'Oh really?' I say. 'Did he mention when?'

Luke shakes his head. 'Or with who?' Luke shakes his head again and digs into the Pringle tube with such force his hand is, for a few tense moments, stuck. As he wrestles it out I abandon all semblance of dignity and ask, 'So is Tom going out with someone? Apart from me,' I add hurriedly, seeing his confused expression, 'he's not going out with me, remember?'

Luke blurts, 'Doesn't he fancy you any more?'

I say, with effort, 'No.'

Luke crunches loudly, becomes aware of the deafening crunch-crunch sound echoing round the kitchen, and tries to crunch more quietly. He then coughs, spewing a fine Pringle spray over the table. 'Can I have a water?' he croaks. Luke downs the water in one, then says slowly, 'He might be seeing someone, I don't know.' I squeak, 'He *might* be! What does that mean?' Luke pours a caterpillar of crisps on to the table and starts to devour it agitatedly, wodge by wodge. 'Luke!' I say awkwardly. 'It's just that I like him, I just wondered. I think I blew it.' I tell him about Dog's Bottom Night in the hope that the background information will spark a faint light in the dimness of his head.

Luke almost picks his nose, thinks better of it, and sits on his hands and says sadly, 'He didn't say. We talked about football.'

I feel like a sparrow pecking at concrete in the hope of it yielding a worm. I rub at an imaginary smudge on the table and say, 'I don't suppose he mentioned me, did he?'

Luke desperately wants to say yes, because his heart is as soft as a strawberry creme. So when he says 'No' he cushions the blow by offering me a Pringle as he says it.

I grin and say, 'It doesn't matter.' I add jollily, 'As someone else's mother would say, Plenty more fish in the sea!'

Luke smiles and says, 'Yeah, but who wants to shag a fish?'

After this philosophical exchange I decide not to mention Tom ever again ever and we sit on the lounge carpet and Luke plays 'Snake Style v Cat's Claw' with Fatboy – who may look like a sumo wrestler but judging from Luke's ravaged hand has an aptitude for kung fu. I make Luke wash his wounds under the tap, explain that Fatboy doesn't mean to be spiteful, he's just competitive – like a feline Gobbo, I add in a burst of inspiration – and after this Luke cheers up and we chat about Christmas.

Luke hadn't a clue what to get his parents so he rang his dad to ask if he knew what Mum wanted as a present and Dad revealed that Mum had been dropping hints about a pine bathroom and so he'd bought her a pine toilet seat and if Luke wanted to buy the matching doorknob he was welcome. Dad reckoned it 'wood go down a treat!'

I snort and snicker until I notice Luke looks confused.

'What?' he says, half-smiling in an I-don't-get-it way.

'What do you mean, what?' I squawk. 'He's joking, isn't he?'

Luke shakes his head, panic-stuffs in four Pringles and lights a fag at the same time, and says (though the words are muffled), 'Don't you think she'll be pleased?' I slap the table-top and squeal, 'Loooooooke! I swear on my life she will not be pleased! My God now I know where you get it from!' I am explaining to Luke the golden rules of female present-buying (quick guide: Cheap functional jokey token items = Go away you stingy bastard, Thoughtfully extortionate big frivolous items = Excellent you gorgeous man) when the phone rings.

It's Lizzy. Can she pop by? 'Of course!' I boom. 'Luke's here too!'

Lizzy beams down the phone, 'How lovely! I'll see you in a tick!'

I replace the receiver smiling. 'Lizzy bought all her presents months ago,' I say to Luke – whose mind remains derailed by the pine toilet seat bombshell – 'She'll tell you how it's done.'

As it happens, Lizzy doesn't tell Luke how present-buying is done. She shows him. She is still doing self-imposed penance for DBN – even though I have waived the crime about thirty times – and is keen to 'make amends' as she puts it. 'There are no amends to make, you idiot!' I say, as she hands me a large parcel. 'This is very unnecessary,' I add – you have to say that if someone gives you a present and you're over twenty-five – 'but very sweet of you.'

Lizzy clasps her hands and whispers, 'I *do* hope you'll like it! I asked Brian to bring it back from Hong Kong! He found it in Staunton Street, the old part of Central.' Lizzy and Luke watch, breathlessly, as I lift away the delicate wrapping and a heady waft of incense floats into the stale carroty smell of my mother's kitchen.

Lizzy clutches my arm and says, 'It's, well, I – I thought it would be, well, it's more a present for your father than for you! But I thought it would be nice for both of you.' She shrugs.

I stop unwrapping. 'What do you mean?' I stammer.

Lizzy squeezes my arm even more tightly and says, 'I hope I did the right thing! Open it and I'll explain.' I put the wrapping to one side and lift out the biggest item.

It is a cellophane-enclosed pack of confectionary – 'Hichiload creamy milk choco bar with assorted flavour' it reads on the side. The pack is as light as air and purports to contain small boxes of chewing gum and biscuits too. I smile weakly and don't know what to say. Has Lizzy lost it? Her jokes are usually of the most impeccable taste. What does she expect me to do – sprinkle crumbs on the cold stone of my father's grave?

Luke seizes a wad of what looks like toy money, also encased in cellophane. 'One million dollar notes!' he squeaks. 'The Hell Bank Corporation promises to pay the bearer on demand at its Office here *One Million Dollars*!' I look up and he flaps the money about and says defensively, 'That's what it says here!'

I turn to Lizzy who bursts out, 'It's a Chinese buddhist custom!' She grabs at another plastic pack and thrusts it at me. It looks like a child's toy set – a gold pair of glasses, a gold and silver watch with 'Rolex' printed on its face, a silver bracelet, a gold cigarette box, a pen, and a gold ring and a gold necklace, both with green bits stuck on them – all made of stiff paper and set against a bright red paper background.

'You burn it!' cries Lizzy. 'It's a man's gift set! A jade ring! And the money, see! And look, a box of paper cigarettes with paper lighter, and look! a paper Mercedes! I didn't know what car your dad drove so I told Brian to get a smart one! – you put it in a sack and address it to your father, see look, here's the sack' – she sifts through the pile and waves a grey paper bag printed with Chinese figures and burning joss sticks – 'You put it all in the sack and you seal it with this yellow sash – it's a heavenly post office stamp – the spirit will know it's his parcel when he collects it and' – at this point she glances at me and falters – 'You can glue on the sash with Pritt Stick, it's fine to do that, and you write the date you're burning everything on a Post-it note which you stick on the sack and, well, I thought it would be a comforting thing to do. Especially at Christmas. You don't mind, do you?'

She points at the Hell Bank Notes and says hurriedly, 'I know it says Hell and don't think that means he's in Hell, they all say that, all the money you burn says that, it's just, I suppose that, er, people are at different places in the afterlife and um, they're covering all possibilities.' She peers into my face. 'Are you okay?'

I nod, put my head in my hands and wail, 'It's such a wonderful it's such a boo hoo beautiful thing, Liz, it's so sweet of you! Oh God what an amazing thing!' At this point someone hits me on the spine so hard I am flung forward and nearly poke out my eye on a candlestick. 'Thanks, Luke,' I mumble, 'you don't have to pat me on the back any more, I'm okay now.'

Lizzy runs to the side, rips off a square of kitchen roll and hands it to me. I dab my eyes and try not to think of how touched I am because I don't want to start blubbing again. I wipe my nose, scrunch up the kitchen roll, and say snufflingly, 'A candle on a wooden stick.'

Lizzy gasps and says, 'Oh yes! The red candles symbolise food!'

Luke pokes at a long plastic pack and cries, 'Joss sticks! Reminds me of being a student!'

I say witheringly: 'Reminds you of last week more like,' and he grins, relieved that I've stopped grizzling.

Lizzy smiles and says, 'You burn the joss sticks first, three of them, and that gets your dad's attention.'

I say, 'Can't I just pretend I'm about to get a tattoo?'

Lizzy giggles and says, 'Well, if you want to be doubly sure.'

I wave a hand in front of my face to indicate that I'm shutting up, and gesture for her to continue. Then I notice something else in the pack – 'What's this! It's beautiful. Look, Luke, sheafs of silver and gold leaf on funny thin paper!'

I look questioningly at Lizzy who sighs beatifically and says, 'It's traditional Chinese money – you burn it too. You fold it first, in the shape of a gold tael – the Chinese weight measurement thingy for a gold ingot. Look, like this, in the shape of a fortune cookie. There you go! Although I do think it looks too pretty to burn, but it's nice to think you're sending your father such pretty things!'

I nod. It seems a shame to say that my father never noticed pretty things when he was alive – not liking yellow ruled out sunflowers and cornfields and daffodils – so I say nothing. Maybe death will have mellowed him.

'Where do you burn it all?' I say.

Lizzy pauses. 'Well,' she says, 'anywhere really. In Hong Kong you can burn it in your apartment block staircase if you want. You don't have to do it at the grave. You can do it at the roadside, although maybe in England it'd be better to do it in your garden. I thought the cigarettes would be nice for your dad – you said he smoked a lot.'

I say, 'But you hate smoking!'

Lizzy shrugs and says awkwardly, 'Yes, but if he's already dead I suppose it's okay.'

I look at Luke nodding in wise agreement and growl, 'You're still alive! So don't think that ruling applies to you!'

Luke pokes out his tongue and lights up. Lizzy continues. 'You can also lay out your dad's favourite meal or snack – you don't burn it but you can eat it later. But do you want me to write it all down for you?'

I say, 'Yes please,' and smooth a finger across the shiny gold leaf. I stare at the gold leaf for a good three minutes while Lizzy scribbles frantically on a piece of paper. She then hands it to me and I read it and smile. She has written:

Ritual
1. light three joss sticks to summon Dad. Concentrate on his name. Let sticks burn for five mins. (Can be on Chinese New Year, but not essential.)
2. light red candles. Say few words – tell spirit what he's got coming.
3. put stuff in sack, write date on sack, and burn in steel bin, or if easier burn one bit at time. DON'T use water to put fire out. Has to burn out by itself. (Water stops goods getting passed through.)
4. lay out snacks (e.g. peanuts) if wish (eat later).

I sigh and say, 'It's such a lovely thing, Lizzy.' Lizzy nods. She looks as if she wants to speak. 'What?' I say.

She frowns and chirrups, 'You've got to be careful when you burn it. It's the major cause of forest fires in Hong Kong!'

I laugh then look at her suspiciously and say, 'Was that what you were going to tell me?'

Lizzy bites her lip. Then she says, 'I'm not sure if I should tell you this bit but' – I raise my eyebrows – 'Okay,' she says. 'Well, people *do* do this mainly to look after the dead person, but it's also a bit selfish – it's to gain favour with the spirit. So he'll look after you and bring you luck. You also burn items to keep evil spirits away, which I suppose could seem like bribery, but obviously not in this case. But I just thought I should tell you, you know, so you're aware of what you're doing. I always think it's best to be aware of what you're doing.'

I squeeze Lizzy's hand. I don't want to reply in case my voice cracks. I pick up the packet of joss sticks and breathe in their rich scent, then jump up to make Lizzy a decaffeinated coffee. And I don't say this to Lizzy but I am already aware that if I do burn money from the Bank of Hell to send to my father it *will* be a selfish act. It will be selfish because it's not about my father. He doesn't care. He's dead. It's about me. Not wanting him to be dead. And sending him a paper Rolex because I don't want to believe that death is the end. I want him to still be conscious, like me. I want him to be excited at getting a present through the post, like me.

Which incidentally reminds me – this morning I caught the postman effing and blinding and trying to force a medium-sized parcel through my mother's small-sized letter box, so I opened the door and said, 'You could have rung!' So for my father's sake, I hope that postmen in the afterlife are a tad more patient. You could do a lot of damage trying to force a Mercedes through a letter box.

When Luke and Lizzy leave I gather up my death-kit and probably for the first time in my life, feel a girly burst of gratitude – towards *who*, I'm not sure – for my friends. I march to the phone and ring Tina. She answers immediately, in a small voice. 'Tina!' I breathe, lowering my pitch to match hers. 'How *are* you!' I am so delighted to speak to her that I forget I'm sulking. 'What are you up to tonight?' I say.

'Nothing,' she says.

'I'll come round!' I cry.

'Oh no please don't,' she says quickly.

Something in her tone catches at my heart and I say, 'Tina, I'm sorry I said that stuff about Adrian, it was shit of me, and I *am* like a broken record sometimes – but I'm, hah, in the process of being mended.'

May I interrupt myself here to say this is possibly the noblest lie I've ever uttered – but I feel so warmed by the kindness of Lizzy and Luke that I want to be saintly and forgive. Tina says something not a million miles from 'Huf!' She adds quickly, 'Don't be sorry, Helen.'

I wait to see if there's more, but there isn't so I say, 'How about I bring round some Blackadder vids and smoky bacon crisps?'

Faster than the speed of sound Tina is saying no. 'Oh not tonight, no I don't think so, another time I—'

But my wish to forgive overrides Tina's wish that I leave her alone which I suppose is selfish again, but then what isn't? You can't feel other people's pain, only your own. I gabble, 'I'llbearoundinfortyminutesokaybye!' and put the phone down. She rings back immediately but I ignore her. I leave a note for my mother and speed to the video shop.

Forty-eight minutes later – the traffic is preposterous – I'm ringing Tina's doorbell. I know she's there so I ring and ring and when she doesn't answer I sit on the doorstep and wait. After twelve minutes she slowly opens the door. 'What's wrong with you you nutt—' I begin the question but there is no need to end it. What is wrong with Tina is as plain as her cut lip and the ugly purple bruise on her chin. My eyes prickle and even as I deny reality I know the truth. I say, 'God no. Tell me you had an accident. Why didn't you tell me. Tina, Tina, oh my poor Tina, I'll break his neck the fucker, the oh my God.'

The hate wells and I am afraid to touch her, this thin, broken shell of my bright, glamorous friend. I hold out my arms and she collapses into them and weeps on my shoulder and I hear myself mew with pity and anger as she wails, 'But he really loves me.'

Chapter 34

A few years ago I was marching around the heath extension with Lizzy – who has a nasty habit of forcing people out on walks – and we saw a woman trotting along with three whippets. One of the dogs spied us across the field, ran the entire length of it towards us, and cringed against my legs. Flattered by this inexplicable show of trust, I bent and stroked it. Lizzy was enthralled. 'It's as if he knew you would protect him!' she cried. Even though I vastly prefer cats, my ego was swayed by the bittersweet romance of the moment. I became convinced that animals had an instinct for good*ish* people.

Then I bought Fatboy, whose blatant aversion to anyone nice turned my quaint assumption on its dumb head. But I was fond of my theory and loath to let it go. I remained fixed on the magnetic whippet incident as a sign. Preferably, a sign that I was special. Maybe I had a raw sensuality that animals could relate to? ('I've got it! You smell!' exclaimed Marcus.) I chanced upon an idea that suited me. What if I was spiritually attuned to vulnerable souls and the whippet sensed this? After all, I realised that my mother was needier than anyone else on the planet at the age of six. That was it! I was blessed with a unique insight! I really was.

I sporadically indulged this twaddle until the day I faced Tina and saw that her pink-and-white cherub of a boyfriend – who I'd blithely assumed was delightful because he looked good and had a posh job – was bashing her to a pulp. That wiped the smile off my face, I can tell you. The ludicrous words 'But Adrian's not the *type*,' leapt and danced and chased around my head in circles. 'I want you to swear you won't tell anyone,' begged Tina. Only when I'd sworn on 'your mother's – no, Fatboy's life' would she speak.

She sat stiff on the edge of her yellow sofa and her eyes flicked about. She reminded me of a lizard trapped in a jar. I listened in silence. I found it hard enough to reconcile my glowing impression of Adrian with the man she described. And I found it almost impossible to reconcile my sassy successful friend with this piteous wreck of a woman hunched in front of me. She spoke in a whisper and directed her words to the floor and I had to strain to hear what she was saying.

'I don't know if this counts, because it was just a row. Everyone has rows. And he was so sorry he cried. And I'm a right harpy when I get going. You can't blame him. It was the car. I should have had it serviced but I was penny-pinching. Trying to save money. We'd been to Adrian's boss for dinner and I'd eaten a, a braised pea off my plate. With my fingers, before everyone was served. It was embarrassing for Adrian. Like he was going out with someone common.

'Anyway we got outside and he was distant. And cold. I didn't know what I'd done. It might've been okay except the car wouldn't start. I thought the battery was flat. And we hadn't brought our mobiles. Adrian didn't want to go and ring on his boss's door to call a cab. I'd ruined everything. He started screaming at me and kicking the car. I shouted back and so he pulled my hair to calm me down. I know he didn't mean to, but it hurt – a big clump came out – and my eyes watered. He says it was just a joky tug.

'He was so sorry though, he cried too. He only did it because he hated to see me make a fool of myself in public. He was really really upset. He punched the dashboard and then the engine started and so he forgave me. The next day he brought me flowers and breakfast in bed. He's a doll like

276

that. He really cares! He was sad that we argued so I tried to comfort him and make him feel better about it. He hardly ever hits me. It's not continuous. Certainly not more than once every, hmm, six weeks. Most of the time it's great, you know – he's funny. He cracks me up. And so clever.

'I've never met anyone like him. He's under a lot of stress at work. It's tough for him. It's crucial he makes the right impression and I'd jeopardised that. So you can understand. We were fine after that. Fine. Until, until I did this stupid thing. I should have realised. We'd gone to the Dog & Duck up the road from me. We came back pissed and I forgot where I'd put the door key. Adrian was knackered. He had this meeting with a client the next day and it was imperative he got to sleep on time. I'd fucked up. He called me an ugly bitch and kicked me and banged my head into the door. I fainted and I woke up in bed. He'd found the key in his pocket. He was so sorry. He was so kind. Nursing me and put ice and tissue on the cut. And saying it didn't need stitches, it was just a scratch. And getting a headache pill and more tissue from the late-night chemist. And missing out on sleep for me. He bought me flowers and chocolates right through the week. He spent a fortune. He repaired the door. He's so generous.

'I still get headaches but it was a one-off. It wasn't like I didn't deserve it. He only does it because I provoke him. The rest of the time he's so gentle. It's hard to understand if you don't know him. I can't explain it. I know it will get better. It will be okay so long as I cut back on my drinking. And learn a bit more about how to behave in public. So I'm sorry if I haven't seen you and Liz that much. It's that I'm trying to make it work with Adrian, I'm trying, and I know I've been snappy. I want it to get better. So you mustn't tell anyone. It's my business, it isn't a big problem. I frustrate him and it whirls out of control. It's him I feel sorry for, poor bloke. Stuck with me, trying to make a shit out of a shite . . .'

She said other stuff but you get the drift. This month's injuries were caused when Adrian cracked her round the face with the telephone. She'd put milk in his jasmine tea (he threw the cup at her but missed). She must have done a very bad thing indeed because normally he wouldn't *dream* of touching her on the face. Sweet of him, I think, because it really is so vulgar for one's girlfriend to walk around with a broken nose for everyone to see and gossip at – so much more refined to keep all bloody beatings to arms and legs and torso where the telltale weals can be covered up with a smart cashmere top and elegant wool trousers.

I look at Tina's determinedly blank face and gently suggest that Adrian is an evil, violent bully who should be banged up and she hasn't done anything wrong and furthermore there *isn't* anything she could do that warrants being hit. Ever. There is no excuse for it. None. Sorry and flowers don't make it better. And it won't get better. If she tolerates it, he'll keep doing it. Can't she see that? I say this in a quiet, casual way because I'm terrified she will block her ears and order me out. Tina is prisoner to the cult of Adrian and my words are blasphemy. She feels guilty for talking to me, she says. Disloyal. She jerkily folds her arms and mutters that she can't think any more, she's confused, she doesn't know what she feels. She keeps repeating, 'It will get better,' like a chant.

When I try to state the facts in a clear and lucid manner so she cannot deny them, she denies them. It's like she doesn't understand English. With a shock, I realise she is delusional. It is as if she sees the world through *his* eyes. Her reality is an altered state. I can hardly believe I'm talking to Tina. She's like a lost soul in animation. I feel bereaved.

The woman who spent three months trekking alone through Africa, who bullied a Hell's Angel into vacating his tube seat for an elderly woman, who chased a mugger up an alleyway and forced him to return her purse, who led a thirty-strong group of American tourists around Rome having never set foot in the city (she read three guidebooks the previous week), believes she is worthless. But then, considering she believes that a man can hold his girlfriend's head under water in the bath for two full minutes while she splashes and struggles for air 'as a joke' – I suppose her belief system is out of whack.

And she won't let me help her. I ask her, doesn't she feel angry with Adrian for what he's done and she hesitates and says maybe, once, but now she just feels angry with herself. My pulse throbs and I say sharply, does Adrian know she has three brothers, and more to the point, do her three brothers know about Adrian? Then I feel terrible because she is so scared she whimpers and the sound of it chills me and she tells me I have to promise again not to say a word because, because . . . She trails off and my gut clenches and I don't get how she can be like this but I hear her.

Tina tells me she's off work until the New Year now but I'm not to call her. She's fine, really she is, she's a bit run down, she wants to rest and be quiet. When her face is better she's going to go home to her parents. Adrian is skiing in Val d'Isère with friends. He did ask Tina but kept warning her that it wasn't her scene, so she declined the invitation. My diplomacy bubble pops and I exclaim, 'Tina! Just listen to yourself! I can't believe you're letting him abuse you like this!'

I regret my outburst instantly, not least because Tina snaps, 'Excuse me? Jasper? Marcus? Hel-lo! I don't think you're in a position to preach, Helen, do you?'

I can't imagine what she means but I drive home fast at 3 a.m., thinking fuck, fuck, fuck. I am stunned. It is as if Adrian was my boyfriend hitting *me*. I go straight to my mother's computer, log on to the internet and scroll through a long list of books on abuse, which includes the corker *Domestic Violence For Beginners*.

I order four titles. Tina won't like this, but I've just bought her Christmas present. My heart is racing as I announce to the dark silence, 'Tina. You don't know it yet but you are going to leave that vicious bastard if it's the last thing I do.'

On Sunday morning I call the police and ask what they can do if a woman is being hit by her partner. The cold reply is that if the victim herself doesn't make an allegation, nothing. I call Tina on Sunday and Monday and Tuesday because I am determined that she see sense and dump Adrian this week but she doesn't answer and I don't want to leave a message and then it's Christmas.

On the morning of 24 December my mother and I receive a last-minute invitation to Christmas Day lunch from Vivienne. I reject it because I don't feel like being around a complete family. I'd feel like a spare part. Which – now I'm fatherless – maybe I am. My mother also rejects it then changes her mind because otherwise she'll 'just sit at home getting miserable'. This is an understatement considering that even the Grinch would walk in our door and start craving fairy lights. My mother is making a point to God. She hasn't even displayed the cards she's been sent – they lie in a scrappy pile on the kitchen table. I arrange the cards in a neat row before I go to work and suggest we light Chanukkah candles, sod it, *any* candles – frankly I'd set myself alight if I thought it would make the house less gloomy – but she's having none of it. She finds the beauty voucher I bought her hidden in the napkin drawer and sulks and says I've only bought it to make her feel bad. At this point my patience twangs and I reply sharply that the only person making Cecelia feel bad is Cecelia. And I'm right. She's vetoed joy. So yesterday I purchased a small turkey, a bag of potatoes, and a jar of cranberry sauce (I was about to pick a bag of frozen peas when a wave of apathy swept over me and I thought stuff the peas) and dumped them in the fridge in defiance.

*

At 2 p.m. on Christmas Eve I watch my colleagues twirl round the office in a haze of tinsel and mulled wine and goodwill and feel detached. I wonder what Tom's doing now and if I'll ever see him again. I think of us together and it feels like I imagined it. I knew it wouldn't last. I am staring into space when something whooshes through the air and makes a loud thud. I jump and see that Mr Grouch the doorman has dumped a fat bouquet of roses on my desk. *Flowers!* I never get flowers! I am a flower-free zone. 'For Laetitia?' I bleat in disbelief.

Mr Grouch scowls, says, 'You're Helen, incha?' and stumbles off.

The blood fizzes in my head and I think, Tom? Tom! Flowers from Tom to say he likes me again! I take a sidelong glance at the fire escape just in case he's climbed up the building à la Richard Gere and is loitering with the intent of whisking me away. He hasn't. But roses. The symbol of romantic love! He's sorry for bellowing! He's contrite and I'm right! I fumble for the card and rip open the envelope. My hands are clammy and shaking as I read the message:

Darling Helen. It's been too long. Love Jasper, xox.

My hopes shrivel and I feel like James of *The Giant Peach* fame when he drops the magic bag of life-enhancing grubs and they wriggle and disappear into the soil. Marvellous things could have happened to me but I messed up and now I have nothing. I stare at the note and wonder what Jasper wants. I expel an angry little puff of air through my nose. He's got a nerve. Still. Nice flowers. I smile reluctantly. Cheeky sod. I suppose he isn't *that* bad. He is nothing like Adrian. He's just a rogue. At least he doesn't hassle me about my living arrangements. I sniff the roses. I don't suppose it'd do much harm to meet for a drink. I touch the soft pink petal of a rose. Pink roses. Does this mean I'm gay?

I am breathing in the scent of my pink roses like other people breathe in oxygen when my mother rings to tell me in a grumpy voice that she's sorry for being grumpy and if I don't want her to go to Vivienne's tomorrow she won't go. She doesn't want me to spend Christmas in an empty house, she knows for a fact that Morrie wouldn't like it. (For a non-believer he was surprisingly fond of Christmas.) When she says this I feel like most normal mothers feel when their child takes its first step. 'Mum,' I say softly, 'that's very considerate of you, but I'd feel awful if I stopped you going to Vivienne's. I *want* you to go.' To which she replies 'Oh good!' and puts the phone down. I am wondering if it's possible to pinch oneself and awake in another dimension, when Lizzy bounces up and asks if I want to help her and Brian decorate her tree tonight. The plan is to eat wholemeal mince pies, arrange baubles, and attend Midnight Mass. Although I'd love to, I feel she's asked out of compassion and I don't want compassion so I pretend I'm busy.

'But I'll come with you to the soup kitchen tomorrow!' I burst out, before I can stop myself.

Lizzy's hand flies to her throat and she exclaims, 'Oh Helen! But you can't! I rang and they've already got more seasonal volunteers than they can cope with!'

I blush scarlet and mutter, 'Doesn't matter. I'd have depressed the tramps, anyway.'

Lizzy pauses then retreats, and I see a cartoon in my head of me as a human turkey eating turkey alone. With a heavy heart I ring my grandmother to see if she wants to join me for what I confidently predict will be the most depressing festive meal of my life.

To my relief Nana is spending the day at her friend Nora's thank you, they've plotted their television schedule and they're playing bingo in the evening with people from the Fellowship Club. As she says, there's nothing to celebrate, you won't find her pulling crackers, not this year. She'll be at home on Boxing Day if I want to visit, but I shouldn't come between two and three thirty because she'll be watching a Cary Grant film. And if – as Cecelia's

282

mentioned – I've bought her a china ornament of Princess Diana's head, she doesn't want it because she's got five already and her mantelpiece is full up.

When Christmas dawns I am feeling Grinchish and consider cooking the turkey, slinging it in the Toyota, speeding to the cemetery, and hurling it at my father's grave.

Well, if this mess isn't his fault, whose is it?

Chapter 35

Owning a large gob and a short attention span, I remember very little of what I learned at school, which leaves me with not much. But I *do* recall a story we translated in our French class because, as they say in fairytales, it smote my heart. It was about a factory worker who was so poor he couldn't afford to buy his little girl a Christmas tree. So he postponed Christmas. And when all the rich families threw out their Christmas trees in the New Year he crept to the rubbish dump and took one. And so his little girl got her Christmas tree and had the best Christmas day ever.

I don't have much in common with that little girl except that this year my Christmas comes late too. The day itself isn't bad either. Surprisingly peaceful. I act as wardrobe consultant to my mother, who is desperate to out-glam Vivienne. 'Are you sure you won't come too?' she says, in a rush of excitement. 'There'll be people your own age – some cousins, I think, and Jeremy and his friend Simon.'

I sigh and say, 'Jeremy and his *boy*friend Simon. Vivienne's in denial.'

I briefly consider going – Jeremy is warm, cuddly and irrepressibly cheerful, Prozac in human form – then decide that Vivienne is sulphuric acid in human form and I need to be alone. I give my mother the beauty voucher and she gives me a static pair of blood-red silk pyjamas. 'You shouldn't sleep in a tatty old T-shirt,' she explains kindly, 'men don't like it.' Neither of us refer to my father. We tiptoe around his absence, which pollutes the air like a thick smog. The effort is draining and I wave my overdressed mother out of the door with relief. Then I wrap myself in my duvet and read my present to me – *The Black Dahlia* by James Ellroy – with the television on mute.

I can't be bothered to cook the turkey so I make potato wedges and dip them in cranberry sauce. I break up the reading and eating with naps. I wonder what Tina's doing. I pray that Adrian skis into a tree. And I try and fail to interest Fatboy in his new clockwork mouse (he sits down next to it, lifts his leg high like a ballerina, and starts licking what Luke refers to as his 'willy case').

Boxing Day is quiet too. Nana Flo rings to retract our invitation as she has an upset tummy. This is not a huge surprise as she *always* has an upset tummy on Boxing Day because she treats Christmas lunch as if it were the Last Supper. So I challenge my mother to a game of Monopoly which is a mistake as she bunks jail, resents me buying Mayfair, and defrauds the bank. Peace is only resumed when I lose. Then I read my book and my mother opens the door because she thinks it might be snowing and sees that Fatboy has brought us a seasonal gift, a sweet little dead robin redbreast. Peace is in chewed bits, until I spot that an *Only Fools And Horses* repeat is about to start on BBC1. And that's the jingle bells over with.

The real excitement starts ten days later.

My mother returns to work. I find a flat. Michelle forces Marcus to get his back waxed. It's all too much – where shall I begin? Actually that's a rhetorical question because if I keep Marcus's Discovery Of The Meaning Of Pain to myself for one moment longer my head will explode from pent-up gloating. I hear the tale from Lizzy, who heard it from Brian, who heard it from Sara, a beauty therapist at their health club. And I think, glory be, there is a God.

Marcus was sent by his fiancée to get his back waxed and it took Sara forty-five minutes! And she was mortified because he was screaming! Screaming! The B-word and the F-word *so* loud when there were people in the other rooms having massages! She put the wax on him and he screamed that it was *scalding*! When it was hardly even hot! Sara said, 'Now you know what women go through!' and he said no way did a bikini wax compare to this, because it was 'just two strips'! And Sara stopped feeling sorry for him and said, 'I assure you it's not just two strips!' And he was so hairy that afterwards he looked like he was wearing a tank top! She didn't know if she should carry on down his arms! And then it turned out he worked at another gym but was too embarrassed to have it done there! And he only did it because his fiancée had made him!

Lizzy rarely gossips but waives her morals on the grounds that this isn't hearsay, it's reportage. Secretly I suspect she's never forgiven Marcus for forcing her to admit in public that her ex-boyfriend's penis was 'medium'. This peek at Marcus's new life in bootcamp almost arouses my sympathy. But I manage to quash it and am recoiling at the thought of my one brief tussle with Gorilla Back and wondering what – apart from desperation – possessed me when the phone rings.

It's my mother. She is calling from the staffroom. Everyone has been *so* lovely. They all missed her. Her children have made her a Welcome Back banner out of coloured tissue paper. They're all on their best behaviour. She thinks Mrs Armstrong's had a word with them. She's *so* pleased to be back. And Mrs Armstrong has made her promise that if at any time she even begins to feel she can't cope she's to say so *instantly* and Mrs Armstrong will do all she can to assist. She has *heaps* to do, the schedule is crazy, but she doesn't care. Anyway she's got to go now, she's about to take a maths lesson.

As my mother clanks down the phone, I marvel. Either Prozac or Cliff are agreeing with her. Or today is a fortuitous day. Marcus gets his comeuppance and I get to hear about it. All thirty four-year-olds in Cecelia Bradshaw's class refrain from vomiting down their tops, wetting their pants, or poohing down their legs. It's got to be fate. I consult my star sign to see if it agrees with me. (I believe my horoscope for as long as it flatters – the moment it starts chiding is the moment I dismiss it as gobbledygook.) Apparently Jupiter 'the planet of growth and opportunity' is busybodying around in my sign, so I should expect 'exciting developments'.

I hunch over the page, nodding. Fact is, when you live at home, do a menial job, and have no love or social life, the torture of a former fling and the fleeting contentment of a problem parent assume thrilling proportions. I gnaw at my lip and wonder if I should have another go at Tina this afternoon. She has successfully avoided me and my self-help books for the last fortnight but *her* star sign says that Jupiter's muscling in on the portion of her chart that 'accents the structure' of her existence and is 'likely to bring changes'. Perfect. I'll ring her after lunch.

It's 12.02 and I'm about to start work when the Joop!-drenched Adam calls to say that he's found the perfect property for me, it's right up my street, I gotta view it immediately, it's well cheap, no chain, cracking use of space, it's spot-on, it's in a much-sought after location, handy for public transport, could do with updating, hundreds of people are interested, if I don't hurry it'll go, and there's sod all else around and I'll be stuffed. By now I am well acquainted with Adam's freestyle interpretation of the Property Misrepresentations Act and don't believe a word. But seeing as Jupiter is breathing down my neck, I decide I should see this (from what I can gather) bite-sized, ramshackle, prehistoric flat situated under a railway bridge.

'Okay,' I say. 'How about six forty-five tonight?'

'Yeah?' says Adam, who doubtless expected me to put up a fight. 'Lovely jubbly! It's a date!'

'No it isn't,' I say.

Lizzy and I meet him in his office at 6.32. Adam ignores me and leers at Lizzy who is wearing a short skirt. I don't mind – partly because I've been shunned by men a lot higher up the food chain than Adam, and partly because if I was a bloke I'd choose Lizzy's tall tanned elegance over a pale-faced shortarse too. But mainly, my indifference stems from fretting over whether I should tell Lizzy about Tina. I know I promised to keep quiet and that Fatboy's corpulent life depends on it. But. I am convinced that if I *was* to tell Lizzy about Tina, for once I'd be divulging classified information for the right reason. Because when I rang Tina this afternoon she tentatively agreed to meet me tomorrow at my house on the condition that I 'don't have a go at' her. So I'm wondering quite how I am going to have a go at Tina without her noticing and as Lizzy is the diplomacy queen and I'm the diplomacy pauper, I need her advice. Yet however I justify it, the sharp stark words 'but you promised' peck at my brain. Eventually – just as Adam spies a parking space and swerves violently into the kerb – I settle on a compromise.

I say in a low voice, 'Lizzy. You know Adrian, Tina's bloke? Well, what would you say if I said that I'd spoken to a woman who went out with him a while ago, and who said that he'd, ah, roughed her up a bit?' Admittedly, this is a feak weeble adaptation of the truth and I'm aware that anyone else would decode it in a picosecond. But Lizzy's intolerance of evil (she's the direct opposite of Fatboy in that sense) is a guardian angel that wards off unpleasant imaginings. It wouldn't occur to her that I was talking about Tina.

As it is, she pulls an astonished face and says briskly, 'I can't believe it! Adrian's so nice! It can't be true!'

Surprised by her vehemence, I say mildly, 'Well, that's what she said.'

Lizzy retorts – in the incredulous tone of a child on hearing that babies aren't delivered by storks – 'Is she sure?'

To be honest, I'm taken aback. I expected shock, horror, and flapping ears. Not obstinance. I say, 'I don't think she made it up, Lizzy, I honestly don't.'

But Lizzy says firmly, 'Adrian is so nice! And polite! She must have imagined it. And really, I don't think it's good of this person, to tell you nasty things like that.' With that, Lizzy clicks open the lock, slinks out of the car, and slams the door. I feel like I've just tried to sell her double glazing.

Miserably, I glance at our surroundings. We are standing in front of a neat terraced row of wedding cake houses. They are all white, with beautiful bay windows and brightly painted doors. Adam opens the gate to the pebble-dashed exception. It is truly the cut-glass vase among wedding presents. 'Maybe you could get a builder to scrape off the pebbles,' whispers Lizzy, 'and remove the rusting fridge from the front lawn.'

I nod and smile. I don't trust myself to speak to her, just yet. So I say sweetly to Adam: 'I'm not sure why you've brought us here unless it's a joke, but will you ring the bell this time so the owner doesn't have to run upstairs in his pants?'

Adam coughs and replies, 'The owner doesn't live here any more.'

He pushes open the shabby front door and I understand why. The owner probably looked at the decor one day and died of fright. The stairs are wonky, creaking, and uncarpeted. The walls are covered in what I can only describe as a garish travesty of wallpaper and so, inexplicably, is the ceiling. Despite the breathtaking clash of orange and brown swirls, the effect is drab. Lizzy murmurs, 'How very, ah, unique!' I take a deep breath to stop myself suffocating.

'It's got a lot of potential,' says Adam brightly. I sigh and follow him into what masquerades as the kitchen.

'The owner obviously had a fetish for brown,' I say with a sour look at the stained mud-coloured lino. 'And an allergy to cleaning,' I add, on seeing the grimy sideboard.

'But the joy of this flat is that it's crying out for you to stamp your own personality on it!' replies Adam. 'Under this lino lies a vintage wooden floor!'

289

I glance at him and say hopefully, 'Is there?'

He nods, 'Yeah, well there's floorboards, innit?'

At the same time Lizzy cries, 'Helen! I think this may be an original New World Gas Range cooker! Yes, look it's got two doors! Ohmigod! I'd *die* for a cooker like this! I can't believe it! It must be at least fifty years old! Adam, does this come with the flat?'

Adam looks longingly at Lizzy and says, 'Yeah. Lush, innit?'

I huff and say, 'It's a piece of old junk' but Lizzy insists that it's 'an antique'. Then she discovers the Formica is – underneath its coat of grime – gold-sequinned.

'This is unbelievable!' she squeals. 'It's a treasure! It hasn't been changed since the war!'

I growl, 'Yeah, the One Hundred Years War.'

Adam shows us into the bathroom which is so small that only two of us can fit in it at once. Lizzy waits outside. 'Original tiling!' she whispers, 'Helen, you've *got* to have this!'

I glare at her and snap, 'It's a pit!' But then I see the bedroom and although the plaster is crumbling and the carpet is threadbare and the windows are filthy and cracked, something inside me tweaks.

I imagine ripping up the carpet and polishing the floorboards, repainting the walls yellow, and cleaning the large windows so that the sunlight streams in. 'Let's see the lounge,' I say.

'Original fireplace,' says Adam, as we enter the small, cobwebby room. 'And no chain. Once you've done the necessary you could move in in weeks!'

I say, 'Don't be ridiculous, it's uninhabitable!' but I don't say it with much conviction. My heart is thumping and I feel hot with trepidation. I don't know why but I want it.

The next morning I make an offer on the flat. Adam says coldly, 'I'll get back to ya.' Lizzy says soothingly that he's playing hard to get and gives me the number of her solicitor. And Tina rings from a shoot to say she's sorry but 'something's come up' and she won't be meeting me tonight. I start to ask her how she is but she cuts off. Almost immediately the phone rings again and I grab it. 'Tina?' I gasp.

'Is that the lovely Helen?' says a drawling voice.

My skin prickles. 'Jasper?' I whisper.

'Hey, Babe,' he says, 'you never called about the flowers. Does this mean it's over?'

I giggle. 'Is *what* over?' I say, 'There's nothing to *be* over.'

Jasper breathes in sharply, as if hurt by this observation. 'Ouch,' he says.

'Jasper, you're as thick-skinned as a hippo's elbow so don't pretend,' I say sternly.

He laughs. 'Helen, my Angelsweet, I miss you! How are you? How's the new pad? What say we catch up? What say you to dinner?'

I think, I'd say yes, so long as you promise to talk like a normal person instead of a medieval knight. 'Weeeeeellllll,' I say – he interrupts – 'Tonight! I'll pick you up from work at seven in a cab and spirit you away!'

I am about to launch into coy protestation when the line goes dead. So I think, what possible objection can I have to substituting an evening of ready-cook pasta in front of *The Bill* with an orange moggy farting by my side, for a sumptuous candlelit dinner in front of Jasper Sanderson with his slender foot nuzzling up to my love-starved ankle?

It's not as if I'm going to get off with him or anything.

Chapter 36

Occasionally Fatboy forgets himself and shows me some devotion. These lapses are at his convenience and inevitably occur when I'm busy. Especially when I'm reading the paper. He springs on to the table and sprawls languidly over the headlines obscuring every word. If I lift him on to the floor, he jumps up on to the exact same article and flops again.

The only compromise he'll accept is being sat on my lap. He perches there, bolt upright, digs his claws into my legs, purrs like a propeller, and kneads. The sensation is identical, I imagine, to poking ten sharp needles into your skin, again and again, on the same increasingly tender spot. The action simultaneously draws out little threads and ruins your trousers. But I bear the pain and forfeit the trousers because affection from Fatboy is so devastatingly rare – which in a sellers' market makes it all the more precious.

I suppose I agree to see Jasper for similar reasons. And despite everything, it's pleasant to see him. He's wearing – don't laugh – Egoiste which makes me want to bite him. 'You smell nice,' I say, without meaning to.

'I know,' he says, grinning.

I notice a bit of white gunk caught between his teeth. I run my tongue over my own teeth, and suck, even though I brushed them before I came out. Suddenly I feel clunky and the blithe arrogance of 'I know' resonates harshly in my ear. Jasper is as beautiful as ever but he is also mightily pleased with himself. I decide to give Jasper a hard time.

Or, at least, a harder time than he expects. As we walk down Long Acre he rests a hand on my shoulder. I consider shrugging it off but I don't want to be *too* unfriendly. So it sits there heavy and uncomfortable until we hail a cab.

'So where are you taking me?' I say, as we chug through the London traffic.

'It's a surprise!' he says. 'So how are you! Long time no see!'

I nod and say, 'Fine, fine!' and try not to be irritated by the phrase 'long time no see'.

'So how are *you*?' I say. 'How's Louisa?'

Jasper wrinkles his nose and says, with feeling, 'I'm well, she's a silly bitch!' Strangely – or not – this doesn't surprise me.

'Oh? And why's that?' I say coolly. I feel inexplicably irked on Louisa's account.

Jasper flares his nostrils, snorts loudly, and rolls his eyes. The image of a panicking horse. 'Ah, she winds me up, I can't stand the woman! She' – from his tone I expect a long, whingeing rant but he hesitates then trails off – 'She, oh, she's alright. She's a good girl. She's er, fine, I er, I abhor her taste in music.'

I raise my eyebrows and say, 'Jasper you abhor everyone's taste in music. Why, what does she like that's so offensive?'

He shudders and spits out the name like sour milk: 'Madonna.'

I squeal, 'Madonna! What've you got against Madonna! She's brilliant! I love Madonna!'

Jasper snaps, 'She's a man-eater!'

I purse my lips and say primly, 'I see. That affects her music, does it?'

Jasper – like all good politicians – ignores the question and replies, 'Her music's an abomination!' I think Jasper expects further comment but I am quiet. Eventually he mutters, 'I can't stand girls like that.'

I knew it. A tremor of rage ripples through me and I

blurt, 'I can't stand *boys* with opinions like that.' After this we sit in frosty silence for a full five minutes until Jasper surrenders.

'Hey, Babe,' he says softly, 'I didn't mean to upset you. Did I tell you how great you look. Really well.'

In my vocabulary 'You're looking really well' is a polite way of saying 'You're looking really fat.' So I say scoffingly, 'Huh!'

Jasper perseveres: 'No, really. Have you lost weight or something?'

I'd prefer to stay grumpy but smirk involuntarily. 'I don't know and don't care,' I mumble, 'I haven't weighed myself in ten years.'

Jasper, sensing a slight thaw, says cheerfully, 'You can weigh yourself at the flat if you like.'

I widen my eyes like a Disney chipmunk: 'What flat?' I squeak, 'I thought you were taking me out to dinner.'

'I thought I'd cook you a special dinner at my place,' he says.

I growl, 'Louisa's place, you mean. Is *she* going to be there?'

Jasper replies smoothly, 'Louisa is in Chicago on business. We'll have the, er, kitchen to ourselves.'

I decide to test him. 'So what are you planning to cook me?'

Jasper coughs into his clenched hand. 'Frittata di cheddar e erbe d'estiva,' he says, smiling.

'Wow!' I say, pleased that he's made an effort. 'That sounds amazing! Did you go to a specialist foodstore?'

Jasper laughs. 'I suppose,' he says. Jasper has exerted himself on my account. I'm dumb with delight. For the remainder of the journey we chat about Jasper's job and how he's on the brink of promotion. I tell him I am on the brink of demotion and he tells me that I've got to learn to 'play the game'. Whatever that means. The cab pulls up in a dinky toytown street in Kensington.

'Oof!' I say. 'Hasn't Louisa done well!'

'Yeah,' says Jasper, 'Lucky for some.'

Lucky for *you*, I think. My opinion doesn't change on seeing the flat. Louisa is keen on red. The walls are deep crimson, huge scarlet wool rugs cover the floors, and the windows are adorned with heavy red velvet drapes. The lounge is crowded with ornate candlesticks, elderly wooden tables and chairs, a worn lilac sofa, an overloaded bookshelf – I'd love to loathe it all but the effect is warm, plush, and undeniably alluring. 'This is wild!' I gasp.

'It's like living inside a womb,' shouts Jasper from the kitchen. 'Care for a sherry?'

I shout back, 'Sorry, but do I look like a hundred-year-old aunt?'

There's a pause then Jasper says briskly, 'Suit yourself, I'm having one.'

I poke my nose round the kitchen door. 'Haven't you got a beer?' Jasper shakes his head. 'Wine?' Jasper shakes his head.

'I'll have a glass of water please, then,' I say.

'It'll have to be tap,' he replies. 'Cheers! So, tell me, how's your new pad?'

I sip my water and say, 'What new pad?'

Jasper looks confused, 'I thought you were buying a place.'

I say quickly, 'I am, I am. I'm ah, moving in in about, ooh, five weeks.' This isn't strictly a lie because before I left work today Adam rang to say my offer had been rejected but, between him and me, if I was to up it by six thou, Flat 55b would be in the bag. 'Yeah, and it's so bloody poky it would fit,' I'd muttered, after plonking down the phone.

Jasper indicates his interest in my property venture by raising an eyebrow so I tell him all about the flat (leaving out the fact I haven't bought it yet) while he cooks what appears to be a cheese omelette. Why is it, in these post-modern days, that all the men I know only cook omelettes? 'I thought you were doing something complicated,' I say crossly.

295

'This *is* complicated, Babe,' he replies, and winks.

We eat our omelettes sitting on the sofa, and Jasper is very attentive. He tries to feed me omelette off his fork – I humour him even though I have been perfectly able to feed myself for nearly twenty-five years – and he rummages through Louisa's magazine rack to find a recent copy of *Homes & Interiors*. We pore over it together, and although there is precisely nothing in it I like or can afford, I feel touched by his interest. All is going well, until the clock strikes ten and Jasper tries to kiss me. 'I miss you, Babe,' he murmurs into my neck. 'Babe, I miss you.'

He pushes me gently but firmly back on to the lilac sofa and attempts to remove my top. I lie still and let him kiss me but I unpick his roving hands from my top. Jasper kisses me all over my face, making loud squelchy sounds. My stomach heaves with distaste and I avert my face. I should feel squelchy and kissy back but I feel blank. Maybe the omelette disagreed with me. 'So bashful,' mutters Jasper, twisting my face back into kissing range. 'Very unlike you.'

I sit up fast and pull away from him. 'What do you mean by that?' I say icily.

Jasper rakes a hand through his hair and says, 'Take it easy, Angelsweet, it was a joke.'

I glare and say, 'Well guess what, I don't get it.'

Jasper tweaks my nose and jumps up. 'How's ah, Fatty?' he says.

'Fatty!' I say, shrill with displeasure. 'Fatboy is his name, and he's thriving, thank you.'

Jasper laughs and in a low husky voice says, 'You're sexy when you're angry.'

I shake my head and reply, 'And you're impossible. And don't give me that line, it's about fifty thousand years old. Dinosaurs used it on each other.' Jasper rubs his forehead and treats me to a full-beam grin and I giggle and say, 'Oh stop it! Under normal circumstances I'd leap on you but I'm feeling a bit headachey.'

Jasper looks at me, and without too much regret, says, 'Awww.' Then he adds, 'Hey Babe, I bought you a present.' He rifles through his briefcase and throws a pocket-sized brightly coloured book at me. *Cat Chat*. Immediately I know he's pinched it from work. 'I do have other interests,' I say huffily. He picks up *Cat Chat*, plonks on to the sofa, lies down, rests his head in my lap, and starts reading extracts. As Jasper likes cats about as much as Nana Flo likes cats, I acknowledge the sacrifice.

'Every life should have nine cats,' he declares as if he means it, and my hard-set face softens and I feel the beginnings of an inner purr. I close my eyes, listen to his voice, and stroke his hair. I'm basking in the warmth of our intimacy when he drops the book, grabs my hand, and says, 'Helen. I miss *us*. Please let's get back together.'

I don't know what to say so I say 'Oh!' and tell him I'll consider it. Then I leave.

I'm starting to think that the planet Jupiter was wrong and my late Christmas hadn't come and I'd been tricked by idiots into hailing a false dawn when my offer on Flat 55b is accepted. Adam relays the joyful news like a binman hurling a sack of rubbish on to a dustcart. Then he says do I want to go for a drink and bring that posh bird I hang around with? I tell Adam that Lizzy only goes out with estate agents who deal in properties over three hundred thou. Then I relay my property news to Lizzy who bounces on the spot and suggests I line up a feng shui expert.

'I hate this,' I say, as I put down the phone to the dodgiest mortgage-broker in the land. 'I'm being stitched up.'

Lizzy does her best to look sympathetic and chirrups, 'But just think, it'll be worth it in the end!'

I sigh and say, 'Yeah. I'll be the proud owner of negative equity.' I gnaw at my lip and mutter to myself, 'Well at least Tom will be pleased, the sanctimonious git.'

Tom is like a radio jingle – infuriating and unforgettable. Ever since I saw Jasper – and probably before – I've thought about Tom. I compare the two men obssessively. Eyes, jokes, chests, voices, humour, wit, omelette-cooking skills, penises, tempers, likes, intelligence, waiter-hailing styles, jobs . . . I compare most things about them and the end result is I don't call Jasper.

But I itch to see Tom.

Admittedly, I am desperate to distract myself from the hell of conveyancing and all the leechery that surrounds it. But the main reason is, Tom and I have unfinished business to attend to. And, while a bonk would be an enjoyable bonus, I'm not referring to sex. If I'm to get on with my life – a phrase which I *cannot* stand, as if life is an economy class long haul to be struggled through, but which I'll make an exception for this once – I have to talk to Tom.

I don't want to but I need to. I keep backflashing to his astonished face on Dog's Bottom Night. The feeblest part of me wants to throw myself at his feet and explain but the bolshy rest of me wants to rant at him until he throws himself at my feet. How dare he preach to me about my wrongdoings when he was tarting around behind my back? How could he say the things he said and not mean them?

How could I be so naive as to think just because he said them he meant them? What did he think he was doing being so nice? Why wasn't he honest? Doesn't he realise I can deal with gittishness, so long as it isn't disguised as sincerity? These sly, maggoty questions burrow and squirm and prevent me from attending to the riotous confusion of Laetitia's Invoice Drawer. So I snatch up the phone, ring Megavet, announce that Fatboy is off his food, and make an urgent appointment for 6.45 tonight.

My mother is sulking because I haven't yet shown her the flat – the reason: I don't dare – so I am able to prise Fatboy off the Volvo, stuff him into his Voyager, and speed to the vet without being waylaid. As the Toyota chokes and shudders to a halt on Golders Green Road, I pray that Tom is still on holiday. I take a deep breath, check my hair in the rear-view mirror (as I thought, it's flat), retrieve Fatboy from the backseat, and plod towards Megavet's door. I lean my weight against it, push with my bottom, and stagger backwards into reception. This isn't a dignified entrance and I'm pleased to see that there are no animals and people waiting and Celine isn't standing behind the front desk. Sadly, Tom is.

He is writing something in what I assume is the appointment book, and looks tired and dishevelled. He stares at me, as if he can't quite believe what the cat's brought in, and nods curtly. My neck tenses and I stare and nod too. Fatboy wails and scrabbles. 'So,' I say sourly, 'we meet again.'

Tom throws down his pen, slams shut the appointment book and says flatly, 'You're next. You might as well come in.'

I heave Fatboy into the surgery and Tom shuts the door behind us and I feel frightened. I'm scared of what he might say so I speak before he does. 'Did you have a nice holiday?' I say smarmily.

Tom seems surprised at this civility and says, 'Yes tha—'

I interrupt him with a roar: 'With your girlfriend!'

Anger and shock vie for supremacy on his haggard face and he hisses, '*What?!*'

I am like Fatboy in that being hissed at is not my favourite thing and the fury and resentment fuse and I flare up like a lit match. '"What"!' I snarl, mimicking his surprise. '"*What*"! Don't give me "what" like you don't know what I'm talking about! Your girlfriend! You know, the one you went on holiday with? The one you were shagging while you were shagging me! Just about!'

Tom grits his teeth and growls, 'I don't know what you're talking about! What girlfriend?'

At this point I clutch my hair to stop myself shaking him, and scream, 'Don't lie to me, I'm sick of being lied to! The girlfriend we saw you with in the pub, you moron!' Tom's mouth falls open. 'What?' I say angrily.

Tom glowers at me and shouts, 'You stupid brat, that was my *sister*!'

This is absolutely impossible and I'm about to say so. But then I remember a wheedling comment Lizzy made soon after the pub incident, something like 'she could have been his sister'. Then I also remember Tom telling me about his sister. And suddenly, the idea that the pub woman was Tom's sister is less impossible than it first appeared. If this is true my position is untenable. But I'm not going to give in without a brawl.

'My mother was told that you were on holiday with your girlfriend!' I snap.

Tom shakes his head in disbelief. 'I don't understand,' he says. 'Why was *your* mother discussing *my* holiday arrangements?'

I say quickly, 'Because I was busy at work, Fatboy was ill, so she brought him to the vet.'

Tom says coolly, 'Really. So?'

I shrug, 'So she knows you, so she asked where you were! I suppose . . . Celine told her.'

As I say the slimy word 'Celine' a toe-curling yet plausible theory forms in my head. It forms in Tom's head too. 'O-o-oh!' he says acidly. '*Celine* told your mother that I was away with my girlfriend.' He pauses for a second then bellows, 'Why are you so selfish? Why don't you give anyone a break? There's no pleasing you is there! You can't ask me to my face like an adult! Oh no! That'd be far too easy! You—'

I stamp my foot so hard I nearly break it. My voice is shaky with anger. 'Don't you shout at me, you pompous man, I won't have it!' Secretly I am mortified to the core about the girlfriend error, but I'll be damned if Tom's going to know about it. I screech, 'I can't believe I let you boss me about! You think you're so superior!'

Tom splutters, 'What are you on about?'

I stamp my foot again – less hard this time – and snap, 'Don't pretend you don't know! Preaching to me about what I should be doing, saying to my mum, feeling about my dad! Where I should be living! You—'

Now Tom slaps his hand down on the table and makes me jump. He yells, 'I didn't preach about anything, you little shit! I made a suggestion because you were never going to think of it yourself! I tried to help but you wouldn't let me! You're the one running away! I wasn't going anywhere! So don't blame it on me, sweetheart! You're like a bloody yo-yo! And I'm guessing at what I've done wrong! When I've done nothing wrong! You wanna grow up, darling!'

I am so astounded at the intensity of his rage that I barely hear what he is saying. Not for the first time I feel an urge to slap him. So I pounce on 'I tried to help you' with a shrill squawk of 'No you didn't! You knew I needed somewhere to stay! You never offered! You didn't care!'

Tom smacks himself on the forehead with the flat of his palm. This takes me by surprise and I bleat, 'Wh, what did you do that for?'

He sighs and says, 'Because you make me want to cry!'

I say sulkily, 'Why?'

He says in a slow, tired, heavy voice, 'I didn't offer Helen, because I *do* care. Or did. I'm not a fucking emergency service. Now is there anything I can do for your irresponsibly overfed cat or did you cart him all the way here in a box as an excuse to yell at me?'

Like most petty criminals whose cover is blown, I am glaring and silent.

'I thought so,' says Tom, his blue eyes cold. He rips open the door. I snoot out. 'Your ca-at!' he shouts after me in a nasty singsong tone. I snoot back, snatch the Voyager, and snoot out again. I snoot around to say something horrid but Tom slams the door in my face. I look towards reception and see a Jack Russell and its owner staring at me in beetlebrowed fascination, so I lean my bottom against the front door and snoot into the street.

*

The poison cherry on the plastic icing on the rotting cake is a call from Tina on my mobile. Every time I've approached her at work she's trilled 'Not now, doll, I'm busy!' and waved me away. All my carefully worded e-mails are ignored. But this evening she chooses to make contact. My callback tone rings as I heave Fatboy through the front door. I dial my message service and wince at Tina's high-pitched merriment: 'Hi, Helen! Just thought I'd let you know! Aide has made a big promise to change and it's all sorted and okay! So you can stop fussing! No need to ring! Bye!' I kick the door shut, release Fatboy from portable prison, and say bitterly, 'Jesus, you're even thicker than I am.'

I can't even smile when my mother shouts from the kitchen, 'Darling! Are you talking to me?'

Chapter 37

Nana says that when something bad happens you know who your friends are. Lizzy says that when something good happens you know who your friends are. The upshot is I don't have a clue who my friends are. Jasper is still chasing me like a fox after a chicken, Tina veers from reasonable to remote, and I can't decide *what* has happened.

The only news is that after four knackering, nitpicking, hair-tearing weeks, my solicitor rings to say we're ready to exchange contracts on Flat 55b. I tell Lizzy that in less than a month I'll be a homeowner and collapse on my desk. She can't understand it. 'Aren't you thrilled? What's wrong? Oh my, it's so exciting! We'll have to go paint shopping!'

I'm not sure which is more upsetting – the fact I find paint shopping a happy prospect or that I am now committed to living alone by myself in a titchy derelict terraced box in a scruffy part of Kentish Town. At least the Toyota will feel at home. And the purgatory of argybargying with banks and brokers and wasting cash on surveys and searches and surveyors and getting gazumped by people richer than me and being patronised and bullied is nearly at an end.

But I think of the hovel that is Flat number 55b and my stomach flips like a pancake. When my mother saw it she nearly burst into tears. 'Why can't you stay with me?' she exclaimed. 'This is disgusting! It's like a disused squat.' I was tempted to reply, 'Funny you should say that,' then thought better of it. Adam went white and tried to suggest it had a storming aspect, but hushed up when my mother

303

screeched '*What!*' For once I feel as if my mother's talking sense. What on earth am I'm doing? 'Yes, fine,' I hear myself bleat to the solicitor, 'Eleven a.m., tomorrow, in your office, alright, see you then, bye.'

For the last month I've been working as hard as an Egyptian slave to take my mind off Tom and the cruel things he said, so Laetitia is gracious in granting me the morning off. Her only comment is 'Kentish Town? Wasn't someone stabbed to death there recently?' I laugh nervously.

Meanwhile Lizzy is being as sweet as the sugar plum fairy – she has already given me the number of her 'sensational' builders and 'superb' electrician and 'angel of a' plumber – and it's easy to forget that I'm annoyed with her. I can't help it. I feel sullen because Lizzy is *too* confident – for her own good and for everyone else's. Her way is the only way. She may be kind but she is also alarmingly shortsighted. Lizzy is right about ginger being good for circulation and she is possibly right about peppermint being great for ringworm, but she is horribly wrong about Adrian and her teacher's pet complacency is pissing me off.

So I sneak out of work without saying goodbye, and when she calls me at home in the evening I whisper to my mother to say I'm out. 'She says she's out,' says my mother, forcing me to rip the phone out of her hand and be civil after all.

'Sorry about that,' I say with fake cheeriness. 'She's spent all day screaming at her kids. She's gone deaf.' Lizzy isn't so sure. 'Is anything the matter?' she says cautiously. 'You sound different.'

As I'd rather face a speeding truck than Lizzy's aggrieved piety, I say breezily, 'Nothing at all. I'm a little concerned about tomorrow, you know, big commitment and all that.'

As I expect, Lizzy poohpoohs this and sings, 'Don't worry! It's so straightforward! You'll be fine!' As it happens, she's wrong. Again.

*

304

The day of contract exchange starts badly when my mother storms off to work without saying goodbye. I try not to be annoyed and fail. I know it's only because she wants us to live together for ever as a weird double act – the princess and the bloody pea. 'The madam,' I mutter. 'She wants to stop behaving like a brat and grow up.' As soon as I say this I realise it sounds familiar, and that Tom said it to me. 'Hur!' I say, switching on the TV and falling backwards on to the sofa. 'He can sod off. Sod *off*! Shouting at me like that!' I say this aloud in an attempt to make his loss less aching but it doesn't work. My masochistic mind keeps turfing up cute memories. Hey Helen! Check out that wolf teeth smile! The emergency bunch of blue marigolds! Dissecting Stephen King while eating pizza! The elephant joke! Babysitting on tequila night! Fluffing up Fatboy's fur to make him look like a punk! Kissing off that crumb of cream cheese at the corner of your mouth! Adorable, no?

But it's not so much the little things as the sum of the parts. I can't deny it. I try to work myself up into a rancour against Tom but I can't. I want to despise him for liking me but can't. I want to maintain the things he said to me were said out of malice but I can no longer pretend. You don't spent ages peeling an orange unless you want to eat it. I recall his despair on our last meeting and it pains me. I've hurt him. Which proves me right. To care is to lose. And I'm a bad loser. It's as if I've ripped out my own heart and stamped on it. As punishment I watch the Shopping Channel for ninety minutes to remind myself that there are people out there far worse off than I am. Then I jump in the Toyota and drive to my solicitor.

The solicitor's office is in darkest north London and its frontage is made of glass. This sends me into a panic. Arctic explorers and people who live in Colorado get snow blindness. *I* get glass door blindness. There are six to choose from and as I ascend the steps I start sweating because I know the one I try will be locked and I'll have to scuttle along the steps like a crab pushing and heaving all of the doors in turn while the doorman and the postboy lean on the reception desk and laugh and laugh and think I'm thick.

Sure enough, my prediction comes true and after a flurry of baffling gestures from Mr Jobsworth – who watches my struggle with small-eyed interest but won't leave his seat to assist – I open the fourth door and stamp in, red-faced and fretful. Then I wait on the black leather sofa for seventeen minutes and listen to him sniff. After the twenty-ninth sniff I want to scream 'Blow your nose!' but am summoned to my appointment on the second floor just in time.

Lizzy's solicitor is called Dorothy Spence and Lizzy is forever praising Dorothy as 'thorough'. And thorough she is. Easily an hour thorough, reading through this clause and that clause and do I understand what this liability means and the import of this restrictive covenant and she's queried that and she's queried this but all her queries have now been satisfied and do I have any questions and if not she requires a deposit of nine thousand pounds.

I nearly fall off my swingaround chair. 'What, now?' I stammer.

'Yes please,' says Dorothy briskly.

'But I, I didn't realise.' I bleat, 'I, I thought that was . . . just before completion . . . I misunderstood, I haven't done this before, so I thought . . .' Dorothy shoots me a look – the same kind of look the doorman gave me earlier today – and I falter to a halt. There are times when I have so little faith in my own abilities that I ordain myself to failure.

And this is one of those times. I have made a foolish error. In my tizzy ignorance I assumed the ten per cent deposit was payable on completion. Admittedly, Dorothy sent me a letter a week ago detailing what would be required of me but – as I now recall – I glanced at it, stuffed it in my bag to read later, and forgot about it. (I regularly ignore scary letters, but credit card companies encourage me to confront my fears by ringing sly and early on Saturday mornings.) Dorothy didn't even send me a red reminder. As a result, the cash is breeding in a high interest account and I can't withdraw a penny without giving notice. I am a clueless fraud aping a dependable adult and the worst has happened.

I've been exposed for what I am.

'Can I make a call?' I ask Dorothy in a small voice. She glances at her chrome clock, nods sharply and reclines in her plump leather chair. I call my mother's mobile and pray she answers. She doesn't. So I call the school and ask to be put through to the staffroom. 'Is Cecelia Bradshaw there?' I say breathlessly. 'It's her daughter.'

A distant voice replies, 'One moment.' Forty moments later, I'm still waiting and Dorothy Spence is tapping her foot.

Then the line goes dead. I bite my lip, smile weakly at Dorothy, and redial. 'I rang a minute ago and got cut off,' I say, keeping my voice hard and loud so it doesn't break. 'I need to speak to Cecelia Bradshaw. It's urgent.' Thirty seconds later, my mother is on the line. I feel weak with relief. I pinch my nose to stop myself crying and explain. The humiliation throbs through me in shockwaves. When I finish declaiming my mother is silent.

Then she says in a wonder-of-you voice, 'It's not a *problem*, darling. I'll call the bank right now and get an electronic transfer to the relevent account. Let me speak to the lawyer woman.' I sink into a grateful trance and hand the receiver to Dorothy.

Fifteen torturous minutes later I am driving home in the Toyota. As any form of reflection is painful I spend the entire journey saying 'La la la' in a loud monotone to ward off thought. I slink into the office at 2.30 p.m. and start typing Laetitia's rejection letters to all feature ideas sent in on spec without faffing needlessly for two hours first. To my relief Lizzy isn't in the office – and as Laetitia wouldn't dream of asking how my morning went any more than she'd dream of buying shoes from C&A, I work undisturbed until 6.36.

Then I leave without speaking to anyone. As I sit on the tube I feel naked. I am convinced everyone is peering at me, talking about me, jeering at me. I feel claustrophobic and I want to scream.

By the time I'm home I am a gibbery quivery wreck. I intend to curl up in bed and sleep but as I tiptoe upstairs my mother appears like a shimmering genie in the hallway and exclaims, 'Helen! Come down here and talk to me!' Wordlessly, I swivel and descend. I feel as hunchy and evil as a tarantula. My mother, meanwhile, is as glowy and zingy and zesty as a teenage beauty queen. The only difference is she's not wearing a sash. She beams and pats her hair and lifts her hands and says in a joyous voice 'So?'

I stand before her and my lower lip starts to tremble. I scowl at the patterned carpet and clutch my arms behind my back. And I say fiercely, 'If Dad was here he'd have known what to do.'

I dig my nails into my palms and wait. I don't know what I expect. Huffing. Tutting. Not laughter. But my mother tee hee hees and says, 'Yes, but I managed okay didn't I?'

I nod and whisper, 'I miss my dad.'

My mother is quiet and I feel like a fart at a wedding. Then she looks at my face as if for the first time, and says softly, 'I know you do, darling, and I'm sure he misses you too.'

And suddenly, she takes a step forward and hugs me tightly and I am lost and found in a waft of Chanel. The range of sound effects available to me as a human seem inadequate and I wish I were a wolf so I could tilt my head and howl, owwooww owwwwwww, surrender my body and soul to the resonance of grief.

Instead I close my eyes and wail silently, absorb the warmth of my mother's purple jumper and feel her thin arms firm around me.

Chapter 38

I cling to my mother like, I imagine, a rescued mountaineer clinging to a St Bernard. Oh God, I wail inside, why is it so bad, *why*? No one said it would be like *this*. I am a hollow skin stuffed with razor blades that slash my body from the inside until I choke on my own blood. I cling to my mother so heavily that her knees buckle and we gently crumple to the floor, where she strokes my hair and makes soothing noises. 'I don't know what to do,' I sob. 'I don't know what to doo-hoo hooo!' Even as I bleat the words I feel horrified at this pitiful collapse in front of the one person who needs me to be invincible.

But my mother rocks me and says, 'It's so hard, darling. And I know I haven't been much use. But you've been so brave,' and suddenly I am five years old again and being consoled after falling over and cutting my knee. I smile weakly and wipe my eyes. 'Cry if you want to,' orders my mother briskly. 'The children bawl constantly and I always say, better out than in!' The tears fall hot and fast and I shake my head, wordlessly. This unexpected fortitude is like finding a shiny brown chestnut amid autumn's decomposing mulch.

My mother smiles at my stupefaction and says softly, 'Come on, darling. I'll make you a hot drink.' I meekly allow her to drag me to my feet, and suddenly she bursts out angrily, 'Stupid hot drinks! Your father's dead and all we can do is have a bloody hot drink!'

I snivel-giggle and say, 'It's shit, isn't it?'

My mother makes a face and fills the kettle. We sit in

silence, drinking hot chocolate and contemplating the fact that death is a monstrous affront to the living and shouldn't be allowed. After a long time my mother pats my hand and says softly, 'Remember, darling. Daddy may be gone but he'll always be with you.'

I look up, the corners of my mouth trembling, and see that she is crying too. And I realise that even amid the rubble, we've salvaged something.

I think my mother realises it too, because in the weeks that follow my outburst, our relationship slips from fraught to placid like the stunned quiet after a flash thunderstorm. When she recounts a success she had at work and I tell her 'well done', I notice with surprise that she *blushes*. It's as if we're on honeymoon after a speedy romance – tipped into intimacy after the pink whirlwind of lust has settled – and she's suddenly shy because what I think of her matters. I scramble upstairs, grinning to myself, and consider the inconceivable: that when I move into my flat tomorrow, I am going to miss her.

It's strange. After I completed on the flat, I expected my mother to shun me for at least a fortnight but instead she offered to help me interview builders for quotes. I assumed this was for bicep ogling purposes but she turned out to be a shrewd, efficient ally. Her enthusiasm didn't fizzle out like it usually does. She dismissed Lizzy's recommendation (he wanted cash) and called the firm that Vivienne had employed to refurbish her kitchen and build a conservatory. 'Vivvy couldn't fault them!' explained my mother. Naturally I assumed they must be excellent – as most people employed by Vivienne are sued to within an inch of their livelihoods – and to my relief they *were* excellent.

Last year Laetitia moved to Barnes and *her* builders dragged out a two-month job for five months, turned up when and if they felt like it, drank their weight in sweet tea (Laetitia had to purchase a bag of sugar especially) then peed it out over her turquoise mosaic toilet floor, cracked her extortionate new cast-iron roll-top bath, chipped her antique gilt wall mirror, botched her Swedish style trompe l'oeil panelling, installed her boiler in such a way that it emitted poisonous gas into the kitchen, dented her Aga, scratched her Provençal armoire, spilt paint on her Aubusson carpet, forgot to tighten the nuts connecting two water pipes thus transforming the flat below into a large designer swamp, drilled through the electrics, blocked off access to the gas mains, installed a dimmer switch in the bedroom that dimmed lights in the lounge and study too, and gave her an estimate of £3,500 but charged her £19,000. Laetitia marched into work most mornings shaking white dust out of her hair and muttering that it was 'like being in a war'.

So I appreciate my beginner's luck.

After six backbreaking weeks, *my* builders have re-plastered, re-plumbed, re-wired, and resuscitated my little flat. They have been masterminded by Terry who, in his own words, 'runs a tight ship'. And my mother and I have spent at least thirty hours trawling Greater London in search of – as she puts it – 'fitments'. While I am as skilled in sourcing glass bricks as I am at completing *The Times* Crossword – no, I won't lie – any crossword, my mother has been astounding. She's approached the flat refurbishment like a school project. She bought a pile of glossy interiors magazines, and ordered me to scour them and make notes. Every time I saw something I liked, she'd fill the Peugeot with petrol, and force me to plan a route. Equipped with a tape measure and a sketch of the kitchen and bathroom dimensions, she'd then speed to the relevant store and *barter* with its sales staff.

She has the business scruples of a kidney broker, and if a shop didn't offer her a loss-making bargain, she'd walk out. (I'd already *be* out, having run into the street purple with mortification.) Personally I wouldn't query the price of beads in a Moroccan flea market and would have forked out a premium for granite floor tiles without a squeak. My mother, however, would shout down God over the cost of a halo and shame Him into a discount.

311

I won't say it hasn't been stressful. Especially as Lizzy had assumed that the role of Assistant Foreperson would fall to her. I pacified her with a paint shopping trip and – while she struggled to accept that all purchases were to be made from Crown rather than Farrow & Ball – she accepted my mother's superior involvement as widow's compensation. This excuse to Lizzy was partially true.

Following her husband's demise, my mother has a loose bunch of emotions rolling about that she needs to put somewhere. Until recently, she hasn't been capable. But the key has been jiggling in the lock for the past month and it seems, finally, to have turned. The electronic transfer and its tumultuous aftermath has helped my mother realise – on some vague level – that if she keeps pushing me away I will eventually go. So yes, her interest in my flat is in her interest. But it would be more truthful to say that she understands I genuinely need her.

Consequently, for the first time in – at a rough estimate – twenty-six years, she has been humouring *me*. When I threw *Elle Decoration* on the floor and announced I was sick of stick women in Nicole Farhi flouncing around their cool empty homes, smirking over their solid oak chairs which they'd 'picked up for two pounds each from a thrift store' my mother rose to the challenge. Three days and twenty quid later – she handed me the receipt – I was the proud owner of two solid oak chairs. (She hadn't bought more as there wasn't enough room in the flat: 'Aren't I clever!')

When I decided that multi-million-pound steel kitchen units were imperative or I'd be too embarrassed to invite people round, she consulted *Living Etc.* and suggested a visit to 'The London Metal Centre – look, darling! They sell stainless steel sheeting from about five pounds per square foot! You stick it on top of that MFI cardboard stuff and it looks exactly the same!' I caught Terry chortling to himself but I think he was secretly impressed.

I'm just thankful that she's fizzing with energy. I'm

determined not to think about how long it may or may not last. Mostly, I'm succeeding. So maybe I have changed too. I feel calmer. It's as if I've had my nose pressed up against an abstract painting, fighting, panting, pushing for a brilliant view. But it's only now when I step back that I can appreciate the picture. It's an unexpected revelation and when I recall the incongruous sight of my mother in animated chat with Terry over architectural suppliers, I feel an airy flutter of delight.

I expect moving in to feel ceremonial, but though I carry Fatboy over the threshold, it doesn't. Possibly because I possess only seven large items: two chairs, a table, a television, a bed, a dartboard, and a clothes rail, so it takes Luke and myself about seven minutes to hoick stuff up the creaky stairs and arrange it. Now the builders have gone the flat looks stark – in the same way that a pinhead looks stark. 'Helen,' says Luke, 'this is *so* tidy for you!'

After Luke leaves – he has an urgent date with Gobbo and a PlayStation – I walk around from room to room (it takes me nine seconds) touching the yellow walls, sniffing the chalky newness, stroking my craftily crafted steel and MDF kitchen units. Then I boil water in my shiny new kettle – courtesy of my mother who inveigled it out of John Lewis as compensation for a faulty plug – make myself a coffee, sit on a chair, and look at the polished wood floor. Silence.

Then, after three labour intensive hours of arranging my duvet, moving four mugs and three plates from a high cupboard to a low cupboard, shoving forks into a drawer, lining up my murder collection in a row on the bedroom floor with piles of bricks as bookends, scrubbing the bath, bleaching the toilet, sweeping the floor, placing my blue toothbrush next to the sink, and making a list of items I need but can't afford without a new credit card, I tire of homemaking and ring Lizzy.

I have pasted over my disappointment in Lizzy. She

313

sensed my coolness and was palpably hurt. A week ago she said – in a stiff rehearsed voice that made me suspect she'd been brooding – 'Helen, I do hope you don't think that you can't ring me any more just because I'm going out with Brian. We're not one person. We don't do *everything* together.'

I laughed guiltily and said, 'Lizzy, of course I don't think that. I've just been mad busy with the flat, that's all.'

The pathos of this exchange stayed with me and I began to wonder if I'd been harsh. After all, I hadn't presented Lizzy with the brutal facts so maybe it wasn't fair to condemn her. Of *course* she would have wanted to help Tina if she'd known the truth. And – holier than thou considerations apart – I missed Lizzy. I missed her for the same reason I resented her. I wanted Miss Twinkletoes back in my life sprinkling fairydust. The next day I approached her at work and asked if she'd like the New World Gas Range cooker because it was rusting to dust and about to be dumped on the skip. She flung her arms around me like I'd offered her eternal life, and collected it that same evening. Amen.

Lizzy is thrilled at my call and bounces round clutching a bunch of daffodils and a sleek glass vase. The vase is beautiful – a warm burnished orange, like captured sunshine. 'It's gorgeous,' I squeak, 'it completes the room!'

Lizzy beams. 'It's my pleasure! Now show me round!' she exclaims. 'I can hardly believe it's the same flat. It's so dinky!' To my shame we spend the next two hours earnestly discussing glitter paint and sugar soap and sanding machines. I find myself gabbling desperately, incessantly – as if building a wall of words could prevent her from leaving. But at 6 p.m. Lizzy wrenches herself away (Brian's aunt is throwing a houseboat party) and Fatboy and I are alone. The evening looms ahead like a dark tunnel.

I switch on the TV, am confronted by *Songs Of Praise*,

switch it off, wonder if the flat is bigger than a Wendy house, flop on the bed, stare at the ceiling, spot a money spider in the corner, run into the kitchen to find a broom to poke it with, realise I don't own a broom, run back, can't see the spider, know it's scuttling about the bedroom, suspect it's pregnant and laying spider eggs, and start panicking. I am about to ring my mother when I remember that Vivienne has taken her to an organic health farm for the weekend. I slump back on the bed and feel miserable. When the phone rings I almost swoon with gratitude. 'Hello?' I whisper, hoping it isn't a wrong number.

'Babe?' says a clipped voice.

'Jasper!' I squeal. 'How *are* you!'

I am well aware that I sound inordinately keen. Unbeknown to Jasper my delight is nothing personal as I'd have greeted a BT salesperson with the same shrieky degree of elation. But Jasper being Jasper, he takes it personally.

'Hey, steady there, Angelsweet!' he exclaims.

As I believe any man who says the words 'Hey, steady there, Angelsweet!' without irony should kill himself instantly to dispel the shame, I choke and pause before answering.

I say, 'Hey yourself, Smug One! Do you want to come and see my new flat?'

There is a silence and I wonder if Jasper is going to cut me down – and it has been known – with a cry of, 'I'm devastated Angelsweet! I'd adore to but alas I can't! [ascending pitch as if asking a question] I'm escorting Monique the supermodel? The one with a Harvard doctorate? Who writes books on Jungian theory? to, hum! Paris? [he'd pronounce it '*Paree*'] for a night of pash at the Georges Cinq? What *crippling* timing!'

Instead, he replies, 'Absolutely, Babe! Where are you? I'll hop in a cab now.'

An hour later, Jasper and I are sitting at my table on my solid oak chairs, prodding at the remains of a Chinese takeaway. Jasper is wearing a blue-and-white baseball cap, which I cannot see the point of. Even so, he looks ravishing. I am explaining how laying tiles at a diagonal will give a feeling of space when I notice Jasper stifle a yawn. 'Sorry,' I say indignantly, 'am I boring you?'

Jasper's eyes widen and he drawls, 'Babe, I could listen to you for ever.' I tell him he's a liar. He sighs.

'What?' I say, surprised that I've made an impact.

'Oh nothing, Babe, *rien.*'

He shakes his head mournfully.

I snort. 'If you're resorting to French something is definitely up. What is it?'

Jasper leans on his elbows and says slowly, 'I'd rather not say.'

Naturally, I am agog. 'Jasper,' I gasp, 'you *must* tell me!'

I rack my brain to think of how to say this in French but there's a large vacant space where the knowledge should be.

Jasper shifts in his chair and mutters, 'It's not fair.'

I clutch the sides of the table to stop myself flying at him and prising the secret out of his mouth manually. 'Is it your job?' I say.

'NO!' says Jasper in a loud voice. 'God, no! The job's A1!'

I try again. 'Is it, uh, not being able to drive?'

Jasper looks piqued. He croaks, 'Helen, you don't think I'd care about a plebeian thing like that, do you?'

As I know from rifling through his bedside drawer that he's failed his driving test at least six times (it's why he's constantly broke) I decide not to answer. I say, 'hmm,' and then, 'Is it . . . Louisa?'

Jasper rakes his hand through his hair and leans back. I hold my breath. 'In a word,' he says.

At this point I realise a pool of saliva has collected in my mouth and if I don't swallow instantly I'm going to drool like a basset hound. I gulp and squeak, 'What happened?'

Jasper stretches his lips into a grimace and the tendons in

316

his neck appear like tent ropes. Then he says, 'She ah, wanted to get back together.'

My mouth drops. '*No!*' I say. 'What, what did you say?'

Jasper sighs again and says, 'I said, if I could, I would. But it wouldn't be fair on her.' He stops. Then adds, 'Because I'm keen on' – he sighs – 'someone else.'

I gaze at him and he blushes. And immediately I know that Jasper has a belated crush on me. My eyes are like gobstoppers. I try to keep my voice level. 'Oh no!' I squeak. 'What did Louisa say to that?' Jasper looks uncomfortable. 'Well?' I demand.

He says quietly, 'Ah, I'd rather not say.'

I bang my fist on the table. 'Come *on*!' I bellow. 'You can't not tell me now!' I force the details out of him. Although he doesn't mention my name, he doesn't need to. I watch his mouth as he talks. And as he relates the woeful tale of his ex-girlfriend's unrequited love, I find myself wanting to kiss him.

I'm the same with jumpers. I was hovering by a black V-neck in Warehouse, fingering the material and wondering if it would itch, when a tall tanned woman sashayed over and plucked it from the shelf. Immediately I craved the V-neck like a nicotine addict craves a fag on a no-smoking flight. I tailed V-neck Woman around the shop, into the changing rooms, out of the changing rooms, and when she shot me a nasty look and dumped the jumper over a rail, I snatched it up and, trembling with excitement, bought it. I am the gullible materialist that advertisers dream about. I am indifferent to a person or a product until someone else wants it. Then, immediately, I want it more.

So when Jasper tells me that a week before Christmas Louisa gave him three months to move out because she couldn't stand the agony of seeing his face and not being able to snog it, I exclaim, 'Jass! Jass! I've had a brilliant idea! Until you find somewhere – why not stay at *my* place for a few days?'

Jasper stares at me as if Fatboy has spoken. 'You can't

mean that?' he says in an awed voice. I nod vigorously. Anything is better than living in poky isolation. His chiselled face breaks into a dimpled smile and he grabs my hand and kisses it. 'Angelsweet,' he murmurs, 'you're a shining star.' And then, 'Hey! I know! Why don't you drive me to Kensington and we can get my things now! It'll be fun!'

Though I cannot see how taxiing Jasper across London and lugging his gloomy ship paintings up my stairs will be fun, I can hardly refuse. As there is precisely nowhere to park in Kensington, I wait in the Toyota while Jasper fills it with his belongings. Clothes. Paintings. Stereo. And two hideous wicker chairs and a wicker coffee table. I blurt, 'I thought the crap furniture belonged to your landlord!'

Jasper laughs and says, 'Babe, these are original colonial pieces! Anyway I don't know what you're complaining about. They'll look ace in your lounge!' I am not so sure and my suspicion is confirmed when the chairs are in place. They hunch over the floor, each one like a preying mantis, and their mean scratchy wickerness dominates the room. Even though it's great to have company, I feel cross.

I feel even crosser when Jasper snakes up behind me, grabs my hips, and whispers, 'Hey Babe, what say we christen the flat?'

I sternly imprison his hands in mine and say with forced sweetness, 'Sure, Jass. Only I should tell you I'm having a really heavy period. Whew, talk about a flow! Honestly, it's like my uterus is being dragged out of me, so I'm warning you it'll be very messy, like having sex in an abattoir, but I see you've brought your Egyptian cotton, we can lay it over the bed like an absorbent plaster to soak up the effluvia . . .'

Jasper sleeps on the lounge floor and doesn't bother me again.

318

Chapter 39

I was about fourteen and walking down the road when a paunchy, wisp-haired, middle-aged man stopped me and said, 'If you don't mind me saying, that jumper doesn't suit you.' Taken aback I squeaked, 'Oh! er, thanks for telling me.' I ran home, stared in the mirror at me and my round shoulders in my red-and-white striped sweatshirt, and thought, ugh, yes the state of you.

It was a good few years before it occurred to me that an adult who stops a plump teenage stranger in the street to criticise her dress sense has got to be a thick chauvinist fruitcake. Then again, I had to ask myself – what the hell was I doing wearing a red-and-white striped sweatshirt? Did I work at a barber's shop? Was I a pouting Lolitalike superwaif who could wear doll's clothes and call it ironic kitsch? When I ventured out disguised as a comedy bollard did I have even a splash of self-awareness? No.

When I see my pristine white bath defiled by Jasper's shaving stubble and my freshly tiled floor transformed into a penguin's paddling pool and my big square mirror steamed up like a microwave door and realise there's going to be no hot water for the fourth time this week and it's only Thursday, I scowl and think in the last twelve years have I learned anything at all? Obviously not.

Although the last four days have been interesting. My romantic notions of living – as Jasper might say – *à deux* – were shot to pieces within minutes. In the foolish seconds preceding my rash invitation I fantasised about a host of cosy things. Changing the message on my new answer machine to 'HelenanJasper aren't in right now'. Filling my supermarket basket with Jasperish items like smoked venison and freshly squeezed OJ as well as Dime bars and cat litter. Snuggling up on the floorboards in front of *Lethal Weapon*. The edible scent of Egoiste lending a blast of masculinity to my bachelorette flat.

What was I thinking? The moment I saw those grubby wicker chairs polluting my territory I knew I'd made a mistake. I *liked* having an answer machine message all to myself. I didn't want a dead Bambi in my fridge. I preferred watching *Lethal Weapon* on my own, especially as – unlike some people – I would never exclaim loudly at a crucial point, 'This is preposterous, facile pap, let's watch a decent film like *Citizen Kane*.' And if I was that desperate for a masculine blast I could feed Fatboy a large helping of turkey & giblets pâté and await the stinky inevitable. What is it with me?

'But I can't tell him to leave,' I bleat to Lizzy over lunch. 'He's got nowhere to go.'

Lizzy, who is carefully inspecting her green salad for slugs, says, 'Really, Helen, I don't know why you asked him in the first place. He's a selfish man who, if you ask me, is emotionally constipated, and he's not been nice to you.'

I poke my lasagne with a fork and think how prettily two-faced Lizzy is. I remember a time, not so very long ago, when she shared a flat with her psychologist friend in a stuccoed street in Camden. The shrink went away for a conference, returned two days later, and discovered – rather like Daddy Bear – that someone had been sleeping in his bed. It emerged that Lizzy had taken pity on the young homeless man who slept on a bench at the end of the road. She couldn't understand why the shrink was annoyed. 'But *you* weren't using it!' said Goldilocks. 'And I was going to wash the sheets but I didn't expect you back until tomorrow.'

I dismiss this episode from my mind and attempt to answer her question. Why did I ask Jasper to stay? 'I felt lonely after you'd swanned off to your boat party,' I say sulkily. 'And it was rainy and I was by myself in an empty flat.'

Lizzy shakes her curls and says, 'But that's my favourite thing! Being all cosy in a warm flat, watching the rain! And it was your first night in your own home. Weren't you excited?'

I sigh. Then I say in a grumpy voice, 'Yes, but I saw a huge spider. And I felt sorry for him. Jasper, I mean.'

Lizzy purses her lips. 'Why?' she says.

I feel hot and cross. I snap, 'Because Louisa turfed him out!'

Lizzy retorts, 'But she gave him notice. Couldn't he find his own flat?'

I growl, 'No.'

'Oh,' says Lizzy. 'Why not?'

I shrug and say, 'I think he's short of cash.'

Lizzy isn't convinced. She says, 'Well, he's lucky that he had you to fall back on. You're very kind, Helen, but I do think it's your right to tell Jasper to go if you've changed your mind about having him.'

Something Lizzy has just said chafes at my composure. I say huffily, 'We're fond of each other. And I feel sorry for him because I know what it's like to be living with someone you've been involved with and for it to go sour.' I say.

Lizzy emits a neat, ladylike snort and replies, 'Well, Helen, you certainly know now!' I tut and ignore her.

Lizzy is in a bad mood because she's twenty-eight tomorrow. Normally this wouldn't be an issue but she has booked a private room in a restaurant to celebrate with friends and yesterday afternoon Tina e-mailed her to say she would be unable to attend. She didn't give a reason. This shocked Lizzy and she rang Tina at home in the evening to ask why. Adrian answered. I can only assume that Lizzy charmed the bastard because he and Tina are now attending.

But Lizzy remains upset. She counts Tina as one of her

ten closest pals and has made infinite excuses for the fact that recently she's been as friendly as a traffic warden with gout. According to Lizzy, Tina has been 'incredibly pressurised' because the deputy fashion editor has landed a job at *Cosmopolitan* and hasn't yet been replaced so Tina is 'snowed under with work'. Also, Tina is 'mad about Adrian' but 'they both work such long hours' and so 'Tina wants to spend every precious minute with him.'

It has been easy for Lizzy to believe her own hype as she is one of those repulsively popular people who isn't possessive of her friends (they're two a penny and always ringing her). But while she's a liberal pal she is a birthday fascist. This is because Lizzy's family have always made a huge fuss of birthdays – hired halls, magicians, clown cakes, balloon sculptures, fancy dress, ribboned presents, goody bags stuffed with sweets (I didn't get any of that when *I* turned twenty-six) – and Lizzy continues to regard birthdays as sacrosanct. So Tina's attempt to wriggle out of Lizzy's birthday dinner is an unpardonable sin. And that Tina's now been forced into attending doesn't erase the snub. I open my mouth to say 'How many people have you invited?' when Lizzy opens *her* mouth and says, 'Helen, do you mind awfully if I don't invite Jasper?'

I am astonished. Lizzy blushes and adds hurriedly, 'It's just that I don't think he'll enjoy it at all. Oh I do hope you're not offended, it's just that—'

I overcome my surprise and say, 'Liz, honestly, it's fine. In fact he *can't* make it, he's going out with the guys from his college cricket team tomorrow night. So don't worry.' Even as these words drop glibly from my lips, a thousand more rough and tumble inside my head. Do I believe my ears? So Jasper is blackballed but the wife-beater is cordially invited! This is heresy! It's tantamount to God telling Adam that Eve isn't invited to his Garden party but the Snake is.

I smile thinly and try not to look offended. I don't *want* Jasper to come to Lizzy's – he'd only bitch about the food and the guests and the music and the venue – but Lizzy not wanting him to come is another thing entirely. It's my right to discriminate against Jasper as he's *my* ex. But Lizzy has no past-ownership entitlement to Jasper's reputation and so I am forced to declare her out of order. (In my head, of course, I wouldn't dream of saying so to her face.)

'I've invited Luke, though,' says Lizzy, 'I know you adore him, and he's such a sweetie.'

I am astonished for the second time in two minutes. 'Oh!' I say. I'm not sure if I am pleased (at least Luke won't talk about karmic astrology all evening) or annoyed (Lizzy's got a billion friends, why is she appropriating *mine?*). I tell Lizzy that's fine, but if she'll excuse me I've got to make a phone call. Then I stalk back to the office and sulk. My mood doesn't improve, even when I get home and see that Jasper has made himself a cheese and tomato sandwich in the kitchen and eaten it in the lounge – the cutlery drawer is open, a crumb-encrusted plate is abandoned on the table, a bread knife is lying by the sink, a spider-resembling tomato top has been dropped on the floor, and the remains of a hunk of Cheddar (unwrapped) is turning stale on the side.

'He's got a nerve!' I say to Fatboy, who is biting his claws and pays no attention. I wonder if Jasper has left me a note to say where he is. After a three-second search in which I comb the flat, I discover he hasn't. I wash up the plate and knife, slam shut the drawer, pick up the tomato top and the cracking Cheddar, and hurl them in the bin, all the while muttering under my breath about slothful loutish flatmates who hurl their weight around like Henry VIII, expect other people to tidy up their filthy mess, *and* leave their Earl Grey teabags in the stainless steel sink and stain it. I pound around for forty minutes fussing and dusting, become bored, and call Tina.

I know I shouldn't. The last time I rang her and enquired after her health she told me coldly that she knew I was trying to break up her relationship and furthermore she knew it was because I was jealous of her and Adrian's 'amazing love' for each other, and I didn't understand it. I – according to Tina – am eaten up with bitterness because the men I date are all wankers who couldn't give a shit about me (only she didn't put it quite so nicely).

Hurt though I was, I reminded myself she'd been hypnotised by the evil wizard and merely said, 'Damn right I want to break up your relationship! I'd love to get you away from Adrian. He's a—' but she put the phone down on me. She's ignored me ever since and the self-help books are mouldering away on my bedroom floor. I hate it, but I'm scared to call in case I get her into trouble. But I think, I can pretend I'm ringing to see what she's buying Lizzy for her birthday. Just this once won't hurt. Tina's mobile isn't working so I call her home number. 'Hello?' she whispers.

'Tina?' I say nervously. 'It's me, Helen. Do you know your mobile's not working?'

Tina coughs, and says, 'I don't have one any more.' As Tina is – or used to be – famed for the scale of her mobile phone bills (approx £300 per month) I am taken aback.

'But,' I stutter, 'how can you live!'

Tina coughs again. She seems to have a sore throat. 'They're bad for you,' she says flatly, 'they give you brain cancer.'

I reply, 'But isn't it essential for your job?' Tina says nothing. I feel a stab of rage and I say heatedly, 'It's him, isn't it? He's trying to take you away from us! Why—'

She interrupts me. Her tone is fierce: 'No he's not! It's only because he cares about me, and you can't deal with that! Why won't you stop interfering and leave me alone! *Please!* He'll be here soon, he's got a key, and if he catches me, he'll press one-four-seven-one and if he'll want to know who I spoke to and for how long and what we said and—' her voice cracks.

I grimace and try to understand. I tell her I'm her friend and I want the best for her and she's got to trust me. I tell her (and here I keep my fingers crossed) I respect her and

324

Adrian's relationship but a relationship should make you happy and I don't think she's that happy. I ask her if he's hit her recently and she tells me he hasn't hit her in a long time. But something in the way she says it alerts me and I ask if he's done anything that he wouldn't do if say, *I* was in the room.

Which is when I find out that last night, after Lizzy's phone call, Adrian took a plastic spatula from Tina's kitchen drawer, a plastic M & S bag from under the sink, locked Tina in her flat (saying he *might* call at any time so if she rang anyone he'd know), sauntered down the road to the park, shovelled three fresh dog shits into the M & S bag, returned to the flat, donned a pair of yellow rubber gloves, then smeared dog shit all over Tina's face and into her mouth, while hissing, 'That's what *you* are.'

Apart from that, he's been a real dear.

Chapter 40

I was raised to believe that good vanquishes evil. Cinderella's ugly sisters, Cruella de Vil, the sneering shop assistants in *Pretty Woman* – they all got their come-uppance for no better reason than because they deserved it. So when I hear about Adrian's latest atrocity I expect justice. I want a storybook hero to sweep to the rescue and save the goodie and punish the baddie. Yet, when I beg Tina to let me call the police, she hesitates then says 'No'. She says real life doesn't work like that. I don't know what Adrian is like, he's smarter than the law. When she says this, I feel helpless and weak and sick to the stomach. I am robbed of speech and two decades of complacency.

I don't sleep well on Thursday night and wake up on Friday morning feeling groggy. I drag myself to work and try to wake up. But I can't. I drink two double espressos which make my body jangle but have no effect whatsoever on my dopiness. I see Tina slink into the office, head bowed. My heart lurches, and I decide she doesn't need to avoid eye contact because today I am going to ignore her. I know it's childish of me, but I'm so angry and frustrated that if I spoke to her I'd find it hard not to shake her. Listen to me – I'm as bad as Adrian. I force a smile as Lizzy bounds up and tinkles, 'Are you looking forward to tonight? What are you going to wear?'

My smile dissipates and I say, 'Er, this.'

Lizzy looks at my baggy, faded grey top and frowns. 'You can't wear *that* for my birthday! It's my *birthday*!'

Grow up, I want to say but don't. 'Well I haven't got anything else,' I growl. Lizzy peers under my desk. 'Oi!' I squeak.

'I wanted to see what shoes you were wearing,' she explains, 'and I have to say, those stack-heeled boots aren't my favourite.' To be frank, my stack-heeled boots aren't anyone's favourite. A while back, when Tina was still herself, she took one glance and said they looked like calipers. But *I* like them. 'I know!' sings Lizzy. 'I'll ask Tina to lend you something fabulous from the fashion cupboard. I'm sure she will when she—, I'm sure she will.'

Lizzy tootles off, consults with Tina and, four minutes later, reappears at my desk brandishing a pair of strappy black stiletto sandals and a yellow wraparound top with mauve lace edging. 'Ay carumba,' I say crossly.

'Don't be silly!' snaps Lizzy. 'These will look gorgeous with your black trousers.'

I reply, 'Yes, but what about with me in them?'

Lizzy ignores my grumblings and forces me to try everything on. I stare dourly at my reflection in the Ladies mirror while Lizzy skips around me like a demented pixie, pulling and tugging and brushing at the top. Then she says, 'Helen, you look divine! Wait there!'

She slips out of the door, and two seconds later is back, with Tina. 'What do you think?' she crows, flinging her arms wide like a cabaret singer.

'Great,' says Tina, smiling wanly and addressing the words to my left ear.

'Good!' says Lizzy. 'That's that then.' She allows me to put on my grey top for the remainder of the day but confiscates my boots 'because I don't trust you'. She dances out of the door, leaving Tina and me alone.

I feel as awkward as when Michelle's grandmother set me up on a blind date with her dog-walker – who was Russian ('from *Rrrr*ussia weez love!' he threatened on the phone) and had a mullet. 'Hello,' I say.

Tina nibbles at a fingernail and blurts, 'Helen, please

327

don't be off with me, or Adrian tonight, he'll get suspicious and, and—'

Instantly I feel cruel and ashamed, so I touch her upper arm, trace my finger down it gently, and squeeze her hand. Her eyes fill with tears and she turns and walks out.

As I don't wish to disappoint Lizzy – and because when she leaves the office I search frenziedly around her desk for my calipers but can't find them – I walk into the restaurant bang on seven thirty wearing my black trousers, carnival top and strappy sandals. And the first person I see is Tom. He is standing in the far corner of the room, and is in conversation with Brian, who is wearing stonewashed dungarees. I'm so astonished (not at the stonewashed dungarees, they complement the green dayglo T-shirt perfectly) I double take and nearly drop Lizzy's present on the floor. The birthday girl skips over. 'Surprise!' she squeaks in my ear.

My face feels hot and red. 'Oh my God, you maniac! Keep it down!' I mutter, trying to keep the inane grin on my face under control.

Lizzy clamps a hand over her mouth to muffle a loud giggle. Luke appears at my side, digs an elbow into my ribs and winks.

'That was subtle,' I say.

'Tom came with Luke, so don't blame me!' exclaims Lizzy happily.

Luke chirrups, 'We went to loads of trouble so don't bugger it up this time.'

I stare at my strappy sandals and murmur delightedly, 'You meddling kids!'

Luke takes this as a sign of approval and cries, 'I'll go and get him, shall I?'

He is only prevented from doing so when I grab his shirt, drag him backwards by the scruff, and hiss 'No!' But then Tom walks across the room, gazes at me for a second, and says boldly, 'Hello, you.' And I know he's being bold because when he says it he turns pink and his voice trembles slightly. I open my mouth and realise it's as dry as stale toast, so my 'hello, Tom,' emerges as a faint croak.

Tom blushes again – not least because Luke and Lizzy are staring at us like Muppets – and starts to say 'I, uh, you look ni—' when he is interrupted.

Luke nudges him in the back and exclaims, 'Aren't you gonna kiss her then?'

I freeze as the godawful words boi-oi-oing around our ears like a boomerang at a funeral. Lizzy – who I conclude didn't *quite* understand what she was dealing with when she went into cahoots with Luke – looks aghast. Tom's horrified expression cracks and he roars 'Arrrrrgh!' and pretends to throttle Luke.

'Come away now!' orders Lizzy sharply, like a nanny who is watching the rhinos with a five-year-old when they start rutting.

Tom and I are left to face each other. My hands dangle awkwardly by my sides and I don't know what to do with them. The rabbit foot is thumping away crazily in my chest, and I look at his face and all I can think of to say is 'How've you been?'

Tom tilts his head and nods and mutters, 'Okay thanks, and you?'

I nod too and say, 'Fine, thanks. Just fine.' *Just* fine! Who do I think I am? Dolly Parton? I bite my lip and wince and because I am starting to panic, blurt, 'Luke says funny things, doesn't he?'

Tom nods miserably and says, 'Yeah.'

Suddenly he looks as if he might cry and my insides squeeze and I take a deep breath and I say, 'But sometimes he says things I think but don't dare say.'

I say this, can't believe I've said it, stare at the floor and screw up my face, thinking, fool, fool! prat! fool! When I dare to look at Tom again, he's looking at me like he's starving and I'm a large kebab, and we step forward at the same moment and he gently holds my face to his and we kiss. We kiss as soft and warm as velvet on velvet and I close my eyes and feel choked with joy and when I open them for a quick peek *his* eyes are shut, so I glance around the room to see if anyone has seen us – twenty people are ogling – so I close them again and sink deeper into the kiss.

'Everyone's looking,' I mumble.

'So what,' whispers Tom and holds me tighter, and I hug him back hard, and I gaze into his blue eyes and feel a headrush and it seems madness that we've been apart – mad, stupid – and I think 'this must not happen again' and the warmth hits me like sunshine after rain. I love you.

It's not like anything else, ever. Everything that has gone before Tom is all very nice and fine but nothing. Tom is it. I look at him and I think of that old-fashioned phrase 'I love you with all my heart' – if I recall, it's what the handsome prince says to the flaxen-haired princess – and that is what I feel. He kisses my face, my hair, and says into it, 'Sorry for being a git.'

I rear back so fast I nearly knock out his teeth on my skull. '*You're* sorry!' I squeak. 'Don't be! You were right! Everything you said. *I'm* sorry.'

Tom shakes his head. Then he smiles. 'When you fell into the pub that time with Lizzy, even though, what she said' – at this point I nod hastily to encourage him to gloss over it – 'I wanted to run after you and kiss you to death.'

I glow and say, 'Did you!'

He nods and kicks at the floor, like a small child, and says gruffly, 'It was shit without you. I hated it.'

I can barely believe it's Tom saying these things – not some balding, smelly-breathed goon, the sort that usually trap me in bars – but *Tom*. Tom who I lust after. Tom who tells it like it is. Tom who fancies me, Helen, even if I do have flat hair and drive a Toyota. Oh God, please let it be real.

Dare I say it, I think Tom is thinking along similar lines, because we sit next to each other during dinner and he keeps beaming at me, and kissing me, and squeezing my

330

hand, and he barely eats a thing. And, in an unprecedented scene, neither do I. We just talk.

Tom wants to know everything, like what I did for Christmas, and did I think of him at all, and how my job is, and how Laetitia is treating me right now (like a serf), and how Fatboy is doing (so spoilt that if I stroke him much more a genie will emerge from his arse), and Nana and my mother and how are things with me and her – although I don't have to tell him – and how I found my flat and how I did it up and did I miss him and how long it took and what I chose and how I feel and if I've seen Marcus and he keeps gazing at me as if I'm some unimaginable beauty and I want to know everything about what he's been doing, if Celine is still working at Megavet (no, she was sacked for gross incompetence after dropping a hamster then treading on it), if his sister is okay (great: only yesterday she said to her boss Mr Higgenbotham 'The thing with your name is, you don't have to pronounce it Higgen*bottom* – you can get over that by pronouncing it Higgenbo-*tham*!'), if he's still doing his boxing (sort of, if you count watching *Rocky I, II,* and *III*), how his family is (fine: his stepdad had a smallish win on the pools last week and is taking Tom's mum to the Lake District), and if he's got over his fear of painting (nice of me to remember), and if he's had sex with anyone since me (the cheek, and can he ask me the same question?), and has he read *Déjà Dead* yet (yes, he has – it's as juicily gruesome as a Pot Noodle), and can we go to the heath extension again in the Honda and eat bagels?

When I ask him about the heath extension, he stares at me and says, 'I'd do anything for you, Helen. I mean it.'

And I don't bleat 'Ah but you didn't let me stay in your flat' because now I understand. I gulp and whisper, 'And me for you.' (I am not so liberated as Tom because the full sentence 'And I'd do anything for you too,' sticks and although I want to say the words, they feel more comfortable in my head. Anyway, he seems content with the abbreviation.)

I keep gazing at him and grinning and thinking he likes me, and what the hell was I doing rejecting his advances like a cat refusing cream. We smile at each other until our mouths ache. And until I catch Luke's eye across the table and he immediately opens *his* mouth wide (without bothering to swallow the chewed up burger inside it) and sticks a finger into the gunk to communicate his repulsion at the fact his closest female friend and one of the lads have mutated from normal decent people into a nauseating pair of twittering lovebirds.

Tom sees Luke and tauntingly feeds me a chip, mouth to mouth. Luke puts his head in his hands as if in great sorrow. Tom sighs and says, 'You know he's going to blackmail me for ever?' and I nod and say, 'So, can we have sex later?' and he grins. I promptly stand up, scraping my chair. Tom looks at me, raises an eyebrow, and jumps to his feet – and a waiter brings in a huge pink birthday cake and we all have to sing happy birthday dear Lizzy. Tom and I squawk it with gusto. We are exchanging sneaky 'shall we, now?' looks when I glance across the table to see if anyone has noticed and catch sight of Tina.

And the happiness drains away. She looks terrified. Cringing, servile, like a starving dog. She is sipping water and her hand is shaking. She won't look up. The person to her left has given up trying to engage her in conversation and is talking to the person on *his* left. The person to her right is to blame. Adrian is dapper in a pale green shirt and a beautifully cut dark grey suit and his teeth are whiter than white and his blond hair is styled just *so*. He is in animated chat with the woman next to him. He touches her hand, lightly, to emphasise a point, and she throws back her head and laughs prettily. I want to stab her.

'What's wrong?' says Tom, following my line of vision.

'Oh, er, nothing,' I say. 'I think Lizzy's on to us. We'd better, ah, save it for later.'

Tom glances at me and says, 'Something's wrong.'

I shake my head and say, 'I'm just going to talk to Liz for

332

a sec, you'll be alright, won't you?' At this point, Luke appears behind Tom and tries to poke a bean in his ear, and Tom shouts with laughter, grabs his wrist and twists it so that Luke is forced to his knees.

I grab my chance and hurry over to Tina. I say 'hi' and she looks horrified. She says feebly, 'I see you and Tom got it together.'

I smile and say 'yeah!' and 'why don't you come over and have a chat?'

Tina glares at me as Adrian swivels round, an ingratiating smile tacked to his face, and croons, 'Helen! How *excellent* to see you! You look terrific. And I love your top, it's so you.'

Much as I'd like to spit in his eye, I can see Tina quaking, so I force the corners of my mouth upwards and say, 'Yes, it's a nice top.'

I pause and add, 'Don't let me interrupt you – I was just about to drag Tina over my side of the table for a sec to see Tom and Luke.'

Adrian's smile remains fixed as he replies, 'We'd love to, but' – show glance at the Tag Heuer – 'my lady's been nagging on all night about being exhausted, so I'm sweeping her home to beddybyes, right now. Rouse yourself, darling, the cab's waiting outside!'

Tina stands up like a robot and says in a strained voice, 'Goodnight, Helen.'

They kiss and hug Lizzy, then leave. I can't relax. Lizzy skips over and says that she and Brian and some others are going on to a club and would I like to come too. She adds quickly that she won't be offended if I wouldn't. I start to apologise but she squeezes my shoulder, nods towards Tom, and whispers, 'Be happy.'

Tom sees that people are dispersing and he turns to me and says bashfully, 'Would you like to share a cab?'

I reply, 'Of course.'

Luke sticks his head between us and exclaims, 'Great! I'll cadge a lift!' Tom and I glare at him and Luke smiles and says, 'What?' then, 'Don't worry, you can drop me off first!'

Tom growls, 'You got that right!'

We tumble into the street and Tom hails a taxi. Luke puts his feet up and lights a fag, and Tom strokes my hand and says, 'You've gone quiet.'

I nod. I can't speak. There is nothing on this earth I want more than to tape up Luke's mouth and drop him at Swiss Cottage then speed home with Tom and tear off his clothes and make mad passionate love on the hallway floor and then again on the lounge table. I *need* it. I need to make love to Tom, to feel that connection, like I need to breathe.

But how can I knowing that Tina's gone home with Adrian?

If this is a bright shiny new beginning, I want it to be perfect. I think of my friend's terror and the thought impedes my libido. What's he doing to her now? It pains me to consider it. There's no option. I tap Tom on the leg and tell him the truth about Tina and Adrian.

Then I divert the cab to Tooting and I pray we get there in time.

Chapter 41

Although I look odd in a bikini and inevitably get burnt to a crisp, I love beaches. I like watching the sea and thinking unchallenging thoughts like 'Wow, all that water', or 'God, the sea's really big.' I like seeing the waves froth and fizzle on the shore. Or digging my feet into the warm sand and feeling it grainy between my toes. I love looking for shells – those curly ones like tiny unicorn horns – and smooth grey pebbles with white streaks of marble running through. I love closing my eyes and listening to the crashing waves and people's laughter. And smelling the salty air, tasting it on my lips. My favourite thing is to paddle in clear water, searching for gold. I'll see a glinting speck, and try to pinch it up. Of course it never *is* gold, just another grain of sand made shimmery by sun and water. But I don't mind because the joy is all in the seeking.

That's not how I feel when I lose Tom though. After all that searching I stumble on gold and let it slip through my fingers like sand.

Yet as we hurtle to Tina's defence like a squadron of black knights, there isn't a clue it will end like it does. I burble out the sorry tale and Tom says, 'Fuck!' and asks a thousand questions. Luke splutters and says, 'I don't get it.' They bristle and say poor poor Tina, and Adrian's got it coming to him.

'This isn't a boy's adventure game,' I say stonily, because I'm terrified of what I've started.

Tom says, 'Helen, we're only going to check she's okay. You're right to be looking out for Tina. We won't do anything stupid.' He squeezes my hand.

Luke adds earnestly, 'You did the right thing.' I'm not sure I have.

I soon change my mind. When the taxi stops outside Tina's flat – 'Adrian drives a Beamer!' squawks Luke, 'how *dare* he?' – and we tumble into the street, I can hear the screams. A vile miracle, as my heart pounds loud enough to deafen me. Luke wants to kick the door down, but Tom doesn't want to give Adrian warning. We sneak in the main door via the woman who lives downstairs. Curiously – or rather, uncuriously – she doesn't ask who we are. Then again, her neighbour is screaming like a pig who's just been offered his cousin in a bacon roll, and that doesn't bother her so maybe I shouldn't be surprised.

We clump upstairs and Tom rings the doorbell. A whimper, a rustle, then silence. He rings again. He stands with his back to the door so if Adrian looks through the peephole he can't see who's there. 'Who is it?' barks a tense voice.

Tom barks back, 'Are you the owner of the black Z3 outside with slashed tyres—'

There is a loud exclamation and a clack-clack of bolts being drawn and Adrian rips open the door and as he does so Tom gives it a hefty boot and Adrian staggers backwards. Tom and I rush to Tina, who is cowering in the corner. Luke flings himself at Adrian in what I presume is a textbook rugby tackle – or maybe he just trips on the edge of the rug – and before I can say 'harder than that', is sprawled on top of him and shaking him so that Adrian's head makes a pleasing bonk-bonk-bonk sound on the floor.

When Tom sees the state of Tina his face goes taut. Adrian asks what the fuck's going on and bleats that we've misunderstood the situation and Tina and he were merely having a tiff and *yelp!* Adrian's rant ends swiftly as Tom squeezes an apparently sensitive point on his neck. 'Shut up,' says Tom in a hard voice. Adrian shuts up. I ring the police on my mobile as the phone has been ripped from the wall and Tom runs to fetch ice and a towel for Tina. Adrian is struggling for breath under fifteen-stone of Luke, so the sterling effort my friend has put into building himself up on pepperoni pizza and chicken korma and cheese & onion crisps for the last decade is paying off beautifully. 'Tina,' yodels Luke from his elevated position, 'are you okay?'

Tina has seven fresh cigarette burns on her stomach and is far from okay. Her head wound has re-opened. Tom strokes her hair out of her face and gently dabs at the blood trickling down her forehead. He says, 'Christ, Tina, this is terrible. You don't have to put up with this.' In a quivering voice she jokes that she won't be wearing a crop top this summer then starts crying and clinging to me and Tom.

'Tina,' I say, trying not to cry myself, 'I had to, I couldn't leave it any longer, I'm sorry.'

When the police arrive Tina stops weeping and freezes. The police want to hear what happened from all of us, but especially from Tina.

'Please say,' I urge her. 'Be brave. We're all here.' She quakes and glances at Adrian who stares ahead like he thinks he's the Maida Vale Terminator.

Silence. Tina says nothing and I hold my breath. Luke steps forward and Tina jumps but he only wants to offer her a scrumpled piece of toilet paper on which to blow her nose. 'I've only used it once,' he explains kindly.

Luke's gentleness steels her. After much snuffling and gulping, Tina points at her boyfriend and says, 'He – Adrian – he said cigs are bad for me, which they are. He, he st-stubbed them out on my belly.'

The male officer – whose stern expression is compensation for a faceful of freckles – writes this down in his notebook. Then Tina goes quiet so the female officer, a woman with bright yellow hair and a steel aura, ushers her into the next room. Freckles turns to Adrian. Adrian starts to say, in his plummiest, chummiest voice, that Tina has a drink problem. To my great joy, Freckles cuts in with, 'Right now I don't want to hear your explanation.'

I want to tell Freckles that Tina has stuck to orange juice ever since Adrian nearly drowned her for 'flirting' with a guy in the pub (as if Tina would ever fancy a man in a boiler suit). But I don't want to be reprimanded in front of Adrian so I save it for later. Instead, I point out the ashtray full of stubs which, I assume, are riddled with Adrian's fingerprints, even though he doesn't smoke. Freckles obligingly pours the stubs into a plastic bag and I whisper excitedly to Tom, 'I saw this on *The Bill*. Even if it's not forensically tight, it's circumstantial evidence!'

I then go into the kitchen because Tina wants me with her. I sit at the kitchen table while Blondie takes pictures of Tina's stomach and scalp with a Polaroid camera. She seems to understand that Tina is overwhelmed by her presence and its implications and says firmly, 'You're doing the right thing, love. You've done nothing wrong. This isn't what should happen in a normal relationship.'

I'm not sure if I'm allowed to talk, so I nod supportively behind Blondie's back, and try not to retch at the sight of Tina's injuries. Blondie then tells me to take Tina to hospital. I ring for a cab. Then I think sod it, I'm busting to give a statement and I will. I haven't been so keen to blab since I overheard Laetitia one lunchtime making hushed enquiries about liposuction.

Blondie indulges me and I dictate until she shakes her hand as if she's got cramp. I feel frustrated because I am forced to admit that I have never actually *seen* Adrian lay a finger on my friend. 'I've seen the results though,' I say fiercely, and then, 'Aren't you going to take a statement from Tina?'

She says she'll get a statement from Tina tomorrow morning. Tina, who's gone as quiet as a mouse in felt slippers, nods. Tom and Luke also give short statements. As the cab arrives, the Blondie marches downstairs to interview Tina's neighbour (which I am spitefully pleased about) and Freckles says to Adrian, 'I'm arresting you for assault occasioning actual bodily harm,' and handcuffs him.

'Careful of my cufflinks!' Adrian snaps which – I am delighted to note – doesn't go down well. Freckles becomes, if anything, less careful of Adrian's cufflinks. Adrian shoots me a bully-boy look and I taunt him with a curly-fingered wave. I am hoping to goad him into saying something incriminating like 'Honest, officer, I hardly touched her!' but Adrian isn't stupid. He doesn't say a word. I was also hoping to hear a hearty boom of 'You're nicked!' but the heartwarming sight of Adrian in chains will do nicely. He and his Savile Row suit are to spend the night in a police cell and tomorrow morning he'll be interviewed. Then he'll be up in court.

And, if I might borrow a phrase from Nana Flo, not before time.

Tom wraps Tina in a blanket because she's shivering and carries her to the cab. All the way to the hospital we tell her well done and she's so brave and this is the end of Adrian. Tina doesn't seem to hear. She mutters into her hands, 'I'm so ashamed.' Tom and Luke and I chorus, 'Don't be!' and Tina smiles because we sound like berks then winces because her stomach hurts.

In Casualty, the baby-faced doctor says as if he can't quite believe what he's seeing, 'Your boyfriend did this?'

Tina replies, as if this explains everything, 'I smoke.'

The doctor – who has piercing green eyes and might have sprung from *ER* if only he had more colour in his cheeks – looks suspiciously at Luke. Luke has appointed himself Tina's bodyguard and is standing beside her with a bulldog expression and folded arms.

'It wasn't *me*!' he blurts. 'I'm Luke! I'm looking after her!' Tina smiles at him tearily and Tom smiles at me. I glance at my watch and discover it's 3.23 a.m. – which means we waited in Dante's Hell, sorry, Casualty for three hours. Peely walls. I feel a swell of exhaustion. I mutter that I'm going outside for a second.

I stumble towards the door. The thickly sweet smell of A & E is having an effect on my ability to breathe. And the swingy hospital doors, with their neat rectangular glass windows, the bright glaring lights, and the screeching children, and the shouty drunks, and the old people shuffling down grey clinical corridors, and the rushing staff in white and blue and sensible shoes, the whole lot converges and spins around my head like a small tornado and I am watching my father die again and the monitor is bleeping and curtains are being pulled and trolleys being pushed and I'm being yanked away and there are screams of 'he's arresting' and my mother is wailing and my father died and I sat there and missed it and I never told him I loved him because I couldn't say the words. The blood drains from my head and I feel nauseous and tottery. I need to sit down or be sick and I'm not sure which so I collapse on a bench – next to a ragged man swigging from a bottle – then I say 'Urgh' and vomit on to the pavement. Understandably, the man moves to another bench.

I clutch the side of the bench while the world sways. Then Tom is holding my hair off my face and rubbing my back while I retch and spit. I keep retching. Loudly. 'Romantic, this,' I mutter, the latest burp ringing in my ears as I stare down at a yellow puddle of bitty sick.

'Nah,' replies Tom cheerfully, 'this is nostalgic for me. It reminds me of our first date.'

I would look at him to laugh but I have dribble on my chin. I wipe it on my Ay Carumba sleeve. 'How's Tina?' I say.

'Still in shock, I think,' says Tom. 'She said she felt bad about Adrian. But the doctor wasn't having any of it. He told her men like Adrian don't change. He was kind but straight down the line. I hope he made some impact, poor Tina. Oh and Luke's in love. He wants to stay and guard her.'

My eyes bulge. 'Luke's in *love*!' I squeak.

Tom grins and nods. 'Very,' he says. My brain is twisting in an attempt to absorb this when Tom adds, 'Has Tina got family? Do you think someone should phone her parents?'

I joke, 'What, to warn them about Luke?' Then I add, 'I suppose so. She needs all the support she can get. And I want her brothers to know. We should ask Tina though.'

Tom nods. 'Tom,' I say, 'I'm scared for Tina.'

I'm scared because I want this to be the end and I'm scared it won't be. I'm scared because a few weeks back I rang a refuge and talked to the woman in charge to ask how I could help Tina. She told me about women like Tina. One tale she told me stayed in my head. This woman was married to a man who shoved her down the stairs and urinated on her wounds. He also tied the family dog to a tree in the garden and starved it to death over three weeks. She and her two children, aged four and six, were made to watch. Once or twice they managed to sneak out and feed the dog scraps but this only prolonged the agony. This woman only reported her husband when she became afraid for her kids.

Then she withdrew her statement. The police prosecuted anyway but her husband was bailed to live at home. He kept his job because he was a 'key worker' in his firm and negotiating an important contract which his (male) boss was loath to lose. The (male) magistrate decided not to send him to prison as – he said – he was not in the habit of wrecking people's careers. He wanted offenders 'rehabilitated'. Eventually his wife fled to the refuge but he traced her and . . .

The knowledge is polluting me. So I tell Tom. 'I bet Adrian has a good lawyer,' I say miserably.

Tom replies, 'Yeah. I bet he does. But, see how it goes. At least we all know about him now. He can't isolate her any more. And I know this sounds weird, but Adrian strikes me as a man who cares very much about his reputation. And you don't know what Adrian's boss is like.

And Tina has three brothers. *Three.* I reckon Adrian's in trouble. Fuck, if anyone did that to my sister—' Tom shakes his head. I shrug. I feel so despondent I no longer trust anyone to do the right thing.

'Listen, Helen,' says Tom, 'it's four in the morning. Luke's stuck to Tina like a lovestruck leech. They're not keeping her in, and Luke's going to stay with her, you can visit her at home, first thing. You can stay here but you're near delirious. Why don't I take you home. I'll sleep on the floor.' I reluctantly agree. I run to see if Tina minds then sprint back to Tom. A small mercy in a mean world: I see Tom's found a black cab. He opens the door and I clamber in and sprawl like a rag doll on the back seat.

'Fuck,' I say.

'What?' says Tom.

'I hate this,' I burble, 'I hate what's happened to Tina. I did sod-all too late.'

Tom shakes his head. 'Helen,' he says, 'only Tina can see off Adrian. You couldn't force her. But you stopped her from getting hurt, well, more seriously hurt, tonight. You did a good thing, be proud. You're a good friend.' I recoil from his praise because I feel tarnished and undeserving. There will be no personal gain from Tina's pain. I don't want it. Tom senses my misery because he says, 'We'll all help Tina.' Then, inexplicably, he grabs my hand and kisses it.

I close my eyes. There is a vague, elusive thought buzzing at my brain but I can't be bothered to identify and swat it. 'Wake me when we get there,' I whisper and fall asleep.

I awake as we pull into my road.

'Which one is it?' says Tom.

'Mm, it's too dark to tell,' I say, rubbing my eyes – and louder – 'If you stop here, please, that'll be fine!'

We hop out and I spy pebble-dash and realise my flat is the next one along. I am about to open the gate when Tom tenses and I stop instinctively. I peer into the shadows and see a figure slumped on my doorstep. And it is only as the figure jerks and stumbles to its feet that my vague buzzy thought pings into focus and hammers sharp and fast and deep into my still fuzzy brain.

Jasper.

I stand as frozen as a particularly dim-witted pillar of salt while Jasper blinks at me. Then he blinks at Tom, and growls, 'Who the hell are you?'

Tom replies coolly, 'No, who are *you*?'

Jasper says, 'I'm her fucking live-in boyfriend, you prick.'

Tom drops my hand from his grasp like a dead thing. To Jasper, he says icily, 'My mistake.' To me, he says nothing. He whistles at the departing taxi – which screams to a surprised halt – and steps in.

I watch him speed into the night and I know he's gone for ever.

Chapter 42

Being the least attractive teenager in my class (so you can imagine) spectacles were not an option. I spent two years squinting before my maths teacher – a spiteful man if there ever was one – cornered my mother at a parents' evening and told her I was as blind as a retired bat and rubbish at sums. The next day she dragged me to an optician who asked me to read out 'the letters' on a blank white board then mysteriously declared that my eyesight was 'minus five and a half'.

When, soon after, I was presented with the monstrosity of an NHS pair of glasses I came close to tears. But when I put them on I felt like Dorothy entering Munchkinland. I could *see*! The world was crisp! It had sharp edges! Trees weren't fuzzy! They were precise! They had millions of individual leaves! Car number plates! They had numbers on them! The transformation was total and miraculous. After so long living with the vision of a cheap underwater camera, here I was – abruptly blessed with the potent wonder of perfect sight.

And, as Tom leaves my life, I relive that seminal moment where everything looms into focus. All that is blurred becomes clear. But this time it's as painful as if I were rubbing crushed glass into my eyes. Meanwhile Jasper shouts and shouts, but his words wash over me and leave me untouched.

'Who the heck was that tosser i've been waiting here since one a.m. i told you i lost the key i'm freezing my arse off here where the hell have you been it's a ridiculous hour how dare you leave me out here all night it's unacceptable i won't stand for it i need to change i was walking home from the station and some spotty little oiks drove past in an escort and threw eggs at me this area you live in its like a housing estate who was that git how dare he ask who i am who's he i want an answer i won't—'

I hardly hear him. I watch the taxi shrink and disappear, taking all my tomorrows with it. This can't be real. It's not allowed. It's not what I deserve. I stare at the horizon in the hope that Tom will do a Mills & Boon and come beetling back. He doesn't. Fuck. How can this happen. I take Jasper in out of kindness (mostly) and the toad repays me by scuppering my life. To lose Tom once, ouch. To lose him *twice*. That's not carelessness, that's obscene.

How could I forget that I was sharing my bathroom with the worst flatmate since *me*? How could my honeycomb brain sieve through the relevent facts and let the queen bee slip through? And Jasper. How could he? It becomes mortifyingly obvious that he fancies living rent-free but hasn't fancied *me* for the best part of a year. To describe himself as my live-in boyfriend is not only a wilful contravention of the Property Misrepresentations Act, it is a large, malicious, havoc-wreaking lie.

As my future crumbles, I stand still. As if a sudden move might shake my frozen emotions from their cubbyholes and create chaos, like a thousand ball bearings thrown on a marble floor.

My unspeakable grief will stay put while I deal with its catalyst. Then I walk slowly to the front door – each step is like wading through glue – unlock it and look straight at Jasper.

'I'm so sorry,' I say calmly. 'There was an emergency. But wait there. I have a surprise for you.' Jasper opens his large mouth to object as I shut the door on him. I glide upstairs – thinking how did I ever date a man with a jaw like a velociraptor? – and walk into the lounge where his wicker chairs await. I walk to my pile of CDs and search for a suitable soundtrack. Ah yes. Then I heave open the bay window.

Jasper steps backwards, stumbles over a stray piece of wire embedded in the lawn, and shouts angrily, 'What the heck's going on?'

It's like someone's pressed a switch on my back marked 'insanity'. A fusion of shock from Tina's cigarette burns and Tom walking away. I sing, 'It's a surprise! You'll find out in a moment!' I survey the devastation that is my new lounge. Jasper's clothes are strewn over the floor. I press 'play', pick up a pair of white Y-fronts and throw them out of the window. Surprisingly – I was reserve for the netball C team – they hit Jasper full in the face. He looks as shocked as when he first saw me park the Toyota (I am, quite simply, brilliant).

I lean from the window to watch what he does. And, as an anthropological exercise, it's worth it. Jasper rips the pants from his face and screams, 'What the heck was that for? You' – he pauses in disbelief as I retreat inside – 'Let me in, for heaven's sake! What the heck are you playing at?' He soon finds out. I stagger to the window with his suitcase, position myself against the ledge so I'm stable, and sling it out on to the grass. It lands in a large puddle. Jasper leaps nimbly aside to save his head from being crushed.

'Stop it!' he bawls. 'What are you doing, you madwoman? Say something! Why are you doing this?'

He scrabbles frantically about the garden trying to stuff shoes, socks, trousers, vests, pants, and shirts back into the case, and I laugh and sing 'Ja-spaar! Ready or not?'

He looks up and screeches 'Noooooo!' as I fling the first of the nautical paintings into the road like a frisbee. It makes a pretty tinkle as the glass shatters.

I turn up 'Heart of Glass' as loud as it will go and – in a mad, bitchy sort of way – crow, 'I love the sound of breaking glass!'

Jasper drops his college scarf – which hails from a college

346

he didn't attend – and runs into the road gibbering. He tenderly cradles the bits of gilt frame and I almost feel sorry for him. I drop the other two ship paintings so they land on the flowerbed. Then I trot back to the stereo, pray the neighbours will forgive me, and change the CD. Preferably something upbeat to stop me tailing Jasper's possessions out of the window. After a minute – during which I can hear squeaks of rage emanating from the front garden – I find what I'm looking for. The music that has the same effect on Jasper as sunshine on vampires. Oh yes. Country music.

Jasper's wicker chairs fall to their deaths to the tune of 'Let Your Love Flow'. He begs and pleads from the pavement but no deal. I hum along (even though I know it's vastly uncool) and – when I find another stray pair of Y-fronts – twirl them around my finger and ping them into the atmosphere while belting out the words to 'Ring of Fire'. Fatboy, who is washing himself on the table, stops licking, paw mid-air, and stares. I hit a high note and his ears flatten in fright. La la la. Jasper's wicker coffee table takes flight to a rousing background of 'Stand By Your Man'.

'Stop it!' sobs Jasper, nursing a detached piece of wicker. 'Turn it off! I'm sorry! Please!' Reluctantly I blip off the music.

'Thank fuck,' gasps Jasper (and everyone else in my street.) I lean out of the window and smile. I am the Ice Queen and loving it. Jasper brandishes the snapped wicker leg and yells, 'Look what you've done! You, you . . . wicker killer!' I laugh nastily, which makes him stamp his foot. He bellows, 'Shut *up*! Oh heck, look at my stuff! Helen! Stop it! You're being weird! Please! I've got nowhere to go! Be reasonable!' I disappear from the window to retrieve Jasper's Egyptian cotton which – I suddenly remember – is sitting sodden in my washing machine. I carry it to the sill and drop it on him. 'You bitch!' he shrieks. 'What are you doing?'

I shout, 'What does it look like, wanker?' I see the blue-and-white baseball cap slung over a chair, snatch it up, and roar, 'Catch!'

Jasper leaps into the air, but alas, it lands on a lamp-post. He clutches his head in despair and yells, 'Okay! Okay! I'm sorry! Please! Let me in! I've got no transport! Just till tomorrow?'

I stick my head out and sing, 'Learn to drive! You've got your crap furniture and your pointless hat, now fuck off!'

Jasper strikes a pose reminiscent of Hugh Grant at his most piteous. 'But where?' he bleats, spreading his hands wide.

I bellow, 'I don't *care*! Goodbye, Jasper!' Then I slam the window and draw the blinds. I feel briefly elated – as if the albatross round my neck has eaten the chip on my shoulder and flown off – and blip on 'Sea of Heartbreak'. I am free. I snatch up Fatboy and whirl him around my de-wickered lounge in a dance of defiance, but he struggles, whines, claws me in the chest, and runs off. Story of my bloody life.

I switch off the stereo and walk into my bedroom in silence. Then I sit on my bed and think of Tom. Tom is gone. What have I done? What *have* I done? I am seized with dread – a dread of having made the most terrible mistake of my life. I only have one life and I've fucked it up! My head swirls with the irony of Tom and me in a taxi zooming away from Tina's doom towards mine. All I can think is that I was standing at the beginning of the rest of my life and I tripped over the starting line. The tears fall and I clutch my stomach and scream. I scream and scream until my throat hurts (and the person next door bangs on the wall). Then I stare dully at my bright yellow walls and think, what's the point? I wonder if this is what bereave-ment is like? To feel that the truth is unacceptable.

I sit on my bed until sunrise and ache from the heart. I tell myself Tina's pain is worse but the ache throbs worse than ever. I pull the curtains, curl up under the duvet and try to lose consciousness. When sleep comes, it's a relief.

It's not that I can't go on. That I can't live without Tom. People die and the people who love them go on living. And Tom isn't dead. Just dead to me. So if I said that I couldn't live without Tom it wouldn't be true. Of course I can live without him.

It's just that it isn't going to be much fun.

Chapter 43

If I had an electrode attached to my toe which buzzed every time I did something stupid, maybe I'd be more efficient at learning from my mistakes. As it is, I make the same idiotic blunders again and again and again and again until I get so sick of the consequences I annoy myself into changing habit. For example, if I get up in the night to go to the toilet and jab my foot on a spike-heeled shoe, it will take a dozen stabbings before I pick the stiletto off the floor and stick it in the wardrobe. If I set my alarm for 7.30 with the intention of going for a run, I have to fall asleep again at 7.31 and be late for work at least nine times before I stop pretending I can face anything other than a pillow before 8.00. Laetitia's verbal warning also helped.

But Tom and Jasper's unscheduled meeting was in its own league. I didn't need a next time. My plans for the next six decades were botched, which piqued me sufficiently to draw up resolutions. Never again would I be caught out by auto error. No longer would I mismanage my life. Fatboy would eat at 8.15 a.m. and again at 7.30 p.m. with a veterinary-approved snack before bedtime. From now on grazing would be outlawed (for both household members). I'd shop at the supermarket weekly instead of paying a daily premium at the corner shop. I'd b- b-ugh, *budget*. I'd only get drunk on occasions. I'd give more to charity, in particular unglamorous causes. I'd visit museums and Nana Flo. I'd teach myself Italian with a tape. I'd stop picking my lip and learn about car maintenance. I'd drink twelve glasses of water every day and be hydrated.

The list was long and imposing, but that week I was on time for work every day and forcibly courteous to Laetitia, even when she exclaimed, 'Not again! Your bladder must be the size of a thimble!' (I bit back the reply, 'I wouldn't know, I've never seen a thimble.') My flat was pristine to the point that I reached the neolithic stratum in my linen basket. I stopped discussing other people's relationships apart from to tell Lizzy about Tina (with the heroine's permission). I listened to the forecast on Radio Four every night and was appropriately attired for the weather. Although if I'd dressed to suit my mood I'd have worn sackcloth. Not even a visit to see *Grease* with my mother cheered me. Not even when she bought the soundtrack and said, 'Darling, do you think I'm too old to wear my hair in a ponytail?' Not even when we went for a pizza and I told her about Tina and she cried, 'And to think you used to be such a selfish girl!' As Vivienne's son Jeremy is fond of saying, Get *her*!

I even joined Lizzy at her gym and spent thirty-five minutes doing up my laces in the changing rooms and listening to a pair of papier mâché women squeak at each other, 'I'm huge, you're tiny! . . . No, *you're* tiny! . . . No, *I'm* huge! . . . No you're not, you're *tiny*!' etc. My heart wondered if there was a tiny chance that Tom might listen if I called to explain but my head crushed all hope flat. From nowhere I recalled a rule of baseball – three strikes and you're out. I'd blown it. By Friday I was as miserable as sin and as dull as godliness. I tore up the list and threw it in the bin. But I still felt dead inside.

On Saturday though, I cheer up. Not much – I'll categorically never know happiness again and the best I can hope for is to become a rubbish-hoarding recluse – but a little. I ping from suicide watch (metaphorically, as no one seems to care enough to watch me) to common garden depression. The reason for this mood twitch is that I hear from Luke.

Since last Saturday Luke hasn't budged from Tina's side.

351

Whereas *I* haven't seen her since the hospital. I wanted to visit last Sunday but, Luke informed me, she was resting. When I rang back later, Luke told me that a plain clothes officer had come round but Tina had decided not to give a statement. 'But *why*?' I cried.

'She doesn't want to,' he replied.

'But she must!' I exclaimed.

'We can't make her,' said Luke.

'I suppose not,' I said sadly. 'Can I speak to her?'

Luke said, 'She's not up to being bullied, so only if you promise not to nag her.'

I promised and was passed on to Tina, although I was a little hurt by this. (Luke thinks I'm a nagger when we've never even dated? My reputation precedes me.) Tina informed me she was feeling better. And that the police were probably going to prosecute anyway. And that she had told her family. And that her parents were on their way over. Oh, and that she was *almost* sure she never wanted to see Adrian again.

Ideally, I'd have preferred Tina to drag Adrian through the courts, for the national press to pounce on the case and broadcast it far and wide, complete with screaming headlines and front page mugshots, and for Adrian to be drummed out of Maida Vale and ostracised from Aquascutum. And to lose his job *not* because it was bad publicity for the firm but because his male boss would – as he'd ringingly tell the clamouring reporters – rather cut off his own bonus than employ a violent criminal. And for Adrian to lose his job anyway because you can't work as an architect when you're spending the next forty years in a dank prison.

But I suppose I understand why Tina didn't want to pursue it. What I didn't understand is why Adrian pleaded not guilty and was instantly bailed as if his crime was forgetting to pay a parking ticket. 'But it's unbelievable!' I screeched, when Luke relayed the scandal. 'She'll never be safe! He'll probably come round tonight and blow up the house! Jesus! Don't you dare let her drive the Escort without testing the brakes.'

Although that last warning was applicable with or without Adrian's interference, Luke objected to my pessimism. One of Adrian's bail conditions was not to contact Tina. And maybe by the time the case came to trial in three or four months, Tina might have decided to testify. And if *I*, Helen, were to testify – 'you bet your bottom I will' I interrupted crossly – maybe justice would be done. 'One would hope,' I said bitterly. Meanwhile, he, Luke, was watching out for her now.

'Luke,' I snapped – more meanly than necessary – 'As I'm sure you're aware, Tina has just been dragged out of a stifling, abusive relationship with a domineering tyrant. The last thing she needs is to be dragged into another one.'

Luke was, predictably, upset. 'Shhh!' he wailed. 'She'll hear! It's not like that! She doesn't think of me like that. She's fragile, Helen, she's nervous of being alone. She's scared. I'm *good* for her! I'm helping her to stay away from Adrian. I'm protecting her, I promise! She's still keen on the bastard! I'm distracting her! It's the truth! Tina's confused. But she trusts me. We talk. We've got a lot in common.'

I was tempted to reply, 'Don't make me laugh, your accessory of choice is a Head sports bag and you pronounce Gucci "Goo-ky".'

But in keeping with my new ninety-eight per cent spite-free personality I restrained myself. After all, if Luke was hardening Tina's heart against the Evil One, he was not a tactless, bumbling goof but a talented miracle worker who should be left alone to complete the proselytising process.

This realisation didn't stop me being a teensy bit jealous of Luke's abrupt conversion from *my* ever-hopeful platonic friend to Tina's.

Excepting this emergency call, I don't hear from him. I don't ring Tina as – according to her new interpreter – 'She's knackered and not up to chatting. But when you see

Lizzy can you thank her for the fruit and the, the er, St John's wart stuff and the tea pee oil.'

I do as I'm told, sit tight, and pass on the message. When I tell Lizzy, she says, 'Oh I feel terrible, *terrible*! Adrian was so smiley! And all those flowers! And all the phone calls! Who would have thought it? Do you think I should send Calendula too?'

I say it's a kind thought but Tina already has a diary. And anyway, I'm sure she'll be in touch if she needs anything. She doesn't. So when Luke rings on Saturday I am gagging for information. And my, do I get it. Although Luke is so hyper and gabbly it takes all my concentration to understand him.

'Okay, Tina's brothers, Max, Sean, and Andrew, were *spitting blood* when they heard about Adrian. They went mental, Max especially, he's the youngest, he was gonna go round and sort him *right* out. But Sean said no, they had to be clever about this, yeah, because Adrian sounded like the sort to press charges, so anyway, Tina doesn't know it, but Sean calls this mate of his, Tony, who knows this bloke Ray, and Ray is one mean bastard, so Tony has a word with Ray, Ray runs a security firm, providing bouncers for clubs and shit, he's ex-army, he used to be a bodybuilder, he's a big bloke, like about eighteen stone and *menacing* and you can pay him to warn people of the error of their ways, yeah, and he'll send somebody round, and so right, Sean tells Ray about Adrian and Ray hates wife beaters, it's his worst thing, he calls himself The Equaliser, and two of his men turn up at Adrian's door at two in the morning and they burst in and strap up Adrian's hands with his belt, and Adrian shouts that he'll go to the police and Ray says in a soft way that *Adrian* doesn't talk unless *Ray* says so, *Ray* is the person who decides who talks around here, and he doesn't give a toss about the police, and what's more the police don't care about him, and as is apparent Ray knows where Adrian lives and Adrian will know when he's coming and anyway there's another ten of him out there, and then Adrian goes dead quiet and they rip up his living room carpet, right, and they roll him up in his own carpet and stuff a hanky in his mouth and they *remove* him, okay, and they drive him off in Ray's black 4 × 4 and it's got leather seats yeah, because people cack themselves, and Adrian cacks himself! It stinks! And they take Adrian to this dungeon thing, like a cellar but worse, and they *warn* him, Sean'd said don't hurt him, just warn him, and Ray, Ray can lift a man by his neck with one hand, he's got hands like plates of meat – like a big steak, I think, rather than a chicken drumstick, or maybe his thumb muscle is like a really big drumstick, I dunno – anyway, and Adrian was down with them for three hours and then they dumped him naked in the road outside his office and Ray spoke to Tony who spoke to Sean yesterday and said that Ray didn't think Adrian would be telling tales to anyone. Or bothering Sean's sister again.'

Dear me. Maybe Adrian should have listened when Tina asked him nicely.

Unsurprisingly, I think about Tina for the rest of the afternoon. I will her to come through this. Maybe one day she'll look back and wonder at how it happened. Imagine. To be *so* blind to a person's true nature. To wave away their crimes as involuntary, like epileptic fits. To be so optimistic that when that person is killing you, you smile as they wield the knife. I sit and marvel at the measure of Tina's madness. And then it strikes me. We're both mourning relationships we wanted but cannot have.

I can't understand why Tina loved Adrian but she did.

As for me, I am and will always be in love with Tom. But for the moment my thoughts aren't about him. I'm thinking of the other man, not in my life. And I think the same thing over and over, like a chant. I think, I never was a Daddy's girl and now I never will be.

Chapter 44

When a relationship breaks down, people always declare, 'It isn't the big things, it's the little things.' And if the relationship in question was Marcus and Michelle's, I wouldn't hesitate to agree with them. But in my case, the little things were fine. My relationship with Tom breaks down because of a big thing – my endless stupidity. Following that, it's the little things that break *me* down.

For instance, I open the *Observer*, read the first line of a report by a journalist who has travelled to the Arctic with a Greenpeace ship, glance at the adjacent photograph, see it is captioned, 'A starving polar bear begs for food from the ship', and burst into tears. I buy a large packet of posh crisps from the supermarket, stuff six into my mouth and think 'hmm, these aren't very crunchy,' stuff three more in to make sure, think 'these crisps taste funny,' peer into the bag and see what appears to be a large crushed cockcroach but is more likely a mass of black rotting potato. I have flashbacks all day and can't eat my Dime bar.

And I visit my mother, and notice a folded card on the side table. It looks like an invitation to a seventies club night so I open it and see a faded picture of a tanned man and a pretty woman laughing and feeding each other spaghetti – my parents, twenty-five years ago, eating at a tacky restaurant in Portugal. The pain curdles as I realise she must have hunted for it, in a moment – an hour? a day? a week? – of loneliness. I have an image of my mother desperately digging through boxes in the attic for this wisp of memory and – much as I try to banish it – it won't go away.

We haven't spoken about my father for ages. It's as if, after months of fighting it, my mother has retreated into her pain. I know the sadness is swelling inside her like a cyst but I am scared of prodding it in case it all pours out in a hysterical rush and I'm unable to finish what I started.

'Maybe you should have another supper party,' suggests Lizzy, 'It might cheer her up.'

I sigh and say, 'Liz, she'll be cheered up for five minutes then she'll go home and feel even worse. And also, I don't have any friends left apart from you. And I've only got two chairs.'

Lizzy retorts, 'People can sit on your floor, on cushions!'

I say quickly, 'That wouldn't work – I'm a one-cushion household.'

Lizzy perseveres, 'You, and me, and Tina, and Luke, and er, your mother, it would be lovely!'

'It would be awful,' I say. 'It worked as a one-off because everyone knew they'd never have to do it again. It would be like, oh, I don't know, like trying to recreate the Beatles.' Lizzy doesn't see the connection and says so. I ignore her and say, 'So would Brian be forced to attend this torture evening or is he excused by his doctor?'

Lizzy pouts. 'We're no longer an item,' she says breezily, 'I ended it.'

'*What!*' I shout. 'Why? Why haven't you told me? How dare you! Not tell me, I mean.'

Lizzy explains that closure was only reached yesterday and she was going to tell me but we'd been talking about Tina and Luke, and me and Tom. 'You and Tom.' Me and Tom. Even being in the same sentence as him makes my blood rush. How sad is that? I sigh and demand an explanation.

'Was it something Brian did?' I ask.

'Sort of,' says Lizzy.

'Something offensive?' I suggest.

'Kind of,' says Lizzy.

'Offensive to you personally?' I enquire.

'Yes,' says Lizzy.

'Repellent?' I bark.

'Awfully,' says Lizzy.

'Something his own mother would be ashamed of?' I say, squirming with pleasurable distaste.

'Definitely,' says Lizzy.

'Jesus!' I say, my mind overrun with wild scenes of t'ai chi orgies and punch-ups in the Gap over a last pair of dungarees. 'What on *earth* did he do?'

Lizzy pauses. 'You'll think I overreacted,' she says hesitantly.

'No I won't,' I say.

'Yes you will,' insists Lizzy.

'Elizabeth!' I squeak. 'Look at me! I'm in an agony of not knowing! End it! Just say!' I feel beads of sweat on my upper lip. I *hate* it when people dangle a pearl of self-disclosure in front of your nose then whip it away on the specious grounds that you'll judge them.

'Okay,' says Lizzy reluctantly, 'but only if you—'

'I promise!' I screech. I clasp my hands as if in prayer and fake an innocent expression. Lizzy falls for it and reveals that she dumped Brian – kind, generous, gentle Brian who buys her figs and kisses her hand – because she was irritated by the sound of him eating. And I thought I was shallow.

Once I would have been comforted by Lizzy's revelation. I'll live in solitude and die alone, but yippee, at least I'll have back-up. But the news doesn't even dent my misery. If anything, I feel sorry for Brian. The punishment seems disproportionate to the crime. 'Couldn't you have asked him to chew more quietly?' I say.

Lizzy huffs and says crossly, 'There was more to it than that.'

I can't resist. 'What?' I say.

'The way he swallowed,' says Lizzy. I give up.

Later though, at home, I try to fathom the peculiar workings of Lizzy's mind. 'You see, Helen,' I say aloud to the silent room, 'she wouldn't mind this. She'd love it. She *prizes* her own company.' It's only when I say the words that I realise. I don't mind it either. After listening to the excruciating mindwarp of Lizzy's rationale, the stillness of my own company is a relief.

I put on a Kate Bush CD, and spend the remainder of the evening erasing every trace of Jasper from the flat (flecks of shaving foam on the bathroom mirror, two copies of *Country Life* by the toilet, three yellow toenail cuttings on the lounge floor, and – from the kitchen cupboard – an Oxford University mug bought from a gift shop off Leicester Square). By 11 p.m. I feel better than I did. I realise that if I can't have Tom I don't want anyone, just me. For a second I consider unplugging the phone as a symbol of my new independence. Then I think, don't be mad. I go to bed early and read *C is for Corpse*.

The next day I ring my mother and invite her round for coffee. 'You don't need me now you've got your flat done,' are her first words.

'Now Mummy, you know that can't be true,' I say sternly, 'or why would I be inviting you over?'

There is a sullen silence before she replies, 'I don't know. You want some more chairs?'

Her obstinacy should frustrate me but it doesn't because I guess that right now, she needs to do this. And our honeymoon was bound to end sometime. Not that I plan to nurture the return to dysfunctionality. I say in a gratingly jolly tone, 'Actually, I invited you purely for the pleasure of your company, but I'd hate it if you felt you *had* to come—'

'I'll be round at five,' snaps my mother.

She shows up, ready for battle. I knew it wouldn't last. I offer her coffee ('only if it's decaff' – it isn't); I offer her tea ('only if it's Earl Grey' – it isn't); I offer her water ('only if it's mineral' – it isn't). Then I realise that tap water contains minerals so I shout 'Okay!' and pour her a glass.

When I present it she sniffs it suspiciously and gives it a small push away from her.

'Aren't you going to offer me anything to eat?' she says.

'Yes, of *course*,' I say in an injured tone, trying to recall if I ate that Dime bar or if it's still in my bag. 'Hang on a sec.'

I rush to the bedroom, tip the bag's contents on to the floor, and snatch the Dime bar from the smoking heap. I unwrap it (it looks nicer) arrange it centrally on my best plate (the best of two) and present it with a flourish. She inspects it from a distance, craning her neck slightly but otherwise not moving a muscle – precisely the way in which Fatboy inspects supermarket own brand cat food. I say briskly, 'This is a very superior confectionery, it—'

She rudely interrupts with, 'It's a Dime bar.' My discomfited expression makes her smile for the first time and she adds gruffly, 'Bernadette Dickenson always has one for lunch. She's got twelve fillings.'

I take this friendly snippet of information as a peace offering and say, 'You don't sound very happy, Mum.'

She reacts as if I've just sworn. "Happy!" she spits. 'Happy! No I am not "happy"! I am extremely *un*-happy. My husband's dead as a dormouse! How can I be happy? I'm a widow! My whole life's unravelled!'

I wince and mutter, 'Sorry, bad choice of word.'

My mother glares. Then she blurts, 'It was your father's birthday and you didn't call me!'

I blurt, 'So why didn't you call *me*?' I feel myself tensing.

My mother folds her arms and bawls, 'You can't criticise me, I'm too upset!'

I grit my teeth and say, 'I tried you, twice, and you were engaged both times. I thought if you wanted to speak to me you'd call. You know, like a grown-up?' My mother gasps as if I've slapped her. Immediately, I feel bad. I say gently, 'I'm sorry, Mum. I didn't want to upset you more than you were already upset. I know highdays and holidays are tough.'

She replies wearily, 'It's not the high days and holidays. It's the every day.'

'Oh Mum,' I say sadly. I lean across and touch her arm. She covers her eyes with both hands and weeps into them. I grimace, and wait. After approximately six minutes (an age in weeping terms) the weeping halts. She tells me she spent three hours on the internet eavesdropping on a chat-room for the bereaved. 'Oh,' I say warily. 'And it didn't make you feel better?'

My mother shakes her head like a dog emerging from a pond. 'It was *terrible*!' she cries. 'Everyone'd been shot!' Ah. 'They'd all had worse deaths than me!' she exclaims. 'Much, much worse! I felt like a fraud! And then, the Christian said look to God, and they all started rowing with her!'

I feel it's advisable to move on, fast. 'Mum,' I say, searching for a grain of wisdom and, in my haste, finding a platitude, 'grief is a private, internal thing. No one can say their pain is worse than yours because they don't know. So maybe it's not good to compare. Maybe it's better to talk to people who know you. You can always talk to me.'

My mother squeezes my hand silently, and nods and sniffs. Then she splutter-laughs through her tears and says, 'The only person I liked was Emma from Kansas. Her teenage daughter died in a farm accident and they had an open coffin, and one of their friends looked in and said to Emma, "She looks good though . . ."! It was like when Harold Reel's mother told me I should be relieved because divorce was worse.'

I laugh in shock and exclaim, 'For Christ's sake!' Then we laugh together at the senselessness of some people.

And we start talking about Dad. My mother tells me about their first date. He took her to a French restaurant where they ate snails and got food poisoning. 'It wiped me out for a week! My mother insisted I move back home. Your father had to take me on three more dates to make up for it!' she cries, flushed at the memory. 'Of course, my mother didn't believe it was the food! She thought I had morning sickness. My own mother thought I was "fast"! She didn't say so to me, of course, but I crept to the bannisters and heard her whispering to my father. Morrie used to say my mother had a whisper that could shatter eardrums! Oh he made me laugh. Although' – she frowns, almost to herself, and I can tell she's immersed in her own little world – 'I never could get him to put his teacup in the sink. Never! And God forbid I should speak to him when there was golf on television. "You don't need to *hear* golf, do you?" I'd say!'

My mother chuckles and I pitch in with, 'Mum, he wouldn't speak to us when *anything* was on the telly. He was worse than Nana! Remember when he took time off to watch Wimbledon and I ran in to show him a mug I'd made in pottery – what was I? Eight? – and I ran in front of the TV and he missed a match point and scowled at my mug and said, "That's sod-all use, it's the shape of a pine cone! How are you going to drink from it?" I threw it on the floor and ran upstairs!'

My mother tilts her head. 'I don't remember that,' she says. She pats my hand and says softly, 'Don't take it personally, darling. He could be very rude sometimes. I told him off for it. Like when he told Vivienne her mink coat stank.' She sighs. 'Oh Helen, I miss him. The ache. It's always there. You understand. Some days it fades and then, I'll see his spectacle case in a drawer, and it'll be back with a vengeance.' I nod dumbly. What else can I do?

My mother sighs again. 'Oh well,' she says, snapping a large corner off the Dime bar, 'that's the price you pay for love.'

I think about what she's said long after she leaves. (Vivienne is due round for advice on which dress to wear for Jeremy's latest première. 'I don't know why,' grumbles my mother. 'They're all red and sequinned.')

I feel *I'm* paying the price for love despite it bolting back to the shop before I could get any use out of it.

362

Chapter 45

My mother didn't set out to be a bad parent, she just didn't know any better. Her support has been erratic, to say the least. When I was eleven she made a big deal about taking an afternoon off work to watch me compete in a school swimming race. She attended, and I came third. Out of four contestants.

'I was sure you were going to win,' she said as I slumped, sodden and defeated, in the car home. I brightened at this show of faith, until she added, 'The other children looked so scrawny. What a shame you did so badly!'

Wary after more than two decades of this, I hesitate to tell her about Tom. I'm too delicate to cope with her booby-trapped reassurances. However, when I give in and confess, my mother is surprisingly optimistic.

'He'll come crawling back!' she says. 'They all do eventually!' She suggests we go shopping instead. 'You could do with wearing brighter clothes,' she says, 'No wonder you're such a mope.'

While we are closer, her ability to ricochet from gushing to crushing never fails to astound me.

When I'm not being insulted by relatives, I sulk indoors. I have added a lamp to my living room and rude magnets to the fridge, and the flat feels warmer and more mine every day. I like to be in it. And I get every chance to be in it because I don't feel much like partying. If I do see my friends, we meet in the day. (They don't feel much like partying either.)

Talking of which, yesterday I saw Tina. She returned to

work and while she looked fragile and on edge, the first thing she said when I bounded over was, 'Alright, you big tart!' I beamed and replied joyfully, 'Hello, slapper!' Then we hugged. It was a blissful cross between Romford and New Jersey.

Later on we snuck out for a coffee and Tina said she was feeling stronger. 'I take it Luke's still cooking for you then,' I said teasingly, looking at her gaunt face.

To my surprise, Tina said fervently, 'That man is a gem. Everyone's been great, especially you. And the police were good. They gave me pamphlets. I'll never forget what you did, Helen. I, God knows, I needed the push. I – *ugh* – even to talk about it. I can't. It's too raw. Maybe later.

'But Luke. I don't know what I'd have done without him. He's been solid. Because this hasn't been easy, Helen. It's frightening, being out in the world again. It sounds mad but I felt safe with Adrian. And I, I haven't heard from him but I'm scared I will. He's got to be madder than hell. I'm almost resigned to it. Sometimes I think, I've survived this many beatings, what's one more? But Luke says I won't see Adrian again. He's confident of that. I half believe him. I should feel happy, but I'm not sure how I feel. It's like there's a void where the feeling should be. I might feel different when the case is over. But I don't know if I could have stuck it without Luke. I can't tell you. Every woman deserves a Luke.'

Humbled, I said, 'No Tina, *you* deserve a Luke.' Not wishing to sound soft I added, 'A Luke with good hygiene and some vestige of dress sense.'

But Tina said quietly, 'He's cool.'

Instantly, I felt mean. Trying to sound joky – but wishing to procure serious information – I croaked, 'Oh! So it's like that, is it?'

Although Tina insisted that it wasn't like that and that she planned to remain single for a long while, I knew it was only a matter of time before it *was* like that. And this morning, as I hunch over my marmalade on toast, I think, why can't it be like that for me? I would say I'm always the bridesmaid, never the bride, but I've never even *been* a bridesmaid. How dare bridesmaids complain! They don't know how lucky they are in their puffy lilac.

As I brood on the ungratefulness of some people, I hear a thud. Yet another crippling bill. I stomp downstairs to be financially damaged and see a large white envelope lying on the floor. I snatch it up, rip it open, and inspect its contents. A scrawled note: 'Darling, look what I found!' And a faded birthday card. The illustration is of a baby penguin wearing a woolly hat and scarf and carrying a flower (as they do). The message reads 'For You Daddy On Your Birthday'. I open it and my eyes prickle. 'To dear Daddy', a little girl has written in her neatest handwriting, 'With lots of love and kissis and hugs and best wishis lots of love forom Helen xxxxxxx ooooooooo.'

I wait till 9.32 then ring Laetitia. 'Hello?' I whisper, forcing out a weak cough. 'Laetitia, it's Helen, I'm [*groan*] not well. I've [*wheeze*] got a cracking headache and [*choke*] I feel sick [*sniff*]. I'm going to [*snuffle*] have to drag myself [*rasp*] to the doctor. I feel [*gasp*] terrible.'

I await the fearsome cry of 'Don't lie to me, you skiver, get in here this minute or you're out on your sodding ear!' But Laetitia merely says, 'Don't come in until it's officially not contagious.'

I agree, plonk down the receiver and crow, 'And the Academy Award for Best Actress goes to Miss Helen Bradshaw! For a *staggering* performance! Ta naaaaa!' Then I pack what I need, grab my metal bin from the bathroom, jump in the Toyota, and speed to the cemetery.

I'd forgotten how quiet it was. Quiet except for the insolent drone of aircraft every five minutes. It's less windy than on the day of my father's funeral, but the sky is grey, not blue. I survey the desolate landscape of white stones and sigh. Who would have thought it. I hope no one sees me carrying this bin. Or wearing trousers. I glance around, then crouch

365

and read the inscription on an ancient-looking headstone. 'Thy Will Be Done.' I suppose that's called resigning yourself to someone else's fate.

I walk around, hugging the bin and peering at strangers' graves. I frown at 'Not lost but gone before'. Bloody optimists. I decide that 'Watch, for ye know not when your Lord doth come,' is spiteful scaremongering. And it hurts me to read the inscription for Joey Steadman, aged twenty-two.

'To the world he was only a part.
To us he was all the world.'

It's a long while before I approach my father's grave.

Finally, I stand and stare at the name. 'Maurice Bradshaw', etched in granite. And my first thought is, what the fuck is my father's name doing in this graveyard! I stare at 'Maurice Bradshaw' for a long time, and scowl. Slowly I reach out and touch the cold stone. I trace my finger along each solemn letter. Maurice Bradshaw. His row is nearly filled up, with people who have died since. But the grave itself looks stark. I stare some more, and see a dandelion struggling to survive in the soil. 'He hates yellow,' I murmur. Something about being here immobilises me. I feel I could stand here staring until dark.

I stare and stare. Then I kneel on the ground next to my father's grave, rummage through my bag for my notepad and my pen, and start scribbling. Pebbles dig into my knees through my trousers, but I don't mind. I like feeling the sharpness. When I've finished, my trousers are wet with mud and my knees hurt. I brush myself off – which smears the mud – and read what I've written.

'Dear Dad,
    I hope you're well.
    I'm not. I miss you and it has been awful. I wish that it had been different. Of course, the family have been no help at all. I hate Cousin Stephen. He has disgraced

himself. He was so greedy at the will reading that Nana had to tell him to shut up. He had egg mayonnaise at the corner of his mouth, it was disgusting. No one can see beyond themselves to a bit of compassion and decency. Nana Flo hasn't heard from Great Aunt Molly for ages. But we've tried with Nana, and I think she's a bit better. She's a strong woman. Mummy is slightly less strong but I think you'd be proud of her (apart from the wrist business). She was brilliant when I moved into my flat. You'll be pleased to hear it's in a good location.

I lost confidence when you died. I didn't know who I was, suddenly. What to do. And if you must know, I don't feel too good at the moment. Maybe your death YOUR DEATH YOUR DEATH YOUR DEATH YOU ARE DEAD YOU ARE DEAD I CAN'T BELIEVE IT WHY CAN'T YOU COME BACK WHY WHY WHY WHY NEARLY A YEAR AND STILL NOT BETTER. Not many people understand. They decide how I feel, should feel, ought to feel, in relation to how bad Mum feels . . . I'm twenty-nine years younger than her, therefore subtract grief to the power of two, add one for . . . I don't mean to complain. They mean well. It's useless trying to convince them it isn't like that. Like trying to convince Nana that gay people aren't doing it to spite their parents. But Mum and I are getting on better, which is good.

I wish we'd got on, Dad. I was hurt that you called me the Grinch. I tried hard with you, Dad. I loved you. I wanted you to love me back. If you don't mind me saying, it was like trying to force the Toyota up a steep hill. I meant to say I love you at the hospital, and I was saying it inside. I hope dying wasn't too bad, leaving us and sinking alone into the dark. I hope you play golf with Grandpa and get to know him. It must be nice for you both to meet at last.

I have wondered what I did to make you not care but now I see you did, in your way. Mum says you were rude in general so it's good to know it wasn't all me. No offence, but not all men are like you. Some try harder. Which makes me feel better about things.

Anyway, I hope you don't mind me saying this, but it was time. I still love you. And I feel better now. With lots of love and kissis and hugs and best wishis lots of love forom Helen xxxxxxx ooooooooo

(Remember!?)

I don't want to over-romanticise the moment but I feel like I've just had an enema.

I sigh deeply and fold the letter. Then I turn to my death-kit. I open the grey paper sack and place the letter inside. I also put in the paper Mercedes (to ferry Dad to a heavenly golf club), the gold and silver watch with 'Rolex' printed on its face (he likes to be on time), the Chinese gold leaf, and the Bank of Hell notes (to buy a drink at the bar). And the five ripped-out end pages of *Single & Single* by John le Carré (he hadn't finished it). I stick in the glasses, the pen, and the cigarettes. Then I write my father's name on the sack, make a note of the date on a Post-it note and attach that too. Then I seal it.

I glance around to see if anyone is watching, but the place is deserted. Furtively, I light the three joss sticks – I crouch behind the headstone for shelter – and think 'Dad, Dad, Dad.' Then I realise, shit, I could be summoning *anyone's* dad, so I quickly amend it to 'Maurice Bradshaw, Helen's Dad, Maurice Bradshaw, Helen's Dad.' After five fragrant minutes, I poke the joss sticks into the ground, and light the red candle. 'Okay, Dad,' I whisper, feeling only slightly silly. 'I'm sending you cash, fags and a Merc, because I know that's what you'll appreciate, even if it isn't very zen. I've also sent you a John Le Carré but please read my letter first. Okay, now I'm sending it.'

I jam the red candle in the earth, right behind the head-stone so it doesn't blow out. Then I wonder, do I torch the lot like a pyromaniac or do I play the control freak and

368

burn it item by item? I might as well be organised. I owe it to that stupid list. I tip everything out on to the ground. Then I set fire to the sack first, so that all I send has transport. I fold the Chinese money in the way that Lizzy showed me, plop it in the steel bin, and strike a match.

The money burns and curls, orange cinders squirming over it like bugs, devouring the paper until it is dust. I stare, bewitched. The smell is sweet, heady, almost sickly. I am nervous that the smoke will alert the gravekeepers (or whatever they're called) and keep peering over the headstone to see if any officials are thundering towards me shaking their fists. They aren't. Then I light the Hell notes. I watch and wait until they crumble to ash before lighting the cigarettes (I hope they're not stubs on arrival). Then I light the pen, the watch, the glasses, as I don't want a fire raging out of control. My father would be mortified. Then it's the turn of the Merc, which takes about three hours – not what I'd expect from a fast car. Then John le Carré. And finally, my letter.

'I'm shutting the door after the hearse has bolted,' I joke to the whispery air. My eyes water from the smoke and other things and I wipe them with the back of my hand, before realising it's filthy. Then I glance down and see that so is the rest of me. I look like a charred potato. My face is hot and itchy from crouching over the bin, my throat stings, and my knees are damp and frozen. But I don't care.

My heart races as I watch the cinders fly.

Chapter 46

I drive home in a trance, flames leaping before my eyes, my hands black with soot. I speed along, invincible. There are no tangible thoughts in my head, just an image of ash dancing in the air like a thousand white butterflies set free. I run upstairs to the mirror to see if I look different and a grubby urchin stares back at me. When I breathe deeply it is like I am encased in a steel corset. Slowly I place my hands on my chest and feel the frantic beat of my heart. I stand still. And the ache of loss, dragging on my insides like a devil tugging at my soul, seems fainter.

Later, when I sink into sleep, there are no pursuers thumping up the stairs behind me.

But fate compensates for the absence of nightmares. I open my eyes in the morning and instantly feel [*groan*] not well. My first thought is that I've caught something from the graveyard. All those germs seeping up from the ground. My second is that I'm being punished for lying to Laetitia, in which case God has no sense of justice and shocking taste in women. And my third is, I have just taken a large step towards exorcising a ghost – at the very least, I've sacrificed a Mercedes – I should feel light and springy and full of *zing*.

Instead I feel as bouncy as a dead kangaroo. I heave myself upright in bed and attempt a delicate 'hhu hh'. Suspicion confirmed. My throat is raw, my head aches and my eyes have been bathed in ammonia.

I flop on the pillow and stare at the ceiling. So. The day after I visit my father's grave, I am haunted by the tedious moral punchline of The Boy Who Cried Wolf. I'm too old for this, I think as I wincingly shift position. I've learned all the lessons from fairytales that I need to know. (Thanks to Little Red Riding Hood and The Three Billy Goats Gruff I grew up with an abiding fear of Nana Flo and humpback bridges.)

'I'm as weak as a kitten,' I croak self-pityingly as Fatboy lands on my bed with the force of a small building. I stagger to the kitchen and retch as I open a tin. Then I ring work and leave a hoarse message. I also ring the doctor and demand an emergency appointment. 'He's on holiday,' warbles the aged receptionist. 'You'll have to see the duty doctor, Dr Sands. Eleven ten okay?'

I lean heavily on the reception desk for a full minute before one of the three women behind it stops jawing and deigns to notice me. I am about to say sweetly 'Mrs Cerberus, I'm sorry to trouble you but I'm about to expire,' when all the life exits her voice and she says, 'Can I help you?' I announce myself and am despatched to the waiting area. I sit as far away from all the ill people as possible. There's a *Hello* on the table but the thought of it is too intellectually demanding. I swallow carefully – it feels as if I'm gulping down a golf ball – and close my eyes.

It seems like an age before a gruff voice raps out 'Helen Bradshaw!' I jump up and scuttle into the surgery. The duty doctor and I regard each other and my heart shrinks. Dr Sands is about ninety-three with tufts of yellow-white hair, a curved back, and a disdainful demeanour. I start to describe my symptoms and he interrupts me as if I am simply too dull and stupid to be heard. He glances down my throat and mutters, 'Nothing there.'

I want to exclaim, 'What! no oesophagus!' but lack the strength. His contempt takes my breath away.

I collect myself and say firmly, 'My father died quite recently and I've been stressed and sad, I think, and maybe—'

The doctor says, 'When?'

371

I clench my fists and say 'July.' I add, 'I'm just so tired, and I've had no time to think, and maybe if I had a week off work it—'

Dr Sands cuts in again. He says sneeringly, 'A *week* won't do anything! I can prescribe you a course of anti-depressants—'

It is my turn to interrupt him. 'I don't *want* anti-depressants!' I snarl. 'I want to deal with it not stun it!' I look at his drooping face and see the acute boredom and know I'm wasting my time. 'Oh I'll manage,' I say and walk out.

I rage and fume all the way to the Toyota then drive home at the speed of sound. Patronising old goat. What if I had throat cancer? He'd probably suggest I eat a Tune. I think uncharitable thoughts about Dr Sands being struck off and dying in the near future. 'He's on his way out,' I say meanly, addressing the steering wheel, 'and he wants to take everyone with him.' By the time I get home I've burned the edge off my aggression. I flop into bed and fall asleep.

I wake up at 3 p.m., feeling dazed. I swallow to test my throat. Not bad. If only the fluff would go from my head. I can't go back to work, I just can't. I can't face *doing*. I cannot stomach the reality of chasing Laetitia's laundry. I just need to *be*. I lie back and see the flames as the Hell notes burn. It feels like I imagined it. I grab yesterday's top from the floor and sniff it. It's streaked with dirt and reeks of smoke and incense. I wonder if Dad received his parcel. I can't help smiling as I imagine him opening it. Maybe I should have sent something for Grandpa Gerald too? Nah. He can share with Dad. You can't get too carried away. It's like feeding the pigeons in Regent's Park. Feed one, and it's pleasantly British. Feed two and it starts a frenzy and before you know it you've got birdshit on your head.

Later on I ring work. I choose my words with care. I don't stretch the truth. I merely tweak it. 'Laetitia,' I declare solemnly, 'I've seen the doctor and he's gagging to put me on anti-depressants. The thing is, it'll mean sick

372

leave, and I'm reluctant to leave you in the lurch. Especially as we're so short-staffed. But I'm sure if I take this week as holiday and rest, I'll be fine. Would you be okay with that?'

Laetitia grants me this week *and* next week off without a whimper.

Lizzy is the first to ring. 'Helen!' she peals. 'Are you okay?' Alarmed at her tone – which suggests my death is pending – I reply, 'I'm fine. Why?'

Lizzy blurts, 'Laetitia told the managing editor, who told the beauty director, who told me, that you're unstable and you've got to keep away so you don't contaminate the office!'

As I predicted this, I say cheerily, 'Laetitia is a large, lowing moo cow who should learn to keep her trap shut.'

Silence. Lizzy whispers, 'So is it true?'

I squeak, 'No it isn't! I'm fine. I'm just tired. I burnt your death-kit yesterday. It helped.'

Lizzy nearly bursts through the earpiece with joy. 'That's *wonderful*!' she shrieks, 'Was it amazing? spiritual? intense? a release?' Lizzy – amid a host of other talents – is mistress of the superlative and I immediately fret that the posting ritual wasn't as emotionally extreme as specified.

'It was *quite* intense,' I say warily, 'but I was nervous about being caught by a grave warden.' I know Lizzy is about to reply 'A what?' and I can't be bothered to begin that conversation so I add swiftly, 'It was good. I feel much better *inside*, but also ill, if you see what I mean. Sore throat. Probably from the smoke. So I'm taking time off.'

The Blyton gene kicks in and Lizzy sighs, 'Oh good for you! The pain is probably psychosomatic. I'm sure you got masses off your chest.'

This happens to be an expression I loathe so I exclaim, 'I hope not – with my figure I can hardly afford it.'

Lizzy ignores me and resumes, 'Just relax and consolidate what you've achieved.'

This makes me imagine myself as a nesting hen. I yawn and say, 'I plan to sleep.'

Lizzy – who's even more evangelical than normal – says, 'That's fine, but you mustn't sleep more than nine hours. If you do and you're still lethargic you could be lacking iron. And have you heard from Tom?'

I reply stiffly, 'No.' And then, 'What about Brian?'

'Oh *no*!' says Lizzy, who never looks back.

In the following days I take calls from my mother ('fresh air, darling, and drink milk'), from Tina ('I'll bike you crisps'), from Luke ('I saw Tom the other night and he didn't mention you. Has Tina mentioned me?'), and from Nana Flo.

'Cecelia tells me you're poorly,' she says. 'Is it your monthlies?'

If I wasn't lying flat when I answered the phone I would have keeled over in shock. As it is, I want to burrow into the ground like a mole. 'No,' I say, making a grim face. 'No. I had a sore throat but now I'm fine, Nana. I'm having a holiday from work.' If not my relatives, I add silently. There is a long pause, so I say, 'I'd like to visit. Maybe when I'm better?'

Nana replies shortly, 'I'll be here.'

After speaking to Nana, I keep myself to myself for ten days. I stop expecting Tom to call, which means I stop lifting the receiver to see if the line's dead. I sleep ten hours every night *plus* a leisurely afternoon nap (mainly to spite Lizzy) and – for the first time ever – I have a manicure. It is *exquisitely* dull.

I also spend a lot of time on the heath extension. I take *A Taste For Death* and a blanket and a bagel and a tube of hairspray to spray at muggers and sit on a wooden bench and eat and read and watch people walk their dogs. And I stare at the sky a lot. In the evenings I play darts in my front room – I've got the nails for it – to the sound of the Sandpipers. Surprisingly, the song 'Guantanamera' reminds me of my father – I can only imagine that he must have liked it. At first it makes me cry but I play it twenty times in succession and become immune. (Listening to the lyrics also helps.) Two days before I'm due back at work I tire of bellowing 'One hundred and *aaaytee*!' and decide to be more active. I ring Tina and ask if she wants to go ice skating.

'Ice skating?' says Tina in a tone that makes me wonder if I accidentally said 'Potholing.' I tell her I saw it on TV and it'll be glamorous and fun. She surrenders, but 'only because you've been a recluse for the last fortnight'. Two hours later, the pair of us are slithering around Queens Ice Rink on rubber legs and getting cut up by eight-year-olds.

'I'm getting the hang of it now!' says Tina, arms flailing like a windmill.

'I'm knackered and boiling and faint from exertion,' I gasp after nine minutes of staggering. 'I need some Kendall's Mint Cake. I assume they sell it at the bar.' We hobble to the edge for a breather, which leads me to an exciting discovery. 'Look! I can skate backwards!' I crow, clutching the siderail and clonking into it.

'I want to do *that*,' declares Tina, pointing at a teenage madam in a glittery skirt and white boots who has positioned herself at the heart of the ice and is spinning like a top.

'Go on then,' I say.

'*You* go on,' says Tina.

'But,' I bleat, 'she's got white boots and I've got these blunt blue things. And she's on the smoothest bit of the ice. My bit's scuffed up. And I'm wearing a puffa jacket and padded trousers. I'm incapacitated.'

Tina huffs. 'Dressing like a doughnut has nothing to do with it. Don't make excuses,' she says.

'Fine!' I exclaim. 'Fine! You've pushed me too far! Just watch me!'

Approximately three seconds later I am wobbling to the lockers with a bruised ego and a cold wet bottom. Tina is staggering along behind me like a small yeti. 'Your ha ha legs *literally* ha ha ha flew right out from ha ha ha under you,' she cries, crippled with glee, 'you looked a right berk!'

In my prissiest voice I reply that I am not a penguin and therefore am going home to change into civilian clothes and drink a hot chocolate and walk on the floor like a normal human being and if she has nothing nice to say then I suggest she say nothing at all.

But in truth I rather enjoyed it.

Chapter 47

Yesterday I returned to *Girltime*, paid my electricity bill, rang Nana Flo to check she was alive, took the work experience girl for a coffee after Laetitia made her cry, asked the bank to extend my overdraft (it refused), bought bleach and cling film, traipsed to three shops in a hapless search for a mobile phone earpiece, made an appointment with the optician (number plates are blurring again), attended a features meeting (suggested fifteen ideas to show up Laetitia), booked the Toyota in for a service (the garage was getting shirty), and thought, now I see why Dad always boomed, 'Schooldays are the happiest days of your life!'

I muse on how draining it is to be a grown-up, and think back to my schooldays. I remember reading aloud from *Henry IV* and being laughed at by the entire English class for pronouncing 'discretion' discreeshun. And hating net-ball. Then I think, give me debts and a trundly car any day. At least I owe and drive badly how *I* want. And I'll never have to sit another exam. At college my tutor used to say, 'When you get the exam paper I want you to look around the room and smile knowingly to yourself. It'll psyche out the opposition!' I followed his advice and I'm sure the opposition would have been psyched out except they were all miserably smiling knowingly to themselves too. This psyched me out and I got a 2.2. Never again. Thankfully I ignored my father and I didn't try to become a lawyer. (The law's reputation is bad enough.)

I take a large swig of espresso and feel calm. As if I've let something go.

Laetitia is safely engrossed in *Tatler* so I start making a list of who I took orders from aged ten (my mother, my father, Brown Owl, nine teachers, Michelle, equals thirteen) and who I take orders from aged twenty-seven (Fatboy, Laetitia, the bank, the garage, Lizzy sometimes, equals four and a half but feels like eighty-four and a half). Which means that technically I am just under two-thirds less downtrodden than I was seventeen years ago. I have nearly twice as much control. No, *three* times! I always was a klutz at fractions – another point in favour of the present. I must go to the theatre more.

I shove the list in a drawer, then return to fretting over the first ever feature Laetitia has been coerced into commissioning me. She was most reluctant and reminded me of a spaniel I once saw being dragged into Tom's surgery on its bottom. Tina saw us exit the meeting and e-mailed me remarking that Morticia looked red in tooth and claw and was it because she'd missed her rabies injection? I replied, 'Rabies antidote rendered powerless by potency of subject's venom. Morticia irate because after years of meek submission the deodorant monitor has turned.'

Tina messaged back, 'Like it. But caged animals lash out so go easy. Victim Support number here, if needed.'

In a burst of flamboyance, I retorted, 'Save it for Morticia. Her broomstick's busted! Her goose is cooked!'

This was such a kick-ass thought (albeit untrue) that I struck the enter key with a loud *pank!* and Laetitia looked up. 'What are you doing?' she snapped.

'Research for my feature on bullying,' I replied happily. Laetitia swelled like a puff adder with PMT, but turned back to *Tatler* without another word.

Tina and I have a drink after work to, as she says, celebrate. I'm not so sure. Laetitia would rather publish a feature written by a spider monkey than anything composed by me so my picture-byline is far from won. 'But since when did you care?' asks Tina.

I shrug. 'Since I became bored of dressing as a tampon.'

378

Tina nods wisely, and says, 'Makes sense.'

I add gloomily, 'And I need a raise. I'm sick of not being able to afford my lifestyle.'

Tina snorts, 'Well one feature won't swing it!'

'Tina!' I squeak. 'I am being positive in the face of doom. You're not being helpful.'

Tina replies, 'Sorry. What I meant to say is, you go, girl! Keep at it and maybe in a year you'll get a rise that'll allow you to upgrade deodorant.'

I grimace and say, 'You never know. Maybe if I get a feature printed in the mag I'll be headhunted.'

Tina replies, 'That would be impossible.' Actually what she says is, 'That would be nice,' but it comes out in the *tone* of 'That would be impossible.'

I slump – bar stools are made for slumpers. 'How are you about Adrian now?' I begin, but Tina shakes her head and crunches hard on an ice cube.

'Don't want to think about it,' she says.

I see the tension in her jaw and say hurriedly, 'Have you heard from Luke?'

This elicits a half-smile. 'I'm resisting,' she says. 'He's a doll but I need a break.'

I sigh and say, 'It must be great to be pursued, though.' Then I think about what I've just said and stammer, 'I mean, by a nice bloke.'

Tina gives me a playful kick which – from a steel-toed Prada shoe – feels about as playful as a kneecap.

'Ow,' I say, as Tina exclaims, '*You* were being pursued by a nice bloke. I don't get why you're not together. And you seem so laid back about it. Did you go off him?'

I think of Tom and feel a pang. I growl, 'No, I didn't go off him! I'm pining here! Haven't you noticed I'm off my Dime bars? I can barely eat for lolling and moping like a great big plank. The only reason I'm not whining on about it is that I've bored myself.'

'Bloody hell!' says Tina. 'I didn't realise! Why didn't you say?'

My bravado dissolves and I say sadly, 'There's no point. The look he gave me when Jasper said he was my live-in boyfriend. You wouldn't wish it on anyone, even Laetitia. It was as bad as when I tried to eat a plastic grape out of Vivienne's fruit bowl.'

Tina looks piqued. She says, 'But Jasper was only kipping on your floor! Have you rung Tom and explained?'

I sigh and say, 'I've agonised about calling him a million times. But there *is* no explanation.'

Tina clunks down her beer bottle so fast a small plop flies out. 'Yes there is!' she cries.

'No there *isn't!*' I exclaim. 'Whether we were shagging isn't the issue. It's that I'd invited Jass to stay at all.'

Tina frowns. 'But why?'

I say, 'It's to do with me needing Jasper there. It was stupid.'

Tina huffs, 'For Christ's sake!' she says. 'Tom's a sorted out bloke. He'll forgive you one—'

I interrupt with, 'No, it's not that. It's not that. There were *multiple* mistakes. I know he's a, sorted out, but it's not that. It's to do with' – I pause to search for the correct word – 'trust.' Tina falls silent. I say – feeling only a *tad* Mills & Boon and wishing I was wearing something more suitable, a cape perhaps? – 'It's not so much to do with him not being able to trust me. It's about me not being able to trust myself.'

Tina looks queasy and says, 'Stop it, you're churning me up.' But she means it kindly.

She then does her best to cheer me by flimsifying the conversation – which makes me feel like a grizzling toddler being desperately bounced on a knee. Tina watched *Men In Black* on video last night and don't tell Luke, but she's defected from Rob Lowe to Will Smith, who is definitely the prototype of man. This, as we both know, is the cue for me to say what I've been saying for the last decade: *I discovered Will Smith's potential way back when he was fuffling around as The Fresh Prince of Bel Air, and I was* spreading the word *years* before he got A Grade famous and all the fickle hoi polloi jumped on the stargazing bandwagon, and if anyone has the right to Will Smith's perfection it is *me* and only *me*. 'If I've told you once I've told you a million times,' I say primly, 'and anyway, Rob's like the Escort. It would be disgraceful to desert him after all these years, just because you got a whiff of a Porsche Boxter.'

'Just checking,' grins Tina.

After she leaves I sit on the bar stool and wonder if I should phone Tom. As a fantasy it's a kick. I imagine a tearful reunion, me flitting towards him across a buttercup field, my hair – blonde for the occasion? – streaming in the light breeze, the sun shining golden upon us, Tom love-struck and smiling and tall, me not treading in a cow pat, and no ramblers. But if I made it reality the dream would crumble. Buttercups and breezes apart, I do not want to announce myself and be snubbed. But faint lady never won fair knight. Well actually she *always* won fair knight, but these days knights are lazier and ladies more proactive. At least, if I rang him, I'd know. Maybe it's better to know, and pine with conviction. I'll phone him.

In a bit.

If I go home now, I'm honour-bound to call Tom. So I'll do something else. What? A walk? Better not – I could sprain an ankle. The theatre – oh tut, everything's started. Nana's? There are limits to my masochism. After five minutes during which I realise I have no imagination I decide on something that I've never done before. I will eat dinner, in a restaurant, by myself. And, unlike those friend-less men who inevitably order paella then spill it down their grey suit, I won't take a novel to shield me from the horrified stares of *paired* people.

And the venue can't be Spud U Like. It's got to be proper. Preferably, fashionable. My solitude must be flaunted. I'll walk into Garfunkels, head high, and demand the centre table! No – even better – a window seat! Let them *try* to squirrel me away in a dark corner and I'll sue them for discrimination! The might of Alex Simpkinson will crash down upon them like a ton of writs! And I'll eat three courses! I'll string it out, chewing every mouthful fifty times! I'll laugh aloud at my own thoughts, should I find them amusing! Helen Bradshaw will carry the banner for lone dining females!

Then a stocky man knocks past me, spilling my drink, and I realise I am sitting on a highly uncomfortable bar stool with flushed cheeks (all four, I imagine), and sweaty palms. I think, I've virtually dined! I've as good as done it! I may as well go home.

I force myself into the first place I see which happens to be the Noodle Bar. I stomp in, glaring and quaking, angrily plonk myself down in the window like a large pink dummy, order plain noodles from the utterly polite waiter, ignore everyone, stare fixedly at my mobile phone until the food arrives, wolf down the noodles in one minute while feigning fascination at the menu and feeling like the biggest geek in the entire universe, pay cash and bolt.

Triumph! I think, puffing from the effort of running away from the Noodle Bar faster than I've ever run from anywhere in my life. *Now* I can phone Tom.

I ooff-ooff-ooff to get my breathing straight. I tilt my head from side to side until my neck feels less like concrete. I sing 'La la!' to ensure my voice is working. Urgh, I stink of garlic. Hot, foul-mouthed, and trembly-fingered, I flick to Tom's number in my address book. 'Come on!' I bleat to myself. 'You just ate alone in a restaurant! This is a cinch!' I place the book on the sofa, and sit on its arm. Then I dial.

Brrt-brrt! Brrt-brrt! Brrt-brrt! Brr—

I smirk with fright.

'Hello?'

The phone is suddenly slidey in my hands.

'Hello Tom?' I gasp.

'Who's this?'

I gulp and close my eyes. I've never sky-dived but this is what it must be like.

'Don't you remember?' I joke feebly. 'Me, Helen.'

Silence.

'Tom?' I whisper.

'Yes?' His voice is ice.

'It wasn't what you thought with Ja—' I begin. I can hear the sickening desperation in my own voice.

'I'm—' says Tom.

'*Please* listen!' I beg. Begging. Always works.

'Helen,' says Tom.

'Jasper and I weren't—' I say. He said my name. It's a start.

'*Helen,*' says Tom again.

'Yes?' I breathe, hoping.

'No,' says Tom.

'No what?' I say in a small voice.

'Sorry,' says Tom.

'What?' I blurt. I think, he doesn't get it. I should be more specific.

'I—' begins Tom.

'I'd like to ask you out!' I exclaim.

Silence.

'Tom?' I whisper.

'Thanks,' says Tom. 'But you're too late.'

Clunk!

Chapter 48

Ever since I emergency-babysat for the neighbours and their child bit me, I've firmly believed that no good deed goes unpunished. The sadistic truth is proven again and again. Lately, I've noticed Fatboy showing interest in the small grey tabby who lives next door. Unfortunately his orange paunch terrifies her. So this morning I tried to bath him to boost his chances and he yowled and squirmed and bolted. 'I'm your owner!' I screeched after his vanishing bottom. 'I won't be treated like a casual acquaintance!'

And this afternoon I get my comeuppance for being civil to Vivienne. My mother rings me at work, as I polish my feature *How To Beat A Bully (When You're 24)*. Currently, it's 8,236 words long so it may need a slight edit. Laetitia is already muttering about lack of space in the issue. 'Darling?' says my mother in a voice I recognise as wheedling.

'Yes?' I say suspiciously.

'Darling, I have a favour to ask you. But it's a *fun* favour.'

My disbelief proves unwilling to suspend itself, but I say, 'Really?'

My mother launches in to what is obviously a pre-prepared introduction:

'This Sunday Vivienne is having an afternoon tea.'

The words 'afternoon tea' explain my mother's tone. Vivienne's afternoon teas are legend. Vivienne adores giving afternoon teas. They provide her with an excuse to splurge on a new sequinned red dress. Her husband falls

384

asleep in his salmon pink leather armchair, presumably wiped out by the expense. Vivienne flirts with her current hunk of arm candy, thus providing every guest with sufficient gossip for the week. And she trawls the crowd for a young woman to marry her son.

This is where I and the afternoon tea connect. Not that Vivienne would dream in her worst nightmare of matching Jeremy with *me* – my mother once heard via a friend of a mutual friend that Vivienne considers me unsuitable for marriage as I'm too 'volatile'. This offended my mother but was fine by me as I consider Jeremy unsuitable for marriage as he's too 'gay'. But Jeremy's mama refuses to twig, and I and the afternoon tea connect because even the volatile have friends.

'It's catered,' adds my mother, unnecessarily.

'Mum,' I say, 'it always is. The last time Vivienne baked was when she fell asleep on the sunbed. Go on.'

Pause, then my mother blurts, 'A cold *and* hot buffet.'

I sigh, 'Very nice. And what's the gimmick this time?'

Vivienne always insists on a superfluous element. Last year it was Morris dancing and everyone under retirement age left early. The year before it was a group of Jeremy's actor friends doing improvisations. I recall my father telling a man in a leotard to 'piss off'.

My mother says testily, 'It's not a gimmick. It's finger painting. *I* suggested it!' I am reflecting on what a sweetly typical and terrible idea this is when my mother gabbles, 'andshedloveitifyouandallyourfriendscamebecauseshelikes havingyoungpeopleabout.'

This is such a brazen hussy of a lie I emit a derisive squeak before I can stop myself. 'Mum, you *know* that's not true! Vivienne loathes young people, they make her look old! Unless they're sleeping with her. The only reason we're invited is because she wants Jeremy off the shelf – even though he's having a perfectly nice time out of the closet.'

'Darling,' says my mother, 'Vivvy doesn't believe in all

385

that. She has her heart set on a wedding. She was *very* helpful when you were looking for builders, wasn't she? And I was invaluable, you said so yourself!' Admittedly I did, and I belatedly realise that my praise will be held hostage until the seas run dry. 'And Vivvy has been very kind to me so it's the least we can do. And it'll be *nice* to go to a party, and I don't want to go by myself with all those married people saying "haven't you found anyone yet?" and I haven't seen Lizzy and Tina and Luke for ages and I don't want to be stuck with Nana Flo the *whole* time, I want to go with a pussy!' The strain of hard work has affected my hearing.

'Pardon? You want to go with a what?' I say.

'A pussy!' bawls my mother.

'Fatboy?' I say, stumped.

'No!' shrieks my mother. 'A group!'

'A posse,' I say solemnly.

'As I said,' says my mother airily. 'So will you?'

I say, 'Yes, alright. It'll be nice to see Jeremy. I'll have to see what the others are doing though. I'll call you back.'

My mother says, 'It's okay, I'll call you.' When she says this I know that she wants us to attend Vivienne's afternoon tea very much indeed.

'Finger painting!' trills Lizzy. 'How creative! It sounds delightful! I *was* going to go have an extended session with my cranial osteopath but I can always reschedule.'

Tina says, 'Ooh, matron. *I* wouldn't.' Then Tina and I snigger at Lizzy's unamused face.

'Please come,' I say. 'I won't be forgiven if you don't.'

Lizzy chirps, 'I'm coming! I *love* this sort of thing!'

I reply, 'Actually I don't think you do,' but I say it in my head. Aloud, I exclaim, 'Lizzy, it'll be great. Tina?'

Tina wrinkles her nose, remembers Lizzy is present, and unwrinkles it before she's told off.

'There's free food,' I say shamelessly.

'I'm not a student!' snaps Tina.

'Sorry,' I say quickly, then 'Do it for me? For *meeeeee*?

Oh go on, please? *Pleeeeeeze?* Pretty pleeee—'

'Oh bloody hell, alright!' shouts Tina.

'Yesss!' I bellow, and attempt a victorious high-five with Lizzy who doesn't know what to do and botches it, making us both look stupid. 'No, like this, berk,' I say, grabbing her arm and showing it what to do.

Tina covers her eyes, 'Stop it,' she begs, 'I can't believe you're my friends. You're so square.' Outrageous!

'*I'm* not square!' I say indignantly. 'It's her! I *know* how to do a high-five—'

Tina looks at me from under her eyelashes. 'Darling,' she says, 'that you even *call* it a "high five" is embarrassing. It's so plonky. Stop digging.'

Tina and Lizzy have agreed to come to tea. So, graciously, I stop digging.

All that remains is for me to ask Luke. Here's how I predict the conversation will go:

Me: 'Hi, I'm calling to ask you to come to a tea party on Sunday hosted by a friend of my mother.'

Luke: 'Are you having a laugh?'

Me: 'Tina's coming.'

Luke: 'What's the address?'

When I do ring Luke, the conversation evolves as I expect. Which makes me all the more miserable that I didn't foresee Tom's new girlfriend before I ate a thankless meal in a noodle bar and rang *him*.

Naturally Tina and Lizzy have been supportive of me and dismissive of Tom. Not. Lizzy was 'disappointed' in him, but maybe he was going out with someone 'as a joke'. And Tina was even slower to condemn. I think she remembers how sweet Tom was after he'd booted in her door. She said, 'You broke his heart, Helen.' I was about to bristle when she added hurriedly, 'But he's still a prat.' The upshot is, I'm officially in mourning. This has one advantage – it entitles me to the fluffy treatment. I'm not that daft. If it wasn't for Tom, they wouldn't have accepted Vivienne's tea invitation in a million years. Not even if Will

Smith *and* a chanting troupe of Gregorian monks were invited.

Sunday dawns and Tina rings to cancel. She can't spend a quarter of her weekend with a bunch of gin and catatonics, it's not very rock 'n' roll. 'It's only an eighth if you count the nights,' I argue. 'And Luke will be devastated,' I add, 'and so will I.' Tina goes silent so I say – my voice starting to whine like a mosquito in a dark hotel room – 'We'll stay for twenty minutes, then we'll go to the pub.'

All Tina says is, 'Bradshaw, – your mother doesn't appreciate you. And right now, nor do I.'

Lizzy is the first to arrive, chic in a black cotton shift. 'It's washable in case I spill paint on myself,' she trills. 'It will be water-soluble, won't it?'

I say, 'Don't know, don't care.'

Tina turns up at three fifty, grizzling that north London is 'confusing'. At four, I ring Luke's mobile. He sounds flustered, and I can hear shrieky voices in the background. 'I got held up, I'm nearly with you!' he says.

'And who's with *you*?' I reply.

Luke's voice soars proudly like an eagle in flight. 'Marcus and Michelle,' he sings. 'Michelle wanted to see you, she said you'd be pleased. I thought it would be a nice surpr— bollocks!'

I croak, 'Nice surprise! What, to see the landlord who turfed me out and my ex friend?'

Luke pauses then says, 'I can't say anything bad about them, they're with me.' At this, the shrieky voices get shriekier.

I shout, 'serves you right!' and blip off the phone. Tina and Lizzy are consoling me – 'maybe wear higher heels and tartier make-up?' . . . 'chant a self-affirming affirmation' . . . 'when she asks about Tom say you ditched *him*' . . . 'or say "I suppose, being engaged, you find single women threatening because we're innately powerful"' – when Luke's Fiesta judders to a halt outside the door.

Michelle spills from the Fiesta, all puff and flounce, like a cloud of candyfloss. 'Helen, honey, it's been yonks!' she cries, her hair and bosom bouncing in unison. 'Say, you're looking healthy, did you put on weight?'

I am trying to drum up a wittier riposte than 'possibly' when fast as a well-mannered bullet Lizzy blurts, 'Silly you – Helen's a slip of a thing!' and Tina chimes, 'But Michelle, aren't you filling out! A bit of what you fancy and all that!'

Michelle's fluffy pink coat trembles as if it's about to explode and she snarls, 'I don't even *touch* what I fancy!'

Tina glances at Michelle's fiancé who is standing behind his future wife as meek as a heavily sedated lamb, and croons, 'Poor Marcus!'

For the safety and sanity of all concerned, we proceed to Vivienne's in two cars. 'Oh come *on*,' I shriek at the car in front which is dawdling along at 40 mph, 'it's like she's driving a hearse!'

'We're okay, aren't we?' says Tina.

'I said I'd meet my mother outside the house at four,' I bleat, 'she'll be incandescent.'

Sure enough, as we approach Arcadia I spy an irate leprechaun doing a war dance on the pavement. Closer up, the leprechaun morphs into my mother in dark green sweater and matching trousers. Nana Flo is sitting in the Peugeot chewing what appears to be the cud but is probably a mint. I wave and clamber out of the Toyota singing, 'Luke's fault!'

'Hurry *up!*' roars my mother, face flushed under a fierce layer of foundation. 'All the fishballs will be gone! Oh! Hello, Luke! Tina! Lizzy! And you two! Goody, everyone's here. Where's Tom?' My face and heart turn to stone and Michelle's ears flap like kippers in the breeze.

'He's catsitting Helen's cat,' says Tina.

'He's meditating,' says Lizzy.

'I ditched him,' I say.

'I thought he ditched *you!*' says Luke.

389

'He ditched you!' says Michelle. 'Gee, you must be devastated!'

'You must be devastated,' murmurs Marcus, resurrected as a faint echo.

The only dignified response is for me to laugh breezily and mutter 'tiny penis,' under my breath. Then I gesture towards Arcadia, pinch my nose and nasally intone, 'Okay guys, I'm going in.'

There is a collective gasp as Vivienne swings open the door, sausaged into a straining red dress.

'Wow, that dress looks tight,' says Luke in awe. Tina treads heavily on his foot.

'Your dress is to *die* for!' breathes Michelle. Vivienne recognises a kindred spirit and smiles broadly.

'Vivvy, there's lipstick on your teeth,' says my mother.

'Versace,' murmurs Tina. 'Six grand, easy.'

Nana Flo shuffles and says, 'Are we going to stand here all day? My legs are killing me.'

Chastened, Vivienne ushers us into her hallway where we are accosted by a pinafored waitress carrying a tray of champagne.

'Come into the garden, darlings, here,' – gesturing to a bronzed creature with fluorescent teeth – 'Zak will take your coats.' My mother looks narked and makes a swigging gesture behind Vivienne's back.

'Do you have cranberry juice?' says Lizzy politely.

'Never,' replies Vivienne coolly.

'Vivienne is aiming to be the Raquel Welch of mother-in-laws,' I explain as we step into the garden, 'so you've just been ruled out as a potential wife for Jeremy. You're too picturesque.' I point out Jeremy, who is chatting to a waiter.

'Jeremy *is* dashing,' says Lizzy admiringly.

'Nice too,' I say glumly. Lizzy and I retreat to a shady corner and watch the spectacle.

Vivienne is brushing a piece of fluff off Zak's brawny arm – the piece of fluff totters angrily off on clicky heels to console herself with a vodka. Michelle and Marcus argue hissily by the trestle table. My mother flirts forcefully with Luke, who clings to Tina's sleeve like a nit clings to clean hair. Nana Flo eats a gargantuan wedge of lemon meringue then graduates to trifle.

'Shall we do some finger painting?' giggles Lizzy, after twenty minutes' captivating surveillance.

'Why not?' I sigh, and follow her to the huge blank canvas, propped towards the back of the garden at a safe distance from the conservatory.

Vivienne's party organiser has squirted a rainbow of paints into plastic basins and placed them in a neat row on the lawn. There is also a bucket of soapy water plus paper towels.

'Do you think we're allowed?' whispers Lizzy.

'Vivienne will be thrilled,' I say. 'Mum says she wants every guest to contribute a hand print and make a collage. Then she'll frame it, or sell it to the Tate.'

Lizzy gingerly dips a finger in red paint and, bang in the middle of the canvas, draws a heart. 'What fun!' she simpers. 'Go on, Helen! I can't be the only one!'

I look at Lizzy's heart and say, 'Tom used to paint.' Lizzy smiles sympathetically. I sigh deeply, dip a finger in the blue, and add a dagger to the heart.

'Oh *Helen*!' says Lizzy crossly. 'Don't be destructive!'

I scowl and say, 'I thought being creative was about expressing your feelings.'

Lizzy dips both hands in the purple and prints an odd-looking butterfly above the heart.

'You two are crap!' says a cheerful voice. 'I'll show you how it's done.'

I roll my eyes at Luke – who is high with relief at escaping my mother – and say, 'Stand back for Leonardo then.' Luke dips his right hand in the bowl of black and in huge sprawling letters, which cover at least half the canvas, writes

'Luke 4 Tina 4 Ever.'

I glance at Tina who covers her mouth with mock embarrassment. 'Luke,' she says, 'this isn't school.' But she smiles the luminous smile of a woman who knows she is adored. My throat constricts. And in a rush I think, 'Luke used to like *me*.' I look at Luke, who has swivelled round for applause. He has a black splodge of paint on his forehead. His shirt is rumpled and there is a dubious stain adjacent to his jean zip. I look at my favourite human labrador but he doesn't see me because he is blinking shyly at Tina. And the truth washes over me in an ice-cold ripple.

I love *Luke*.

Chapter 49

If I remember correctly, and I probably don't, a dog in a manger is a person who can't make use of something but doesn't want anyone else to have it. I think it's a biblical reference – as I explained to Jasper, after calling him a dog in a manger for refusing to lend me his driving gloves. 'But you don't *drive*,' I squawked, 'and I want to see what it's like to drive wearing the correct gloves!' Jasper insisted they'd be too big for me. 'I don't care!' I said. 'I'm only going to drive round the block!' Jasper suggested I buy my own pair.

'Don't be mad,' I snapped. 'Only nerds actually *buy* dri—'.

Jasper glared and said, 'You can't borrow them so don't ask me again.' So I called him a dog in a manger and he said, 'What the hell's that?' I said I thought it was to do with Joseph and Mary looking for a manger in which to have Jesus and a dog refusing to let them have *his* manger.

Jasper suggested I didn't know what I was talking about and it was probably allegorical – Jesus being a lamb, and a dog being a dog, and a lamb belonging in a manger and a dog belonging in a kennel, and was I sure the dog *was* in a manger and was I sure it wasn't that the dog wouldn't let Mary and Joseph have Jesus in his kennel? By then I was nearly screaming with frustration. 'Jasper, I don't care, they got the manger in the end, now can I borrow the gloves?'

I remember this particular row with a distinct lack of fondness. I remember it because I am wondering if *I* am a dog in a manger. I might possibly be the biggest dog (not literally, of course) in the biggest manger in the whole wide world. For instance, have I wanted Tom purely because I like attention and selfishly didn't want anyone else to have him? Has it been a mere crush? Have I been obsessed by Tom when all the time I was subconsciously in love with Luke?

It makes sense. Lots of women fall in love with their best male friends. Partly because that means you actually get on, and partly because the freedom to fart at will is so enticing. With an ordinary boyfriend you have to hold it in for the first six months.

Clasping my guilty secret and the *Daily Mail* to my chest, I shuffle into work on Monday hoping to avoid Tina. I'm not fit to breathe the same air. Happily, I learn that she's out of the office today, and that Lizzy is on a shoot. I sit at my desk like a Stepford employee and by lunchtime I've ruthlessly slashed my bullying feature to a miserly 1,200 words. That kind of thing is easier when you hate yourself. (Last week, when I didn't yet realise I wanted Tina's man, I regretfully hacked twenty-three words off it but Laetitia threw it back and threatened to kill it unless I cut the feature to a 'readable length'.)

I deposit a hard copy on her desk and say tonelessly, 'I'll start my feature on *How To Get Ahead When Your Boss Hates You* this afternoon. Do you want anything from outside?'

Laetitia glowers at me and snaps, 'I'll get it myself, I'm not a frigging cripple.'

I glance aghast at the Editor, whose eight-year-old son has MS. Laetitia follows my gaze, sees the Editor standing by the photocopier with folded arms, and blanches. 'Hasta la vista, baby,' I think, wave at Laetitia, and walk out. She doesn't say a word. She's said enough already, I think coolly, as I step from the stuffy building into the cold air.

I wander around Covent Garden like – I fancy – a lost soul but more realistically, a lost tourist. After ten minutes of wandering I can no longer bear my own droopiness so I banish Luke from my head and walk briskly to Broadwick Street in Soho. I dash into the first art shop I see and start prowling. Aquamarine blue, deep violet, and ivory black – the paint names are richly seductive but I know less than nothing about art and can't choose. Wistful watercolours or passionate oils? A vast expanse of canvas or a small sketch book? A huge bristle brush or a pencil? I check the price of a large canvas and – forget passing out, I nearly pass on.

Less is more, I tell myself sternly – despite fervently believing that more is more – and reach for a small palette of paints and a square canvas. Then I race back to work. Laetitia is not at her desk, and doesn't reappear all afternoon, so I am excused from the usual errands and get a wodge of work done. At a conservative estimate, *How To Get Ahead When Your Boss Hates You* looks like romping home at 9,000 words. It is 6.02 and I'm wondering if I shouldn't stay late – six ten perhaps? – to work on it, when the phone rings. 'Yes?' I say dully.

'Helen?' says my caller. 'You alright? You sound like an old woman.'

I feel joyful and irked all squashed into one big dizzy ball. 'Luke!' I exclaim. 'How are you?' Luke tells me he's fine. But he sounds as antsy as an ant in a pant. 'What is it?' I say.

'I need to see you,' says Luke. 'Urgently. Can we meet?'

The blood roars in my ears and I squeak, 'Yeah, sure, what, tonight?'

Luke says, 'I'll see you outside your office in fifteen.'

I tell him I'll see him then, and do a full three minutes of working late. Urgently. What does *that* mean? Luke has realised that I am The One and wants to profess his undying love? He wants to borrow a fiver? If his affections have reverted to me, he must feel dreadful about Tina.

Suddenly I remember I have a shiny face and unplucked eyebrows so I spend nine minutes performing emergency cosmetic surgery. At 6.17 I stand back to survey the results and see I look exactly the same except matt. I gallop into the street cursing and run smackbang into Luke. 'Whew!' he gasps. 'Check out the blusher! Wotcha Mr Punch!' Then he laughs (alone) at his hilarious joke. 'We'd better go to the Punch & Judy!' he continues. 'Ha ha!'

Am I really in love with this man? I wonder, confused. Tom wouldn't be so crass. Not that crass is *so* bad. And Tom does have the capacity to be crass. The ketchup trick wasn't exactly sophisticated. But then, Tom's crassness makes me laugh and want to kiss him whereas Luke's doesn't. Probably because Tom knows me well enough to understand that I graciously pardon crimes of crassness against others but will in no way forgive them against myself.

Luke and I descend into the bubbling cityboy cauldron of Covent Garden's Punch & Judy and I am tongue-tied with confusion. Luke grins wickedly and says, 'I've got news for you that you're going to like.' Oh God. I *am* The One. He trots off to buy me a drink and there is a sick feeling in the pit of my throat.

I watch Luke jostling at the bar and picking at his backside (I assume his briefs have ridden up) and I think, no. I can't do this to Tina. Not now, not ever. There are some rules you don't break and I don't mean wearing leggings in public. Naturally I am agog to hear Luke's declaration, as I am a woman who *never* gets proposed to, not even by mistake. No man has ever said he loves me, and I can count the number of Valentine cards I've received on the thumb of one hand. (It was from my mother, the year I turned sixteen and decided that this February I was going to do what all the other girls did – only *I* had to buy it, stamp it, and address it.) Still. I've survived this long without an I love you, I think I'll be able to struggle on. I won't let Luke embarrass himself – it would be gratifying but unfair.

Luke waves a beer in front of my nose and sits down, still

grinning like a maniac. You don't smile in London! As Luke sits, I leap up like a spring salmon whose bottom has just been groped by a trout and gabble, 'Luke, I know what you're going to say, but I think it's best I don't hear it. What you did for Tina at Vivienne's party was very sweet, if a little naff, and I'd hold out for her because I know she's keen, it's just that she needs time, alright, okay, bye!' As I flee the besuited crowds I glance back, once, at Luke and see he is still clutching the two beer bottles. The expression on his face is utter incomprehension.

But curiously, no trace of devastation.

I collapse into a cab, still clutching the box of paints I bought earlier. I hold the art shop bag tightly and think, no Bud for me thanks – just a bloody martyr on the rocks. I might as well burn myself at the stake. Hey, maybe if I incinerate myself in a sack my father will pick me up at the other end. 'Yeah, Mr Bradshaw, parcel for you, we had to unwrap it to check the contents, it's labelled "your daughter" but she looks like a pointless heap of ashes, shall we return to sender?' I imagine my father's irritation at being distracted from a heavenly hole in one, and slump in my seat. Oh, me and Dad are alright, but I'm still a reject. I've spurned Luke's advances about as elegantly as a ballerina in wellington boots. I was an ego-shimmer away from betraying one of my closest friends. Well, at least everyone else will have a nice life. I feel a vicious urge to conpound my misery, so I redirect the cab driver.

'This is a surprise,' quavers Nana Flo, undoing the heavy chain on her flimsy door. 'And what can I do for you?' A rhetorical question.

'I didn't get a proper chance to talk to you at Vivienne's yesterday,' I shout over the television's volume, 'so I came to see you.' Nana Flo glances longingly at the screen and says she'll set the video. 'Shall I make tea?' I say, hoping she'll say no. My voice sounds strange because I'm breathing through my mouth – Nana doesn't believe in opening windows and her flat pongs even by Luke's standards.

'The teapot's on the side,' says Nana. Her ankles click as she clutches the *TV Times* and kneels painfully on the carpet.

'Shall I set it, Nana?' I say anxiously, but she banishes me to the kitchen. Five minutes on, Nana is sitting back in her recliner chair and I am perched like a paralysed parrot on the edge of her sofa.

But I know why I'm here. I want to talk to Nana about Grandpa and it can't wait.

Maybe I'm a parasite who wants to soothe my pain by leeching off hers. Maybe understanding a fraction of her loss will diminish my own. Or maybe I just want to talk with my grandmother because I'm sick of the silence in our family.

Understandably, Nana is surprised at my interest. She wants to know why I want to know. I tell her a vague but piquant tale about having lost the love of my life. (The tale is vague because I'm not sure if the love of my life is Tom or Luke but the cliché neatly covers both eventualities.) I suspect Nana doesn't believe me – the rolling snort is some indication – but at least it gets her talking.

Florence and Gerald met at a bus stop. He told her he was a confirmed bachelor then three days later gazed into her wide blue eyes and asked her to marry him. They were engaged for ten months as Florence's father wouldn't allow them to marry sooner – and went to Torquay for their honeymoon. 'There was barbed wire up, but I got through it and went in the water. I was so much in love, I was bouncing along,' says Nana, sipping her tea. The picture is so unlike her that I stare at her skinny, wizened face, trying to imagine my grandmother as a young woman so much in love that she was bouncing along. After Gerald died, she knew she'd never remarry.

I gulp. 'Why not, Nana?' I say, sniffling.

'He was such a wonderful husband, the short time I had him,' she replies. Then, dry-eyed, she looks straight at me, weeping on her sofa, and says softly, 'I couldn't replace him.'

398

Nana is sharper than I give her credit for. She knows I am crying half for me. 'So what's wrong with *you?*' she says, brusquely reverting to the Nana I know. Feeling ashamed in the presence of a woman who possesses the courage I lack, I tell her about Tom and I tell her about Luke. 'Luke?' she exclaims, her reedy voice so loud and incredulous that my china teacup clatters on its saucer. 'Nonsense! That long-haired fool! He's not for you! You're jealous is what you are! Oh he's pleasant enough, but I know feckless when I see it!'

As a minicab ferries me home, I wonder why – even with a hundred and twenty quids' worth of new prescription lenses – I am always the last to see the obvious. Honestly. Talk about a prat.

Chapter 50

There's a time in your life when you have to stop looking back and start looking forward because otherwise you're going to walk down the road one day and bump into a lamp-post. But it's not easy. When my father died I felt like the smooth carpet of my existence had been carefully positioned over a large hole. Until then I'd skipped carelessly around it, blind to its fateful presence.

And one sly day I stepped on it and fell, down, down, like Alice in a merciless Wonderland, dragging precarious everything in my wake, all of it chaos, toppling, crashing, falling, and I was consumed by madness, irrational whirling emotions from nowhere, I was wrenched from the assumed safety of my paper house, engulfed by a freak wave that lunged without warning from a glassy sea, wrecking all that I believed in and forcing me to start again at the beginning. How could I make sense of that lot if I *didn't* look back?

And when I looked I saw that grief is a murky pool of endless depth, and in a year of wallowing you might barely dip your toe in the water. Me, I was afraid of drowning. I learned to swim slowly and I'm still learning. Now I realise that sometimes it's only possible to go forward if you do look back. But not for ever. Talking to Nana Flo I realise how a person can be paralysed by their own past and stay bitter for a hundred years. So the evening after we speak, I decide to indulge in one last backward glance before plodding onward like a little donkey. As opposed to a big ass.

I bolt home feeling sparky. Laetitia is still under a cloud and ostentatiously talking about opportunities elsewhere, and suddenly the office is less of a gulag. And tonight I have a date with Tom. Admittedly, he doesn't know about it but, as I don't want a bucket of scorn tipped on my head, I don't *want* him to know. I plan to come and go like the tooth fairy on a one-night stand. I wish him happiness and I need him to know it. But I can't quite bring myself to wish his girlfriend happiness. I try to be gracious in defeat but keep hoping she'll go bald. Possibly I wish Tom happiness on the condition he lives like a trappist monk. (Although he can keep his flat and I'll allow civilian clothes.) He can't reasonably expect more from me – in fact he should count himself lucky. Why, other women would be threading prawns into his curtains! This isn't an option for me because I don't sew.

I wait until dark. Then I tie my hair back, curl my eye-lashes (he isn't going to see me, but I've made the 'I won't score tonight, I'll wear my grey period knickers' mistake once too often) and dress in black. I look like a young Italian widow. Not. Then I scamper to the car carrying the art bumf. As this is an undercover assignment I briefly consider wearing sunglasses and wish the Toyota didn't look so much like an unlicensed minicab. But I don't and it does. I drive to Tom's road speedily enough to make all four tyres and one pedestrian squeal. As I approach I slow to a crawl and click off my headlights. (Which is such a thrill I decide that if I don't blossom at *Girltime* in the spring of Laetitia's inevitable resignation I shall retrain as a private investigator. I've read the books.)

I check that the street is deserted, then slide out of the car, shut the door gently, and tiptoe towards Tom's ground-floor flat. Warm yellow light spills from his windows although the curtains are tightly drawn. Holding my breath, I inch open the metal gate. It squeaks like a mouse at the mouse dentist. I wince, and creep up the garden path. The rabbit foot is hammering hard in my chest and I don't

401

know if my face is damp with drizzle or sweat.

Softly, I prop the bag containing the paintbox and canvas against the side of Tom's green front door. I have stuck an envelope addressed to him on the bag. Should I ring his bell and do a runner? Leaving it for him to find by chance is risky – what if the postman's named Tom? I'll make an informed decision. First I need to assess the subject's location and how long I have to make my getaway. I glance up at the chink at the top of the curtains and feel peeved at Tom for *having* curtains. He thinks he's so fascinating to the outside world? He's paranoid someone will spy on him?

At this point, I wonder if I shouldn't have worn sensible shoes. A thought I dismiss instantly, as I regard sensible shoes on a par with bum bags. They mark you out as staid. I'm staid enough without advertising the fact. That said, sensible shoes are useful if and when you decide to climb on top of a metal bin to peer over the top of your ex-lover's curtains. I check the bin is stable, and clamber up, using the window frame as support. I crouch on the slippery surface and, wobbling like a jelly on a surfboard, attempt to stand.

The lid instantly collapses and I and the bin crash to the ground in a great cacophonous din that rings through Kentish Town loud enough for the neighbours to prosecute.

I lie stunned on the grass with a chicken carcass resting on my stomach and a stinky crush of eggshell in my hair for three dizzy seconds before the front door swings open and Tom jumps out. I don't know what the protocol is when found trespassing and spying *and* coated in rubbish so I say 'Hi.' Tom stares at me like I'm naked and I am about to tell him it's rude to stare when he exclaims, 'What *are* you doing?'

'A bin project, what does it look like?' I say crossly, moving my ankle to see if it's broken.

'Are you okay?' he says, stooping. He has a strange expression on his face and I can't tell if he's smiling. I nod.

Tom removes the chicken carcass from my stomach and drop-kicks it across the lawn. It leaves a patch of grease and flecks of old skin on my black top. Well thank heaven I curled my eyelashes. 'Why didn't you ring?' says Tom, crouching.

'I *did* ring,' I squeak indignantly, 'You told me to piss off!'

Tom looks embarrassed. He glances at his feet and stutters, 'No, I meant ring the door, just now.' My confusion must show because he blurts, 'Luke didn't tell you!'

'Tell me what?' I say, trying to wipe the rain off my glasses without smearing yolk in my eyes. I was hoping he'd notice the art bag but he's walked straight past it. Which means instead of him romantically discovering it and bursting into nostalgic tears, *I* am going to have to plonkily point it out to him and it'll be as awkward as sex in a bath. Your stomach bunches up and the aesthetics are ruined.

'Tell me what?' I repeat, as Tom seems to have lost the power of speech.

He recovers it, abruptly, in a babble: 'I wanted to tell you, I was going to tell you but I didn't know how you'd react so I asked Luke yesterday and he said don't chance it, *he'd* tell you and then the fucker disappears and I didn't know if he'd told you and I couldn't get hold of him and I wanted to tell you myself and—'

'Tell me what?' I shout, screwing up my face and trying to recall Luke's exact words.

Tom picks a baked bean off my shoulder and says, 'So if you don't know, why are you here?' Here we go.

'I bought you a thing,' I mumble, 'it's by the door.'

Tom looks as startled as if I've just bopped him on the head with a wholemeal bap. He jumps up, sees the bag, and rips open the envelope containing the note. He reads aloud,

'*It's about time you started painting again,*
love Helen'

and to my dismay – although I knew this would happen

and rue the day that Tom purchased a cheap bin – his mouth trembles and he blinks furiously. This makes me want to cry.

'Your nose is running,' I say sternly, trying to lighten the atmosphere, 'do you want to wipe it on my sleeve?' My binside manner obviously requires polish, because Tom covers his eyes with both hands and shakes his head. I look longingly at his square shoulders and tousled hair but decide it's best to wait this one out. Feeling like a gorilla, I pick chicken bits off my top and eggshell from my hair. Then I gently touch Tom on the arm and say, 'I didn't mean to upset you.'

Tom looks up and smiles in a way that thrills me. He says softly, 'You did a kind thing.' Even though the rest of me is as sodden as a British Bank Holiday, my throat feels parched suddenly. My God! You don't pick a baked bean off the shoulder of someone you despise *or* smile thrillingly at them (unless you roar past their Mini in your new Testarossa) – could it be that after months of banishment from the kindgom of love I am being ushered back to within its hallowed portals! I gulp and stare at Tom, willing him to speak. And he does.

He says:

'Helen, I wanted to talk to you about my girlfriend.'

The End.

The soppy grin taking shape on my face vanishes like a lemming off a cliff, and I scramble angrily to my feet. 'Thank you,' I hiss, 'but I don't want to know.'

Tom says, 'No, wait, Helen!' and tries to grab my arm but I shake him off and hobble to the gate. My dramatic exit is scuppered somewhat when I skid on the chicken carcass, but I manage to regain my balance, and storm towards the Toyota. 'Helen, please!' shouts Tom, as I jiggle the key in the lock. Why do I bother? I *want* someone to steal this car, they'd be doing me a favour, I think miserably.

'Oh go *IN*!' I roar at the key. Tom catches up as I wrench

404

open the door, which hits him on the knee. Good.

I slam the door.

'Helen!' he gasps, as I turn on the ignition. 'I made her up!'

What.

I wind down the window.

'What!' I screech.

Tom assumes the expression of a puppy that has just weed on a sofa. He mumbles, 'I was going to tell you but I was embarrassed.'

'I would be,' I say sternly.

Tom sighs and adds, 'I was a berk.'

'You said it!' I crow.

'Luke didn't blurt it out then?' mumbles Tom.

'Certainly not,' I say, blushing.

Tom purses his lips and looks sorrowful. 'I was jealous,' he says, eyes lowered in penitence.

'Really,' I say primly.

'Of Jasper—' he says, wincing.

'Jasper—' I begin.

'I know that now,' says Tom.

I turn off the ignition.

'Thanks,' says Tom, 'I'm choking to death out here.'

I smile.

'I'm sorry,' says Tom.

I nod regally.

'Do you forgive me?' says Tom.

I raise an eyebrow. (Well, I try to, I've never quite mastered it and forcibly holding down the other eyebrow detracts from the allure.)

'Depends,' I say.

Tom squats so his face is level with mine.

'On what?' he whispers.

'On how many other lies you've told,' I say tartly.

'That's the only one!' he cries. 'I'm a very honest person!'

'Are you sure?' I say. 'This is important.'

Tom pauses. Then he says, 'When I was twenty, I um,

405

used to tell women I was a Navy diver. Does that count?'

'Should I stay or should I go,' I murmur.

Tom rests his arms on the Toyota's window frame.

Then he leans in and hugs me and drags me out through the window!

'The Dukes of Hazzard's lazy cousin,' I say, clinging on.

'You stink of old egg,' says Tom, tightening his grip.

'That's too honest,' I say, wriggling free.

I gaze at Tom, he gazes back, and we both blush.

In the silence that follows, I squeeze my hands into fists to give myself courage.

'Tom,' I say slowly, 'I never told you.'

'What did you never tell me?' he says softly.

'About my father,' I say. I smile tightly and nod, more to myself than Tom. 'You helped me,' I say. 'Really, you did.'

Tom looks stunned. 'What did *I* do?' he gasps. '*You* helped you.'

I bite my lip. 'All the same,' I say, 'you said things that helped.'

Tom says, in a whisper that's barely there, 'I was out of my depth.'

Shakily, I say, 'So was I.'

Tom says, 'I wanted to make it better. I knew I couldn't,' – his voice cracks – 'but I so wanted to.'

I can't speak for a second. Then I say, 'You didn't try to, to distract me.'

Tom gulps. 'There was so much pain trying to get out,' he says.

I wince. 'Better out than in,' I murmur.

'You,' says Tom, 'are stronger than you think.'

I shake my head. 'I couldn't face it,' I say falteringly. 'Not for a long time. Not brave at all.'

Tom looks straight at me and replies, 'Strong, I said. "Brave" is different. Overrated.'

He lifts a hand and strokes my face. Then he gestures to his front door.

'Helen, do you want to come in and, um, I'll make us

some coffee?' he says finally.

'Yes. Yes please,' I reply.

'How's your leg?' he asks.

'Not great,' I say.

'As a doctor,' says Tom suddenly, 'I don't think you should drive with a bad ankle.'

'Sorry, do I look like a chinchilla?' I say.

But I smile as I say it.